The Smart Kid

A Novel by
Bob Miller

Copyright © 2015 by Bob Miller

All rights reserved. This book or any portion thereof may not be reproduced or used in any manner whatsoever without the express written permission of the author except for the use of brief quotations in a book review.

ISBN: 1505562767
ISBN-13: 978-1505562767

Bob Miller
31 9th St. NE
Rochester, MN 55906
Bob@ChrysalisChronology.com

Get free research archiving software at
www.ChrysalisChronology.com

The Smart Kid

1. The Trap at Lincoln

They attacked in late May, during his phy-ed class at Lincoln Middle School, beside the Arkansas river.

Tom Howardson felt fresh and energized, ready to begin the workout. He enjoyed phy-ed. It was the one class where he didn't pretend. He couldn't. His body, although slightly smaller than the other sixth-grade boys, was solid and muscular. His muscled legs where visible below his gym shorts. But his loose-fitting t-shirt, with the bright lettering of *The Beatles* hid the contoured muscles of his chest. It secretly amused him to show off his strength, especially on the ropes challenge.

Tom and another boy faced the two ropes and waited for the whistle. He clambered up the rope without using his legs. The other sixth-graders watched, with open-mouthed amazement, at his easy climb and cheered when he reached the top. Tom, the victor, looked at the student below struggling to get to the halfway mark. "SHAZAM!" he yelled.

From his vantage point, he saw the assistant principle and the two government agents enter the far side of the gym. Instantly, Tom knew who they were. They paused by the door, and the assistant principle motioned for Coach, the phy-ed teacher, to join them. During their temporary distraction, Tom plunged down the rope, burning his hands red.

He had three choices: the two gym exits or the locker room exit. Without saying a word, he hustled to the nearest door, into the locker room. As the door closed, he looked back. An agent pointed in his direction and yelled, "Stop!"

Tom ran through the locker room, set on escaping through the exit into the school hallway. He jumped past two boys huddled in conversation. He nearly collided with another who had abruptly bent forward to tie his sneakers. A last-second dodge, and Tom banged against the lockers as he passed the surprised boy. He slammed against the exit door's push bar with his full weight— and came to a dead-

The Smart Kid

stop.

He groaned in pain as his shoulder took most of the force. For the first time, the exit was locked. He tried to ignore his shoulder pain and stinging hands, and scanned for an escape route. The only other door led to the pool, which would be unused at that time of the day.

In the gym and the locker room, students and staff had been present, limiting the agents' public actions. But an empty pool area would be a perfect place to forcefully abduct him, again.

What waits behind this door?

He ran to Coach's open office and grabbed the desk chair. It had a high metal back and most importantly— wheels.

Tom pushed it through the locker room, toward the ramp leading to the pool door. His palms on the seat, the back of the chair forward like a shield, he crouched, and forced it down the ramp with increasing speed and banged open the door.

They were waiting for him.

A muffled shot echoed as the tranq dart ricocheted off the back of the chair.

Tom shoved the chair toward a surprised agent. He had no time to react before the chair pounded him in the gut.

The agent staggered back, slipped on wet tiles, and plunged backward into the pool. The chair followed, splashing and crashing on top of him— the tiled floor slippery with water.

Tom lost his footing and skidded to the floor, just in time to avoid another dart shattering the wall tiles above his head.

The shooter stood in the open doorframe of the only emergency exit— the one that Tom had been hoping to use. Two other dark-clothed agents stood beside him, hand-cuffs ready.

Tom recognized one of them— Stephen, the 'student teacher' who'd started last week.

That should have been a red flag.

Tom scrambled for a few feet, unable to get traction on the damp tiles. He ran west toward the uninspiring gray door of the maintenance room. It might be a dead-end. Tom ran in any way, slamming the door behind. He paused while his eyes adjusted to the dim light, his hand on the door knob. Then his finger touched it— the small thumb-knob which he turned to lock the door.

Many round, lighted dials encased in the heating and filtration units delicately illuminated one side the room. But shadows remained at the far end.

The large room wasn't just for pool maintenance, as he had thought. An old furnace, and hot water tanks lined the dark walls.

Tom frantically scanned the grayness looking for anything that he could use as a weapon. He took a few steps toward the shadows and studied the floor.

It was an access panel— a door in the floor.

Tom slid his hands over the rough metal surface for a few seconds before finding the flush, circular latch handle. He jerked up on the heavy metal floor panel. He stuck a foot into an opened crack of darkness and struggled to lift the thick door until it swung back hitting the wall with a loud clang.

Tom paused for a second to catch his breath.

The room reverberated with the thunderous pounding of agents outside the maintenance door.

A dart of fear paralyzed him.

Get moving! Go, go!

Tom crouched in the darkness, peered into the darker hole and saw a ladder. He jumped down the dark square as he grasped the rungs to halt his plummet. His feet kicked around until they found a footing. With hands and feet pressed on the outside edges of the ladder, he slid into the darkness; distance unknown.

His burning hands gave out and released their grip. Tom fell backward unhindered— fortunately just a few feet— and jarred against a solid floor.

He stood and made a dizzy stumble backward in the blackness.

Tom wavered in the darkness, disoriented, looking for direction.

The agents busted through the maintenance door.

A fuzzy shaft of light from above turned the blackness to a dim gray.

Tom stood in a small, hot utility room lined with strange shadows of mechanical equipment. An empty light socket protruded from the low six-foot ceiling.

The Smart Kid

The only exit: a narrow cement-walled hallway with pipes and wires lining the ceiling.

I'm a rat running through a maze.

With the light behind him, he ran blindly into the dark corridor with hands extended.

He had no idea how long the corridor might be, until he smashed into something that knocked him to the floor, his head striking hard.

Ears rang as fingers felt for damage. It hurt but wasn't bleeding.

Sitting on the floor, thin light filtered past Tom and lit his obstruction: a dark door.

He could see a hairline of light under the door— it led outside.

The G-men had expected him to run into the empty pool room. But had they known about the access panel in the maintenance room? The corridor could be a cattle shoot, with a big cage outside that door, surrounded by armed agents.

He caught his breath and considered his two simple choices: the certainty of the past or the uncertainty of the future.

He grasped the door knob.

It didn't open.

Tom intentionally searched for the protruding thumb-turn. He turned the lock and pushed, with no effect. He shoved hard, but the door shoved back harder.

A door that doesn't open is as useful as a wall with a door knob. A dead-end. They had planned it.

An agent's distant voice cut through the dark, "OK, put that arrogant punk to bed!'

A closer voice came from the utility room, "Ooww! These ceilings are low."

Shuffling feet moved cautiously near the corridor's entrance.

Tom was trapped, hunted by an invisible predator. He was powerless to do anything in the darkness but listen to his pursuer approach. He tried to silence his nervous breathing, and steady himself, when his hand touched a deadbolt latch—

Escape! Run!

No.

His first instinct was always to run. But if he ran out to the daylight, the agent would just follow close behind. He had to stop the attacker, or it really would be bedtime.

Fear clamped around his heart.

The shuffling, unseen feet were moving faster, closer.

Think.

Tom remembered a magic illusion which required a flash of light to temporarily blind the audience.

He flipped the deadbolt and pushed.

As he swung the door open wide, Tom closed his eyes to the blinding light of the afternoon. He used the sun as a weapon against his pursuer. He promptly reversed his motion, slammed the door shut and ducked.

From behind, a gun fired and a tranquilizer dart stabbed into the door.

Tom had remained in the corridor and was crouching in front of the door, invisible to the agent.

He reached for the dart, finding it at once, just a few inches above his head. He yanked it out and carefully probed it with his hands like a blind man. It had a long metallic needle, with a micro-canister attached.

Fast footsteps approached the door. Tom remained cowering in the pitch-black until the agent was a step away…

With ferocious force, he swung his hand upward and jammed the sharp metal tip into the oncoming sound.

"Aaaaah!" was the next sound he heard.

Tom hoped that the dart still had a dose of its venomous drug, otherwise the only result of the effort would be a really pissed-off agent.

Large hands clenched Tom's small neck and squeezed hard, choking him.

Tom struggled and swung against the unseen, murderous hands. They remained on his throat, fingers digging into his esophagus.

They finally got me …

A familiar voice said, "I'm so glad that I get to— arrgh …"

The agent's body slumped forward, crumpling on top of Tom, who fell back, forcing the door open, lighting the corridor.

The Smart Kid

It was Stephen, the way-too-friendly student teacher— with a dart lodged in his chest.

The student pushed the fake teacher's body off with disgust. *He's the cause of this chase!* Stephen had pretended to be a friend. But his smiles were a disguise. Tom vowed to never again trust a friendly adult— if he escaped.

Out of rage, Tom kicked Stephen in the gut. The agent didn't complain.

Tom jumped to his feet and got his bearings in a second. He stood about three quarters of the way down a grassy hill. A narrow gravel path, for an occasional utility truck, gently curved down from the higher parking lot a few hundred yards away. Surprisingly, no sign of agents. *They hadn't planned for this.* The thought pleased him.

Two choices: up or down?

A large white van labeled *Child Welfare Services* skidded to a stop in the west upper-parking lot. Four men jumped out and began to descend on Tom.

Nope. Only one choice.

The sloping grass slowed them considerably. One man's black dress shoes lost traction and he slammed to the ground.

Tom pounded down the hill toward the corner of the building. As he pivoted passed the south corner, he glanced back.

A man pointed a gun at him.

Tom looked forward as an explosion of brick sent pebbly shards into the side of his neck.

That wasn't a dart!

For a moment, Tom foolishly thought that he had outsmarted the G-men and that side of the building was unguarded. And it was, for a reason: behind an eight foot chain-linked fence streamed the Arkansas river. The stunning view that Tom had seen every day from the school cafeteria, became his final barrier.

It's the end of the maze for the rat.

The long drop to the monstrous, sharp rocks littering the steep ravine would certainly put an end to Tom's flight— not that the G-men would care. They could still use him, even crippled for life.

Tall leafy trees framed the sides of the dead-gray rocky slope. As he anticipated his capture, a branch of the nearest tree scraped against the window above him.

The high-pitched grating noise reminded him of Mrs. Jackson's chalk on the board of his fifth-grade classroom. Fifth grade. Before he knew who he was; what he was.

Tom's eyes traced a path along the branch to the crossing limb of another tree, further down the ravine. If he could— hell, even if he couldn't— it was his last and only choice.

He was seconds from capture.

The safety fence was no problem for Tom. Balancing on it was.

This was the toughest phy-ed workout of his life: Rope Climb, Mad Dash, and a round of Darts. Then Gymnastics on the high beam. Coach would be proud of him— that is, if Coach didn't think that he was a juvenile-delinquent run-away.

With his left hand on the building, he steadied himself on the fence. The sharp rocks threatened fourteen feet below his head. Even the wind was against him. His wobbly legs hardly supported him.

He heard the approaching shouting of his pursuers.

His target swayed in the wind.

He jumped.

Outstretched hands grasped the thin branch.

He hung on the end of a long, narrow limb; not strong enough to support even his light weight. As it began to sag, he pulled himself along; hand over painful-hand.

His body dangled high above the rock-strewn ravine.

His pace was fast, but slowed with each strained stretch of his arms. Every limb ached.

The sound of the gun shot startled him. He almost let go.

The shooter was at the fence, only missing because Tom was a swinging target in a carnival game.

Shoot the monkey and get a prize.

But they were playing for his life. His life.

What right do they have?

Anger boiled up and energized Tom. He finally reached the strong, supportive limb of the next tree.

He moved with greater speed along the sturdier branch.

The Smart Kid

Tom glanced toward the window of the cafeteria.

Wide-eyed, little faces pressed against the glass. Children pointed and laughed.

Only a dozen feet away were innocence, peace and freedom. They had no idea he was running for his life.

The eighth-grader, Michelle Hanson, in her pretty blue dress, gazed wide-eyed, both palms pressed against the window. No smile. It seemed as if she knew that she'd never see him again.

I'm going to miss her.

Tom reached the next tree; the leafy branches giving him temporary cover. He stepped around the thick trunk, from branch to branch, toward the river. Like a high-wire performer, Tom traversed a sturdy limb until it began to bend from his weight. He stooped, grabbed the branch and swung his body below it, pulling himself farther over the river.

Hanging below the branch, his view was unobstructed. He saw the G-men stopped behind the safety fence— and they could see him.

A man struggled to snip the wires with a large metal cutter.

Oxfords aren't good for climbing.

Tom stared at the flowing water. It seemed as cold and uninviting as death.

He was at the end of his rope.

The cramped muscles of his hands finally gave out.

The second that he let go, another shot rang out.

He flailed his arm to keep upright. His last vision: dozens of young faces with surprised expressions.

Deep breath.

The shock of cold water nearly forced his breath out of him.

His light body didn't plunge far into the water. But he swam deeper, toward the middle of the river. He stayed under water until the threat of breathing in death forced him to the surface. His head popped out of the water and he sucked in great breaths of life.

The cold river current moved faster than he expected.

Tom brushed his wet, blond hair from his eyes and saw agents stumbling down the rocky ravine. They were losing their rat. Drowned rat.

He let the river carry him downstream, and away. Away from his school haven of the last nine months. Away from Michelle Hanson. Away to his unforeseeable future.

Part One
The Counselor

2. Students

TWIN OAK TREES behind the chain-link fence surrounding Jefferson Elementary swayed in the gentle, silent wind of a bright, blue day. The tallest loomed over the playground as if it were protecting the kids running around in its shadow playing Tag, and Four Square, and teasing, shouting and doing things that children do while on their own. It was morning, Monday, Oct 1st, 1979. School had been in session nearly four weeks. And the daily rhythms of classes, lunch, recess, and more classes had been repeatedly rehearsed.

Wayne Z., a lean, well-dressed boy with straight brown hair, was next to Dave Brewer, his curly-haired side-kick.

"Crust on a Log!" Dave said in a swearing-tone, when he lost in the card game to Joe, the nerdy kid.

Fat Pat, as he was known to the kids, held an unlucky third-grader in a head lock and rubbed his chubby palm on the young boy's noggin until he screamed. "Take that Johnson!" yelled Pat.

"Hey! Pick on someone your own size," yelled Wayne at Pat.

"There is no one his SIZE!" laughed Dave. That brought howls from everyone. Pat scowled and wobbled away.

"I don't want to play again," said Joe, dropping his cards on the deck.

Dave said, "Hey, we need at least three to play this game." Joe walked away, ignoring Dave's pleading.

"Hey, what about Janson?" asked Wayne.

They both peered in his direction. "Good luck asking him," said Dave. "He never plays."

Matt Janson was a thin, blond-haired boy who wore a faded sweatshirt with a Beatles logo. He kept to himself, occasionally talking with other students one on one. At the moment, he sat on the wooden bench with Niki, a sixth-grade acquaintance, who was puzzling over a math book she'd brought to the playground. He pointed to the book and explained something to Niki.

"Ooh, that Niki is nice." whistled Dave.

The Smart Kid

"Jealous, Brewer?" asked Wayne.

"Me, no. She's nice— but too prissy." replied Dave, as he rubbed his hand over his curly, brown hair.

"Yeah, right. I believe you." He added, "Want a Hurtz Donut?" as he hit Dave on the upper arm.

"Hey, Wizzee!" yelled Dave, rubbing his arm.

"Hurts, Don't it?" Wayne smirked and walked away. "I'll go ask him."

From a distance Dave watched Wizzee walk up to Janson and Niki. Her pony tails tied with the pink ribbons swung back and forth prissily as she turned her head. Matt pointed to Niki's math book. Wayne stood there with his hands in the pockets of his light tan pants.

He could hear Matt explaining to Niki, "Dividing by one half, is the same as multiplying by two."

"Thanks," said Niki, as she closed the book and walked away.

The bell rang, abruptly killing all fun. A group moan of disappointment rose like a co-ordinated song of mourning. Wayne's intentions were moot, so he just said, "Hey Janson."

"Hello, Wayne," said Matt. "How's your dad?"

"He's still in the hospital. How'd you know?"

"I read about the car accident in the paper."

"You read the paper?"

"Sometimes," said Matt as he walked toward the school.

The kids sifted back into the building to their homerooms.

Matt, and other sixth-graders belonged to Mrs. M.'s homeroom class. She was a nervous, older teacher, past her prime teaching years.

The partially closed sliding wall had a doorway's space remaining. Educational posters, charts and pictures of presidents, decorated the other three walls. Jimmy Carter's portrait held a prominent place on the front wall of the classroom.

Three people Matt had never seen entered the room. A winsome woman with short, dark hair, spoke with Mrs. M. for a minute. Mrs. M. gestured toward the students seated in the classroom. The new woman stepped forward with a student on either side, her hands on their shoulders in a gentle, motherly fashion. Each student had hair as black as onyx and their eyes were just as hard. The girl, nearly the same height as the thirty-something woman, had thick eyebrows and was also very pretty. But unlike the woman, she was not smiling. She appeared defiant, with her mouth closed tight. The scowling boy was shorter. It was obvious that they were brother and sister.

Both Matt and Dave were instantly attentive, for different reasons.

"Hello students," the woman said displaying a gorgeous, sincere smile. "My name is Ms. Therry. I'm your new school counselor. I started here last week. I'll tell you more about me tomorrow, but now, I'm here to introduce two new students to your class." She paused and scanned the room. She had the attention of every student.

"This is Greg and Karen Urban. They just moved here."

Looking at Greg and Karen with a worried expression, Mrs. M. said, "I'm sorry but you may be a bit behind in your class assignments."

"So what!" said Greg. Several students laughed at that. Mrs. M. frowned and glanced at Ms. Therry. Greg changed position, moving away from Mrs. M., and stood next to his sister.

"Class," said Ms. Therry, "Greg and Karen are brother and sister — twins." Karen wore bluejeans and a matching denim vest buttoned over a white long-sleeved blouse, but Greg's shirt was ripped, wrinkled and untucked. He carried a permanent scowl on his face. Karen spoke in low tones to her brother as he fidgeted at the front of the class while Ms. Therry introduced them. His sister nudged him; he stopped fidgeting.

Even though she appeared to be older, she was in their grade. Dave Brewer kept his eyes on her. He whispered, "Hey, Wizzee, she don't look prissy at all." Wayne smiled, his eyebrows raised.

The boy sitting in front of Matt, wrinkled up his face and said, without getting permission, "What do you mean 'twins', they look different, and she's taller." A few other students nodded in agreement.

"Students, do you know the word for twins who look different?" asked Mrs. M. The whole class stared at her.

Matt raised his hand. "They are called Fraternal Twins. But the technical term is *dizygotic* meaning *from two eggs*. In contrast,

The Smart Kid

identical twins, formed from one egg, are *monozygotic*." A few of the students made questioning faces at the teacher for confirmation of these weird science-words.

"That's right, I think," said Mrs. M. She glanced at Ms. Therry, who showed no surprise and continued smiling.

Fat Pat said in a loud whisper, "You stupid idiot, Matt! People don't come from eggs. Except for you maybe because you're so chicken!" That got the desired laugh from the other kids.

Matt just smiled.

As the Urban twins found a seat, Ms. Therry regarded Matt for a moment, and then exited the room.

Through his blue eyes, Matt also regarded her, as he watched Ms. Therry leave.

He sat in the fourth desk of the middle row of Mrs. M.'s class. He was one student among hundreds in the school. This school was one among thousands in the state; and one among the tens of thousands in the mid-west; and one among more than 100,000 schools in the country. With more than 30 million elementary and middle school students in the entire country, someone would have a very difficult time searching for this one special student ... he hoped.

3. Charleen

"Class," Mrs. M. said, over the sound of chatter and laughs, as the sixth-graders got settled for the start of their day. "Ms. Therry, the school counselor, is here to talk with you." Mrs. M. nodded to Ms. Therry and stepped to the side of the classroom.

Charleen Therry stood in the front of the classroom, with one hand resting on Mrs. M.'s desk, as she scanned the class with piercing eyes. She was dressed more formally than yesterday, wearing her gray pant suit. She remained quiet, until every student noticed the counselor staring them down to silence. In a minute every student gave their full attention.

"Hello, students," Charleen said with a charming smile. "As your school counselor, my job is to guide you to the best experience possible here at Jefferson Elementary School. My main purpose is to help you to deal with things that might prevent you from reaching the three goals that I have for you: to challenge yourselves academically, to become skilled socially, and to have fun. School isn't about working all the time."

As Charleen surveyed the room, her trained eye looked for any visible issues with students: bruises, unkempt clothing or hair, or lack of eye contact. The whole class stared back at her, except for one student: a blond-haired kid in the middle of the room. She recognized him as the smart kid from yesterday. He was writing in a notebook. As if he could tell that her thoughts were focused on him, he shut the notebook and placed it into his desk. He looked directly at her, and gave a slight nod. She felt that they'd made some type of connection.

She focused on Greg and Karen, the Urban twins. The twins each slumped in their desks. When they saw Charleen looking in their direction, they looked out the window.

She continued, "This will be your last year at this school before you move on to one of the Junior High Schools, so I'm here to help. We can talk about anything- either school things or family stuff. I will be inviting each of you to my office over the next few weeks. When

The Smart Kid

you get called, that doesn't mean that you're in trouble. In due course, I'll meet everyone, so don't worry about coming to see me. I just want to get acquainted with you. OK? Any questions?"

Matt raised his hand.

"Yes. What is your question?" asked Charleen with a smile.

"Why did you start school late?"

Charleen's smile disappeared. "What's your name?" she asked.

"Matt Janson."

"OK, Matt. I meant, are there any questions related to what I just said," Charleen said as a frown flicked across her face a moment. No other students raised their hands.

Charleen looked at the homeroom teacher. "Thank you, Mrs. M."

As Charleen turned to leave, she glanced back at Matt. He was focused on his notebook again.

When she got back to her office, she dug through her stack of student folders. She found the one labeled *Matthew Janson* and placed it on top of the stack. Then she did the same with the files for Greg and Karen Urban.

Top priorities.

Later that Tuesday, after reviewing the upcoming parent conferences with Principal Heim, Charleen went to the staff lounge, 'for a break,' she told herself. But it was also a good place to socialize with teachers, and maybe, meet a new friend.

It was a small, windowless room in the center of the building where the teachers could escape from students to eat lunch, have coffee, smoke, or do all three at once, as demonstrated by Donna Nessler, a middle-aged, fifth-grade teacher. The result was a smoky haze that smelled of coffee and cigarettes. Three other teachers were in the room, seated around two small round tables.

Charleen entered in the middle of a conversation, and walked to the coffee pot. The aroma of the brewing coffee stirred a memory of early mornings with Garrett. She poured herself a cup and stood there, breathing in the memories.

"So anyway," said Donna Nessler, "my cousin is an actor in the

Paramount Theater, and will perform *The Importance of Being Earnest*. It's a classic farce written by ... What's his name?"

"Oscar Wilde."

Everyone turned toward Charleen. The sudden attention surprised her.

"Oh, I'm sorry for interrupting," said Charleen.

"No, that's great. It is Oscar Wilde. Anyway, I'm inviting any staff to go with me. What do you think?" She said this to no one in particular, and no one in particular was giving her their full attention, except for Charleen.

"Yes! I'll go. Let me know the details."

"Oh great!" Donna said to Charleen. "I'll post a sign with the dates and times, for any staff that want to go." Other staff in the room ignored Donna.

Charleen had thought that she wanted to meet the staff but as Donna walked toward her, she noticed how confining the room was. She glanced at the exit as Donna approached.

"Charleen Therry, right?"

Charleen nodded, and sipped at her coffee. She eyed Donna over the edge of the cup.

"So you knew the author was Oscar Wilde?" said Donna pointlessly.

"Yes, I've seen it years ago ... with my husband."

Donna nodded and smiled. "Oh, nice. Have you been married long?"

"Oh, I'm so sorry, but I must get back to my office," said Charleen. She escaped with her coffee for the safe solitude of her office.

In the afternoon, Charleen wore a long jacket, buttoned up against the chilly, October breeze, as she walked through the school yard, guarding the kids, during her weekly playground duty. Unlike many teachers, who thought it a waste of their time, Charleen enjoyed it. She considered it part of her job caring for her students. And there was no fear of invasive questions.

There was so much energy, activity and noise among the

The Smart Kid

children. It did come as a surprise to her, when she realized that she was *not* bothered by the smiling faces of the carefree kids, as they played with friends. She had her mind buttoned up against chilly memories, she believed.

The mild temperature didn't demand gloves. Charleen stood near the school, her back to the building, scanning the children like a security camera. A small, cold hand touched hers. She jerked her hand back, sucked in a lung full of chilly air, and discovered a first-grade girl, innocently smiling up at her. Charleen stooped so she was eye to eye, and greeted her, exhaling a cloud of relief.

Charleen rubbed her hand across the girl's head and continued her walk around the school yard.

A few sixth-grade boys played cards. A curly-haired boy threw down his cards. "Oh Wizzee! You win again." A lean boy, with straight brown hair, smirked as he collected the cards.

Matt Janson, the smart kid, sat on a bench by himself writing in a notebook. Timmy Iverson, a sad-looking, small boy, wearing an oversized gray jacket walked toward him. Matt reached into his pocket, removed a red yo-yo and handed it to Timmy, who smiled, obviously happy to receive the gift. Timmy worked at the yo-yo, trying to make it climb back up the string. Matt said something and pointed to Timmy's wrist. He stopped tossing the Yo-Yo and rubbed his wrist. They talked for a few minutes before Timmy walked away.

Timmy turned back, raised his voice and said, "Hey Matt, I'll ask my dad if you can come over tomorrow. Bye." Matt wrote something in his notebook.

On Friday, Charleen sat at her desk, neatly stacked with student folders on one side. Her office had a tall wooden shelf filled with counseling, psychology and social-work books and magazines. Another, smaller bookshelf by the door, held her favorite and most used counseling and reference books.

She was extremely thankful for her job and for Mr. Heim's flexibility with her starting date. She realized that, in Minnesota, elementary school counseling was not yet mandated by the legislature. But fortunately, a few foresighted school districts took a proactive approach and created budget appropriations for elementary school counselors.

Her office window faced the back of the school, south toward the teacher's parking lot. The bright sunlight of the chilly October day, deceptively warmed the office. For the fifth tedious day in a row, she was reading the files of her new students. In reality, *she* was the new person, trying to get acquainted with a couple hundred kids at once. However, most of her student time focused on the older students, and their adolescent challenges.

She had the Urban files open. It was hard to believe that they were the same age. Karen, age 13, and Greg, 13.

They should be in seventh grade ... held back due to academic under-achievement. *They really stuck together.*

They had been transferred from Minneapolis to a foster family in St. Cloud because their dad was in the nearby prison, and their mother was deemed to be unfit to parent them. Their test scores were average. They just didn't *do* much at school except cause trouble. Fights ... Stole a car too.

The intercom buzzed, followed by the secretary's voice. "The Urbans are here."

"Holly, before you send them in, could you come in here?" Charleen said toward the intercom on the wall.

Holly entered Charleen's office, quickly closing the door.

"What is it, Ms. Therry?"

"You've lived here awhile ... What's the story on this prison in town? Is it for really bad people, or what?"

"Well, no. It's like a first step, some prisoners stay here, others get sent to more appropriate facilities after an evaluation."

"What's with the giant rock wall around it then?" Charleen asked.

"Oh, the granite for the prison came from the huge quarry outside of town. That's why this is *The Granite City*. It's the longest granite wall in the world and one of the oldest prisons. —Right here in St. Cloud."

"Oh, and that's why they're here. It's so sad," said Charleen. "Send them in, Holly."

The Smart Kid

Holly stepped out and spoke to the two sullen-faced teens who reluctantly shuffled into the office. Karen's black hair hung straight. She was pretty, but didn't try to be. Greg had wavy, dark hair. A small bruise marked his face.

"What did we do now?" asked Karen. Her bright green blouse was a stark contrast to the darkness of her mood.

"Oh, you're not in trouble. I wanted to personally welcome you to the school." Charleen tried to convey care and acceptance, to these kids, who obviously needed it.

The twins just stood there, unsmiling, looking uncomfortable.

"Please, sit down," said Charleen. She could see the relational walls on their faces and wondered if she could break through.

She waited while they looked around, then flopped and slumped in the two farthest chairs against the wall. Two empty chairs and the desk stood between her and them. Charleen walked around to the front of her desk. She turned one of the chairs intended for the Urbans and sat much closer to the twins. They sat upright in their chairs.

"I know that you're from Minneapolis; how do you like St. Cloud?" Charleen asked, smiling, and wondering who would speak first. *Start with something easy...*

"It sucks!" said Greg. "It's too small! They don't even have a decent bus system like they do in Minneapolis. How are we supposed to get around?" He shot a defiant scowl in her direction.

"Well, why do you need to *get around*? Don't your parents—foster parents drive you where you want to go?"

The twins looked at each other and smirked. Charleen knew that twins had a special way of communicating with each other in a manner that was nearly psychic.

"Sometimes we need to go to the mall during the day, but they're both working, and it's too far to take our bikes," complained Greg.

"Now during the day, you're supposed to be in school, right?"

Karen straightened up and scowled at Greg. "Oh yes, Ms. Therry. Greg just whines sometimes. Can we go now?"

"Wait a minute. How are you adjusting to your new foster family?" *Get more personal.*

"They suck!" said Greg, in a loud voice. "I don't know why we can't be with Mom. They won't even take us to go see her."

Oh, you poor, angry boy. Charleen understood his anger. From his young perspective, his family had abandoned him. Her heart went out to him. She felt the same pain.

Karen scowled at him. "Because she's in Detox right now, you idiot!" She crossed her arms in an exasperated pose and looked away for a moment. Then she looked at Charleen with a softer expression on her face and said, "Ms. Therry, our parents aren't dead, so we're not orphans. But what's the word for children who don't live with their parents? There must be one, right?"

Abandoned, thought Charleen, who got a small glimpse behind the girl's facade, and saw a vulnerable, hurting child. "I'm sorry, Karen, but I don't know."

Karen just nodded, and then the wall went up again.

"Listen, I understand what you're going through, but you two are fortunate that you've got each other for support. Right?"

Charleen smiled, hoping they'd find something positive to say.

The twins said nothing.

"Greg, I understand that you were in a little altercation today in the schoolyard," said Charleen.

Greg crossed his arms and looked at Karen.

Karen, unfolded her arms. "Um, we don't know what an 'alcartation' is."

"Oh, I'm sorry. I mean, did you get in a small fight, Greg?"

He scowled.

"Greg gets kinda protective if a boy talks with me," said Karen.

"Oh. Do you want to talk about it?" Charleen didn't expect a positive response. *Please share your pain. Express yourself.*

Greg shook his head.

I took this as far as it could go. "If you ever want to talk, you may come to my office. I mean that. Just ask your teacher for a hall pass. All right?" Charleen gave a soothing smile to the impenetrable twins.

Charleen stood to open a desk drawer and removed a Polaroid camera. "We need a photo for your files … smile."

The twins didn't smile.

The Smart Kid

She took an instant photo of each of them. They blinked at the flash. "Thanks. You may return to your class."

After they walked out with evident relief, Charleen made a few notes in their file finishing with: *Unhappy living in St. Cloud. Check into possible visitation with their mom or dad.*

She hoped that their mom sobered up and realized how she's damaging her children. Charleen began to get angry at their mother, someone she didn't even know. But she did know that children were hurting because of her.

She shelved the manila folder and her angry thoughts, and moved to the next file, Matt Janson's.

Then there's this model student, Matt Janson. Test scores are good. Completes his assignments. A's in every class. She made a mental note to be sure to meet the parents of this little genius during parent-teacher conferences. *He should be waiting by now.*

Charleen opened the office door and saw the blond-haired kid with the notebook, seated and waiting.

The Urban twins were standing over Matt, menacingly. Greg had his finger an inch from Matt's face. "You think you're so smart."

Matt, showing no trace of intimidation, smiled at him. "Greg, you don't have to always act so tough. It will be easier to make friends if you're nice."

Greg removed his finger from Matt's face and just frowned at him.

"Hello," said Charleen.

The twins jerked their heads in her direction and then zipped out the door.

Matt watched them leave and turned to Charleen. He smiled.

She wanted to meet this bright young boy, it would be a happy contrast from the twins.

He was ready to enter her office when Holly interrupted, from behind the registration desk, "Ms. Therry, it's time for that meeting with Mr. Heim."

"Oh. Tell him I'll be there soon." She turned to the boy. "Listen Matt, I'm sorry but my other tasks and meetings took longer than I anticipated— ran out of time. Could we please meet on Monday?"

asked Charleen, with a friendly smile.

"I look forward to it, Ms. Therry," Matt said.

"So do I, Max— Matt." Charleen turned abruptly and walked away.

Charleen parked her Coupe in the slush-filled parking lot. She turned off the engine, but remained in the car. She shook her head, started the engine, and began backing out. The loud, close car horn shocked her. She jammed her foot on the brakes and saw the side of a white truck in her mirror. She sighed, eased the car forward a few feet into the parking spot, turned off the engine, and removed the keys.

By the time she shuffled into the room and flopped in a chair, Dr. Lansing was introducing himself. He appeared to be in his late 50s, wore glasses, and did not wear a suit coat or tie. He smiled intermittently as he finished his introduction.

"You can share as much as you are comfortable doing. It's our first meeting, so just give us a general introduction and tell us why you're here." He nodded to the group of adults who sat there, unsmiling, in a circle, on uncomfortable plastic chairs, looking uncomfortable.

A guy named Mike started. He was a stocky, brown-haired, white man in his mid-forties. His father had died of cancer. He'd known it was coming, but he still didn't have the courage to tell his dad that he …

Then Maija, the attractive brunette, spoke. Her son had been only a few months old when he died of SIDS. She sobbed, "I was holding him, trying to wake him, and he just hung in my arms." Charleen watched her tearfully. Her heart went out to her, since she felt the same pain. Everyone remained quiet. Dr. Lansing put his hand on her shoulder. After she calmed down, others shared.

Each person shared their name and reason for attending. Charleen was unable to focus her attention; the names and stories blended into a cold soup of sorrow; Mona, Sharri, someone, another person … death of parent due to old age, death of someone else, death, death.

The room was quiet.

The Smart Kid

Suddenly alert, Charleen realized it was her turn. She sat upright, took a deep breath and plunged into the icy waters of self-exposure.

"I'm Charleen Therry. I was married to a wonderful man, Garrett. We had an eight year-old son, Max. This summer I chose ... *I chose,*" She sighed deeply and swallowed with difficulty, her throat dry, "... to attend an educational consortium for school counselors. My husband and son brought me there, and then left for home."

Oh, God, help me through this.

Tears welled up in her eyes. "I had no idea it would be the last time I saw them ... alive," she choked out. "There was a car accident ... and ..." Charleen began to sob. It was the first time that she'd had to explain it to strangers.

The memory of caressing Max's small, cold hand was nearly unbearable.

She calmed herself, took a deep breath, and swam onward. "I'm lost and abandoned without them. I was a wife for twelve years. And a mom. And now, what am I? A widow and a ... What's the word for a mom who's lost a child? There's a word for a child without a parent. Shouldn't there be a word for a parent without a child? It's just as important as being a widow or an orphan. I'm ... childless."

She couldn't say another word. But she had said much more than she expected. The opportunity to vent revealed unexamined thoughts.

As she sobbed, the older woman put an arm around her. "We're here for you, honey."

Charleen sipped from her water glass and regained control of her emotions.

After everyone had introduced themselves, Dr. Lansing spoke.

"Listen, I understand what you're going through. I've been through it too. But you are fortunate that you've got each other in this group for support, right? Make use of a couple of friends, you'll be stronger as a result."

Doctor Lansing explained the grieving process as five stages: Denial, Anger, Control, Depression, and Acceptance.

"Not everyone goes through these stages in the same order or at the same speed," said Dr. Lansing. "If you purposefully work through these steps, you may reach the final stage of Acceptance. But some people never do, they live in continual avoidance of the pain."

"Doctor," asked Sharri, "could you please explain the control stage?"

"Survivors try to control everything. Suffering a serious loss makes them realize that they are not in control; as if Death has pushed them out of the driver's seat and now they are simply passengers in their own life. In response, survivors over-compensate by trying to control too much. Avoidance is also a control response, in an attempt to keep the pain away."

After further discussion, the meeting ended. Charleen began to leave the room when Dr. Lansing asked, "Charleen, may I speak with you a moment?" She nodded and they stepped away from the exit.

"Charleen, you are suffering double the grief of any of these others," said Dr Lansing.

She crossed her arms. "I know."

"Yes, I'm sure you do. I'm offering my assistance to you because of that. Do you want to discuss it any more tonight?"

Charleen shook her head.

"That's fine. But if you ever want to talk, you may come to my office, or call me. I mean that. All right?"

Charleen uncrossed her arms and offered a handshake as she said good-bye.

"One more thing, Charleen. Because your grief is so extreme, please be sensitive to how it controls you," he cautioned.

She nodded and left the room with evident relief.

It is much harder being the subject than the counselor. She empathized with the Urbans.

Charleen returned home emotionally drained.

That was way too hard. Retelling the tragedy only brings up the pain, it doesn't bring a solution, because there isn't one.

Charleen skipped dinner and got ready for bed early. She laid in her large, soft bed and tried to read student reports, but her mind couldn't focus. Tossing the papers onto the end table, she tried to recall the meeting, which was mostly a depressing blur. But she did remember the Stages.

She sensed that she had left Denial in her past when she stopped searching for Max's face in a crowd of children. She rarely awoke and reached for Garrett, surprised that he wasn't in bed. Anger, Control, and Depression, were stages that she could understand. But Acceptance seemed an impossibility.

Charleen knew that she was on the Grief Journey, and she was a long, long way from her final destination.

She fell asleep with the light on, holding Max's Teddy Bear, staying on 'her side' of the Queen-sized bed, her remaining concession to Denial.

4. Matt

MATT LIFTED HIS head from the pillow. The digital clock radio glowed 7:00 in green neon.

Monday— appointment with the new counselor. *New? It is already October. Where has she been for the last few weeks?*

He planned to investigate because...*You never really know who they are working for.*

He leaned over the edge of his bed, until his outstretched hands touched the floor, and did 100 pushups.

Matt stood on the playground in the crisp October air. The morning bell rang, officially starting the school day. One of the teachers ushered students into the school and told them to take off their boots and hang up their coats— orders they heard every day.

He walked to his homeroom and listened to Mrs. M. explain what they would be doing that day. Blah, blah.

At the top of the hour, the English teacher entered and told the students to open their English books and to blah, blah, blah.

Next, the math teacher entered and distributed worksheets to the students. He said, "This is a practice sheet; you won't be graded on it." So Matt answered every question wrong.

A half hour before lunchtime, a student volunteer delivered a note to the teacher. She passed it to Matt and told him to go meet the new counselor, Ms. Therry.

Finally, escape from the tedium.

He did want to meet her. Something about her drew his interest. She presented herself in a professional manner by the way that she dressed and by her demeanor with the kids. But he had seen a crack in her protective facade when he had asked why she started late.

Matt walked through the hallways of the school. Artwork from each grade adorned the halls. Several of the sixth-grade drawings were sophisticated, realistic depictions. He saw pictures of roller skates, Star Wars characters, race cars, the moon landing, and landscapes. As he

The Smart Kid

meandered past the fifth- and fourth-grade rooms, the drawings became more childlike: Kermit the Frog, trees, bicycles and baseballs. Some of the drawings were black art scratchings, with multi-colored images scratched into the black waxy surface. The artwork surrounding the younger grades were messy, enthusiastic doodles with cracking, flaky paint, or they were simplistic artwork made from dried macaroni glued to the pages. Matt imagined that he was walking back in time, getting younger and younger.

Mr. Beacham, the Social Studies teacher, hobbled toward Matt. He asked Matt what he was doing in the hallway. Matt showed him the note from the office. He was told that he should "hurry along then."

Matt carefully smoothed the *St. Cloud School District 742* inscribed note paper, and saved it in his back pocket for its next mission.

When he entered, he was told to wait in the outer office for Ms. Therry. He waited for several minutes. She opened her office door and shined her bright smile on him, warming him inside.

"Hello, Matt, please come in." Wearing a yellow blouse and light green skirt, she looked like a sunny day in a green meadow.

He approached Ms. Therry with his hand extended. She raised her eyebrows in surprise. He gave her a firm hand-shake, and sat in a wooden chair facing her desk. She left the door open and sat behind her desk.

"Well, Matt," she grinned. "You must enjoy school. Your grades are very good."

Matt smiled. "Knowing the correct answers doesn't mean that someone enjoys school. But I do like the kids here. They are nice. Minnesota Nice."

Ms. Therry smiled at that comment. "Yes, I've noticed that too, since I've moved here."

"So you moved to Minnesota after school started?" Matt asked.

She paused for a long moment before she answered his probing inquiry, her voice quieter. "Yes, I did start late. I didn't want to discuss this in front of the whole class when you asked because it's a personal issue."

"OK, I'm sorry to have pried."

"Well thank-you for being so polite," she said with a charming smile.

He evaluated her apparent sincerity, as she smiled at him. The bangs of her short hair were just long enough to rest over her eyebrows. Her eyelashes flicked at a few strands when she blinked. She brushed her hair back.

It was not an act. Her smile wasn't masking anything. Ms. Therry was sincere. Then it was Matt's turn to pause a long moment before he opened up to her.

"I'm not really here to learn. I'm here to help." He studied her reaction.

"Wow," said Ms. Therry. "That's a very good attitude."

Her sincerity rang true. Matt smiled inside. *She is the one.*

He made eye contact before he said, "Thank-you, Ms. Therry." Matt felt that they'd made a connection for a moment. Then she put on her professional demeanor, again. She adjusted herself in her chair and flipped through a file folder.

"I was looking at your reading scores, and they are very advanced. You should be in a reading environment that is more of a challenge for you. How do you feel about that?" She looked up from her folder.

"What do you mean? There isn't a more advanced class."

"Well, that's true," said Ms. Therry. "but Mrs. Reilly, the librarian, said that she'd be willing to read through an advanced novel with you."

"Do you mean, it would be only me and her-- none of the other little kids in the class?"

"Yes, doesn't that sound nice?" Her persuasive smile begged him to agree with her.

He looked into her eyes, thinking a moment. "No. I said that I'm here to help these kids. How can I, if I'm in a class by myself?"

"You're here to help the other students?"

Matt took a deep breath.

OK, here goes...

"Yes, like a superhero; everyone needs one at some time, to do what they can't do themselves." Matt waited for a reaction. It didn't

The Smart Kid

register with her.

"Well, fine. You said that you've met kids at other places. I read your admission paper and it says that you moved here from Oklahoma. But I couldn't find your school records from there. They aren't in the file. I guess we're still waiting for them to arrive." As she said this, she paged through his folder.

"Yes," said Matt. "You'd think that coming from Oklahoma, they'd have arrived *sooner*!"

"Yes ..." said Ms. Therry, still reading notes in the folder. Ms. Therry yanked her gaze from the folder to Matt's smiling eyes. She appeared more surprised than amused.

The secretary, who had been standing at the open door for a minute, rapped on the frame.

"Oh, what is it, Holly?"

"The special-ed teacher is ready for your appointment."

"Oh. Well, Matt, thanks for visiting. I hope school goes well for you this year. One more thing ..." She removed the Polaroid camera from her desk. "I want a photo of you for my file. OK?"

Matt didn't respond. She pointed the camera and pressed the button. Matt jerked his head at the bright flash.

"Oh, that's bright!" he said, eyes blinking.

The photograph popped out. At first, it was an indiscernible, questionable image but it slowly began to morph toward clarity.

"Thanks, Ms. Therry." Matt shook her hand again and left.

Charleen turned to the young secretary and slowly shook her head. "That was a subtle joke, coming from a twelve-year-old, wasn't it?"

"I don't get it," Holly said.

"Oklahomans used to be known as 'Sooners' because when they had the land grab in 1889, many of them sneaked in early and staked their claim *sooner* than the legal starting date."

"Oh, funny," said Holly unimpressed. Holly shrugged her shoulders.

Charleen continued, "And I gave him an opportunity to do advanced novel reading with Mrs. Reilly and I was surprised he turned it down. He's way beyond sixth-grade reading levels."

"Some kids don't want to be challenged," suggested Holly.

"No. ... It's something else with him. ... I'm going to have to investigate him further ..."

Charleen looked at the fully-developed photograph, which she still held in her hand.

Matt's face was blurry.

A week later, Charleen was in the staff lounge, drinking coffee, with three other teachers, when Mr. Beacham entered. She had noticed his limp before, but didn't know the cause.

He said, "Could any of you please take my playground duty today? My stiff leg is acting up again, and this chilly weather is bad for it."

"I will!"

Once again, everyone in the teacher's lounge turned to look at Charleen.

"Thank you," said Mr. Beacham. He settled himself into a chair with a big sigh.

Later that day, Charleen bundled up and went outside for playground duty. She wore her long jacket and gloves. She surveyed the kids running around, playing kickball, and jump ropes and other games, seemingly unaware of the temperature. Matt Janson sat on a bench writing in a notebook. He looked up and called to a girl. Charleen recognized the third-grader as Deena Swenson. Matt was asking her questions. She shook her head. Charleen shuffled in closer to eavesdrop.

"No, no. I promised not to tell. And you shouldn't break a promise, should you?" said the cute curly-blonde girl.

"That depends on *why* you shouldn't tell. If someone's getting hurt, then it's right to tell, because it helps them, and— " He stopped and looked at Charleen. Deena saw her and ran away, scuffling through the thin layer of snow.

"Is everything OK?" Charleen asked with sincere concern.

"Not certain," said Matt with a frown. He adjusted the stocking cap on his head.

The Smart Kid

"Ms. Therry!" someone yelled. She turned to find Donna Nessler waving at her. When she looked back, Matt was writing in his notebook.

As Charleen walked toward Donna, she passed the two boys who had been playing cards last week. She heard the name 'Wizzee' again.

"Hi Donna," she said, glad to be developing a friendship with another teacher.

"Hi. Are you enjoying playground duty?" Donna asked.

"Yes. I love it! It thrills me to watch the kids play. Oh, I heard one boy call another one 'Wizzee'. Do you know why they call him that?" Charleen pointed to the boys.

"Oh, yes. That's because his name is Wayne and his initials are WZ. So you know how kids create nicknames," Donna explained with a smirk.

"What's his last name?"

"Zimmerman,"

"Zimmerman! Is his father Colin?" Charleen asked, alarmed.

"Yes. Why? What's wrong?"

The frigid breeze was already stinging her tear-filled eyes as Charleen abruptly turned and walked off the playground.

As the month matured, the school days progressed with a variety of classes: Math, Science, English, Physical Education, and Social Studies.

It was the last hour of the day, mid-October. Mr. Beacham was returning their graded Social Studies tests. Matt barely glanced at the page he was handed. A voice behind Matt whispered, "What'd you get, another A?"

It took a second before Matt realized the whisper was directed at him. He turned to Joey. The pimply-faced kid gave a questioning look.

"I got a C!" whined Joey. "What for?"

"Let me see it," said Matt. Joey handed him the paper. He had several questions wrong. Matt scanned question 20:

What important historical event occurred on Nov. 23, 1963?

A. The end of the Vietnam war

B. *The first man on the moon*
C. *The assassination of President Kennedy*
D. *None of the above*

Letter C was circled with a pencil. In red pen, it was X'd out, a big 0 written next to it.

"The answer is *D. None of the above.* But it's a trick question. Kennedy was shot on Nov. 22nd, not the 23rd," said Matt, shaking his head. "I hate it when teachers write questions in this way. There's no educational value in them."

"Do we have a problem, gentlemen?" asked the gruff voice of Mr. Beacham.

Joey looked straight ahead as if he were a military cadet responding to his C.O. "No, sir."

With a slow deliberateness, Matt turned to the front of the classroom and looked directly at the teacher. "Yes, sir."

Mr. Beacham's eyebrows raised, along with the attention of every student in the room. Mr. Beacham stood— usually a difficult task for him, so he didn't often do it. The room quieted.

Mr. Beacham took an intimidating step forward. "Well, Mr. Janson, what is it, this time?"

"In my opinion," said Matt with confidence in his voice, "The purpose of question 20 is to trick students into selecting C because the date is one day from the correct date of Nov. 22nd."

Mr. Beacham didn't hide his surprise, letting his mouth drop open for a second. "First, it was an extra credit question, so it's supposed to be hard. And second, I don't 'trick' my students, Mr. Janson," said Mr. Beacham. Every student turned to Matt.

"Sir, A and B were so obviously wrong that it made C appear to be more correct, but it wasn't." The students turned to look at Mr B.

"Obvious?" echoed Mr. Beacham, frowning.

"Yes. We learned that the Vietnam war ended later. And everyone knows that the moon landing happened in 1969, in our lifetime. It was the biggest event of the decade. So why try to trick us with a date in November that is one day off?"

"Well, that's the point, to make sure that students didn't confuse the important date of the 22nd with the unimportant date of the 23rd."

The Smart Kid

During this interchange, the heads of the students turned left and right as if they were watching a tennis match. But no tennis match ever held their interest like these volleys.

"So how's it working?" Matt stood and turned to the class. "Who here got question 20 wrong by selecting letter C? Raise your hands. Come on!"

Mr. Beacham blinked his eyes a couple of times. Nineteen of the twenty-two students raised their hands. Matt turned to Mr. Beacham, who looked as if he was going to speak, but just closed his mouth and frowned.

"But," said Matt, "the 23rd of November, 1963, *was* an important date in history."

"Oh?" said Mr. Beacham in a condescending tone. "Educate me."

"One of the most important TV shows in the history of the world began on that date."

There was no more condescension in his voice. "What show is that?"

"Dr. Who," said Matt with a smile, as he remained standing.

"I've never heard of it," said Mr. Beacham defensively.

"It's a British show, and it's only on the public television channels. But it's been running every single week, for nearly 16 years. And I wouldn't be surprised if it was still on the air in another 30 years," said Matt.

"What's it about?" asked Mr. Beacham.

Every student tuned in to this unusual exchange.

"It's about a man who is a time traveler. He is called Dr. Who because no one truly knows who he is. It's as if he has no history."

The bell rang, ending the class and the discussion.

After school, a group of sixth-graders were hanging out in their usual spot at the back of the school yard. Dave, Wayne, and Joe huddled together joking with each other. Pat sat on the cold ground unwrapping a Slo-Poke, chocolate sucker he had removed from his coat pocket. Other students leaned against the chain-link fence. A boy wearing a striped sweater tried to climb the fence with little success.

Matt exited the school building, glanced at the group of students, and started walking away.

"Hey Brainiac! Come over here," yelled Dave across the school yard.

Matt approached the huddle.

A few students stepped closer to listen.

"Hey, Janson," said Wayne, "You sure made Mr. Beacham shut-up today."

"And stand up!" said Dave. All the kids laughed.

"Who are you going to be for Halloween?" quizzed Joey.

"I don't do that anymore," said Matt. "What about you?"

"Maybe Superman," Joey replied.

"I'm going to be the strongest guy of all— The Hulk," said a boy, bending his arm to create a muscle that was impossible to see under his sleeve.

"No! Everyone knows that Superman is the best superhero," yelled Pat. "That's why he's called Super."

A few of the other students nodded in agreement.

"I think Batman is great because of his cool car, and cave," said Dave.

"What? He doesn't even have any superpowers," yelled Striped-Sweater Kid.

"Well…" said Matt, "You could say that Batman's superpowers are the cool gadgets that he uses: the car, hooks, ropes and especially his knowledge." Every student in the group went silent and listened to Matt. Matt ignored their surprised looks.

"Knowledge isn't a superpower!" yelled Striped-Sweater Kid, leaning against the fence.

"Who's your favorite: Batman, The Hulk or Superman?" asked Wayne.

"None of the above," said Matt. "My favorite is Captain Marvel."

"What? Who the hell is he?" yelled Pat.

"He is a boy named Billy, who can become a powerful, smart, grown man whenever he wants, simply by saying the word SHAZAM." The audience of kids still gave their full attention to

The Smart Kid

Matt.

"What does SHAZAM mean?" ask Dave.

"It's spelled from the first letters of gods from Greek mythology and powerful men of history. S stood for Solomon, who was very wise. He became so well-known for his wisdom, that people visited him from around the world to get their difficult questions answered. Solomon used his knowledge and experience to help counsel people," explained Matt.

"He used his knowledge— as a superpower!" announced Wayne. He grinned at Striped-Sweater Kid, who stuck out his tongue.

"I like Superman," said Joey. "I'm collecting his comics. I've got a bunch." He looked down and scraped his boot on the ground.

"Oh yeah," challenged Pat. "How many?"

"Um, twelve, I think," said Joey.

"TWELVE!" scoffed Pat. "There's, like, a thousand of them! My dad used to read it when he was a kid. Twelve? That's a lot— Not!" Pat left, laughing.

Joey sniffled, wiped his sleeve across his nose and looked at his feet.

"Don't let him bother you, Joey," said Matt. "Twelve is a whole year's worth, so that's a good start. Listen, I may have a few copies of Superman comics at my apartment. I'll try to find them for you. How do you feel about that?"

At this, Joey looked up, smiling at Matt. "Yes, that would be great!"

Matt turned away to walk home, as he always did, never with any book bags. He smiled to himself and said, "SHAZAM!"

5. Mysteries

A STUDENT ENTERED Matt's homeroom and handed a note to Mrs. M.

Matt was surprised when Mrs. M. gave him the unexpected note to see the counselor. "Don't worry. I don't think that you're in trouble."

As Matt walked the long hallway again, he smoothed the logo-imprinted note between his hands, and hid it carefully in his back pocket.

He greeted Ms. Therry with a handshake, sat in the wooden chair facing the desk, and waited for her to make her request, or whatever she wanted.

"Hello Matthew, how are you doing today?" she started.

"I'm fine. How are you?"

"Oh, well, I'm doing fine too."

Matthew said nothing.

She rubbed her hands along her skirt to smooth it out. "Principal Heim said that Mr. Beacham, the social studies teacher, was quite impressed by your intelligence."

"Yes?"

"Do you know about the state Knowledge Bowl contest?"

"No, I haven't heard of it."

"It's a new competition between high schools. Teams of students take a test of advanced questions and compete against other teams in their brackets. Several Minnesota schools are planning to model the high school contest for elementary schools. Mr. Heim wants to send a team from Jefferson, and he wants you to be on it."

"No."

Ms. Therry blinked at the sudden answer. "Oh. Well, you don't have to worry about grades, because it's not a graded test. It will be a fun way for you to meet other exceptional students—"

"No, thanks." Matt shook his head. "Anything else?"

Ms. Therry pressed him further. "Wouldn't it be neat to have

The Smart Kid

your team photos published in the paper? You could gain recognition for your abilities. Plus Mr. Heim thinks it's a good way to demonstrate the quality of the St. Cloud School District."

Once again, Matt felt her pleading smile begging him to agree with her. He gave a big sigh and stared her down with a frown. "I'm not interested. All right?"

"Whatever you want to do is fine. I'm just making this request for Principal Heim. You can go now, Matthew." She didn't smile.

"Have a nice weekend, Ms. Therry." He stood and left the room.

Monday morning, Charleen strolled through the hallway, her handbag filled with student's files that she'd reviewed over the weekend. She wasn't required to work at home, but she wanted to complete this task as soon as possible. Focusing on work kept her distracted from personal sorrows.

She saw a group of boys kneeling on the floor around a cardboard box labeled *Pall Mall Cigarettes*. The box brimmed with 50 to 70 comic books. The four boys sifted through the box, intently focused, as if it contained valuable treasure.

"Hi, boys. What's going on?" she asked with a smile.

Dave Brewer said, "Joey just got a whole box of Superman comics, and they're really old!"

Charleen held out a hand, "May I see one?"

Dave handed her a worn Superman comic. The cover depicted a man resembling Superman named Bizarro. Issue #202. Price 25¢.

"Wow, that is old," said Charleen, honestly surprised. "Where'd he get them?"

"Matt Janson," Dave said. "He just gave him the whole box. Lucky dog!" Dave turned back to the box of treasures.

Joey, sitting in the middle of the group of admiring boys, had a huge smile on his face.

"Wow! Cool!"

"Joey, you've got the record now for the biggest comic collection."

"Hey Joey, can I come to your house to look at these after school?"

Bob Miller

Charleen scanned the hall in vain, looking for Matt Janson, the absent Comic Book Benefactor.

For the third time, Charleen called the Janson home. Once again, a man's voice on one of those new answering gadgets, "We can't come to the phone right now. Please leave a message." A beep sounded. She hadn't left any messages because she didn't like talking to these ridiculous machines. It made her self-conscious. Knowing that she was being recorded, she measured every word.

"Hello, Mr. Janson," said Charleen, "um ... This is Ms. Therry, the counselor from Jefferson Elementary school. Could you call me?" She paused. *What now?* "Matt's not in trouble. I want to discuss his placement in a class and his participation in a district competition. Please call this number."

They are so hard to get a hold of. There may be advantages to being able to leave a message. Don't have to keep calling every day. As she pondered this, the phone rang, startling her.

The voice at the other end said, "This is Mr. Janson, Matt's dad. Apparently, you're compelled to talk to us about our son. What is it?"

Wow, that's weird. Was he listening?

Charleen ignored the demanding tone of his voice. "I want to talk to you or your ... wife about Matt's placement in a class. At Principal Heim's request, I'd like to discuss a state-wide competition for gifted students. However I also wanted to discuss Matt's unusual interactions with the other kids in the school and—"

The voice interrupted, his tone was much softer. "Ms. Therry, are you calling from your school's public line?"

"Yes, I guess that's the main phone line. Why?"

"Could you please meet my wife at the diner on Fifth Street, downtown?"

"Yes, but why?" She was glad that he couldn't see the frown on her face.

"I can't explain now. But you wanted to meet us, right? Her preference is to discuss this in person. The phone isn't an adequate medium for discussions such as this. Can we meet you tomorrow at 4:30?"

The Smart Kid

"Well, yes," said Charleen. "That works. Will she recognize me?"

"Undoubtedly. Good, that settles it. Good-bye."

She held the phone receiver in her hand for a moment. As she gently replaced the receiver on the phone cradle, a satisfied smile appeared on her face.

Finally!

The intercom buzzed, startling Charleen. "Yes, Holly?"

"I have a student who wants to talk with you. Are you available?"

"Yes, I've got time now," said Charleen.

Wayne Zimmerman shuffled in and gently pushed the door shut, with none of the enthusiasm or energy he'd exhibited on the playground when playing cards.

Oh my God. I can't face him!

Charleen crossed her arms and remained in her chair. "Can I help you with something, Wayne?"

"Um, you said that if we need to talk, then we could come to you. So…"

"Well, I'm sorry, but I thought this would be a quick question. I'll contact you again when I have more time, OK?"

Wayne's mouth formed a silent, surprised, "Oh."

She opened the door to allow him to leave.

Holly watched him walk out.

"Done already?" Holly asked.

"We rescheduled for a later time," said Charleen.

Charleen shut the door, and dumped herself into her desk chair. She dropped her head on her folded arms and closed her eyes, breathing deeply.

After Charleen calmed down, she went to the teacher's lounge for a break. Most of the staff were complaining about the usual school politics and administrative red tape. Charleen rarely joined in these discussions, even though she didn't enjoy all the paperwork that she had to do as a government employee, either.

Donna Nessler was there, eating a sandwich.

"Did you hear that Jack Iverson got arrested for child battery?" she said. She took a tiny bite of her sandwich.

"I've heard that, since school started, there have been three parents that have been questioned by the police about the same thing," another woman said. She took a long drag on her cigarette.

"Wow, three families in two months? That's a lot."

"Is it some kind of undercover sting?"

"How could they do that?"

Charleen Therry wondered the same thing.

After school, the next day, Charleen drove downtown to The Crash Diner on Fifth Street. The small, outdated restaurant had a row of backless, pedestal stools with red vinyl seats along the counter. Several booths lined the windows. The walls were adorned with baseball mementos and photos from the Minnesota Twins and the three local high school teams: the Tech Tigers, the Apollo Eagles and Cathedral Crusaders.

For this time of the day, it was unsurprising to find it empty. A waitress stood behind the counter and greeted Charleen. A woman sitting in the farthest booth in the back waved to Charleen.

As Charleen approached, the woman stood and smiled. "Hello, I'm Matt's mom. It's so good to meet you!" She clasped Charleen's hand in both of hers, giving an overly-enthusiastic shake.

"Well, I'm glad to meet you, Mrs, ur, what should I call you?"

"Oh, yes. My name is Mrs. Janson, but you may call me Barbara." She held her closed-mouth smile like she was posing for a photo.

"Um, I wanted to tell you how well Matt is doing in school," said Charleen.

"Oh, that's nice!" She smiled, showing teeth. She stared at Charleen and waited.

"Have you and your husband considered moving Matt into a more advanced reading class?"

"Oh, Matt told me that you'd ask that," said Barbara. "But Mr. Janson said that we are definitely not going to move him. Matt likes where he's at, with all his little friends."

The Smart Kid

"Yes," said Charleen frowning. "He said something like that."

"He's a very particular boy," said Barbara. "He's quite articulate and smart."

"I've noticed. That's why he should be in an advanced class," said Charleen.

"Yes, well. Sorry. He's staying where he is. That's all I can say." She put an overly-apologetic look on her face, as if Charleen had just said that her dog died.

Strike One.

"We have another opportunity. The school principal is inviting Matt to take part in a competition for elementary school students. It's —"

"Oh yes. I'd heard that you wanted to discuss that, too. My husband and I don't want Matthew to do any extra-curricular activities like that. Sorry," she said, with a finality in her voice that indicated to Charleen that this discussion topic was done. Mrs. Janson stared out the window.

Strike Two.

"Well, OK. It's your choice, of course," said the counselor, giving a weak smile.

Barbara Janson turned to Charleen and pitched one last fast ball.

"Also I won't be able to come to the Parent-Teacher conferences next week. Sorry. Thanks for meeting with me." Barbara stood and grabbed her purse. She looked at her watch, then walked out the back door.

Strike Three, and she's outta there.

Charleen sat in the diner for another minute, staring through the emptiness formerly occupied by Matt's mom.

Charleen wondered what the hell had just happened.

Why even meet me, if all that you're going to do is say 'no'?

At home that night, Charleen was kneeling on her living room carpet, digging into one of the moving boxes. The words 'Living Room' were scrawled on one side of the box. A stack of four other boxes waited against the wall. One had the words *Garrett's books* written on the side. Another box was labeled *Max's Toys*. The others were labeled *Kitchen Junk Drawer* and *Stuff*. She paused and stared out the large window. The long shadows on the street and the orange glow of the sky hinted at the imminent sunset.

Charleen removed a photo of a fifteen-year-old Charleen with her mom and dad standing in front of Mount Rushmore. She studied it. Her mother's smiling face was turned close to her dad's, as if she were telling him a secret. The four stone presidents, with their unmoving faces, stared over her parent's shoulders, apparently eavesdropping on the conversation.

The phone rang.

"Oh. Hi, Mom. Wow! You made me jump," Charleen said.

"What are you up to tonight?" asked Mom.

"Just unpacking another box." Charleen gave a sigh.

"How are you doing, Sweetie? I worry about you, up there by yourself."

"I know, Mom. Thanks for your concern. I'm OK. I enjoy it here. I'm getting to know some of the staff too. In fact, tomorrow I'm attending a play with other teachers." She tried to sound enthusiastic for her mother's sake.

"That's nice. I'm glad," said Mom. "How's work going?"

"You know, there's good and bad in every job. But I'm getting to know the students. Tonight I met with the mother of one. Her son is a twelve-year-old prodigy," Charleen said.

"Was his mom smart too?"

"No, the opposite. She was flighty. And the dad is mysterious."

"Mysterious?" repeated her mom. "Well you always liked a good mystery."

"What do you mean?"

"You used to love reading those *Nancy Drew* books, didn't you?"

"Well, yes ... it is a mystery," said Charleen.

"I'm sure you'll work it out, honey," said Mom. "I'll call you again, Charleen. Good-bye."

Charleen thought about that meeting again. Her mom was right, it was a mystery. Something about Barbara Janson wasn't right. With a weird mother and a gruff father, it's a wonder that Matt turned out to be such a genius.

She realized that she wasn't going to get any help from the parents. And the school district in Oklahoma still hadn't sent Matt's files.

I'll have to investigate this myself, just like Nancy Drew.

6. Revelations

CHARLEEN SAT AT her desk Thursday morning reviewing her schedule for the day. *Carry On Wayward Son* by Kansas, quietly played on the radio. She wondered how was she going to do it all. Besides the meetings, unique student issues appeared each day, interrupting her well-intentioned schedule.

In addition, she was still meeting individually with students. She'd plan out her schedule and send memos to the teachers. The students would enter at their scheduled times and she'd have an informal chat with them. She'd ask strategically-planned questions, probing into possible trouble areas. After they left, she'd write a few notes in their case files.

Charleen had playground duty again that day.

Matt sat on his usual bench, holding his notebook. He called to Wayne, who, surprisingly, wasn't playing cards, but sat by himself, his back against the fence. He pulled himself up and plodded five steps to Matt.

Charleen wanted to retreat from the emotional incursion of Wayne's presence, but she forced herself to stay. Her curiosity about Matt compelled her to stand her ground and watch the scene play out. Charleen could tell that Matt was leading the conversation by asking questions. Wayne scraped the toe of his shoe on the snowy pavement as he nodded. They talked for several minutes. Matt handed Wayne a small piece of paper. Wayne returned to his spot against the fence and Matt began to write in his notebook.

"I'm really here to help..."

Charleen had ignored those words at first, thinking it was something students say to teachers because they think that's what the adults want to hear. But she realized that Matt was doing what she was: holding counseling sessions and recording notes.

He wants to be a counselor and is practicing on his friends. That's so cute!

Charleen recalled when she had decided to become a counselor.

The Smart Kid

In high school, many of her friends had difficulties with parents, or boyfriends, or eating disorders, and they all came and talked comfortably with her. She loved helping them. But she was twenty before she had committed to a career in counseling. This kid is twelve.

But that explains why he was always meeting one on one and writing in his notebook. Charleen thrilled at uncovering that little mystery, and she was relieved that his obsessive writing was motivated by a rational desire to help others.

As she recalled the uneasiness the Urban twins had demonstrated toward her, Charleen envied the natural advantage that Matt had as one of their peers. *Students probably talk more easily with Matt than with me.*

The clock in the dining room chimed 6:00. Charleen looked up from her photo album. It was time to go.

She parked her car a block away and leisurely strolled along the sidewalk to the Paramount Theatre. The posters for the upcoming shows indicated that the theater used mostly local actors and an occasional semi-pro from out of town, for the four or five performances they offered each year.

Charleen's pace quickened and her smile broadened in anticipation of a fun social evening with new friends.

"Charleen!" Donna Nessler called. She stood by the box office window with another woman.

"Hi," said Charleen with a sincere smile.

"Charleen, this is Marissa," Donna said.

After the women greeted each other, Donna continued, "My cousin plays Cecily, it's a big role and she's very psyched about it."

After a few minutes of idle talk, the three women walked into the theater.

A young woman stood in front of the double doors at the entrance to the theater hall and distributed the play programs. When they found their seats, Charleen glanced at the program: *The Importance of Being Earnest by Oscar Wilde*. At the bottom of the cover page was an advertisement for videotapes of the performance for $10.

There's no way that I can afford a videotape player on a teacher's salary.

The large, old theater exceeded Charleen's expectations. It had been built at a time when fully equipped, grand theaters were popular. She scanned the catwalk above the stage lights, and noted how deep the stage seemed to be.

Even though Charleen had seen this play years ago, she found herself thoroughly entertained and distracted from school and student issues.

JACK
"Well, my name is Ernest in town and Jack in the country, and the cigarette case was given to me in the country."

Charleen was enjoying it, even though the humor was quaint. It was fine— a relaxing diversion.

ALGERNON
"You have invented a very useful younger brother called Ernest, in order that you may be able to come up to town as often as you like."

Like a home-run baseball, Charleen thoughts were knocked from the Paramount Theater all the way back to The Crash Diner when Lady Bracknell walked onto the stage. The actress was Barbara Janson, Matt's mother. Charleen snatched the play program and looked at the list of actors. She found the name of the character, *Lady Bracknell*. The actress' name: *Sandy Otis*.

What?

She looked again.

This must be a mistake.

She paged to the back of the program for the actor biographies: *Sandy Otis is a character actor who is new to the St. Cloud community. Originally from Duluth, she hires out for retail store promotions, as an acting coach, clothing demonstrator, and other acting opportunities.*

JACK
"But you don't really mean to say that you couldn't love me if my name wasn't Ernest?"

GWENDOLEN

The Smart Kid

"But your name is Ernest."
JACK
"Yes, I know it is. But supposing it was something else? Do you mean to say you couldn't love me then?"

The words coming from the stage became a distraction to Charleen as she tried to understand this discovery.

She's not Matt's mother. She's an actor.

But his father had said that she would meet Charleen at the diner and she did. So she *must* be his mother, because his father had told her. He had told her on the phone. On the phone. She had called for days. She hadn't met the father.

Could he be an actor too? No, not likely. But it also wasn't likely that someone would impersonate a student's mother.

Is Matt doing this? Orchestrating a grand deception? No, it was not Matt's voice on the phone. It was definitely an adult male. But who? And why?

Charleen wasn't even watching the play. She stared, her eyes unfocused, at the theater program.

"Are you all right?" whispered Donna. "Charleen, are you feeling OK?"

Charleen turned her head in Donna's direction, without focusing on her. "Um ... no. I have to go." She stood and eased her way to the aisle. As she walked out of the theater, she heard Lady Bracknell, Matt's fake mom, say, "Now to minor matters. Are your parents living?"

JACK
"I have lost both my parents."

Charleen paced the empty lobby as she waited for the play to end. She hadn't wanted to remain next to Donna and Marissa since she was fidgety and unfocused and didn't want Donna asking questions.

The distant voices of the actors were interspersed with the intermittent laughter of the audience. Occasionally, Charleen recognized the voice of Matt's fake mom.

What does it mean? She wondered if it was something criminal, or just a big misunderstanding. For an irrational moment she considered that she might be the victim of a practical joke: *"Smile, you're on Candid Camera."*

Yeah, right.

She left the lobby during the final applause— not wanting to be seen by Donna and walked into a side corridor through a door labeled *Staff Only*. No one questioned her as she sat near the dressing rooms. After a tense, long wait, Matt's fake mom came around the corner, smiling and talking with some actors. When she saw Charleen, she stopped smiling.

"Hello again," said Matt's fake mom, stopping in front of Charleen.

"Hello, Sandy Otis, or should I call you Mrs. Janson?"

"So you didn't like the trick, huh?"

"Why the trick?"

"The man on the phone said that a teacher kept calling the house and he didn't have time to argue with her— er, you, so he hired me."

"What man? You mean you saw him? He paid you?" Charleen stood and faced her.

"Of course I got paid; that's what I do for a job! It seemed harmless enough." The actress crossed her arms.

"Harmless? You're jeopardizing a little kid's education!"

"What little kid? Matt? I didn't do anything to him. How would keeping a kid in school jeopardize his education?" asked Sandy spreading her arms, palms up.

"Well you ..." Charleen started to point at the actress, but dropped her hand as her voice also dropped while she considered what harm this woman had done.

Impersonation. But in truth, she had just stopped a kid from leaving a basic reading class. Or was it to prevent Charleen from meeting Matt's real mom or dad? She changed tactics.

"Who hired you?"

"Matt's dad." The actress, pointed her finger as if she'd just scored a point in an important legal debate.

"So you saw him?" Charleen cross-examined.

"Well ... no. I talked to him on the phone."

"How did you get paid?"

The Smart Kid

"Matt brought the cash before you came to the cafe," said the Faker.

Throughout this conversation, Charleen became increasingly indignant at the carelessness and lack of concern being demonstrated by the actor.

"So a little kid brought you cash paid by a man that you never met, to lie to the kid's counselor? Doesn't that seem wrong to you? Why would you trust this man?" challenged Charleen, with her palms open, but her mind grasping for understanding.

"Well, the purpose, he said, was to save him time and not rock the boat for his boy. And the subject was trivial: advanced reading class or not? Big deal." Sandy glanced around, as if she might find supporters in the jury who agreed with her. "Besides, he's paid me before."

It was as if a gavel had smashed down, convicting the defendant who had made an accidental confession. It echoed in Charleen's mind as she gasped, "What do you mean *before*?"

"Never mind."

"I WILL mind!" Charleen shook her finger at the actress. She raised her voice. "You tell me right now, or I'll report you to the authorities, and I'll report your immoral activities to the theater board and its sponsors!"

Sandy sighed deeply and confessed, "The dad called me before the start of the school year. He said that he was too busy to register the kid at school and asked me if I could do it. Apparently, the poor little boy's mother died."

Charleen was dismayed at this news.

"Now I'll admit that it's a little weird acting as a student's mom, but probably nothing criminal happened. I just registered a kid for school. And the dad paid me well, in cash. I was new to town and needed the money. So why not?"

"And you never saw the dad at that time either?"

"No."

"Have you *ever* seen the dad?" asked Charleen, suspecting not.

"Well, um, I guess not," Sandy mumbled.

A few of the other actors stopped their conversations and looked at the arguing women.

"Are you sure that it was a man and not the kid?"

"Oh my God! Get real! You think I can't tell the difference between a grown man and a kid trying to sound like a man? I can tell when someone's acting. I am an actress, you know."

"Not really. You were over-acting as Matt's mom." Charleen turned to leave.

Of all the things that Charleen had said to Sandy, this comment appeared to offend her the most. Charleen turned back and added, "Your days of acting as Matt's mom are over! If I find out that you did this again, I'll report you for child endangerment!"

"Who the hell are you to tell me what to do?" yelled Matt's former fake mom.

"I'm his counselor. My job is to care for and protect my students!"

"If you're questioning the legitimacy of his enrollment in your school, then perhaps he really *isn't* one of your students and you're *not* really his counselor!" The actress turned abruptly and walked out.

As Charleen drove home that night, a hundred thoughts sped through her mind.

Is he enrolled at school under false pretenses? But his dad authorized it, so it should be fine. His dad. Has anyone seen his dad?

And legally, what form of proof does an adult need to enroll a child into school? Children don't have picture IDs. They only have a parent verifying that the child is theirs. Even a birth certificate isn't a true proof of identity since it has no photo. They only need an address in the district. The law says that the school can't deny enrollment to a child if the parents bring proof of residency. And that proof could be as ordinary as a utility bill with the home address on it.

Yes, an address. She would go to his house, meet his dad and get this straightened out tomorrow.

At home, Charleen had difficulty falling asleep. She tossed and turned and wondered and eventually dreamed of Matthew and Ernest and lost loves.

The Smart Kid

At the first opportunity on Friday morning, Charleen retrieved Matt Janson's file. The contact information included a phone number, a P.O. Box and…Yes: a home address. During a break in her schedule, she left the school through her back office door with the intention of driving to the address: 605 10th Avenue Southeast in St. Cloud.

The residential neighborhood, populated with ranch-style starter homes, was unfamiliar. As she drove north on 10th avenue, the numbers on the houses started getting smaller … 1010 …907 … 825 … The last house was numbered 801. The road ended at a set of railroad tracks, with no crossing in sight.

She drove back the way she had come and tried to get around onto 10th on the north side of the tracks. But the avenue had been eliminated north of the tracks due to a major highway and a commercial district.

It didn't exist. It was a fake address.

No home. No mom. Unseen Dad. A Nancy Drew Mystery: The Case of the Mysterious Boy.

When she returned to the school, she entered her office through the outside door.

What would Mr. Heim think of me, devoting so much time to this one student? But what if it was fraud, or a child abduction?

She considered calling the police but, if Matt was a run-away, he might need protection from cruel parents, or foster parents

Sitting at her desk, she flipped open Matt Janson's file. *Is anything correct in here?* Under previous school, it said, 'Roosevelt School, Altus, OK.' *Why would this be true when everything else is fake? Maybe I should call the kid into my office and demand answers? I will, but not yet.*

The man's voice on the phone had a slight western twang to it. The assistant principal of Roosevelt School in Altus, OK, said again, "I'm very sorry ma'am. I'd help you if I could, but we've not had any recent student by the name of Matthew Janson."

Exasperated, Charleen said, "Yes, I understand, Mr. Williams. But could you just do this for me: look at the students who were in fifth grade last year and see if any of them were named Matthew. I don't care about the last name."

"Well, I suppose I could, but it's going to take a few minutes to find the file and search through the list because we have more than 30 kids in each grade. And we got all grades from first through eighth here," said Mr. Williams.

Charleen couldn't suppress a chuckle.

"What's so funny, ma'am?"

"Oh, I'm sorry. I know that you're kind of a small town school. But here in St. Cloud, we have about that many students in just one classroom."

"Well, our school is big enough for our town. Now, should I do that search?"

"Mmm. If you wouldn't mind, please? But you only need to check the fifth graders," said Charleen, in her sweetest voice.

"OK, just a minute. I'll check the fifth-grade list."

Charleen listened to the sound of the phone getting clunked on a table. She rapped a pencil on the table as she waited.

After a few minutes, his twangy voice came through the phone again. "Nah, Just Matt Kellum, and Matthew Lingen. Both those boys are nice kids."

"Is either of them a thin, blond boy?" asked Charleen.

"What? Well I should say not. You couldn't find a kid much fatter than the Kellum boy. And I know where he gets it from too. Whew! You should see his daddy!"

Charleen imagined him slapping his knee as he made that comment.

"All right, and the other Matt?"

"The Lingen boy is a freckle-faced redhead. Takes after his momma. And he's a tall bean pole too."

"Oh. Thanks anyway, Mr Williams. I'm so sorry to bother you. We've got this student named Matthew Janson who seems to have a mysterious past. And we can't get any school records on him."

"It don't bother me none. I'm just sorry that I couldn't help you," said Mr. Williams.

Charleen apologized for wasting his time. *Another dead end.*

The Smart Kid

Mr. Williams added, "I know just how you feel; we had a fella like that, an eighth-grader, last year. Couldn't find his records either. Hey, come to think o' it, his name was Matt too! And he was a thin blonde boy, too."

"What?" Charleen exclaimed. "What was his last name?"

"Selah."

"Thanks," said Charleen hanging up, after she had him repeat the name and spell it.

Selah, Selah. It didn't make sense. It couldn't be the same kid, because he was in eighth grade a year ago.

Charleen sat in her office, resting her head in her right hand, elbow on the desk, staring blankly at nothing, as she considered the possibilities.

What am I thinking? This twelve-year-old attended a previous school as an eight-grader, using a fake name? ... and his dad is in on it ... and he has a fake mom ... and a fake address?

Not very likely.

A little more digging may get to the real answer...

7. Matt's Face

On Monday, Charleen's alarm clock woke her at six. Last night's questions about Matt Janson still lingering in her thoughts, she laid in bed for a few minutes and looked toward the window. It was still dark; she had time yet. Matt's file said that he had attended Roosevelt School in Altus. But they had no record of a Matt Janson, only a Matt Selah. The only thread connecting them was first names and no history. It may not even be the same boy. How could it be?

Her determined response to this mystery made her question her own motives. She glanced at the photo of Max.

Charleen hoped that she'd be able to get to the school library to research this mystery student. The library must have phonebooks or encyclopedias or something that could aid in her search. As she considered it, she didn't know how to search for a student at another school, but Maureen Reilly, the librarian, would.

After she arrived at Jefferson, Charleen wasn't able to spend any time on the mystery, though. She had more pressing issues: meetings with staff and with the parents of the fourth-grade mentally-handicapped boy. Since Congress had passed the Education for All Handicapped Children Act of 1975, it was required for public schools to mainstream every disabled student to the extent possible. This added to counselors' responsibilities. But she didn't mind the extra work. She supported the law. Charleen was amazed that it had taken so long for these kids to finally get a free public education, the same as everyone else. It was the right thing to do, no matter the cost.

Charleen wasn't able to visit the school librarian until almost the end of the day. She walked past the rows of books and the study tables with child-sized chairs, some of which still contained students, reading.

She found Maureen in the back, checking in a stack of books. Maureen searched for a book's checkout card from a large wooden index-card box. She crossed off the student's hand-written name and

The Smart Kid

re-inserted the card into the pocket inside the back cover of the book. Then she moved the book to a different stack and repeated it with the next book.

Almost forty, Maureen was a several years older than Charleen. She fit the typical librarian stereotype, with her gray-blonde hair tied behind her head in a bun, an open sweater over a white blouse, and a pair of reading glasses hanging from a chain around her neck.

"Hey Maureen, sorry to interrupt. I'm hoping that you can help me find a student as easily as you find those check-out cards."

"Finding something is easy if there's a retrieval system in place. What do you need?"

"How can I research a student, a boy, who attended a school in Oklahoma?"

"Can you get his school records?"

"No, they aren't available."

"Hmmm ..." Maureen rested her elbow in her left hand and tapped her lip repeatedly with her right forefinger. "Does the school have a student directory or yearbook?"

"Oh my. I never thought of that. Of course, there should be pictures of every student."

"And if it's not in a book, most schools take a class photo."

"You're amazing! Thanks, Maureen." As Charleen turned to leave she said, "I hope they'll be willing to mail it to me."

"If you need the information today, you should ask if they have a facsimile machine."

"A facsimile machine?" Charleen repeated as she turned back to Maureen.

"You know, that's how someone can send a copy, like a mimeograph, over a telephone line in five minutes. You've heard of those, right?"

"I know of them, but I assumed that only big corporations had them. Would a school have one?"

"Well, the prices for fax machines have dropped substantially, so they are becoming more commonplace. The one at the St. Cloud public library is old, but it works fine. So if that school in Oklahoma has one…"

"But it's a tiny school."

"OK. But maybe there's one at the town library."

"Wow. That's worth a try. OK, I'll call Mr. Williams and see if I can sweet-talk him into sending a ..."

"Facsimile."

"Yes, a facsimile of the class photo." Charleen smiled to herself. She was solving a mystery just like the Hardy Boys or Nancy Drew books on the nearby shelves.

"By the way," asked Maureen. "I don't usually ask, but who is it that you're looking for?"

Charleen scanned the library for any adults. "His name is Matt, Matthew Selah." Charleen turned to leave but stopped when she heard Maureen laughing. She walked back to Maureen with a questioning frown on her face.

"Is that," Maureen chuckled. "Is that actually the poor kid's name? Wow!"

"What?"

"Oh, you don't get it? Say it again as one word: matthewselah."

Charleen sounded it out. "Methu-selah?"

Maureen stepped over to a shelf to retrieve a book, which she handed to Charleen. The cover read *Methuselah's Children by Robert A Heinlein*.

"May I borrow this?" asked Charleen.

"This is a library."

"Oh, of course. Thanks." As Charleen walked to her office she considered the name: Matthew Selah ... Matt Selah. She wondered if Mr. Williams just made up the name to get back at her laughing about his tiny school— *oh, Mr. Williams!* It was 3:30. *He might still be there ...*

Charleen dialed the number for the assistant principal in Altus. He was just as twangy and cordial as before.

"Mr. Williams, does your school take class photos each year?"

"Yes, ma'am. Yes we do." He sounded proud.

"OK, does the school own a facsimile machine?" Charleen held

The Smart Kid

her breath.

Mr. Williams did not hold his. "Whewee!— a facsimile machine? Now what would we do with one of them things? I mean, we're a modern school and all, but why would someone ever need to send a document somewhere in less than ten minutes?"

"Yes, I figured it was a long shot."

"Ma'am, can I ask why you need that, please?"

"Well, I'm afraid that we might have a student in trouble, and I need to know if he's the same Matthew Selah that you had, and— Hey, is that *really* his name, or are you doing a joke on me 'cause I'm bothering you?"

Mr. Williams sounded offended. "Now listen here, I don't do jokes on strangers on the phone. That *is* his name. And we *do* have his picture in a school photo. And I *will* send it to you today— by facsimile!"

"What? But I thought that—"

"Well, we're not as backward as you might think. I'll just bring the photo to my friend at the newspaper office and he will send it to you right away. So what do you have to say about us now?"

"Oh, thanks. You're the best, Mr. Williams!" Charleen could almost hear his smile as he took the number for the public library's facsimile machine.

As Charleen drove out of the teacher's lot, she noticed a mix of students lingering behind the school.

She drove to the St. Cloud Public Library to retrieve her facsimile. The city librarian directed her to a large gray printer in the back. But nothing had come through yet. After several minutes, the machine hummed to life, screeched tones resembling a choking bird, and printed out a grainy black and white photo. She pulled it out of the machine and studied the fuzzy images. Thirty-four little student faces looked up at her. She searched for the name 'Matt Selah' and found it in the alphabetical list. But the image was blurry, as if he'd moved. It could be him, but it was inconclusive. She scanned the faces of the other students in the photo once more.

If he's there, he's the blurry kid.

* * *

Greg Urban scowled as he stood a couple of steps outside the circle of fifth- and six-grade students who were hanging around the playground after school. Greg's sister, Karen, was there along with Dave Brewer, Wayne Zimmerman, a few fifth graders unknown to Greg, and that smarty-pants Matt Janson, who was showing off.

"OK, what's 24 times 210?" asked Dave, looking at Matt.

Matt paused and said, "5,040."

The kids looked at Wayne, who sat on the ground with a notebook and pencil.

"Well, Wayne, is that right?" asked Dave.

"Just a second … um, yeah, I think so," Wayne said.

Several students cheered at this impressive display. Even Karen smiled and said, "Wow, that is amazing. You did, like, three in a row."

"I just break it down into parts: 24 times 200 is easy. Then do 10 times 24, and add the results together." He looked back at Karen. "Don't you like math?"

"I do OK at it. It's harder for Greg."

Matt and Karen looked his way.

Greg motioned for his sister to leave. She ignored him.

"Hey Karen, have you been to the Skatin' Place yet?" asked Dave in a loud voice, from the other side of the circle.

Greg watched with annoyance, as she turned and took a step toward Dave to answer, "Our foster parents haven't taken us there yet."

"What are *foster parents*?" Dave asked, taking a step closer to her.

She looked around and said in a lower voice, "They are fake parents who take care of us because our real mom can't, because she's… sick."

Greg seethed with anger at the obvious interest displayed by Dave.

"Karen, could I ask you something about your mom… and dad?" Matt asked.

She retreated from Dave, who frowned.

Greg watched, even more upset that she stepped closer to talk with nosy Matt. He also noticed that Dave, from across the circle, was

The Smart Kid

eyeing his sister as she talked with Matt. Karen looked seriously at Matt, as they talked in low voices.

Dave walked to Karen and tugged on her sleeve. "So Karen, do you want to hear about Skatin' Place?" She nodded and they talked in quiet voices.

Greg stood, a silent watchman, outside the group, eyeing his sister. He fidgeted as if he wanted to go, but wouldn't without her. He watched her talk so easily with Dave Brewer. The longer he watched, the tighter his fists became.

Charleen returned from the library to her office to retrieve some folders. She sat at her desk and wrote M-A-T-T-H-E-W-S-E-L-A-H, and M-E-T-H-U-S-E-L-A-H. She was pondering the mystery and unconsciously tapping her pencil on the page.

"Fight! Fight!" came the sound of students yelling outside her office. The sudden commotion caused Charleen to jam down the pencil, busting the lead tip. She looked at the page. It was filled with random dots.

She jumped up and ran out the external door of her office toward the sound. A group of students in the back parking lot had formed a circle and were yelling at three boys struggling on the ground. Greg Urban, Dave Brewer, and Matthew Janson were fighting. At first Charleen thought that the boys were fighting against each other. But as she approached, she realized that Greg was fighting and throwing punches, but Matt was simultaneously trying to stop Greg from hitting Dave and holding Greg back without punching him. Matt's face was bleeding.

Short, stocky Greg furiously swung punches at Dave and Matt.

Dave flailed his arms ineffectually, trying to block Greg's quick jabs.

"Greg! Stop it! Do you want to get us in trouble again?" Karen yelled.

Charleen tried to get between them, putting her hands up, and yelled at Greg.

"Greg Urban! You stop fighting right now!" She tried to sound as harsh as possible.

He dropped the fist he was about to smash into Matt's blood-spattered face.

Matt pulled away. Greg got up and started to leave.

"Wait a minute, young man! Greg, what would lead you to fight, with Dave and Matt?" Every student started answering at once, except Greg, who remained silent, standing next to his sister.

Apparently, Dave Brewer had been getting too friendly with Karen. Dave had tried to make her sit down and talk with him, and had touched or pulled her hand. Over-protective Greg had tried to defend his sister's honor by jumping Dave from behind. Matt had tried to stop Greg from pounding on Dave.

Charleen examined the physical condition of the three boys. Greg and Dave were only scuffed up, but Matt had a bloody face.

"You kids go home now. I'll be reporting this to your parents." She watched as the kids dispersed, as if an exciting sports event had suddenly been interrupted. "Now go! Except for you, Matt. You must go to the nurse's office, if she's still there."

"That isn't necessary."

"Yes. It is. I can't leave you like this."

"All right," he said. They walked toward the school. "Wow! Greg sure can fight! He's so quick and angry. He caught me by surprise with that first punch."

"I'm sure it's sore," she said, putting her arm around his shoulder. "But we'll get you fixed up right away… Matt, you don't seem like the fighting type. Why would you involve yourself in this?"

"You're right. I don't like to fight. But this time, it was the right thing to do. Wouldn't you try to help someone in need?" He turned the question on her.

"Yes. I guess so."

"But it's embarrassing to get beat up by a twelve-year-old."

"Well, if it's any consolation, he's thirteen." She let go of his shoulder and opened the door.

"Oh, well then it's OK," he said.

Charleen grinned. "I guess it doesn't make a difference, does it?"

Matt tried to grin at her, but grimaced in pain.

The nurse's office was locked. The school was almost empty.

The Smart Kid

Their footsteps echoed in the quiet hallways.

"Let's clean this blood from your face and see how you look." Charleen entered the staff bathroom and came out in a few seconds with a wet paper towel. As Charleen dabbed at Matt's cheek, the cut continued to ooze blood.

Matt winced. "When that little brat hit me I slammed my cheek on the pavement and split it open. It's pretty sore."

"Oh my! We have to stop this bleeding! Here press this towel against it for a moment. Maybe that will help," said Charleen, alarmed. "Wait here, I'm going to call your dad."

Matt just stared at her as he pressed the towel to his cheek.

Charleen stepped into her office and dialed the only number that was on file for Matt's parents. Of course, she got the answering machine. She left a message, exited the office, and checked Matt's wound again. Still oozing blood.

"Matt, there was no answer at your house." Charleen studied his reaction.

Matt just nodded, tight-lipped.

"Here's an idea Matt: I could just drive you to your house ... on 10th avenue southeast." Charleen raised her eyebrows as she waited for a response from Matt.

"I'm impressed. You know where ... my house is," Matt said, looking serious.

"Yes." Then, trying to sound like she didn't know what his answer would be, she asked, "Would you like me to drive you home?"

"No need. I'll walk there."

"No. I don't think that you will."

Matt frowned and looked away.

Charleen was not going to abandon a kid, bloodied and bruised, so she made the only decision that seemed right to her. "My house is close. I'll take you there and get you bandaged. Then we'll worry about getting you home ... to your parents."

8. Charleen's Home

CHARLEEN PICKED UP a few files from her office, before they exited through the back door to her 1973 Oldsmobile Coupe. She opened the door for Matt, and then tossed the folders on the middle of the bench-style seat between them.

Driving out of the parking lot, she noticed Matt focusing on the manila file folders laying on the seat. She glanced at them and realized one of them had his name written on it.

"Oh, what a mess," she said arranging the files with her right hand, and pulling them to her.

Matt, still holding the towel to his right cheek, winced as he smiled at her. "Taking your work home with you?"

Charleen looked into his eyes and caught his meaning. "Yes, I guess I am."

Matt eyed her with a half-smile crossing his face.

She turned on the radio. The new Journey song was playing.

"Oh, you got to leave this town before it's ...
Too late, too late."

They entered the driveway of a small, yellow house on the edge of town. She parked the car behind the house. An old white shed on the far side of the yard leaned toward the corn field.

"OK, let's get you fixed up," she said in a motherly voice.

The back door entered to her kitchen. She told him to sit at the table while she retrieved a first-aid kit. After she cleaned and dried the cut, Charleen put a large bandage on it. "You will need this bandage on your face for a few days, young man." She added her heart-warming smile to the last few words, as she gently stroked his hair from his eyes.

"Thank you."

Charleen breathed out something that almost sound like "Matt" as she jerked her hand from Matt's cut face, and brushed it over her eyes. She stood and turned to face the cupboards. "Would you like a glass of lemonade, Matt?"

The Smart Kid

"Yes. It will give us time to talk."

He always has an agenda, she thought. But she said, "I think I've got cookies too!"

She opened and closed cupboard doors until she found the glass pitcher. After preparing the lemonade, she removed a metal ice cube tray from the freezer. The lever on top was supposed to release the ice cubes. But she worked at it with considerable effort before successfully cracking the cubes loose.

As Charleen prepared the lemonade, she glanced at Matt. He was studying the room.

"Here you go, Matt," she said, as she poured the lemonade. An ice cube slid out of the pitcher and plunked into his glass. She set a plate of cookies in front of him. They ate in silence for a minute.

"Do you enjoy listening to rock music?" asked Matt.

" Yes. I do. How do you know?"

"You had your radio tuned to KCLD, the rock station, so I thought ..."

"Well, you thought right. You are a very astute young man."

"Yes, I am. And I'm astute enough to tell when an adult is giving a vacuous compliment to a little kid. It irks me."

Charleen stopped chewing and stared at him for a second. She was sure that the shock showed on her face.

"OK, Matthew," she said. "You're right. Adults do that sometimes. And I apologize for talking down to you."

Matthew grinned. "Apology accepted."

Somehow, he had just transformed himself from a student to an adult, almost. Charleen felt a connection, the same as she had in the classroom, the first time Matt had looked her in the eye.

"Ms. Therry? May I politely ask you who died?"

Charleen gasped and dropped the cookie onto her plate.

"I'm sorry. I know that it's hard to say the names of people that you've lost. Let me re-phrase the question: How long has it been since your husband and son died?"

Charleen inhaled sharply and tears welled up in her eyes. She looked around the room for the clues that this young student discovered. She did have a family photo on the wall. *Could that have been enough information?*

"How ... how did you know?" she asked, as she reached for a tissue.

Matt paused until she had wiped the tears from her eyes. "First, your name: Ms. Therry. Usually, if someone is married, they designate it with *Mrs.* Although some feminists prefer to hide their marital status with *Ms.*, you don't seem like a feminist. So you're using that title for another reason. Perhaps you don't consider yourself single yet, so you aren't willing to use *Miss*".

"So by that, you concluded that I was a widow?" asked Charleen.

"No," said Matt, drawing out the syllable, as if measuring his next words. "You're new to the school, but you didn't start the first week, so something delayed you. Also, you've recently moved into this house because I can see unpacked boxes in the living room."

She looked toward the living room. The boxes were visible through the doorway. "That still doesn't explain how you knew about my ... family." Her eyes narrowed as she started to view Matt in a new way.

"Well, true. Although you have pictures of your husband and son, there's no evidence that they've lived here. There's not a stray toy anywhere and no men's coat or shoes in that open closet by the door. And there's also ..." He paused.

"What?" She shot him a questioning look.

"I see that you've had at least one group counseling session. But you are still wearing a wedding ring. That means ... recently. And I'm truly sorry for your loss. I can relate."

Charleen's mouth dropped open to say something. Then it closed and she said nothing. She looked away, partially to hide the tears but also to hide the anger. She saw her calendar by the door and the words she'd written on it: *Support Group, 4:00.*

Matt slid his fingertips up and down his lemonade glass. Condensation had formed on the outside of the glass and little tears trickled down it.

Charleen was inside her head, trying to adjust to this emotional affront. *What business did this little kid have saying such intrusive,*

The Smart Kid

personal things? How could a twelve-year-old talk this way, and observe so much, and deduce all this? At the group counseling session, she had controlled what information was shared. But today, this kid just ripped her personal tragedy from thin air, like a magician.

Her anger faded and was replaced by questions about him.

"Matt ..." She was measuring her words. "Matt, are you a genius? A real, true-to-life genius hiding in a boy's body?" *Or a superhero?*

Matt shook his head, as if he had been given a compliment that he didn't deserve. "No, I'm not a genius. But you are half-right."

"Do you have special powers of observation, like Sherlock Holmes?"

"No. I notice things that would be obvious to anyone who is paying attention. But most people don't pay attention."

"What do you mean?"

"Watch this." Matt removed a quarter from his pocket, displaying it in his right hand. He transferred it to his left hand and moved his right hand below the table. He tapped the coin on top of the table two times with his left hand. Then he slapped it flat making a loud WHAP sound. He slowly moved his left hand and showed his palm. The coin was gone. He removed his right hand from beneath the table. It held the coin.

"I don't know how you did that but you didn't *really* make it go through the table," she said.

"No," agreed Matt. "I only made it appear that way."

"But I'm certain that you had it above the table. I saw you tap it before it passed through."

"No, you didn't," said Matt with equal vigor. "Your mind filled in the blanks of what you *didn't see* because you weren't really paying attention. You thought that you were carefully observing but you were looking at the wrong thing. Misdirection!"

Matt did it again, showing how he feigned placing the coin in his left hand. "You can't actually see the coin in my left hand, but your mind made you see it."

"But I'm sure it was there because I heard it tap and slap on top of the table," she said.

"No. You heard it tap and slap from the *bottom* of the table, with my right hand, which was out of sight."

Charleen looked doubtful. "That's too easy. You couldn't have fooled me with that."

"But I did. Think about it: you saw what you expected to see. And your expectations controlled your assumptions, and your final memory of what you saw. And it all started because you weren't paying attention," Matt concluded.

"Tell me more about assumptions."

He smiled at the request. "Assumptions are stronger than facts. They shape your memory of what you think you saw and heard. Your memory will adjust to fit your assumptions."

Charleen contemplated this lesson from a student.

"And you know all this ... how?"

"I've learned it through people's assumptions about me."

"How does this relate to you knowing about me?"

"I didn't do anything extraordinary to learn about you. I just observed carefully."

She studied him with a new appreciation.

Matt took a bite of a cookie and sipped his lemonade.

"Can I ask you about your previous school?"

An alarmed expression flashed on Matt's face for a second before it changed to a calm smile. "Sure, go ahead."

"What school did you attend in Oklahoma?" She watched his reaction.

He showed no surprise. "Roosevelt School, in Altus."

"I appreciate you being honest with me."

"So you knew the answer. You were testing me," he challenged.

They looked into each other's eyes and once again, she felt a connection — until it was eclipsed with suspicion.

She removed the book from her handbag. "Do you enjoy reading science fiction?" Charleen set the book in front of him. "Ever read this one?"

Matt looked at the book for a moment. Without lifting his head, he raised his eyes up. He stared at her until she looked away.

Finally, he said, "Maybe you *are* starting to pay attention. ...

The Smart Kid

That pleases me."

This time it had been Matt's turn to speak down to Charleen. But she didn't mind. They were coming to an unspoken understanding.

They drank their lemonade and suspended the conversation for a few minutes. Matt clamped both hands around his glass as if he were trying to melt the ice with his fingers.

Charleen reached for a cookie. She held it with both hands and stared at it, chewing on her lip. She broke the cookie in half. "Matt, there are so many questions about you. I have to ask you these: What's your real name? Where do you really live? Why is Sandy Otis acting as your mom? Why does your dad aid in this deception?" She became more animated as the questions poured out of her. She hadn't intended to spew all these inquiries but the pressure had been mounting for weeks and here was the person who could give some relief.

"Wow! You know about Matthew Selah, the school in Altus, my home on tenth, and Sandy Otis? You've been investigating, haven't you?"

Charleen thought she saw a frown cross his face for a moment. She just nodded.

"How did you feel today when I revealed that I knew about your family?"

She frowned before she could control her reaction. "You know how I felt about the intrusion. How would you feel if a stranger—" Charleen stopped short. "Oh … " She stared into her glass for a moment.

"It's OK. I'm not upset. But now let me ask you: Are you a person who must have the secret to magic tricks explained, always?"

Charleen had never considered this about herself. She nodded. "It would be nice."

Matt grinned. "You do realize that's a control issue, don't you?"

She laughed. "I'm not that controlling!"

"Well, according to psychologists, after suffering a loss, people try to compensate by controlling as much as they can in their life."

The kid is right. That is *what Dr. Lansing said at the Grief Group.*

Her mood changed instantly. She contemplated how she tried to control her life: Meeting all the students, feeling overly protective of them, attending counseling sessions to control her emotions, and wanting the unanswerable questions answered: *Why? Why Max and Garrett?*

She stared at nothing. A tear rolled down her cheek. "Yes … you're right."

"I'm sorry. I made you cry again," Matt said, as he put his hand on hers.

Charleen startled from the touch of his cold, small hand and pulled away. "OK, let's get you home."

Matt leaned back, the discussion over. "Could you drop me off downtown, near my dad's office?"

"Your dad? You mean I will get to meet him?"

He said nothing.

This is so backward: He controls my access to his parents and information about him.

They drove downtown. Charleen stopped at the corner of St. Germain and 8th street. "Please let me take one more minute of your time before you leave. You know that I want answers."

The student and the counselor turned toward each other.

"I plan to answer your questions. But I need to develop more trust with you."

Charleen frowned. "What has happened in your young life that makes you so distrustful? What has to happen for you to trust me … more?"

"Remember my conversation with Deena Swenson?"

"Yes, I interrupted something."

"Wednesday, she has a gymnastics meet. We can talk there."

"OK, fine. We'll meet there. But could you please answer one little question?"

"Yes. What is it?"

He seems to hold all the cards.

"Why would you choose the secret, fake name of Matthew Selah, but tell the truth about what school you attended?"

He sighed deeply. "To leave clues for someone who's paying

The Smart Kid

attention."

He opened the door and disappeared down the street.

9. Trailing Coach

ON HALLOWEEN, AS Charleen walked through the school hallway, she was pre-occupied with the upcoming conversation with Matt. She hardly noticed the variety of costumes worn by the students. Princesses, monsters and super-heroes passed by her, unseen.
Is it an interview? I'm under scrutiny by a kid.
At her office, Charleen opened Deena Swenson's file. She studied the girl's photo.
She's a cute girl. Is Matt interested in her just because she's pretty? ... involved in girls' gymnastics ... Parents are separated ... lives with her mom who works too much ...
Charleen couldn't guess Matt's motivation. She'd have to wait.

At lunch time, several teachers were in the staff lounge. A few were eating; while others were drinking coffee or smoking. To celebrate Halloween, a couple of the teachers had donned goofy hats and shirts. Miss Battey, the first-grade teacher, wore a hat that resembled a garden on her head, complete with a bee buzzing around the fake flowers.
Mr. Jayes, the janitor, entered the lounge. He wore dark blue, dirty coveralls. Charleen had never seen him wear anything different. He rarely spoke, but when he did he usually smiled. Today, as he leaned against the wall, listening to the teachers discuss school politics and other janitorially-irrelevant issues, he seemed to have something on his mind.
One of the male teachers saw Mr. Jayes. "Hey, I know what you're dressed as today." That got a chuckle from the other teachers.
Mr. Jayes asked, "Has anyone noticed a truck parked out past the playground?"
"What kind of truck?" inquired Mrs. Shelly.
"Dark blue Ford pickup."
"It's probably just a parent checking up on their kid," said another teacher.

The Smart Kid

Mr. Jayes said nothing.

Charleen ate her lunch, thinking that it was a strange question.

In her office, later that day, Charleen called the Urban siblings' foster family.

"Mrs. Mulholland, this is Ms. Therry, the school counselor. There was an incident yesterday after school. Greg was fighting with two other boys."

Mrs. Mulholland gasped, "Oh Lord, I knew something had happened. He's been in scuffles before. I'm so sorry. Are the other boys OK?"

Charleen found it insightful that Mrs. Mulholland assumed that the two boys took a beating. "Yes, they're fine, now."

"Listen, Ms. Therry, you should know that Greg holds grudges for weeks. And he's mad at you already."

"Me? Why?"

"He thinks that you're the reason that they haven't gotten to visit their mom in the rehab unit in Minneapolis."

"That's not true. I made inquiries on their behalf, it just hasn't happened yet."

"Now, he's going to resent you telling me about the fight, too."

"Well, he did jump a boy from behind," Charleen said defensively.

"Oh, it's right for you to report it. It's just that, I'm worried for you. This boy has a temper, and if he sets his anger on you, well ..."

"Thanks for the warning. I admire you for taking them in and trying to help. You're a good person. The world needs more people like you."

"Thanks. But they need a strong parent figure. I hope we can help." She sounded sad.

"I'm sure you already have."

Later, Charleen made a few calls to request a visitor pass for the Urban twins. She left messages with two different agencies.

After school Matt arrived at Ms. Therry's office.

"Thank you for inviting me to watch the gymnastics match,

Matthew," said Charleen, using her adult-to-child voice.

"It will give us a chance to talk," said Matt. He had a smaller bandaid on his face.

"How's the cut?" she asked.

"Oh, it's healing fine. I checked it today and replaced the bandage. It's not as deep as we first thought."

"Oh, good. So no costume today?"

"Oh, yes, always." He wore jeans and a Beatles sweater. He removed a baseball cap from his back pocket and put it on his head. It had a picture of a baseball with the embroidered words, *Minnesota Twins*.

"Nice. We can exit here, and go around the school to the gym. It will be quicker," she suggested.

They walked out the back office door and followed along the side of the building to the gym entrance. Several parents and students sat on the bleachers, watching the gymnastics match. Matt led the way up the wooden bleachers. The steps were tall for his short legs. After a few steps he stopped and turned toward Charleen. She caught up and stood on the step below him. They were nearly the same height.

"I hope you don't mind that I'm leading you ... all the way to the top."

"It's your party." She smiled.

He smiled and led her all the way to the top.

Not much athletic skill was demonstrated, but the girls appeared to be taking it seriously, as did Mr. Easton, the coach. He yelled instructions and encouragements from the sidelines. When a girl performed will, Coach Easton would give her a congratulatory hug.

Matt and Charleen sat on the top bleacher, their backs against the wall, and watched the young girls do a variety of gymnastic routines on the uneven bars, the rings, and the floor. They discussed random unimportant subjects, while they watched. After fifteen minutes, Deena, who had been sitting on the team bench waiting for her turn, walked out to the floor mat wearing pink leotards and a big smile. She did a routine that involved flips and cartwheels.

Charleen thought about that conversation on the playground that she'd interrupted. "She's very pretty, isn't she?" suggested Charleen,

The Smart Kid

watching Matt out of the corner of her eye.

"Yes, for an eight-year-old," said Matt dismissively. "But when she gets older, she may do well in beauty contests."

"I did that," said Charleen.

"No kidding?"

She smiled. "Well, don't seem so surprised, mister!"

"If you used one of those smiles on the judges, I'll bet you won."

"As a matter of fact, I did!"

She smiled again. "My mom had enrolled me in a beauty contest when I was 14. It was a regional event. I got first place."

"See, I knew that you had an award-winning smile!" That comment caused an even bigger charming smile.

Matt and Charleen discussed various topics: Charleen's experiences playing sports in school, her family, and piano lessons.

"You took piano? For how long?"

"Three years, until I was in seventh grade," said Charleen.

"Me too. Just from third grade to sixth."

"Oh, so you're still taking lessons?" Charleen asked.

"No."

Charleen frowned. "I never thoroughly enjoyed it. I didn't do my lessons regularly, because I saw no future in it. I figured, 'What's the point?'"

"There is nothing new under the sun. All is vanity," Matt stared at the skylight above the gym. Charleen also looked up.

"What about the sun?"

"It's a verse from the Bible. King Solomon lived a long life and tried to find its purpose. He found no meaning in pleasure ... or piano lessons."

"I agree. Life should be more than just fun and games," said Charleen.

"Right, but young kids today just want to play. You know: to have fun, fun, fun 'till Daddy takes the T-Bird away."

"I see that you quote a variety of famous philosophers," joked Charleen.

"Singers are modern day philosophers."

"You don't agree with living for fun?"

"I've wondered about that," said Matt. "My brother used to wear a hat that read, 'The person who dies with the most toys wins'"

Charleen chuckled. "Oh, I like that. It's philosophy, pop-culture style. By the way, I didn't know that you have a brother. Where does he go to school?"

"Oh, he doesn't. He's older."

Charleen nodded.

"Here's another verse from that same passage in Ecclesiastes: 'There is no remembrance of the men of old; nor of those to come will there be any remembrance among those who come after them.'"

"Meaning what?"

"Your life won't matter. It won't be remembered by people after you. The best thing to do with your life is—"

A whistle blew, marking the end of the uneventful match.

Students and parents rapidly vacated the gym, waving good-bye and yelling, "Happy Halloween!"

Charleen stood.

Matt continued sitting on the bleacher.

Charleen sat next to Matt again.

"Just watch Deena," said Matt.

Deena and another girl lingered behind to help Coach Easton put away the gymnastics equipment. As he joked with the girls, Easton touched them on the arm, or rested his hands on their shoulders. They picked up their coats and started walking toward the exit. Easton put his hands on the backs of the eight-year-old girls.

"Oh Matt, I've got a bad feeling about this."

"Ms. Therry, I don't drive," said Matt. "Could we follow them with your car?"

Charleen hesitated. "Follow them? Why?"

"This is what superheroes do."

"Matt, I think that we should just call the police," she said, alarmed.

"And tell them what? That he's giving her a ride home?" Matt shook his head. "You trust the government too much."

The reprimand shocked Charleen into submission. She lead Matt

The Smart Kid

to her nearby car. They waited and watched.

With Easton's assistance, the two girls climbed into a black Trans Am, his helpful hands running all over their small bodies.

Charleen sighed.

"Follow them, but don't make it obvious," Matt ordered.

"You don't have to ask me twice!"

They drove in silence, trailing Easton's car. It stopped at a house nearly two miles from the school. The other girl got out, waved to Deena and Coach, and walked inside.

Charleen and Matt continued following the Trans Am, keeping a safe distance.

Charleen glanced at her rearview mirror and saw a dark pickup truck. It reminded her of the janitor's comment earlier in the day, but she dismissed the paranoid thought as a symptom of their current activity.

The Trans Am drove around the block, heading back in the direction of the school, eventually parking on the street in front of a house only a half mile from school. Matt suggested that Charleen pull up a block away, screened by a parked car. The counselor and the student sat in the car and spied on the coach and the student.

There was no car in the driveway of Deena's house. She walked up the front step; Easton trailed her, holding a gift-wrapped package. Deena removed a key from her backpack and unlocked the door. Easton turned left and right, surveying the street. When Deena pushed open the door, he put his hand on her back. They slipped into the house together.

The blood drained from Charleen's face. "Oh my God!" she exclaimed. "I've got to stop him!"

"Ms. Therry, super heroes don't just stop their foes; they defeat them."

"Defeat ... How?"

"We need to get evidence."

"What evidence?" asked Charleen, alarmed at the implications.

"I mean that the police, or Deena's mom, have to find the coach in the house," Matt said. "If you go to the house now, he'll simply say that he gave her a ride home, leave immediately and be free to try this again."

"How do you know all this? And what do we do?"

"I'll go to the door, being the kid I am, and keep him occupied. It won't cause suspicion. You go to the dry cleaning service downtown on Seventh Avenue and tell her mom. It's very close. Deena told me she works there in the afternoons. Then, if her mom hasn't made a prior arrangement for coach to enter their home, she can call the police, if she wants. But just get her. Hurry!"

Matt jumped out of the car, turned his baseball cap 45 degrees, and ran up the sidewalk toward Deena's house.

Charleen started the car, jammed it into gear and sped away.

The dark pickup truck did not.

10. Being Trailed

MATT KNOCKED ON the door, and jammed at the doorbell repeatedly. After a minute, Coach Easton opened the door, seeming flustered. He looked down at Matt.

In his most boyish manner Matt said, "Hi, can Deena come out to play?"

"Oh," said Easton. His relief was clear. "Um ... No she can't play right now, she's getting ready for Halloween. And you should too. So scram!"

Easton started to close the door, but Matt shoved his foot in the opening. "Hi, my name is Matt. I live right over there—" He pointed down the street at nothing, catching a glimpse of the dark truck two blocks away. He turned to Easton and continued, "—so I play with Deena sometimes 'cause she's nice and I don't have anyone to play with too much 'cause my brothers are bigger than me and Mom says that I should go outside and play with kids my own age, but I don't know no one my own age except for Deena so that's why we play together some—"

"She's busy!" yelled Easton. Then he softened his voice. "But I'll tell her that you came over and—"

"Great!" said Matt, with boyish enthusiasm. He ducked under Easton's arm and sprinted into the house.

"Hey!" yelled Easton. "Get out of here, kid. I didn't mean that you can play now!"

Matt didn't stop. He charged through the living room, trying not to make his intentions obvious, as he searched for Deena's bedroom.

First, he ran through rooms on the main floor, with Easton following and trying to grab his arm. When Matt saw the staircase, he dashed up with Easton at his heels, yelling, "Get outta here!"

... *instead of leaving like a smart pervert,* thought Matt.

"Hey kid, um, don't go up there! Deena is trying on her new Halloween costume."

Matt found her room; the pink letters glued to the door daintily

The Smart Kid

proclaimed, *Deena's Room*. He banged on the door. Easton caught up to him and grabbed him by the arm, just as Deena opened the door.

"It doesn't fit—" Her eyes lit up when she saw Matt. "Oh. Hi Matt. Look what Coach Easton got for me!" Deena was wearing a pink princess costume, two sizes too big for her. The collar hung off one bare shoulder.

Easton released the vise-like grip on Matt's arm.

Matt pushed into her room and slammed the door behind them. He turned the lock on the doorknob.

Easton pounded on the door for a few seconds. "Deena, I'm sorry that the costume doesn't fit. ... Let me take it back to the store and I'll get you a new one. And then we won't even tell your mommy about this. OK?" He sounded like a parent who was trying to con a child into eating her vegetables.

"Matt, why are you here?" Deena asked. "I didn't know you were coming over. And why'd you lock the door?"

Matt whispered to her, "Tell the coach that you'll give him the costume in a minute."

"Why?" she whispered back, crouching as if she were in a football huddle.

"So Coach won't leave right away."

"OK," Deena said in a hushed tone, liking the game.

"Hey, Coach," she yelled through the door. "I'll give you back the costume. Wait a minute," Deena smiled at Matt.

"Why don't we want him to leave right away?"

"Because it's Halloween, and there's a costume that we want him to wear," said Matt.

"What costume?"

"A striped prison uniform," said Matt.

"Oh, you mean like those ones with the plastic ball and chain?" Deena asked.

"Yes," said Matt.

"Well, where is it?" Deena asked scanning the room.

"Oh, Coach may be getting one soon ..." Matt said.

Matt and Deena waited in silence for a few minutes and grinned at each other, as if they were playing a great practical joke on a teacher. Matt mentally calculated how many minutes it had been since Charleen drove away. It was going to be close. He had to get Easton to stay for a few more minutes.

"Hey Deena, you didn't let me help you with your costume, so why is Matt in there?" Coach said through the door.

Deena wrinkled her nose at that comment.

"Come on, open the door!"

After a few more minutes, Easton said, "I have to go. Don't tell your mom that I came into the house or you'll get into trouble. I don't want you to get into trouble, so don't say anything. OK? Remember, Deena, you promised not to tell. Deena?" Easton's voice had a pleading tone.

"Matt said that someone has a costume for you!" Deena yelled and grinned at Matt. She held her hands over her smiling mouth, as if she had just told a secret she wasn't supposed to say.

Matt started to say, "Don't tell him, because he'll— "

"A prison costume, like the ones on TV!" Deena exclaimed.

Footsteps pounded down the staircase. The front door slammed. Matt and Deena watched out her window. Easton sprinted to his car and raced away.

Deena didn't completely understand what had happened. Matt explained that the coach should not have been in her house when her mom was gone. He spared her the sick details.

After a minute, the students saw Charleen's car pull up to the curb. Only Charleen got out. Matt said good-bye to Deena and ordered her to tell her mom what had happened.

"No more keeping secrets between you and the coach, or anybody." Matt said. "Don't worry, your mom will not be mad at you for telling the truth. Lock the door and don't open it until your mom returns."

"Thanks for coming to the gymnastics meet and visiting me. You're a good friend, Matt."

Matt smiled. *A friend.*

Before Matt got into Charleen's Coupe, he glanced down the street and saw the suspicious dark truck pull out and accelerate up the

The Smart Kid

street toward them. Old instincts took over as Matt jumped into the car. "OK, let's get going!"

As Charleen and Matt returned to the school, Charleen said, "Deena's mom had left work early to— get this— buy a Halloween costume." She shook her head in dismay, then asked, "What happened to you?"

Matt sat sideways on the seat, facing Charleen, with his back against the door, so that he could secretly eye the suspicious truck.

"I delayed Easton as long as I could. He brought a Halloween costume for Deena to try on…the sick SOB. But he got scared and left."

They turned right.

"Matthew, I've never seen you like this. You're as angry about Easton as I am. I'm going to report his actions to the school. At the least he'll get fired," Charleen said.

The truck turned right.

"You think so?" Matt asked. "Deena's mom must have known that he was dropping her off after the meet, so it's not *that* wrong for him to go into the house for a moment. He can explain that away easily. In fact, you didn't *see* anything incriminating. I *heard* how he was with her, but I won't be seen as a credible witness. And Deena isn't aware that something inappropriate happened. So we don't have much on him."

They turned left onto busy Division Street. The truck followed them onto Division and increased speed.

"Ms. Therry, can we go faster?" Matt asked earnestly.

"Why?"

"Because ... I have to go to the bathroom," Matt said.

"Oh." She accelerated the car slightly.

"But I can report how suspicious the whole thing looked," Charleen said.

"No, you can't, Charleen."

Charleen jerked her head to stare down at the twelve year old.

Her students never used her first name. The shock forcefully drew attention to the import of his statement.

He continued, "You can't even admit that you brought me here, because you'd be accusing Easton of doing the same thing that you did: private time with a minor off school grounds."

The implication of impropriety forced Charleen to view her relationship with Matt from a different perspective. She suddenly had the disorienting feeling of seeing herself from a stranger's point of view. She recalled when she had brought Matt to her house to bandage his cut. It had been completely innocent and necessary to help him. But it could look unseemly.

Conceivably, in a larger city, schools had policies restricting such behavior, but in the small city of St. Cloud, it had not been explicitly discussed or prohibited yet.

"Well, then we only have your word and Deena's against Easton's," Charleen conceded.

"Yes," said Matt. "It might be enough to get an investigation going, embarrass Easton and get him to change his conduct, or even better, to resign. I've seen it happen. Yes, I've seen it."

Matt turned to scan the traffic behind them.

One car in each east-bound lane separated the Coupe from the truck, which alternated between lanes in an apparent attempt to get through. Matt was sure they were being followed. He changed his position and sat in the middle of the bench seat, next to Charleen. He smiled at her as boyishly as he could.

Charleen looked at him, smiling up at her innocently.

The stoplight ahead changed to yellow.

How and when did this twelve-year-old gain intervention experience? Charleen thought of Matt's words again: *"I'm here to help."* "Matt, one day I saw you give a yo-yo to Timmy Iverson, and he said that he'd ask his dad about you coming to his house."

"Yes?" Matt asked with raised eyebrows.

"Did you have anything to do with Jack Iverson getting investigated for child abuse?"

They neared the intersection. The light was still yellow and Charleen was slowing the car.

The Smart Kid

Matthew, his heart racing, looked left and right, and held his breath …

One more second … Matt extended his left foot and jammed it hard on the the accelerator. The light turned red. The Oldsmobile Coupe roared through the intersection, tires squealing. Two crossing cars, screeched to a stop, horns blaring. Matt saw angry drivers behind the windshields of the stopped cars, as the Coupe cleared the intersection.

"Hey!" yelled Charleen, "What the hell are you doing? We could have been killed!" She frowned down at him.

Matt had never seen Charleen so angry. But there was something else in her eyes.

"Why'd you do that?"

He realized the source of her fear. Matt's actions had opened fresh painful memories. But it was done, and he couldn't undo it.

"A truck was following us!" Matt tried to explain.

"What? So?" Her voice boiled with tension. Somehow, she managed to continue driving.

Matt said nothing.

Charleen wiped tears from her eyes.

"I mean it, Matthew Janson! Explain your actions right now!" She was using the same scolding voice that she had used with Greg Urban at the fight. "Well?"

"You're not going to believe me."

"Explain!"

"I'm being hunted by a secret government organization with millions of dollars at its disposal."

Charleen looked at Matt for two seconds and started laughing. She laughed so hard that she nearly lost control of the car. Matt smiled.

It took her a moment to catch her breath. "Oh my gosh! That's a good one. I never expected that! You've been reading too many comic books."

Matt remained silent as he eyed her. He didn't care what she thought, as long as she continued driving. She seemed happy, for a minute. Then she became serious again.

"Matthew, you are taking this superhero persona way too seriously. I should not have indulged you with this spy game." She frowned her disapproval down upon him. "Do you want to tell me the truth now?"

Inexplicably, she had flipped to anger again.

"I mean ... I really have to go to the bathroom!" said Matt, sounding exactly like a twelve-year-old who has to go to the bathroom. He squeezed his legs together for added effect.

"Of course, now you decide to act your age." Charleen was still perturbed about the near accident, but the laughter had tempered her anger. And the anger had tempered her laughter.

"Sorry," said Matt, as he moved back to his original position to view the vehicles behind them. The car which had been directly behind Charleen's Coupe stopped at the lights, forcing the suspicious truck to wait. It was about two blocks back. But after the lights changed, the truck would begin relentlessly chasing them again, no doubt.

"Can we pull into that grocery store parking lot? I can use their bathroom."

Charleen turned the car into the large lot. Matt pointed to a spot between two vans. "Please park there, and hurry!"

Charleen did so, unsmiling.

"Be right back!" said Matt. He slammed the car door behind him as he ran into the store. Inside the glass doors, he turned just in time to see the suspicious truck drive by on Division street. He released his tense grip on the door handle. He waited as long as possible, and returned to the car.

"Well, that took you long enough, young man." Charleen was happy and condescending again.

Matt didn't mind.

They continued down Division Street, with no sign of the truck. Matt sighed with relief again. He studied his new adult friend, as if he could discern her character by staring at her profile. Her short black hair didn't quite hide her ear, adorned with a small loop of gold. Her eyes darted left and right surveying the traffic, and then focused on

The Smart Kid

Matt's inquisitive eyes.

    Charleen was aware that Matt had been studying her.
    He looked up at her. "Ms. Therry, you did your part. I told you that if you helped me, I'd tell you everything. You've demonstrated that I can trust you, even putting your reputation on the line. So the short answer is 'yes,' I did that."
    "Did what?"
    "Timmy Iverson didn't fall off his bike. His dad hit him, again."
    Charleen had to play mental catch-up to recall her question. "But that means that you notified the police?"
    "No, my dad did," said Matt, in his boyish way.
    Charleen said nothing, but she nodded. *That's how the police did it. It was like an undercover sting.*
    They approached the school.
    Matt said, "I better get out here before you reach the school. But Ms. Therry, I'll answer your questions tomorrow, at my apartment."
    "Will your dad be there?"
    "I hope you like him." Matt opened the door and stepped out. "Thanks."
    She drove to the school and parked in the back lot. He walked the remaining two blocks to school.
    After Charleen parked the car behind the school, she remained in it, reviewing the mis-adventure she'd volunteered for. The cloak-and-dagger subterfuge and near-crash had spawned multiple emotions. It was like a comic book thriller; the pages colored with emotions: cautionary yellow backgrounds, surprising splashes of orange, sad blue streaks, and a profusion of angry red strokes.
    Charleen was furious at Coach Easton, Jack Iverson, the Urban twins' mother, and all adults who don't cherish children. She was angry at people that she hadn't even met. She was angry at the very idea that there are people who don't love their children.
    And there are so many people who wish that they still had children to cherish. She flipped down the visor and stared at a small photo of Max.
    She began to cry.

11. Answers

THURSDAY, NOV. 1ST, Charleen had just escorted a handicapped student and his parents from her office. They'd had a productive meeting; they reviewed his education plan and discussed how he was adapting to the regular classes. It was what Charleen lived for. There is nothing better than the satisfaction of helping children and making a difference in their lives, she told herself.

The intercom buzzed. "Wayne Zimmerman is here."

No, not again. Charleen hung her head for a moment. "Send him in, Holly," she said, her buoyant mood deflated.

The office door yawned open and Wayne dragged himself into the room. His head down, he remained at the doorway.

"Hello, Wayne. Please come in and have a seat."

The boy slid in the wooden chair facing her desk. He didn't make eye contact with her.

Charleen raised her eyebrows in a questioning manner and waited for him to explain why he had come to her office. He must have had a reason to bother her twice.

He just sat in the chair and looked at his feet.

She couldn't wait for him. "Wayne, how is your father doing now?" She hated the subject she chose, but it was probably the cause of his two visits to her office. She feared that he was going to say, "He's dead."

"He's still in the hospital. Mom says he's resting good."

"Oh, that's good—"

"—Cuz he's in a coma."

"Oh. Well, Wayne, your father is very fortunate to have survived … to have survived that deadly … deadly … that accident …" Charleen was getting teary-eyed, and began to breath heavily.

"I'm sorry, Wayne. I don't feel very good now. Can we talk later? I'll send a note to your teacher when I have time in my schedule again. OK?" She motioned for him to leave.

Wayne walked out of her office and dropped a small piece of

The Smart Kid

paper onto the registration desk as he left.

With great effort, Charleen moved to shut the door, locked it, and dropped into her chair. She rested her head on her arms and let the depressive fatigue overtake her.

The rest of the day dragged on forever. Like a bored factory worker, Charleen repeatedly checked the clock and hoped for the end of her shift. In contrast to her mundane day, the anticipation of meeting Matt's covert father thrilled her like reading the last chapter of a mystery book.

Shortly after school, Charleen got into her Coupe and drove downtown to the same spot that she had dropped Matt yesterday. He was waiting for her. She parked the car and they walked east on the sidewalk along St. Germain street.

He spoke first. "That's a big car for you, isn't it?"

"Yes. But I feel safer in a large car." Charleen glanced at Matt. He nodded.

She looked at her feet.

"Are you nervous?" asked Matt.

Charleen just shrugged. They walked to an apartment building and paused at the old glass-paneled metal doors. He held the door for her. They rode the elevator to the second floor.

"It's the last door on the left."

Charleen started walking faster. Matt started walking slower. She looked back at him.

"Matt, you're the one who seems nervous. What's the matter?"

"Oh, this just reminds me of a bad dream I had once. I was forced into a long hallway and I feared what was on the other side of the door."

"Well, this isn't a dream, and you don't have to worry about anything scary waiting in your apartment." She flashed a reassuring smile.

She reached the door and watched him shuffle up to her, at apartment 242. Matt controlled the key that unlocked the door, just like he controlled her access to information about him.

She followed him in, sensing how inappropriate this would be if

Bob Miller

Matt's dad wasn't home. Many photos, and few decorative mirrors adorned the walls of the clean apartment. Charleen saw photos of Giant Sequoia trees, a framed comic of Captain Marvel, old black and white photos that looked 40 years old. A small step ladder in the kitchen stood in front of the tall cupboard. The top cupboard door hung open a few inches.

Matt sat on the couch and watched her. Charleen roamed his apartment, studying everything, like an amateur sleuth. She saw a 45 rpm record framed in a glass; Heartbreak Hotel by Elvis Presley. It was autographed by Elvis. Behind the glass, part of a page from a music magazine, listed Heartbreak Hotel at the #1 spot in 1956. A small bookshelf sat on the floor just below the frame, forcing her to lean in to closely examine the record.

As Charleen leaned forward, reading the record label, she glanced toward Matt and noticed that he was studying her. His gaze traveled down her body. If he had been a grown man, Charleen would have known exactly what he was thinking. And if his dad were in the room, she would not have leaned so far forward in her tight skirt.

"My dad really liked that," Matt said.

Charleen immediately stood straight and shot a surprised look at Matt. She ran her hands along her hips to smooth out her skirt.

Maybe he is a mind-reader.

"I mean, he really liked Elvis."

She was relieved. "Oh yes. Speaking of your father, is he here now?" Charleen asked, while she looked at other photos.

Matt said nothing.

Charleen studied the framed issue of a comic book, Whiz Comics #5, dated June, 1940. The front cover had a picture of Captain Marvel pulling a submarine out of the water with a chain.

One of the old black & white photos depicted a family standing in front of a house. The mom and dad stood behind three boys of varying heights. The shortest boy resembled Matt. In fact, the way Matt looked, it could have been taken yesterday.

"Matt, how old is this photo?"

"Wait. You're not ready for that yet," he said.

"What do you mean? And where's your dad?" Charleen's voice

The Smart Kid

grew more stern.

Matt said, "I trust you now. I'll get him." He stood and walked the hallway into a room.

An older man called to her. "Ms. Therry, could you please come in here?"

Dismayed that his dad had been in the apartment without greeting her, she complied.

Following Matt's path, she entered the room, a bedroom, and saw only Matt. Dumbfounded, Charleen looked around the small orderly room. There were low-hanging posters of 50s and 60s rock bands on the wall, and a wooden box on the desk filled with magic tricks. Next to the box, leaned a book: *Handcuff Secrets* by Harry Houdini.

She realized, at that moment, that it was a one-bedroom apartment. But there was only one single bed with one pillow.

"I recognized your dad's voice. Now, where is he?" asked Charleen, as amazed as when Matt had performed the coin trick. She looked over Matt's shoulder toward a closet door.

Matt locked his eyes onto hers until she focused on him. In his dad's voice said, "I'm right here, Charleen."

Charleen gasped in shock and put her hand over her mouth. She took a step backward.

"Oh my! Do that again."

"Hello, Ms. Therry, this is Matt's dad speaking."

Matt's face was emotionless. Charleen's was not.

"Oh my Lord!" Alarmed and afraid, Charleen reacted as if she'd heard a disembodied voice. It was disturbing and incongruous to hear a middle-aged man's voice coming out of this twelve-year-old's mouth. And it was not *"a kid trying to sound like an adult."* It was an adult man's voice. Matt's Fake Mom was right.

"Matt, where is your father?" she asked, with a sense of *deja vu*, fearing the answer.

"He's dead."

"Oh, I'm so sorry." A memory flashed of her father lying in a hospital bed, dying of cancer when she was 31. *But to lose your dad when you're so young must be very hard.*

"So ... are you an orphan?" She was certain he was going to say, 'Yes'.

"Probably. I think Mom is ..."

"Oh, I'm sorry," she repeated. But her empathy quickly morphed into comprehension.

A piece of the Matt Janson puzzle fell into place, and Charleen perceived a much clearer picture of him and his life. A tsunami of implications flooded her mind.

"You live alone?" She repeated it as a statement of understanding, "You live alone!"

The questions poured out her mouth faster and faster like overflowing waters. "*How* could you live alone? How could you *survive*? Where do you get money? Do you have a job? How could the school allow you to attend? Does the school even know?"

Charleen realized that she knew the answer to this last question. Sandy Otis, the actress, had helped Matt enroll in school, somehow. Her questions about that whole process had to wait. She focused on her conversation with "Matt's Dad."

Matt appeared ready to say something, but she continued. "So it was *your* voice on the answering machine! And *you* were the one who hired Sandy Otis. And *you* were the one who talked with me on the phone. *You* pretended to be your dad!" The angry words shot out like bullets.

"Yes, but—"

"You tricked me!" Her mind flooded with more implications. "Yesterday, I brought you to this block because you said your dad worked here. That was a lie! How could you do that to me? I thought that we were ..."

"Friends?" Matt offered.

She *was* going to say that but, instead said, "Oh, I have to leave, right now!"

"No," pleaded Matt, with his boyish voice. "Please don't go!" He held up his hands, as if he could stop her with his small body.

Charleen glared. "Which of those voices is really yours?"

He said, in his kid voice, "I guess this is. The other one is my superpower." He gave a half-smile.

The Smart Kid

"What do you mean *superpower?*"

"Well, every comic book superhero has special powers and a weakness, and usually a secret identity," Matt explained.

She recalled her fear when he throttled the car dangerously through an intersection and blamed pursuing villains. She glared at him and spit out, "You are *not* a comic book superhero! You're a little kid who is lying to everyone! You should be turned in to ... to the county social workers or something. You can't live on your own!"

Her earlier expectations were not fulfilled; she was not happy to meet 'his father' and this was not like the exciting revelations of the last page of a mystery. Instead of being thrilled, she felt manipulated.

It was Matt's turn to spout angry words. "*Yes.* I can. Charleen! I *have* been living on my own for quite some time!" he yelled. "And one reason that I've been able to live by myself is because of this ability. I can call for deliveries of furniture, or food, or for someone to fix the utilities. And I can even talk to my school counselor over the phone as an *adult!*" He jammed his forefinger into the air to emphasize his last word.

Never in twelve years had a student yelled in this manner; reprimanding and correcting her.

His heavy breathing slowed and his face relaxed. He paused. "I'm sorry for yelling," he said in his twelve-year-old voice.

Charleen regretted her anger.

With a softened voice she said, "So you're a comic book hero, and your power is being able to imitate an adult. How did you get this *power?*" She hoped that indulging his alternate personae might ease the tension. He appeared to welcome the question.

"Well, partly through training and partly through maturity."

"Maturity?" The tone of that single word conveyed her disbelief. "I have to go. I shouldn't be here." She stomped toward the door.

From behind her, the grown man's demanding voice said, "Charleen!"

The authority in The Voice compelled her to stop. She didn't turn around because she didn't want to see the disturbing image again.

The Voice continued, "Why should you go? Because it's inappropriate to be alone with a twelve-year-old?"

Charleen nodded. She wouldn't turn to make eye-contact with him and fumed that he had gotten her to stop.

"I am not twelve!"

She heard the four simple words, borne in his childish voice. Spoken by any other young student, they might be followed by "I'm thirteen now," or some other benign sentence. But the implication of these words began to grow in her mind. And she sensed that they were going to surprise her when the explanation was fully mature.

The words were also completely unexpected.

"You saw what you expected to see," he had told her.

Once again, using his twelve-year-old voice, he pleaded, "Please come in and have a seat. I have something to show you. And afterwards, if you still want to leave, I won't try to stop you."

Charleen reluctantly turned to face him. She followed him back into the room and Matt motioned for her to sit on the couch. She looked toward her escape door, sighed, and sat on the far end of the couch.

"There's an article that you should read."

Matt removed a ragged-edged folder from a shelf stacked with notebooks resembling the one that Matt always brought to school. He handed the folder to her, stepped back, and sat on the other end of the couch.

She opened the folder of newspaper clippings. The first two articles were titled *The Girl Who Doesn't Grow* and *The Curious Case of Brooke Greenly.*

"Who's Brooke Greenly?" Charleen asked.

Matt swallowed hard and closed his eyes for two seconds. "She's a girl who ... doesn't grow."

Charleen blinked. "Doesn't grow?"

Matt studied her.

What was he looking for?

She reviewed the article. The girl looked five years old, but was actually 22. Her body was as small and frail as an infant. Doctors were baffled. Her mind had also stopped growing. She still thought and acted as a five-year-old; forever five. Charleen's surprise turned to

The Smart Kid

sadness.

"Oh, that's so sad," Charleen said, not thinking how Matt might respond. She looked at Matt and dropped the folder on the coffee table.

He's looking for empathy and understanding.

She didn't say anything for a minute; just stared, searching for proof in his face. Another puzzle piece clicked into place. She turned in the direction of the window, not looking at anything.

He also looked away, breathing deeply.

Charleen turned to him, her piercing eyes attempting to look into his soul.

"Oh, Matt. I don't know what to— So you're ... like her?" She had to say it out loud finally.

Matt nodded.

She looked at the folder on the table and contemplated this new revelation. It was a lot to accept.

"You don't grow?" She confirmed, for no reason other than to help her to comprehend the implications. She mentally reviewed his demeanor with students and staff. It all had a purpose. It was an act.

Charleen remembered his words: *"I'm here to help ... These little kids ... Just because I get good grades doesn't mean I like school."* She recalled the lonely image of him sitting in the school yard with his notebook. She turned and looked at the notebooks on the shelf. "Are those the notebooks?"

He nodded, looking away.

How many years had he been pretending to be a young kid? She estimated ... There were at least fifteen thick notebooks; each one representing how many months?

"You've been hiding out in elementary and middle schools for many years, right? So that means that you're ... Matt, are you an adult?"

Matt, distressed, breathed heavily.

Charleen could see that he was trying to contain his emotions.

He struggled to say the words that would sound so ordinary coming from any other man. He breathed deep and confessed to Charleen, "Yes. I'm ..." Deep breath. "... a man." He averted his eyes as if he was ashamed; as if he had a hidden deformity that was suddenly exposed.

Matt was having difficulty breathing.

Charleen instantly transitioned from investigator to counselor. She empathized with him. It was only a few days ago that her secrets were uncovered by this boy. She knew it created feelings of vulnerability and shame.

She tried to think of something appropriate to say. "I'm sorry," was not adequate or even relevant. More questions, interrogating a handicapped person wouldn't be right. Charleen finally just reflected his emotions.

"This is hard, isn't it?"

And that's all it took. He started sobbing. His face became wet with tears. Charleen leaned forward to grab a tissue from the coffee table. When she handed it to him and sat back on the couch, she moved closer to the little crying boy-man. She put her arms around him. And he held her like a little hurt boy hugging his mother.

As she held him, she tried to imagine what he had been enduring. She had been so busy trying to uncover the mystery and get her questions answered that she hadn't even considered what this was doing to him. Charleen was ripping off bandages that protected old, old wounds.

Maybe he's never told this to anyone but me. It wasn't only sadness, it was emotional release from holding a secret for so long— *How long?* —And, finally, it was free.

She waited as he cried.

Forlorn, alone.

She imagined how difficult this solitary, secret life had been for him, over so many years. *How many?*

He relaxed his cathartic clasp on her, stood and walked into the bathroom. After a few minutes, he came out, his face freshly washed, his blond hair damp above his forehead.

"Thanks," he said. "I really needed to get that out. It's been buried for too long."

His interest in magic tricks, in secrets, made sense to her. She wanted to ask *the* question. But he'd tell her in his own time.

The Smart Kid

Charleen knew that he— they both— needed an emotional break. She walked to the south window and stared down at the street. Many styles and colors of cars were parked along both sides of the road. In a new appreciation of her own assumptions, she realized that she had no idea what the cars contained. Most people would assume them to be empty. But from this vantage point, there was no way to discern what they hid— just like Matt. She watched cars and pedestrians moving left and right below her. A man danced across the busy street as he dodged traffic.

She turned and asked, "Say, do you have a record player?"

That question cheered Matt. He stood and opened a dark-wood phonograph cabinet.

"What do you like?" he asked.

"You choose." She sank into the couch.

He retrieved an album, gently removed the record, protected by a white slip cover, and centered it on the platter. He pressed the cue button. The tone arm raised, pivoted and eased the needle down to the leading groove of the record. After a few seconds of scratchy static, the mellow voice of Elvis Presley flowed from the cabinet's speakers.

"The autographed record from 1956. Where did *you* get it?" She asked pointedly.

He sat on the couch. He whispered, "Elvis signed it for me at a concert ... in 1957."

Charleen gasped. "If you were twelve, you would have been born in 1967. But you saw Elvis ten years before that ..."

"Yes," said Matt. "I was a teenager when I met The King."

"Oh my, so ... ?" Afraid to ask, she left her question hanging.

"I was born," he looked into her eyes as he finished, "... June 2nd, 1940."

Charleen tried to not gasp. But the shock showed. That was the question that she'd wanted to ask. She studied his face and eyes, looking for evidence of his age. She could describe him best by his non-features: He had no whiskers, nor receding or graying hair. He had no crow's feet bordering his eyes. His skin wasn't worn, or damaged by acne or age-marks. But as she studied him, she noticed three small scars on his neck— but she saw no indication of thirty-nine years.

"So you're older than me," she said, not certain if she believed it.

Matt nodded. He looked at his feet and gave a big sigh. He slumped back on the couch, eyes closed; drained emotionally and physically.

She relaxed against the couch and closed her eyes.

The two adults, 35 and 39, sat silently listening to Elvis sing *Blue Moon*.

12. More Answers

CHARLEEN AND MATT listened to the entire Elvis album as they leaned back on the plush tan couch, each on their own side. As the songs played they discussed hobbies and interests and books they'd read— safe topics. She tried to accept him as a thirty-nine-year-old man.

It is so hard to believe. Questions remained, unasked. *He's a man, not a boy.*

That issue made her fret. It was ironic. He was a grown man, but she still had to treat him like a twelve-year-old boy in public, avoiding any suggestions of impropriety. So she still couldn't be seen with him off school grounds. They'd have to play it safe.

During a break in the conversation, they noticed the needle repeatedly riding the last scratchy groove.

"I don't know how long the record's been over," said Matt.

"Matt, I should be going now."

Matt jumped up. "I just bought the newest album by the Eagles. It's called *The Long Run*. Please, let's listen to it together!" He was beaming as he pleaded with her. She assented.

The record played and they continued talking. Charleen learned much more about Matt than he did about her. If Matt resented her probing questions, he didn't show it. They conversed easily, only aware of the passage of time by the progression of the songs on the record.

In the City started playing.

"How do you live?" She sat up and turned to face him on the couch. He turned and faced her directly.

"I earned a substantial amount of money from a few special investments in the stock market."

"But isn't that risky?" she asked, never having done it herself.

"Not when you know in advance about take-over deals, or important press release announcements of product breakthroughs," he said with a wink.

The Smart Kid

"Matt ... insider trading?" She frowned.

"No. I was not on the 'inside', but I still acquired valuable information."

"How?"

"Have you ever shared secrets in a public place and wanted to make sure that no other adults heard you?"

"Yes, of course."

"What did you do?" He didn't wait for an answer. "You looked around for any adults who might be listening, right? But you didn't pay attention to the kids in the room."

Charleen remembered when she was in the library, with Maureen, secretly discussing his other name; that was exactly what she did. "You're right. So you were practically invisible to adults discussing adult topics?"

"I was a busboy at an expensive, upscale restaurant when I attended college. There was a group of lawyers and corporate managers that ate there regularly. They had the inside scoop on upcoming financial deals, mergers, and stock offerings. I learned advanced information that gave me confidence that I could safely invest much of my dad's money."

"Your dad's? Was he worried?"

"At first, but I told him the details, and the results of other predictions from these men that proved true. So he gave me his whole life savings. By the time of the initial public offering, it went wild, and we reaped huge profits, which we split." He put his hands behind his head, interlacing the fingers. He appeared to be proud of himself.

"Oh, that explains a lot. Thank you for sharing."

Charleen leaned back against the couch, closed her eyes and listened to the music. After a few minutes, she opened her eyes, studied the boy-man, and decided she was ready.

"Matt, could you please talk to me in your adult voice again? I want to get used to it, now that I ... it won't bother me as much."

"OK, Ms. Therry," Matt said in a deep baritone. "What do you want me to say?"

She leaned back. "It doesn't matter. I'll just listen to you talk and try to imagine you as a man. Um, I mean, a grown man."

Matt faltered. "I'm sorry that I'm stumbling here, but I don't know what to say. I'm kind of embarrassed because I've never used this voice face to face with someone."

"Never?"

Matt shook his head, and then continued in his adult voice. "Not since I accidentally discovered it, while I was riding across the country in a blue van filled with Hippies. But that's a story for another time."

She closed her eyes again.

"Oh, I know. The first time that I saw you was when you were introducing the Urban twins to our class. And I sensed at once that I could trust you. I felt a connection. That was the day that I began writing notes about you."

"No kidding?" She opened her eyes. "What did you write?"

"I don't remember," he demurred, sounding like a boy again.

Charleen smiled at him. "I can tell that you do. Now let me see it!"

"See, you do need the secrets revealed! I was right about you."

Charleen just nodded.

"Could you please get the notebook from that shelf?"

She grabbed the nearest notebook on the shelf. It was labelled *Jefferson Elementary, St. Cloud, Minn. Sept - Oct.1979. Grade: Sixth.* She handed it to Matt.

There were more notebooks stacked on the shelf. Charleen reached for them as she turned to Matt. "May I?"

"If you must."

She removed two of them. One was labeled *Roosevelt School. Altus, Oklahoma. 1977-78. Sept - Dec, Grade: Eighth.* "I know about this one. You were there last year, but in eighth grade. How does that work?"

"I acquired some birth certificates with different names and dates. My *Matthew Selah* birth certificate proved that I was 14 in '78. After that I had to start using my *Matthew Janson* birth certificate last year, as a sixth grader."

Charleen frowned at Matt, not totally understanding.

"I don't really want to talk about that now, though."

Charleen nodded, and, once again felt like she was digging into

The Smart Kid

his personal business too much. She examined the other notebook: *Lincoln Middle School, Kansas. 1969-70. Jan - May, Grades: 6th.* Inside, Matt had logged names and dates; stories of children he'd met years ago, some of whom were probably fully grown adults. But not Matt.

"The date on this notebook is ten years ago."

"Yes. I nearly got caught there. That was the year I vowed never to trust another adult. Until I met you."

"Why? Why did choose me?"

"When I saw you, something clicked. You seemed to be looking for something too …"

Charleen stared at the floor for a moment. "So what did you write about me?"

"Here it is … October First— Hey. Do you realize that I first saw you one month ago?"

"It's only been a month? Wow. I feel like I've known you longer than that."

Matt nodded in agreement, then in his adult voice said, "Anyway, I wrote: *Met a new counselor today. She seems sincerely interested in kids. Nice smile. Cute. Could be an asset.*"

"What? Did you write that I have a cute ass?" she joked.

That knocked the adult out of his voice. "Nooo! I said that you could be an asset." He smiled sheepishly. It was the first time Charleen had seen him blush.

"Seriously, what do you mean by *asset*?"

"I've told you that I'm here to help. I figured out a long time ago that, if I'm going to be permanently disguised as them, then I might as well use this secret identity to help troubled kids. And I thought that you might be able to assist me, somehow…" He looked down again.

Charleen sensed his reticence. "So as a *superhero,* your mission is to support kids?"

"Yes," he murmured.

"And you help them by … pretending to be one of them?" She empathized, having tried many times to peer into the minds of her students.

"Yes, that's part of the reason I pretend." He stared out a

window. He seemed to be thinking of something far from the peaceful atmosphere of this apartment, in a small city in the middle of the state.

The song, *Heartache Tonight* began to play.

Clearly, the subject made him uncomfortable, or sad, or something else. She pulled him back to current reality. "And you have a special power, your voice."

"Yes, my voice." He glanced at her.

"And said that you have a weakness?"

"Well, who doesn't?" He stood and walked to the window, his back to her.

"Oh Matt. I'm so sorry. I'm not looking for character flaws. Earlier you had said that a weakness was one of the defining characteristics of a superhero."

Matt turned his head, attentive to her words.

"But everyone has weaknesses," Charleen said. "Mine is being too emotional. And now I'm startled by a ringing phone because that's how I was informed of ... the accident."

Matt turned his body slightly toward her.

"I'm just trying to understand you, as a friend."

Matt turned fully toward Charleen and studied her face. "Yes, the weakness is part of my identity. It's not easy being a lone twelve-year-old kid. Adults don't take me seriously. They're always asking, 'Where's your parents, son?' I can't drive. I can't go to the doctor. I can't use a credit card. There's a bunch of other things too. Society doesn't tolerate a kid on his own."

"But can't you prove that you're an adult, show an ID or something? Don't you have a driver's license?"

"Not any more. In college I tried proving my age with a license, and attempted to get a job as an adult. It doesn't work. People don't appreciate having a little kid try to put something over on them. They'd call it a Fake ID, and they'd call me a Scammer, Liar, or other names. Besides, would you want to expose a physical abnormality to strangers every day?"

"I guess not," Charleen sympathized.

"And do you wanna guess how many times I've been pulled over when I've driven a car?"

The Smart Kid

"A lot?"

"Every time a cop or highway patrol sees me, they stop me. I show them my driver's license, and they call on their radio. Usually, I just wait while my contact information is radioed around the state, but once in a while, I get hauled to the police station until everything is sorted out. So I stopped driving."

She sat in silence and tried to imagine his life. He sat down again and they both leaned back against the couch and listened to the music.

The song *Teenage Jail* played.

She sat up again, turning toward him. In a voice that was so delicate and light, as if she feared the very words might wound him if she brushed them against him too harshly, Charleen asked, "Matt, may I ask you about your ... condition?"

"What's your question?"

"When did it start—or stop. I mean—or, um ... sorry. I don't know if something started or stopped."

"Both," said Matt. "The doctors determined something *did* start: puberty. But then something, perhaps my pituitary gland, sent a 'stop' signal to my body. So I never entered that change to manhood—which, thankfully, saved me from being an eternally hormone-controlled teen. But it's still a jail, nevertheless."

He appeared to be getting morose, so she focused on a positive topic.

"You and I have the same mission: to help kids." Charleen smiled. "I envy your ability to get students to discuss their problems." She looked up at the stack of notebooks on the shelf. "They share openly with you, don't they?"

"Yes. They tell me things that they wouldn't admit to an adult."

"Like what?"

Matt's energy level seemed to increase. "Sometimes, it's the big problems: abuse in different forms. But most of the time, it's advice, or encouragement, like helping a kid to understand his parent's divorce and just letting him vent. It's not a counseling session. But I do ask strategic questions and the kids' answers reveal issues in their home life. I'm glad that I can be there to help them."

Matt picked up the notebook that he'd set aside during their discussion. He handed it to Charleen. "Here. You can have it. You can see what types of things I've discussed with the students."

"Oh, no. I couldn't."

"I need you to know what I've been doing with your students. I need a partner."

She took the notebook. "Thankyou. I was curious."

The Sad Cafe played.

Matt gazed toward the window again. He turned back to Charleen and looked into her eyes with a sadness in his.

"I so appreciate that you're here. I need an allay. I've been considering giving up and leaving again." He looked away.

Charleen said nothing as she thoughtfully placed a hand on his shoulder.

After a moment, he asked, "What superpower do you want?"

She smiled. "To heal people who are hurting."

They both leaned back against the couch and silently shared the music.

The Long Run ended.

She stood and looked for a clock. It was 7:00.

Matt asked, "Are you hungry?"

"Yes, very," she said.

"I'll see what I've got for dinner."

"Well, OK. May I take a look around?" she asked.

"Sure. I've got nothing to hide!" he joke. Matt went around the corner to the kitchen.

Charleen chuckled and headed for the hallway. Two black and white photos of giant sequoia trees hung on the wall. An inscription lined one of the frames. It read, *"These trees, like a life well-lived, will outlast us all."* The photograph was signed by Ansel Adams.

"So you met Ansel Adams?" She raised her voice, half-turning toward the kitchen.

"He was teaching a photography workshop for students. I attended for a while. I impressed him, as a twelve-year-old, with my knowledge of photographic composition. I asked him for a signed photo of a Sequoia."

The Smart Kid

"Why a Sequoia?"

"Isn't it obvious?" He sounded amused.

More photos and memorabilia hung on the walls. "You have *a lot* signed photos of celebrities!"

"Yes, well, it's easy to get celebrity photos when you're a little kid. I tell them how far I traveled to meet them and ask for their autograph." He spoke loudly from the kitchen.

"Travel? How do you travel now?"

"Usually the bus or a taxi," Matt said.

"So people always ask you where your parents are?"

"Sure, but it's OK for a young boy to travel solo on a bus. Besides, I used to carry a note from my mom— my real mom, that said I had permission to travel alone. She gave it to me when I left home. That was enough for a child to travel in those days."

"Buddy Holly?" she asked, while he clanked dishes in the kitchen.

"I saw him and the Crickets perform in early 1958, shortly after his appearance on the Ed Sullivan show. I was 17 at the time. My dad brought Mark and me there. I went backstage and got a signed photo. He was thrilled to have such a 'young fan.' It helped that I intelligently discussed his music performances at the Apollo Theater during the previous year. He was amazed."

"I saw a photo of you and two taller boys standing with your parents. Mark is one of your brothers?" Charleen asked.

There was a pause. "Um, yes. He's my only one now." His voice was soft and close. Matt was leaning against the wall, watching her.

Charleen felt self-conscious under his steady gaze. She walked further along the hall. "I feel like I'm walking backward in time."

"Yes. I know the feeling," said the man-boy.

"President Nixon? You've got an autographed photo of Nixon?" Charleen frowned. "Why him?"

"You do know he was instrumental in ending the war in Vietnam, even if it took him years to do it, right?"

"Well, yes, but he only did it because it wasn't popular anymore."

"He got re-elected in a landslide because he was promoting a peace agenda."

"OK. But why did he send you an autographed photo?"

"Because I sent him a letter saying that I appreciated him working to end the war. I had a personal interest in it. Look at the framed magazine cover next to it."

Charleen studied the framed cover of Life magazine titled *The Faces of The American Dead in Vietnam. One Week's Toll.* The number 242 was hand-written in red ink. It was dated, June 27, 1969. Price 40¢. A young soldier's photo had been inserted into a corner. The label read *Thomas Shale. SP4 ER. Combat Engineer. KIA in a helicopter crash.*

"I remember this issue. They published the photos of American soldiers killed in one week. It's so sad," Charleen lamented. "And I guess it really got the public whipped up against the war. But who's Thomas Shale?"

"He was my brother."

"Oh. I'm sorry."

"No, it's OK. I'm so happy to be having an adult conversation again— really the first since college."

"That's the third time that you've mentioned it. I have to ask: You went to college? How?"

Matt paused. "This was before I had a secret identity. I attended as a regular student. My parents paid my tuition. It was a great time— all three and a half years ..."

"You graduated in three and a half?"

"No. I never graduated. Food's ready."

He pulled out a chair at the table for Charleen. She sat down while he poured water from a pitcher into her glass, which was filled with ice cubes. She sensed a role reversal; a power flip. Only three days ago she had been feeding him cookies as if he were a child, she reflected. And now he was serving her, as an adult. It was a surreal turn of events.

As he finished preparing the salads, her mind wandered back over his words, *"All superheroes have a secret identity ..."*

His brother has a different name. He used a false name in the previous school. Surreal. Secret. False.

The Smart Kid

A flicker of doubt lit her mind, but she made a conscious decision to stop chasing him for information.

During the meal, he asked about her husband and son. She shared how they met, when they married, and how they felt when Max was born.

"He was so cute," Charleen exclaimed with a big smile as she poked at her salad with a fork. "I called him *The little man in my life.*" She glanced at Matt, *the little man.*

"And Garrett had a nickname for me too ..." She waited for Matt to ask.

He smiled. "OK. I'm asking."

She had a big grin on her face. "Charlee."

"Charlee ... that's cute."

"And I called my guys *Charlee's Angels!*"

"That's funny!"

After supper, she prepared to leave. Matt said, "Charleen, um, there's something else that I want to tell you."

"What? More secrets?" she joked.

"Um, no. Thanks for coming."

"It was my pleasure. Thank you."

They said their good-byes, she took the notebook gift, and left his apartment.

Charleen walked out of the building, heading west on the sidewalk.

Behind her, in a parked car, a man snapped photos.

13. Doubts

CHARLEEN WOKE EARLY Friday, looking forward to the new day. Since Garrett's death, the sadness had always remained just below the surface of her consciousness. Her job, and other daily distractions suppressed it, although not entirely. It was there, hiding like a shark waiting to attack. But not that Friday.

She hummed to herself as she brushed her hair and prepared for work. Charleen selected a pretty dress, an anniversary gift from Garrett, and smiled at the memory as she reviewed the woman in the mirror. The sky began to brighten in the east.

The Case of the Mysterious Student had been solved, the puzzle completed. Feelings of satisfaction and relief mixed with the exhilaration of sharing an exciting secret. It was as if she'd figured out an amazing magic trick. *Matt is right about me. But, oh, this is such a secret.*

Plus, having an undercover ally to help the children made her more confident of success. Together, they might even be able defrost the Urban twins…

While she drove to school, she planned how they'd work together. The possibilities stirred her imagination. If students didn't feel comfortable sharing a problem with her, then Matt could talk with them. *Is this manipulative?* At least, he could discover if a child was in danger. *In fact, Matt could encourage them to share with me,* she thought. Charleen hoped to discuss it with Matt during playground duty.

At school, she didn't see him in the halls or on the playground.

She checked with the attendance office and learned that "his father had called him in sick today." Back in her office, she closed the door and dialed his number. The answering machine greeted and beeped at her.

"Hello, Matt, it's Charleen. Please pick up the phone. What's wrong?" Silence.

She banged the handset onto the phone with more force than she

The Smart Kid

intended, sighed deeply and considered her next move. She had no moves. She just had to wait.

Charleen had a long lunch break, so she decided to go home for lunch and call her mom. She had to get *her* opinion about Matt. As she drove, she flipped on the radio and listened to The Doobie Brothers sing 'What a Fool Believes.'

Not pausing to set down her purse, she grabbed the kitchen phone. *Mom is going to be so amazed.*

"Mom, I want to discuss something with you."

"Yes, Charleen. It's the middle of the day. What's wrong?"

"Well, I told you about Matt, the little boy that reminded me of Max."

"Yes."

"I'm going to tell you something, but you must *promise* not to tell anybody else. OK?" Charleen glanced out her window and sat in a kitchen chair.

"Of course, dear. I won't tell anyone, if you don't want me to. But what is it? Is there a problem?"

"No, um, maybe ..." Charleen didn't know what to say first. She leaned over the table and spoke into the handset as if there were eavesdroppers nearby. "Mom, this boy isn't a boy. He's really a man! Isn't that incredible?" Charleen knew her mom would be intrigued.

"What do you mean by 'He's a man?'" Mom was intrigued, but apparently not for the reasons that Charleen expected.

Charleen described his disease concluding with, "He's really 39!"

"That's rather hard to believe. Why do *you* believe him?"

"Well, he can change his voice to sound like a grown man. And he knows history really well," she said. The sound of her own voice explaining it was unconvincing, even to herself.

"OK? And that's it? What proof did he give you?"

Charleen shifted position in her chair. "Um, well, he's very smart and he has these antique pictures and he talks like an adult ...Oh, it's hard to describe."

"Listen ..."

Charleen knew by the tone of her mom's voice that a lecture was coming.

"Ever since you were young, you've been a believer of the good in people. And that's what makes you so caring. But it also makes you ..."

"Gullible? Is that what you were going to say, Mom?" Charleen let a hard edge show in her voice.

"Oh, no. It's what makes you non-critical too."

"It's difficult to explain." Charleen finally concluded.

"Well, first you said that he reminded you of Max, and now ..."

"What?" The hardness returned to Charleen's voice.

"How old would Garrett have been this year?"

"Mom, no. That's not it. I know what you're suspecting is happening to me."

"But isn't it quite a coincidence that Garrett was going to be thirty-nine and this boy claims that he's also thirty-nine?"

"No. I mean, so what? It could happen. Mother."

"Sweetie, have you been going to the grief counseling group?" her mom asked with concern in her voice.

"Yes." Charleen momentarily lowered the phone and looked out a window, irritated by the question.

"That's good. Don't stop attending. I think it will help. Well, it's quite a story. Maybe you should take some time to think about this and decide what you're certain is true about this boy. It sounds like he's trying to mess with you. Be careful. OK?"

"OK, Mom. Good-bye." She waited for her mom to hang up, and then she slammed the handset onto the phone with such force that it bounced off and clunked to the table.

What was I thinking?

Charleen returned to school and entered the office by way of the front door, passing Holly's desk.

Holly said, "Oh, I have a message for you ..." She tore a page from her memo pad. "Matthew Janson's father called ..." Charleen grabbed the note. It read, *"Matthew Janson is sick. Stay away."*

"That's it?" asked Charleen.

The Smart Kid

Holly just shrugged. "Yup. I guess it's contagious."

Charleen closed her office door behind her, tossed the note carelessly on her desk and sat down to contemplate this unexpected event.

Did he regret telling me his secret? Have I been duped? Why didn't I just report him to the district? Does he need psychological help?

Throughout the day, Charleen tried to concentrate on her work, but sobering thoughts intruded. Worries about Matt grew— her mom's questions, the seeds of doubt. She told herself to not think about it. *It's as easy as trying to not think of pink elephants,* she thought.

During the last hour of the school day, the intercom buzzed and Holly's voice announced, "Wayne Zimmerman is here for you."

What? Not again.

She intended to give another excuse to avoid the conversation. As a psychologist, she understood what she was doing. It was a flight response from anxiety. Dr. Lansing would call it the Controlling Step in the grieving process. But understanding her motives and controlling her actions were two different things.

He must have someone else he can talk to about ... stuff.

She opened the door. Wayne was waiting in a chair, sniffling. He appeared small and vulnerable. She sighed. "Wayne, please come in."

As he walked past her, she almost touched him gently on the shoulder, but she pulled her hand back.

She sat behind her desk and studied him. He had been crying. She handed him a tissue. *He is a student under my care*, she told herself. In spite of her discomfort, she pitied the sad boy.

"Wayne. How can I help?"

"What do you mean?"

"I mean, why do you want to talk with me?"

He blinked. "What do you mean? I didn't want to talk with you."

Charleen sat back in her chair and frowned. "If you didn't want to talk, then why did you come to my office?"

He removed a small paper from his pocket and handed it to her. It was a handwritten message on School District note paper. At the top of the paper was a patch of black ink where something had been scribbled out of recognition. The handwriting below it read, *"Wayne Z. Please see Ms. Therry to discuss your fears."*

She had not written this. The handwriting was a man's. The only man in the administration offices was Mr. Heim, and that wasn't his script. Besides, neither she nor he would ever write exactly the topic of discussion on a note for anyone to read. Even though they were young, the students still had a right to privacy and confidentiality.

"Who did you get this from?"

"From my homeroom teacher."

"I mean, who did your homeroom teacher get it from?"

"From you." Wayne frowned at her.

She sighed. "Since you're here, do you want to discuss your fears?"

"Yes."

Charleen had not expected a forthright answer.

"OK." Charleen adjusted her position on her chair. "What are you afraid of?" She knew that he was going to say something about his dad's health.

He looked up at her and said, "Greg Urban."

Charleen was taken off guard by the name. "What about him frightens you?"

"Well, you know how he's always mean and mad and stuff?"

"Yes. I know that he is angry and mean sometimes," she said cautiously.

"Well, I don't want to become like him," Wayne admitted.

"Why would you think that you might become like Greg?" Charleen was confused twice-over.

"Well, if my dad dies, then I'll become angry and mean like Greg, because his dad died."

"Oh, you're mistaken, his— " she stopped. She had nearly disclosed sensitive information about another student. That was against the school counselor's code, and district rules.

Wayne waited for her to finish her sentence.

"Um, I mean …Why do you think his dad died?"

"He told me," said Wayne.

The Smart Kid

She understood now. Of course, Greg wouldn't tell other students that his dad was in prison. That would be an embarrassment. From a dejected child's point of view, it would be easier to say his father was dead. That would earn sympathy from peers.

She still found it difficult to talk with this boy, but she used the barrier of her desk as a coping mechanism.

"Greg and Karen have had a hard life, and there have been many factors that may have made Greg angry. But that will not happen to you if… I mean, you have a mother who loves you, right?"

Wayne nodded.

"And your mother will do everything that she can to … she will do everything that she can to protect you … to protect you … from harm." Charleen stood suddenly and walked to her window. Every deep exhalation appeared as foggy evidence on the cold glass; evidence that she'd lost emotional control again. But it was worse this time.

She stared outside at nothing for a minute. She furtively wiped a tear from her eye and turned back to Wayne.

"Wayne, please don't worry. You're not like Greg. I have to go now …"

She escorted him to the door. He appeared to be in better spirits.

She shut her door and collapsed into her chair. After a few minutes, she calmed down and considered the source of her anxiety.

It is Wayne. No it isn't.

She didn't want to think about him and what he represented.

It was the note. The handwritten note was the cause of her pain. She picked it up and studied it. It was a used note. Someone had blackened out the original message and written something different. Charleen removed a large magnifying glass from her desk drawer.

Nancy Drew, detective. If Mom saw me now … She pulled the desk lamp close and examined the note through the magnifier.

Under the scribbled black lines she was able to discern only three letters: s-o-n.

Son! She dropped the paper and the magnifier and turned away in disgust. Of all the words in the world, it was the one that caused her the most pain.

My son.
Charleen sat at her desk and tried to control her emotions.

When she was calm again, Charleen picked up the forged note and the other note that Holly had just given her, intending to toss them into the wastebasket, when she stopped. She looked at the note from Holly. *"Matthew Janson is sick. Stay away."*

Jan s-o-n.

A memory flashed into her mind: Matthew Janson handing a small paper to Wayne.

Another image took over: The second time that Wayne had come to visit her, he had dropped a small piece of paper onto the registration desk as he walked out.

How many times had she written notes for Matt to come to her office? The first time they almost met. And then the next time when they finally met. That was two notes. Wayne had notes the last two times he arrived.

Charleen tried to remember events from weeks ago. A young student wouldn't be foresighted enough to save and re-use a note. But a clever man who sneaked around his entire life might have developed this potentially useful habit.

"... he's trying to mess with you," Mom had said.

But why? What did he gain from arranging appointments between me and my ... my what? What is Wayne to me?

Charleen admitted to herself that her meetings with Wayne had become increasingly distressing. Even the sight of Wayne caused her anxiety. She needed to talk with someone. But she had no one to turn to besides her mom.

No. That's not true.

Charleen searched her desk for Dr. Lansing's phone number.

"Hello?" said the doctor a second time.

Charleen was paralyzed with fear. She finally forced out a syllable. "Um ..."

"Who is this?" asked Dr. Lansing.

She said nothing.

The Smart Kid

"Five seconds and I'll hang up ..."
"Dr. Lansing?" she said.
"Yes, who is this?"
"I'm Charleen Therry, from the— "
"Yes, Charleen. I remember. How can I help?"
She paused. *Where to start?*
"I have had three ... There is a boy in my school whose father ... was ..."

It was as if Charleen were attempting to run through ever-deepening water. It pushed against her efforts, stronger with each step, each word. She dragged her feet forward but it was pointless. If she were strong enough to push against the water, and complete her thought, she would drown. Her success at taking the final steps into the deep water would kill her.

She was hyperventilating now. The handset banged to the desk. Dr. Lansing's tiny voice was calling to her. She pressed the speaker phone button.

"— you OK? Charleen, can you hear me?"
"Yes..."
"I can tell that you're having a panic attack. What is it that you're afraid of?"
"One of my students ..."
"What about him frightens you?"

She breathed deep, and took another step into cold, wet, darkness of fear. She knew that she was going to say it, express the horror that she was ashamed to admit.

Once again, Dr. Lansing gently asked, "How does he frighten you?"

"By ... living." She sobbed at the admission. The dam had burst.

Dr. Lansing spoke softly. "Charleen, I've read the newspaper report of the accident. Is this boy the son of Collin Zimmerman, the man who killed your—"

"Oh God! You know?" she bawled out. She grabbed a tissue.

Dr. Lansing, her far-away-counselor, patiently waited for her. Finally he asked, "Charleen, you realize that the boy was not in the car with his father at the accident, right?"

"Yes ..." she sobbed. "But I'm ..." She couldn't admit it: the petty, hurtful thought that inhabited her mind. It was a dark thought, that no mother should ever have. Charleen could not bring it to light.

But as long as it remained in the unexamined dark corridors of her mind, it would live to attack her. It thrived in the depths. Only by forcing it out of the deep and exposing it to the light, could it be put to death forever. Charleen would need to use the brilliant light of acceptance as a weapon against it.

"Charleen, are you jealous that Mrs. Zimmerman still has a son and you don't?"

The tears started again.

For Charleen to admit this would imply that she'd be happier if Wayne was dead. Then she wouldn't have to see him every day, and week, and forever ... and be reminded of her lost boy.

But how could she wish her pain upon another mother? How could she even admit that she wanted someone else to carry the pain instead of her? That would be a wretched hope. She would be an evil person to want such a thing, the antithesis of a counselor who protected and loved every student in her care. She would not be a true counselor, or a true mother. She would become nothing. Dust in the ocean.

"No."

The last words she heard before she hung up the phone were, "Your attempt at controlling isn't working, and it's going to lead to—"

Charleen locked her door, plopped into her desk chair, rested her head on her crossed arms, and closed her eyes... for just a moment.

14. More Doubts

WHEN CHARLEEN AWOKE, the school day had ended. She felt much better, refreshed, as if she'd had a full night's rest. She gathered her things and walked through the central office, intending to hurry home. Mr. Heim exited his office just as she passed.

"I'll walk with you to the meeting," he said, carrying his briefcase and wearing his usual gray suit and tie.

Charleen had forgotten about the mandatory staff meeting. She considered her options. If she declined, she'd have to explain herself to the intimidating principal.

She faked a smile and followed Mr. Heim.

Charleen fidgeted throughout the meeting, anxious to get home to call Matt. The doubts were growing and she wanted answers immediately. She needed to challenge him about sending Wayne to her office with forged notes. Maybe she didn't know this man/boy at all.

Finally the meeting ended! She sped home intending to call him one more time, and if he didn't answer, then she'd drive to his apartment, despite his veiled warning. She followed her curving driveway to her backyard. As soon as she turned off the engine, the old shed door squeaked open and Matt came out. He ran to the passenger side, and jumped in, keeping low. His head remained below window level.

"Matt! Why were you in the shed? And why were you not in school?" Charleen demanded.

"Did you drive here directly from school? Don't look at me! Pretend I'm not here," he ordered, his breathing heavy.

"What's going on?" she asked, facing straight ahead, but glancing occasionally in his direction.

"Were you followed from school?" Matt asked.

"Followed? I don't know. Why? Who'd be following me?" Charleen shrugged at the ridiculous question.

Matt's head rested against the passenger door, his expression, serious.

The Smart Kid

"Do you remember that secret government committee that I mentioned?"

"Yes. That was crazy— "

Matt's stare pierced into her. "Charleen, just scan the area. Do you see any people?"

"No, my back yard is secluded. I can only see into the yards of my nearest neighbors." She surveyed the houses.

"Is anyone spying from windows?"

"No." She frowned.

"Are there any workmen, or repairmen on the telephone poles, or — "

"No. No one. No one followed me." She raised her voice.

"They may not know about you yet. But they will." Matt nodded his head with certainty.

"Matthew, please tell me what's happening. The 'secret committee' that you joked about last week is real?" She looked directly at him.

"Yes. And they want me."

"Who? Who is in this committee?"

"Perkins."

"Perk— you mean *John Perkins*, the old guy who's been a Senator forever?"

"Yes." He studied her reaction.

Charleen stared back, as a counselor, evaluating his sanity. He could be suffering from a paranoia fantasy as a result of reading too many comic books, month after month, in his solitary apartment. Senator Perkins was well known, and respected, and a thousand miles away, in Washington, DC. It seemed too fantastic that he was involved. But his notoriety would also make him an easy personality to pin a conspiracy theory on. Suffering a downward, paranoid spiral is like a man falling off the edge of a cliff, losing control and grasping at anything jutting out strong enough to support him and his false worldview.

"Right now, you're wondering if this is true, or if it's all in my head," Matt offered.

"You are good, Matt. I *was* thinking that."

"It's natural for you to wonder. But I can prove it. I've got a letter from him, to my parents. You should read it."

"OK. I'd like to. Should we go to your apartment?"

"You're sure that no one followed you?"

It was too much paranoia for Charleen. "Yes! I'm sure! There wasn't a car in sight on the road when I pulled into the driveway. I'll watch as we leave."

She started the engine, pulled out the driveway, and headed downtown, repeatedly glancing at the mirrors. She made a couple of random turns too, surveying trailing cars, but saw nothing unusual.

Now he's got me playing spy games too.

Charleen asked, "Why now? What's happened to get you so paranoid?"

"Ever heard the saying, 'You're not paranoid if people really *are* out to get you'?"

Her expression indicated that she wasn't amused.

"Anyway," he continued, "I've been expecting something like this for a long time. It's finally starting, again. When I got to school this morning, I saw a dark blue pickup truck. I left immediately because, on Wednesday, someone was trailing us in a dark truck."

"Wait. A dark blue pickup truck? Oh no. There was a dark blue truck. Mr. Jayes, the janitor mentioned seeing it," said Charleen, not certain if it actually meant anything nefarious.

"So they followed us from the school, while we were following the coach," Matt surmised.

"Why didn't you say anything to me?"

"I almost told you yesterday before you left my apartment."

"Oh, that was it."

"And before yesterday, I didn't know yet how much I could trust you. But I did try to tell you that I was being followed, and you laughed at me," Matt countered.

"Oh, you did! I thought it was a joke." She angled her head and gave a half smile.

"I presented it that way just to test your reaction. You weren't ready yet. You didn't yet know the truth about me."

"So that's why you revved us through the red light?" The

The Smart Kid

memory added tension to her voice.

"Yes. Sorry."

Another piece of the Matt Janson puzzle clicked into place. But the picture that was forming just made her more aware of the pieces that were missing.

"If they know where you are, why haven't they caught you yet?"

"I think that they must have *just* figured out that I was hiding at Jefferson," Matt said with an ominous tone.

"How do you know that it's the same dark truck from the other day? And how can you be certain that it's not one of the parents? That would explain why Mr. Jayes saw a dark truck, wouldn't it?"

"It doesn't hurt to be cautious. But if I'm right, it may have saved me from getting arrested."   "That's why you didn't go into school: because you think they'll arrest you?"

"Yes. They might not be certain that I attend this school. Maybe they're still investigating. But they won't just barge into the school and arrest me openly. They don't want to draw attention to themselves," said Matt, sounding overly dramatic, again.

"Oh, yes. They are a 'secret organization', right?" She glanced at him, hunkered below the window.

Matt either ignored or didn't recognize her doubtful tone. "In the past, they've come to the school claiming to be with 'Child Welfare', or 'Child Protection Services.' That's a better cover for them." The chilling tone emanating from his youthful face created an incongruity that made it difficult to take him seriously.

"So they've found you before?"

"Yes. First, a phy-ed intern started school late, was placed to investigate me."

"A government agent posed as an intern to spy on you?"

"Yes, to get the layout of the school and set a good trap. I barely escaped by jumping in the river."

"Oh, the river. That was lucky." She wondered if he sensed her condescending tone. "We're near your apartment, Matt."

"Yes, I can tell," he said, still slumped below window level. She snapped a surprised look at him, and then realized he was referring to their location, not her tone.

"Don't park in front. Park a couple of blocks away, at The Crash Diner. We'll walk from there. No one can know where I live." *More dire warnings*, she thought.

"Yes, I know. I tried to find the location of the address that's listed in your file."

"I couldn't very well list my actual address, could I? No one has ever questioned it before, since I always used a P.O. box."

She parked the car and looked around, mugging for his benefit. "I think it's safe, Matt."

As they got out of the car, he scanned the lot.

They walked into the side door of the diner. A teenage boy, wearing a paper hat, stood at the counter. "Welcome! Can I help you today?"

"No," They strode past and sat in the last booth. Matt surveyed the lot through the window.

"This is so ironic."

"What?" He continued staring out the window.

"I sat in this booth just a couple of weeks ago, and talked with your fake mom."

Matt turned toward her, his head angled with a half-smile, just as she'd done moments ago. "Sorry. Just like the fake address, I needed to deceive you to protect me. But I guess it wasn't you that I had to worry about."

He stood, and she followed him out the back door. In the openness of the parking lot, they picked up their pace. They sprinted to the rear entrance of a furniture store. A mix of furniture filled the large store, which had only a few other customers

Matt breathed a sigh of relief. Charleen followed Matt as he weaved through a maze of couches and cushy chairs. He found a pair of high backed wing chairs that faced away from the doors. He sat, grabbed her hand, and pulled her into the chair next to him. They both were breathing quickly from the exertion.

"Let's just wait here a minute." He leaned back and closed his eyes. They remained in the chairs for several minutes, their breathing slowing to a normal rate. At every sound, he turned to survey the source.

The Smart Kid

Up to that point, Matt's frenzied behavior had scared her. But as she began to relax, she evaluated his chase story. Once again, her mom's questions echoed in her mind. *How do I know he's 39? He can talk like a man. Is that proof? I never saw a birth certificate or driver's license. He had an article about a girl that doesn't grow and claimed to have the same condition. Maybe he's projecting. Yes, he acts mature, but that's not proof. He's knowledgeable, but he might be a well-read genius. Why am I doubtful? No evidence. Nothing conclusive.*

"Hello! Do you like those chairs?" The salesman asked in a loud voice before Charleen knew he was beside her. She jumped.

"No," said Matt, as he stood. Charleen followed him out the front of the store. As they scurried along the sidewalk of St. Germain street, Matt scanned the cars, and people and windows, his head turning like a nervous bird. Once they were in his apartment building, he appeared to relax.

They walked up the stairs to apartment 242. Matt unlocked the door and allowed Charleen to enter first, bringing back the memories of their previous day: All the revelations, the unbelievable stories he'd told. *Stories.*

She walked by the framed magazine cover. *'Number of deaths in one week, 242'.*

Is that a coincidence?

"Have a seat. I'll get us something to drink," the boy said.

"Do you mind if I turn on the TV?"

"Go ahead. It's about time it gets some use. I don't even know why I bought it." He walked around the corner to the kitchen.

She pulled the knob. It was a large television, in a cabinet with speakers on each side. It buzzed, and the image faded in. Channel 4 had 'Happy Days'. She turned the channel knob. Channel 5 had 'WKRP in Cincinnati'. The dial clicked at each channel; Channel 6, nothing, Channel 7, 8, nothing. Channel 9 was too fuzzy to watch. Nothing but static on channel 10. Typical. Out of choices, she stopped the dial at Channel 11, KSTC. It had a local news program.

She studied the apartment with new eyes. Clean. Neat. Big phonograph record cabinet. Nice furniture. Decorative mirrors. *Money.*

Charleen realized something: He had no unpacked boxes in his apartment. If he had just moved here from Oklahoma a few months ago, there should be some evidence. She still had unpacked boxes in her house and she'd lived there for about as long as Matt claimed to have lived here. *And where did all this expensive furniture come from?*

Why did I accept what he said without any proof? Because he has the ability to change his voice? Because his face is too young to hide a psychotic liar?

She remembered a college psychology course about people with multiple personalities. Sometimes it was accompanied by change of voice, or personality, just like in the book Sybil. She started to feel foolish. *Have I been duped by a clever kid?*

The news station was reporting upcoming weather. "… partly cloudy for a few days …"

Matt walked in carrying two bottles of Coke and a bottle opener. He set them on the end table.

"I told you that I've got proof about Senator Perkins. Let me find that letter." The boy left the room. The counselor of the boy sat in the empty room waiting for the boy to present a letter from Senator Perkins proving that he was being hunted for … what?

A image of Matt appeared on the TV news program about a mental patient who escaped months ago and was still on the run. "He appears to be twelve years old … blond-haired boy … but he's actually nineteen … very mentally unstable … a master of psychological manipulation … he may be using the last name of Shale, or Howardson or Selah… he may have accomplices … report his location …"

Her mouth dropped open. She stared at the television in disbelief.

"I'm still searching, sorry." The voice of the boy came from the bedroom and startled her.

Oh, I'm so stupid. It's so classic: counselor falling for a patient in her care. But she wasn't in love with him— she was missing Max. She had transferred her love for her child to this boy, losing all objectivity.

It had started at her house, when she was treating his wounds.

The Smart Kid

Like a mother. First, he made her emotionally vulnerable by asking about Max and Garrett. Then, he demonstrated competence and knowledge by explaining a magic trick. Knock her down, and build himself up. It was so classic.

Plus, there were the forged notes. He understood who Wayne was to her, what he represented; so he purposefully and repeatedly sent Wayne although he knew it would distress her. What could he gain from destabilizing her emotionally? Of course to make her cling to him, as a surrogate child, even more.

"... he's trying to manipulate you." Mom is right: I'm gullible. Charleen heard him approaching and jumped to shut off the TV. The lunatic entered the room.

He wore a short-sleeved shirt. It was the first time that Charleen had seen him in short sleeves. He had very muscular arms; surprising since his body was so small. As she studied him, she realized that his whole body was sturdy. She could see his t-shirt hugging the contours of his chest. His neck also looked strong and thick at the base. It had previously been obscured by heavy shirts or jackets. Her expectations about who she thought he was had prevented her from noticing that he carried himself with the confidence and strength of a man.

"I'm sorry. I've moved so many times that I've misplaced that letter."

"Your apartment doesn't look like you've recently moved."

"Thanks. But I wish I could find that letter."

"Mmmm, that's OK. I believe you." She wondered if she sounded convincing. "The last time that I was here, you said that your brother's last name was Shale."

"That's our original name," the nineteen-year-old man said.

"Not Janson?"

"No. I chose that because I'm Jan's son." He gave a half-smile.

"And not Selah?"

"No. I used that name because it's an anagram for Shale."

"But you purposely used the name Matthew Selah to leave clues for someone?"

"Yes."

"Who?"

"My brother, Mark."

"Yes. You said that you have a brother 'Mark.'"

She recalled another manipulator who claimed to have a brother. *"You have invented a very useful younger brother called Ernest..."*

"Yes. He was imprisoned by Senator Perkins, with me. I escaped. He didn't."

"You both were imprisoned?" She raised her eyebrows, truly surprised at this new revelation.

"Yes."

"Does he have this condition too?" She cross-examined him, like she'd done with his fake mom.

"No." He frowned slightly.

"I thought you said that they *didn't* catch you because you jumped in the river?"

"That was *after* I escaped the first time. You're rather curious now, aren't you?"

"Honestly, I did get more curious after I tried to explain it to my mom"—

"Your mom?"

"Yes, I—"

"You told your mother about me?" He frowned at her.

"Oh, well, I'm sorry. But I had to get someone's opinion about this whole situation because it's so hard to believe—"

"You know what's hard to believe? That you told your mom. And did she believe you?" His frown grew.

"No. And I had a hard time explaining it to her. She asked about proof—"

"Yes. Proof. Well that's why we're here now, isn't it? But I can't find it," Matt said glumly.

"Matt, you're safe now. No one's caught you, so I should leave." *Do I sound casual enough?*

"Oh." The escaped mental patient glared at her unopened Coke bottle on the table, as if it shouldn't be there.

She took a step toward the door.

He intercepted, raising a hand to halt her escape.

She stopped, surprised.

The Smart Kid

"Charleen, you started school late, just like that intern."

"Yes, you know why."

"I know what you *told* me. But I didn't see any *real* evidence."

"What? You suspect I'm working with the 'Secret Government Committee'?"

"I'm saying that I only know about *you* because of what you told me. No proof." He spit out the last word.

The indignity of the implication made her roil with anger.

"Well, what do you want— a death certificate?" she yelled, pained at this sudden attack.

"Well, what do *you* want— a birth certificate?"

He was right; she did want to see a birth certificate. But she couldn't admit that now.

"Oh. You!" She abruptly pushed by him and walked into the hallway, past the signed Elvis record. She looked at it again.

It's not even signed to him— it was signed to someone named Michael. Why didn't I notice this before?

Charleen heard him following her, but didn't look back. She forced herself to not run down the hallway. He was getting closer. She reached for the door, turned the doorknob, and pulled. It didn't move. Locked.

Had he planned this? When had he locked it?

His arm stretched out past her and pressed against the door.

"Oh!"

Charleen turned to face him; the young man pretending to be a boy. He stood too close, looking up into her eyes. Her chest was rising and falling, her breasts nearly pushing against him with each deep breath. He glanced at her chest. Her heart thumped wildly out of control and she feared that he could hear it. Charleen became aware of his odor, like that of a man. She noticed the solid muscles on the arm stretched past her, strongly pinning the door shut.

The sudden awareness that she had spent hours in this apartment with a mentally unstable man eclipsed the impropriety of private time with a twelve-year-old boy. That seemed like a tiny infraction compared to the potential harm and violation that a strong nineteen-year-old man could set upon her.

"Charleen, are you OK?" asked the man of the woman.

"Yes, I'm fine. ..." *Make it natural.* "I'm glad you're home safely now ... here ... in your apartment."

"Don't tell anyone! Not even your mom!" he ordered, moving past her. Perhaps he sensed her doubt.

"No. No, I won't. Of course not." She forced a smile.

He turned the deadbolt and opened the door for her.

She walked out and didn't look back.

15. Division

SATURDAY MORNING, CHARLEEN sat on the living room floor beside the unpacked boxes. She'd been staring at the box labeled 'Max's Toys' for several minutes. After a heavy sigh, Charleen opened the top cautiously, as if she were a child cranking the handle on a Jack-in-the-Box, expecting a scary surprise. The first thing she discovered was a toy baseball and bat. Below it was a baseball cap, the word 'Slugger' embroidered above the bill. As she hugged the hat against her chest, an image of Matt wearing his baseball cap flashed through her mind. The memory was an unwelcome reminder of what had transpired between them. She tossed the hat to the floor, as if she could toss away the memory of Matt.

She removed a wooden, six-piece puzzle frame. She dug into the box looking for the pieces. She found a crescent moon, a star, a cradle, and a mother in a rocking chair. An empty spot remained for a missing piece. She dropped it back in the box and leaned against the wall with a heavy sigh, resting her head in her hands.

Her memories of Max and Matt seemed to be all mixed together.

She dreaded the thought of her mom calling this weekend to check on her.

Mom is right. Matt is an emotional substitute.

It seemed as if losing Matt made her feel the loss of Max even more deeply. It was as if she'd lost her little Max again. Her tears helped her to feel her love for Max.

Sunday, Charleen washed dinner dishes while the radio played soft music. A special bulletin interrupted. There it was again, an announcement about the escaped mental patient who looked like a kid. She switched off the radio and shoved the remaining dishes from the counter into the sink. They crashed and clinked together; maybe a few broke. She didn't look. Her quiet footsteps to her bedroom were the loudest sounds in the empty house. She flopped on the bed crossways.

As she stared at the ceiling, Charleen admitted to herself that she

The Smart Kid

had a duty to report Matt— to open the Matt Janson box and show the authorities what she'd discovered, a nineteen year old lunatic impersonating a student; a false registration in the school district; and fraud by Sandy Otis.

She decided to note the phone number the next time the special bulletin aired.

She also realized that she had to come clean to the school administration about her own infractions: her extensive investigations without school district knowledge and withholding evidence of potential child abuse by the coach.

What will they do to me?

As she wondered, she drifted off. A veil of dreams covered the troubling thoughts. She imagined Mr. Heim popping out of a jack-in-the-box, holding her termination notice.

Charleen woke early Monday morning. Traces of yesterday's mood lingered. Outside, traces of sunlight appeared, reflecting off a fresh layer of snow.

Skipping breakfast, she left for work earlier than usual. While she was still two blocks away, she saw Matt standing beside the road, obviously waiting for her. He wasn't wearing a winter coat— just a thick sweater, sufficient for early November weather.

Do I stop? What might he do to me?

Seeing him standing alone in the street, he didn't seem like a threat.

She braked the car, unbuckled her seat belt, and insured that her door was unlocked, just in case. The lunatic climbed into the passenger seat. Apparently, he'd been waiting for her a long time; his cheeks were a rosy red, and he rubbed his bare hands together for warmth. She didn't drive, letting the car idle in the middle of the street.

"Hi Charleen."

"Hello Matthew ... Janson."

"I wanted to talk briefly before you got to school— "

"Couldn't you talk with me *at* school?" she interrupted, ignoring their earlier discussion.

Matt raised his eyebrows. "No, I can't attend anymore because they probably know about me now."

"They? The Secret Government Organization?" Charleen tried to hide her doubt, but failed.

"Yes. Is something wrong?"

"Is something wrong?" she echoed. "I couldn't even begin to tell you everything that is wrong!"

Matt's mouth dropped open in surprise. "Try. Try to tell me something that's bothering you."

"All right. The forged notes that you gave to Wayne."

"Oh. I expected you to figure that out. But I hope that it helped you."

"Helped me?" She mimicked him again. "Yes, it helped me have a nervous breakdown and become an emotional wreck!"

"Charleen, I'm sorry to have messed with your head, but I knew that you were avoiding Wayne. And—"

"How? How did you know?"

"Wayne said that he went to your office to tell you his fear of becoming like Greg, and that you sent him away. You just blew him off, Counselor!" He paused, as if to imply that she wasn't living up to her title. "I had encouraged him to talk with you. I knew he needed it. And I had hoped that you'd tell him the truth about Greg's dad. He needed to hear it from a credible source. Karen had told me, but neither she nor her brother would tell anyone else. So I made Wayne believe that you wanted to speak with him. The avoidance was hurting both of you," Matt said forcefully.

"Are you pretending to be a psychologist now too?" Charleen asked, her voice bitter.

"No," replied Matt. "I'm just trying to help you face your pain so you can heal."

"I didn't ask for your help, *Doctor* Janson!"

They both remained quiet for a minute.

Finally, Charleen spoke calmly. "Listen, I'm sorry for yelling. I felt manipulated. But I understand why you did it: you want a mother figure in your life."

Matt's jaw dropped open for a second. "How…" Then he shook his head and said, "No."

The Smart Kid

"A lot of patients with your dysfunction try to control others emotionally. It's a symptom of your illness."

Matt frowned. "My illness?"

Using her soft voice, Charleen said, "Oh Matthew, I don't want to hurt you. I want you to get the help that you need. There is a clinic that works with mental patients like you. I'll help you get admitted." She had played her hand and shown her cards.

"So that's it!" He leaned back against the door, nodding to himself. "Charleen, you were angry at *me* for trying to help you. But now *you're* trying to help me. You can give it but can't take it."

Charleen stared out the car window for several seconds before facing Matt again. "For a while I thought that we were friends," she said. "But *real* friends don't lie to your face."

Matt frowned, turned away for a moment before looking her in the eye. "I almost had an adult friend years ago; someone I trusted. It ended badly. I left. But I thought that you were different. I even broke my Vow of Distrust for you."

"What do you mean: 'Vow of Distrust'?"

"I vowed that I'd never trust an adult again."

"You're saying that as if you're *not* an adult," she said.

Matt turned away and looked out the window for a long silent minute. He continued, "I had hoped that, finally, after nearly a decade, I had an adult ally who believed me; who saw the real me. What happened?"

"I saw the news bulletin. I know all about the real you."

"News bulletin? Oh no. It probably said something like, 'He's an escaped lunatic, or criminal. Don't believe him. Call the authorities.' Right?"

Charleen was silent.

"Why would you believe a news report instead of me? Didn't our time together feel real?"

"Real? More like surreal. Once I left your apartment, I started wondering. And then that news report confirmed my suspicions. They couldn't put it on the news if it wasn't true. They even had a picture of you."

Matt shook his head. "That means they know I'm in the city.

They must not be sure which school yet. But either way, they're trying to get someone to report me." Matt stared out the window. Then his sad eyes focused on hers. "Charleen, you were a true friend to me, for a bright moment. You'll never know how much I cherish the memories of our conversations together. I'll always remember you. ... Goodbye."

"... a master of psychological manipulation." Charleen forced herself to be unmoved by his apparent sincerity.

Charleen put the car in gear. "It will be okay. I'll help in your therapy—"

As Charleen started to accelerate, Matt opened the door and jumped out.

After moving forward a few feet, Charleen stopped the car and looked in her mirror.

He was getting up off the pavement. The escaped lunatic raised his hand to wave and ran away.

She sat there for a full minute, deciding what to do.

Well, he is gone. There was nothing left to do but go to school and follow through on her decision. She drove the final two blocks to school. Charleen, preoccupied with her thoughts, ignored the dark pickup truck that approached from the school and passed her.

16. Defense

As Matt walked off the street to cut through a yard, he saw a suspicious dark truck crawling along the road. He could not be sure that it was the same one that had trailed them, but decided to play it safe. Matt dashed through another yard heading north. and passed the corner of a house. As soon as the truck was out of view, he sprinted through the back yard, across the alley, glancing to his left and right, into the next yard leaving tracks in the fresh snow. He cruised through the yard in seconds and crossed the street to the next block. The wider street left him much more exposed than the alley. A moment before he gained cover beside a house, he caught a glimpse of the truck, stalking him along the avenue to the east.

Is it really following me?

Pausing for a moment, Matt placed his back against the house, and paused to catch his breath.

It came from the school. Matt had presumed that waiting for Charleen two blocks from school would be safe. But someone must have been waiting, or circling, or just got lucky. He stooped and peeked around the corner. The sinister truck waited on the avenue, in the middle of the intersection. A government spotter, partially hidden in the shadow of the interior, seemed to look right at him. If Matt was suspected of hiding in St. Cloud, spotters would have been sent to every school in the city.

Matt jumped and ran. He continued north, and ran as if his life depended on it, tearing through yards, hopping over fences, ducking under clotheslines. Instinct had taken control. He was a running machine.

Charleen walked through the school offices, passing Holly sitting at her desk. "Good morning, Holly." Holly wished her a good morning, but not enthusiastically. On Charleen's desk, a memo waited, written by Holly. It read, *"See Mr. Heim."* Charleen walked back out

The Smart Kid

and asked if Mr. Heim was in his office.

Without looking up, Holly replied, "Yes, I'll inform them you're here."

"Them who?" asked Charleen.

Holly mumbled too quietly and pressed the intercom for Mr. Heim's office. "She's here." The fuzzy response was simply, "Send her in."

Before Charleen could knock on the door, Mr. Heim opened it, and welcomed her. Two others were in the room: a man in business attire and Coach Easton. She raised her eyebrows in surprise. She looked back at Holly and met her steady gaze.

"Come in, please, Ms. Therry," said Mr. Heim. "Shut the door."

She felt the apprehension first in her empty stomach. It reminded her of when the doctors came out of the operating room, after the accident, and silently stared, as she sat in the hallway, waiting for the bad news. She sat in the remaining chair.

"Ms. Therry, this is Donald Schroeder. He is the head of the school board. And you know Mr. Easton."

The sight of him fanned the embers of anger into a burning hatred. Easton looked as if he wanted to hit her with a baseball bat.

"First, you should know that Mr. Easton has resigned his position here at the school," said Mr. Heim.

Charleen contained her surprise. *That's good news ... maybe.* "Why?" she asked flatly.

"Mr. Easton believes that he's been falsely implicated in an event from last week and that Jefferson School is no longer a supportive working environment for him," said Mr. Heim. "So I've accepted his resignation."

"OK," said Charleen, expecting bad news. "But why am I here? And why is Mr. Schroeder here?"

"Mr. Schroeder is here as a witness. It's district policy to have a board member present during your disciplinary investigation."

"*My* disciplinary investigation?"

Matt breathed heavily, as he continued to run, his breath exploding into great puffs of white mist. He cut through another yard, and another. The snow slowed his pace. Each time he crossed a street, he saw the dark truck. Matt realized he couldn't outrun the truck. He had to change his tactic. *But how?*

As Matt tracked straight lines north through the yards, the truck followed along a parallel avenue a half block away. If Matt turned to the left and ran *away* from the truck, then it would turn *toward* Matt, and easily catch up to him. If Matt didn't change course, neither could the truck, he thought. It seemed as if the truck were trying to block him in, or outflank him.

Why did this seem familiar?

"Yes," said Mr. Heim, as he put on reading glasses. He looked at a paper on his desk, then judged Charleen over the top of his glasses, which had slid down his thin nose. After a pause he continued, "You are being accused of an inappropriate relationship with one of our students, Matthew Janson."

"What?" This time, Charleen could not contain her surprise. "Why? By who?" she asked and then looked at Mr. Easton.

"I saw you and the Janson boy at the gymnastics match. You sat together during the last part of the match on the top bleacher. When the match ended, you two were still sitting there," said Mr. Easton.

"Well, it's true that Matthew and I sat together during the match. But we were on school grounds with many other people." said Charleen.

"Ms. Therry, the office secretary, Holly, said that Matthew went into your office that afternoon, and stayed there for a long time. Apparently you were still in there when she left for the day," said Mr. Heim.

"No we weren't. Mr. Easton testified that we were at the game. We left through my back office door, and went around to the gym door on that side of the school building."

"I never saw them until the end of the match!" said Mr. Easton.

Charleen saw rage in his eyes.

"But we were there the whole time. I'm sure there's someone who can verify it. And I was performing my counselor duties, getting acquainted with him," Charleen said, angry at the false accusations.

The Smart Kid

"We have been investigating that," said Mr. Heim, "and so far, no one is able to corroborate your story."

"My story? It's not a *story*. Surely, this isn't what prompted this meeting," Charleen exclaimed.

"No, of course not," said the principal, "There's more ..."

It's time to try a different tactic.

As Matthew ran across another street, he looked to his right. The truck mirrored him along the avenue. The moment he passed behind a house, he stopped, paused for a second, and peeked around the corner. The Predator wasn't in sight. Matt changed direction and headed south again. The truck and Matt were moving in opposite directions, he hoped.

His pursuers would soon realize he wasn't running north anymore. That thought incited an adrenaline rush. If his escape tactics didn't work, he'd be captured again.

His thick sweater did its job— he was sweating. The shirt he wore under it was soaked.

He dashed across the street and entered a yard. A second before a house blocked his view, he heard the loud roaring of an engine and saw the truck speeding backward. It drove backward as fast as it had been going forward. The only choice for Matt was to continue running south through the next yard. But amazingly, the truck still followed him backward.

Matt hadn't gained any advantage. In truth, the truck had, because Matt was becoming increasingly tired. And there was no escape route; no river to jump into and float to safety. It was just Matt against a truck, on a giant grid of city blocks.

It's hopeless.

"Ms. Therry, is it true that you had Matt Janson in your house last week?"

"Oh ..." was all that Charleen had time to say before Mr. Heim continued.

"And is it true that you were with him after school hours, and that *you* drove him to your house?"

"Well ... yes. How do you know that?" Charleen asked.

"A number of students told us how you held Matthew as you walked him into the school. And they saw you drive away with him," said Mr. Heim.

"Well, yes. that's true. I was consoling him because he had been in a fight and was bleeding. I was going to take him to the nurse's office, but she was gone already. He needed help; he had a bad cut on his face."

Mr. Schroeder finally spoke. "Ms. Therry, is that your job?"

Charleen looked at the new interrogator, and tried to think of a stronger answer than what came out of her mouth. "Um, I'm not sure, but he needed medical attention."

"Why didn't you just call his parents?" asked Principal Heim.

Because he's a deranged nineteen-year-old mental patient who escaped from an asylum and is living on his own and I fell for his very convincing story that he's actually a thirty-nine-year-old man in a twelve-year-old's body. She practiced the words in her head first.

No, there's no way I can discuss that now. They'll find out soon enough from the news.

"OK. I was going to ... but they ... weren't home," she evaded. She couldn't tell the truth about Matt's non-parents— a truth she had hidden from her employer.

Mr. Heim looked doubtful.

"Have you informed Mr. Janson, um, Matt's father, about these charges yet?" she asked.

"No," he said with a shake of his head. "I thought it best to discuss it with you first, because Mr. Easton has an additional accusation."

Matt looked for hiding places as he ran. The next yard was bordered by a short chain link fence, which he grabbed by the top rail and vaulted over easily. He stumbled on the landing, his bare hands buried in the snow. He looked at his red hands and shook off the cold wetness.

Matt passed through the narrow alley and saw no sign of the threatening truck.

The Smart Kid

Maybe I'm ahead of it ...

He darted to the next yard, and jammed open a tall wooden gate. A large wolf, resembling a dog, barked and ran after him, nipping at his heels. Matt reached the other side of the fenced-in yard and, in one motion, flipped the gate's latch and slammed it open, knocking it against the side of the house. Although the dog was right behind him, Matt stopped short.

The relentless truck roared up the street, loud as a jet, ready to intercept him. Immediately, Matt reversed direction and collided with the dog. They both sprawled to the ground with Matt on top. The dog gave a timid yelp. Matt scrambled to his feet. So did the dog. They both ran for shelter behind the high wooden fence.

The dog chased him with less enthusiasm, until Matt banged through the back gate and crossed the alley. Matt expected to see the truck on the west avenue, but he didn't. He angled east, avoiding the need to jump the chain linked fence again, hoping to create more distance between them ...

Charleen burned Easton with her stare. That was a superpower she really wanted at that moment.

"I saw you with the Janson boy on Thursday too-- downtown! I watched you two enter an apartment building, and you didn't come out for hours!" Mr. Easton had venom in his voice.

"Is that true, Ms. Therry?" asked Mr. Heim, removing his reading glasses and raising his eyebrows.

Charleen found it difficult to swallow. Easton's motives for this attack were a mystery since she hadn't reported him to the administration. He seemed to be attacking without provocation.

"How could you know that?" she asked.

"Because I followed you this weekend, just like *you* followed me last week," said former-coach Easton.

"How do you ..."

Mr. Heim handed her photos that he had removed from a folder labeled 'Evidence'.

"Mr Easton brought these to me this week," said Mr. Heim. He looked into her eyes.

The photos were grainy black-and-whites of her and Matt on the sidewalk outside his apartment building. One showed Matt holding the door open for her, his hand raised behind her back, but not touching it. In another photo, Charleen was leaving the building, and the bank clock clearly displayed 7:40. Charleen gasped.

"Doesn't feel so good, does it? Having someone spy on you?" said Mr. Easton triumphantly.

"Why did you follow me?' asked Charleen.

"If you can take pictures of me, then 'What goes around, comes around,'" said Easton.

"Pictures? What pictures?" asked Charleen trying to catch up with his insinuations.

"After Mr. Heim showed me the pictures, I remembered your green piece-of-shit car from Halloween. Then I put it together; you were the one who put the photos in the school mailbox and forced me to quit," said Easton.

"What photos?" yelled Charleen.

Matt crossed the next street, and dashed through a yard, heading for the alley. He tried to imagine the path the truck would have to take to outflank him: west, then north, and east.

Can I run through *a block faster than the truck can drive* around *it?*

But Matt underestimated the truck's speed. As he crossed the alley, the truck roared toward him, only four houses away. Three metal garbage cans were neatly lined alongside a garage. Matt kicked and pushed them into the alley. They crashed over and rolled; the lids popped off and garbage spilled out.

Matt paused in a backyard to watch the effect of his barricade. He had a plan. Instinctively, Matt knew that the truck wasn't going to stop. But the driver would *assume* that the purpose of the obstruction was to stop the truck, to give Matt time to run north.

Instead of running, Matt lingered behind a garage. He heard a tremendous crash and peeked out at the sound. The truck had rammed two garbage cans. They flew into the air and banged against garages. The third one got wedged under the truck, scraping against the

The Smart Kid

pavement, creating a horrific spray of sparks and a cringe-inducing noise, as the truck continued, full-speed, east through the alley.

The disturbance caught the attention of the neighborhood residents; several ran out to their yards and yelled. The truck exited the alley and turned right, apparently driving away from Matt. This was Matt's chance: he headed south again, in the *same* direction as the truck. He cleared the alley before the truck stopped and backed up for a half a block to dislodge the can. The agile truck did a U-turn in the street and headed north.

The misdirection worked; Matt and his pursuers were once again moving in opposite directions. Sensing he had gained a slight advantage, Matt scanned for a hiding place: doghouse ... playhouse ... shed ... bush ... dumpster ... garage? No.

Beside the garage rested a large plastic box filled with toys and equipment: a deflated wading pool, colored tubes and balls, plastic leaf bags— nothing heavy. The objects were visible through horizontal slots along the side of the box. The hinged lid opened like a piano bench. *Or a coffin,* he thought.

Mr. Heim removed more photos from the Evidence folder and handed them to Charleen. These were sharp, and in color. In one photo, Mr. Easton stood on the doorstep of Deena Swenson's house looking in the direction of the camera. Another photograph showed Deena entering the house and Mr. Easton behind her, with his hand on the middle of her back.

"You didn't take these?" asked Mr. Heim in an accusing tone.

"No!" exclaimed Charleen. "I don't know who did! Where did you get them?"

"You weren't the one who dropped them into the school mail box?" asked Mr. Heim.

"No!" said Charleen, her voice shrill.

"So you weren't there with Matthew Janson?" accused Mr. Heim again.

"Well, um, I ..." she stumbled. She looked at her hands; they were sweating.

"We've talked with Deena Swenson. She told us about Mr.

Easton and the costume gift. Although Mr. Easton has denied the implications, he decided to quit anyway to spare the school any embarrassment," said Principal Heim, looking at her sternly. "And she told us that Matthew Janson was in her house. We know he was with you at the gymnastics meet. He could not have arrived at her house, by himself, that soon. So Mr. Easton has accused you of driving the Janson boy there too. Right?"

Anger forced out her loud accusation, as she pointed to Easton. "But we were following this sleazy abuser because he was planning on playing dress-up with an eight-year-old girl!" She almost stood up from her chair as she pointed an accusatory forefinger at him, like a gun.

Easton pointed at her as he looked at Mr. Heim. "See, I told you that she'd bring up these accusations that she knows nothing about. She wasn't in the house. She's taking the word of a twelve-year-old!" His demeanor was relaxed and his tone indicated that her suggestion was preposterous and not worthy of discussion. He partially smiled, indicating that Charleen's suggestion was ridiculous. He was a masterful liar.

Mr. Heim seemed to be accepting his defense. He looked at Charleen. "Mr. Easton is no longer our concern. He has helped the district to avoid a scandal over what seems to be a simple misunderstanding. In contrast, you have admitted to spending a considerable amount of time with a minor, much more time than Mr. Easton. So you're admitting that you drove the Janson boy from school grounds to spy on Mr. Easton?"

"Yes, I drove Matthew there," she confessed.

Before Matt hid, he looked over the wooden fence into the adjacent yard. A dog of a questionable breed sniffed through the snow. Matt tossed a plastic ball over the fence at the dog, without watching the result. He heard it. The dog ran around wildly and barked. Matt slipped his thin body into the plastic box of junk and wiggled down to the bottom. His heaving chest pressed against inflatable toys and bags. The balls and toys moved in motion to his panting.

The boy is hiding with the toys. Did I find the most obvious hiding place?

He wondered if his breath was creating visible puffs leaking out to the yard.

Then, he wondered if the tracks in the snow would betray him.

And then he realized that he was shaking uncontrollably with fear.

Mr. Heim signed deeply. He stood and summarized, "So you admit that, on at least three different days, you had a minor, one of our students, in your car, off school property?"

Charleen closed her eyes and gave a nod. She couldn't say that Matt wasn't a minor, but really 19, and a paranoid mental patient.

What does that make me? An incompetent psychologist who participates in the fantasy world of a lunatic.

Nor could she say that he wasn't an honestly enrolled student at the school. She had to protect him, to protect herself, and her job. If the truth became known and Matt was in custody, then she'd be able to defend herself. So she said nothing else. She was on trial and Easton was the criminal who snitched on her, in exchange for a reduced sentence. She wondered what *her* sentence would be.

Oh, Lord, I want to talk to Mom right now.

"And Ms. Therry, there is the other issue of Wayne Zimmerman," said Mr. Heim ominously.

This government organization pursuing him was the goad, prompting Matt to move from school to school every year or two. They made him run as if he were a criminal fugitive. He was convicted without a trial. They hadn't gotten this close since Lincoln Middle School in Kansas. Matt thought of Michelle Hanson in her blue dress, watching him as he hung from a tree branch before dropping into the river.

A new frightening thought hit him. The truck was only *tracking* him, like a professional hunter. It was a delaying tactic by the Spotters until the G-men arrived. This truck served the same purpose as 'Stephen,' the student teacher at Lincoln. The real threat was yet to come.

He waited, listening to his own wheezing. If someone were to run through the yard now, they would surely hear him— and maybe see him. He wasn't certain that he was completely camouflaged in the box.

Matt the Rat in a cage.

The sound of a vehicle rumbled through the alley and stopped. Yes, a truck door opened, right next to this yard. Footfalls neared. The back gate opened. Silence. He held his breath. Matt was powerless to do anything in the darkness but listen to his pursuer approach. The dog next door barked. The footsteps walked away. There was a disturbance in the adjacent yard and the dog barked again.

"Get the hell out of my yard!" a man yelled.

A muffled discussion between two or three men ensued. The disturbances quieted.

The misdirection must have worked. But then ...

Charleen hated to even ask about this next accusation. She was depleted and just waited for another attack. She was standing in front of the firing squad too tired to move as they took repeated shots at her.

Mr. Heim aimed his narrow nose at her. "One of our students, Greg Urban, has accused you of sharing private, damaging information with another student, Wayne Zimmerman."

Charleen's mouth dropped open in surprise.

"Did you tell Wayne that Greg's father was in prison?" Mr. Heim accused.

"No! I wouldn't do that!" She looked at the other men, who just silently watched her squirm under cross-examination.

"How else could Wayne have learned it, if not from you? Greg said that he didn't tell the embarrassing truth to any of the students," Mr. Heim reasoned.

"Oh, I know the student who told Wayne," Charleen said. The words were out before she realized that she couldn't follow through with her explanation.

"Really? Who is that?" Mr. Heim asked, crossing his arms.

Oh no! How could she use her relationship with Matthew as a defense for a different accusation?

The Smart Kid

"I don't know."

Mr. Heim focused his gaze on her until she was forced to look away.

Mr. Schroeder spoke like a judge pronouncing her sentence. "Ms. Therry, I'm going to recommend that the school board review your employment with the district. The facts from this investigation will be presented to them so they can make an impartial decision. But until that meeting in two weeks, you will be on temporary suspension, starting at once."

Mr. Heim showed no emotion, but Easton nodded, a half-smile curling on his lips.

Charleen closed her eyes to block the reality of the moment.

Mr. Heim opened the door for her.

She escaped to her office, avoiding eye contact with Holly, and shut her door. She put her head in her hands, and tried to hold it together emotionally. Distraught and fearing for her job, she considered that, since Easton quit over similar allegations, this event has exacerbated the district's sensitivity to abuse charges.

But who took the photos of the coach?

"I'm being hunted by a secret government organization ..." Matt's improbable words suggested an unlikely answer.

Charleen just wanted the day to end. She contemplated the possibility of losing her job, and pounded on her desk. "No ... no!"

Matt heard footsteps approaching the truck again. There was pounding; the sound of someone slapping the hood of the truck.

A man's voice said, "No, no! I give up!"

A voice, as loud as he'd ever heard in his entire life yelled, "MICHAEL! MICHAEL SHALE! MICHAEL SHALE!"

The words reverberated through the neighborhood. Doors and window shades opened in many nearby houses. Matt recognized that voice; a voice from long ago, calling out a name from his childhood.

Matt scrambled out of his hiding place. It appeared that the colored balls and plastic bags came flying out of the box by themselves, until he popped his head out and yelled, "Mark! Mark!" Matt pulled himself up, got a leg over the edge and fell to the snowy ground. The footsteps came near; large, strong hands grabbed him from behind and held him, immobilized. The hands belonged to a full grown man. The grown man lifted the boy-man, his feet off the ground.

"Michael!" yelled Mark Shale. "There you are! Didn't you know I was looking for you?"

Mark lowered him to the ground. Matt hugged his brother. He was speechless for minutes. His heart pounded so hard that his brother felt it.

"Boy, can you run! I had given up finding you today!" Mark said with a big grin on his face.

Matt looked up with tears in his eyes. "I'm glad you found me! What the hell took you so long?"

"You're just too damn good at Hide 'n' Seek!"

They laughed and cried.

Mark, the man, looked down at his brother, Michael.

The short boy-man looked up, smiling, and hugged his identical twin brother.

17. Belief

CHARLEEN'S WORK DAY was only half over, and it was already the worst ever. She was seconds from escaping the school when Holly entered her office, holding a page from a message pad. Holly looked at Charleen, gave an unconvincing smile, and inquired, "How'd it go today?"

Charleen also tried to put on a good face. "Oh, not real great. Easton quit and he blames me for it." She wondered if she should confide in Holly.

Holly nodded. "Listen Charleen, I'm sorry that I said anything about you and Matthew Janson. They were on a witch hunt. I just answered their questions. I had no idea that they were accusing you of — I mean, that's crazy."

She sounded sincere, thought Charleen.

Holly added, "If there's any way that I can help, you tell me. OK?"

Charleen said, "I appreciate that." She looked at the note in Holly's hand, which she seemed to have forgotten.

"Oh, message for you: Please call Mrs. Mulholland. Here's the number. Bye."

Charleen called the Mulhollands. She had met them once, and considered them to be capable foster parents who wanted the best for the children in their care. She had intended to visit them at their home, since they lived in her neighborhood. But now, she realized that she would not get the chance.

"The Urban twins are missing," said Mrs. Mulholland.

"For how long now?"

"Sunday evening, we realized they were gone. We're so worried that neither of us went to work today. My husband and I have called the neighbors and our friends. We think that they went to see their mother; they talked about it all the time— But it was out of our hands." Her strained voice cracked.

"You didn't do anything wrong. Please call the police and give a

The Smart Kid

description. I'll ask the foster agency to call us if— when the twins show up in Minneapolis. OK?"

Charleen tried to sound optimistic, but often, run-aways are never seen again. She made a couple of calls to the Hennepin county foster agency and the social work department. She did as much as she could, at the time— probably ever. Charleen considered that this might be the last caring action she takes on behalf of her students, at this school.

Charleen collapsed at her desk, overwhelmed and exhausted. She didn't know who to worry about: the Urban twins, Wayne, Matt, or herself. She wasn't good at multi-tasking worry.

The single issue with Matt was more than she could handle. First, she believed he was a lonely twelve-year-old student; then, a stunted thirty-nine-year-old man; and finally, a nineteen-year-old lunatic.

And she knew that her job was doomed— over what? A pile of false accusations. She wondered if she should move back home with her mother.

Wait, Charleen, you're getting ahead of yourself. She hadn't broken any *written* district policies, she thought. Maybe she'd only get a formal reprimand put in her file. That wouldn't be too bad.

As she obsessed over her worries, a suffocating anxiety compelled her to escape the depressing office. She could start packing up her possessions later. Right now, Charleen might hide out in the teacher's lounge and have a cup of coffee, or maybe take up smoking.

As she walked by the nurse's office, she saw Wayne Zimmerman sitting on the cot, alone, crying. The nurse wasn't in her office. Charleen scanned the hallway beyond the glass wall. The nurse was talking with a priest. *A priest!*

She turned to Holly, who just sadly stared at her, glanced at Wayne and slowly shook her head.

The worst had happened; Charleen could tell. Shame and guilt instantly filled her heart as if she were responsible for Mr. Zimmerman's death; and had caused it by her dark wish. She knew it was false guilt, but it still distressed her. And she deserved the guilt, she thought.

Compared to what Wayne was going through, her problems seemed small. It was like comparing a heart attack to a scraped knee. Knees will heal quickly. There will be other jobs.

At the end of life, what truly matters?

"All is vanity," Matt's words replayed.

Everyone dies. And all that remains behind is what?

"Your life won't matter. It won't be remembered by people after you. The best thing to do with your life is ..."

Matt had been interrupted before he finished his sentence, but Charleen would complete the thought.

Charleen looked at Wayne: small, forlorn, and crying. Her heart broke for him. She imagined he was Max, missing his dead father.

With a heaviness in her heart, she walked slowly toward the nurses office. Each step felt as if she were pushing through deepening water. It was time. Charleen knew what she was going to do and she resolved that nothing; no fear, no pride, would stop her.

Charleen entered the nurses office and gently shut the door. Delicate tears traced wet paths down her cheeks. She sat on the cot next to Wayne.

Frowning, Wayne asked, "Are you hurting too?"

She nodded. "Wayne, I'm so sorry for your loss. I know how it hurts to lose a father and it's a pain that I wouldn't wish on anyone. If I could take it away, I would."

Wayne stared at her. He had probably never seen a teacher cry.

Charleen looked into his innocent eyes, took a deep breath and said, "Wayne, I have to confess something. I owe you an apology."

Wayne frowned but said nothing.

"I didn't want to talk with you when you came to my office because I was ... um, I was jealous that your mom still had a ... Oh, I'm sorry, just a moment. She paused and calmed her breathing. After a few seconds, she said, "Wayne, I had wrong feelings about your mom. I was jealous that ... that she still had a son, but mine is gone."

"What do you mean?" asked the boy.

"The accident that your dad was in ... Did you know that two

The Smart Kid

other people died in it?"

Wayne nodded.

"Well, they were my son and husband."

The tears that marked her cheeks weren't from sadness— Charleen had enough of that. They were from success and acceptance of reality, finally. She had thought that walking into the depths of her fears would drown her, but the only part of her that died was the vile thoughts, the guilt, and the jealousy.

Wayne cried too. "I'm so sorry that my daddy did that to your family."

That was almost more than Charleen could bear. *He* apologized to her? This small boy had done nothing to harm her. But he was gracious and sincere.

Instead of burdening herself with more pointless, ineffectual guilt, she accepted his apology and his innocent care. It calmed her soul; her breathing slowed. Charleen felt the beginning warmth of healing, like the start of a bright, summer day. She gave Wayne an honest, caring hug. In that moment, Charleen felt a bond with Wayne. They both had lost loved ones in the same accident. As she held him, she wished that he didn't have to suffer the pain of loss.

"Wayne, how are you doing?"

"Well, I guess I'm doing OK. But my knee hurts bad."

"Why? What happened?"

"I fell down outside and hit the corner of the step. It's hard to walk, so my mom is coming to get me."

Charleen didn't comprehend his simple words. "You're in here because your knee hurts?"

"Yes."

A hopeful thought filled her. "Wayne, is your dad …" She paused for a second and asked, "um, is he … asleep?"

Wayne smiled. "No, he's awake from the comma now. He'll be coming home soon! Isn't that great?"

"Oh! That is wonderful! I'm so glad for you and your family."

Charleen was too happy to feel foolish for her assumptions, because they had led her to see Wayne for who he is: an innocent, hurting boy— not the cause of her pain.

But it wasn't *only* her assumptions that had brought her to this point. She had been stepping up, and moving closer to this final stage because of Matt's forged notes. Matt's meddling actions, for whatever motivation, had prodded her gently forward. *"I'm just trying to help you face your pain so that you can heal."* Matt had said. He really had been trying to help her.

The door opened, and Margee, the school nurse entered. "Oh, hello, Ms. Therry." Then, to Wayne, she said, "Sorry to leave you in here alone, Wayne. But my brother stopped by for a short visit. Thanks for sitting with him, Ms. Therry."

"Oh, that was your brother!" Charleen said, laughing.

Margee smiled, but looked confused.

"Margee, don't call me Ms. Therry. From now on, please, call me *Miss* Therry."

Charleen stood and laughed. She opened the door, walked out and laughed again.

It was like a joke: A counselor, a nurse and a priest walk into a bar ...

She entered her office, a completely different woman than the one who had exited minutes ago.

Charleen was still chuckling to herself as she sat in the office.

The door opened and Holly darted in pushing it shut with her back. She wore a worried frown.

"Charleen, I'm sorry to barge in here, but I figured that I owed you, from before."

"What is it?" asked Charleen, leaning forward on her desk.

"I think that whole thing with Matt Janson has jumped to a new level!"

"Why? What happened?"

"OK, these two guys came to my desk with a picture of Matt Janson. And they said, 'Do you know this student?' So of course, I said, 'Yes, I know him.' And then they say, 'What's his name?', which I thought was kinda odd, ya know, having a kid's photo, but not knowing who the kid is. Right?" Holly continued, hardly taking a breath. "Well, I just answered them, and said, 'Matt Janson.' Then he

The Smart Kid

writes the name in a little book, and says 'We're from Child Protective Services.' And so I directed them to Mr. Heim's office ... But I thought you'd want to know."

Charleen stood and cracked open the door. Across the office, two sharply-attired men were walking through the doorway into Mr. Heim's office. It's a rare event when visitors are better-dressed than Mr. Heim. He held the door for them.

Mr. Heim asked, "Who notified CPS about this situation already?"

One of the men responded, "So you were expecting us?" The door closed.

"They'll probably come saying that they are with Child Protective Services ... ", Matt had said.

Charleen pressed her back against the door, forcing it shut. "Holly, is this the normal procedure when CPS comes to school?"

Holly shook her head. "No, it's very unusual. They always know the name of the student. And they've never sent two guys in suits and ties who look like hit men. I've met most of the CPS case workers, and they're all women.

"Holly, I need a favor from you, please?"

"Sure, whatever you want," she responded with open palms.

"Find an excuse to get into Mr. Heim's office, so you can catch a few words of their conversation. OK?" Charleen gave her a pleading look.

"I'll do even better than that. Come to my desk," Holly said.

They snuck out of Charleen's office, scampered around the administrative counter and crouched behind it. Holly motioned for Charleen to keep silent and she delicately pushed and held the intercom button labeled 'Mr. Heim'. The women could hear the men talking.

"...the student calling himself Matt Janson?" a voice said.

Mr. Heim responded, "What do you mean by 'calling himself'?"

"Well, we can't say, sir. But we need to bring him to our department now. It's for his own protection," said a voice.

"Protection from what?" said Mr. Heim, raising his voice.

"Well sir, we're not authorized to say. It's a private, domestic issue. So we need the school records that you have for him, including a home address. Then, direct us to his classroom. And we don't, in point of fact, need your permission," said a voice.

"You guys aren't from CPS! Don't give me this bullshit!" yelled Mr. Heim.

Holly let go of the button. They remained stooped behind the counter.

"Oh my God!" whispered Charleen. "Matt was right! Holly, who do you think would be sent to retrieve an escaped lunatic?"

"I dunno. I guess the police, or the guys in the white suits with the padded truck."

"Yes. It wouldn't be kept secret, with men in business suits who aren't authorized to say anything, would it?" Charleen asked rhetorically.

Holly shook her head.

"Oh no! I've made a terrible mistake!" Charleen exclaimed, raising her voice and her body. "Holly, I need to ask you to help me again."

"OK. Name it," said Holly.

"I should not leave with *my* car because those G-men may be watching for it, so could—"

"Sure. Here's the keys to my car," Holly said, reaching into a desk drawer.

The women moved across the office with a few large, silent, steps. Charleen retrieved car keys from her office. The women exchanged keys. Charleen held a key chain with a silver Ford logo.

"Which car is yours?" Charleen asked.

"It's the little green Ford in the back lot. It's near your car."

"Holly, they are going to come to my office next. Please delay them for as long as possible. And thank you for the car. You're a life saver!"

Charleen ran to her office and locked the door. Out of panic, she tried to push her small bookshelf against the door. But it didn't slide well on the carpet and tipped, leaning at an angle. Her psychology and counseling books piled to the floor.

Charleen scurried out the back office door, locking it behind her.

The Smart Kid

She paused momentarily to study the parking lot for G-men and ran to Holly's car. Driving out of the back lot, she forced herself not to speed. As she curved around the school, two black Town Cars came into view. Charleen saw four men, wearing dark suits, standing by the doors; or were they *guarding* the doors?

She searched for any pursuing cars. Passing by the west side of the school, Charleen saw a large white truck backed against the loading dock and more men in dark suits. Did one of them hold a gun? Her heartbeat and her car accelerated.

No one behind me ... Thank you Holly. Time to warn Matt.

Charleen sped through the city, making a couple of unnecessary turns to verify that she wasn't being trailed. *I'm not paranoid, people really may be out to get me.*

She considered the fact that Matt might not be at his apartment anymore. He may be gone, running for his life again. *And the last thing he heard from me was doubt and distrust. But the last thing I heard from him was 'you were a real friend to me.'*

She was filled with bitter regret.

A more chilling thought filled her with fear: he may have been caught by now. Easton knew where Matt lived, and Charleen was certain that he'd be happy to tell. Maybe the G-men had already discovered Matt's secret apartment. Fear for Matt replaced her own regret. Charleen only had room in her heart for one overwhelming emotion at a time.

When she arrived downtown, she parked the car at The Crash Diner and circled the block to enter Matt's apartment building from a different direction. Too impatient to wait for the elevator, she sprinted up the stairs. She pounded on his apartment door with great urgency. Nothing. She banged again. Nothing. Despondent, Charleen rested her head against the door and stared at her foot, gently kicking at Matt's former apartment door.

He's gone. Did he safely escape, or is he in handcuffs now? I'll never know.

There was a scuffling sound beyond the door. Someone looked through the peephole. She put her ear to the door and heard a man's voice say, "It's a woman!"

That was not Matt's adult voice. I'm too late. They found him!

She jumped to the staircase door and yanked it open. Charleen stomped down the stairs, two steps at a time.

She imagined Matt's voice call to her from above. "Charleen! It's OK! Please Charleen come back!"

If only he were really there ...

Charleen stopped. It *was* Matt calling her.

She raced up the stairs. Matt was waiting for her in the staircase. She paused to look up at him. He had a huge grin on his face. She walked up the final three steps, until she was one step below him.

They stood face to face. She wrapped her arms around his small body and enveloped him with relief and happiness that could only be expressed through the strength of her embrace.

"Oh, hey, I can hardly breathe!" he said.

She could hardly breathe too. Her chest was heaving, from exertion and emotion.

"Charleen, I'm so glad that you came here. I've got so much to tell you!"

"Matthew, listen to me first. I'm sorry! I'm sorry that I doubted. I believe you! I know the Real You. And you know me too. You were right about me avoiding Wayne. I needed to face the reality of my jealousy toward his mother. And guess what? I did, thanks to you!"

"Oh, Charleen, I'm so happy for you!" Matt gave her a crushing hug.

As she accepted his hug, she realized something unexpected. She didn't feel like she was hugging Max. When she gave up her jealousy about Wayne, she lost her need for a child surrogate.

"And Matt, despite *my* hurtful distrust, you trusted me, and told me everything, all your secrets." Charleen wiped away a tear.

"Charleen, thanks for that. But I have to confess now that I haven't told you *everything* about me." He smiled as if he knew she was going to be surprised.

"More secrets?"

The staircase door opened, and a tall, handsome man with a clean-shaven face and wavy, blond hair filled the doorway. Charleen

The Smart Kid

released Matt, grabbed the hand-rail, and took a quick step back in fear.

The smiling man said, "Hey, you two com'n in or not?"

Matt reached for Charleen and led her up the stairs into the hallway. "Charleen Ann Therry, meet Mark William Shale, my brother."

Matt couldn't have grinned any bigger.

Charleen couldn't contain her surprise. "You really do have a brother!" She gave him a big hug too.

Mark stood motionless, hands at his sides, as he looked over Charleen's head at his twin brother's smiling face.

Charleen finally had every piece of the puzzle. The Case of the Mysterious Student had been successfully resolved. Their growing friendship had weathered the storm of doubt. And now, all her questions were answered … except one: *Why* was Matt being chased by a shadowy government committee? But she knew that the final answer was about to be revealed on the other side of that door, and it filled her with overwhelming anticipation.

As they walked into Matt's apartment, and the door closed behind them, Matt said, "Charleen, there's one more, special fact about my brother that you should know. Plus we have a long story to tell you, that started many years ago."

Part Two
The Senator

18. Beginnings

MICHAEL WAS HIDING, again.

He heard *them* searching, but he couldn't see them, from his hiding spot. He waited and listened. His breathing had finally slowed since he'd run and climbed into his haven. Michael had wriggled down and pulled the container's contents over him, hoping he was completely hidden. For ten minutes he cowered in fear of being discovered.

Footsteps came near and one of his pursuers yelled to the other, surprising Michael, who nearly jumped at the unexpected close sound. He held his breath until he heard them walk away. But after a few minutes, they came back and were only a few feet from where he hid, in what Michael feared might be an obvious hiding place.

A loud voice yelled, "OK, Mikey, we give up!" It was his twin brother Mark. That was what Mike had hoped to hear.

He pushed upwards on the gourds, corn stalks and melons that covered him. From his brothers' perspective, it must have appeared as if the vegetables rose and fell out of the large basket by themselves.

He popped his head up, displaying a huge, victorious grin, and yelled, "I win!"

He tried to crawl out, but tipped the basket and spilled its contents, including him, as his brothers ran toward him. They all smashed together and fell on the ground, laughing.

"Got you!"

"No you didn't."

"You are just too good at Hide 'n' Seek! I should have known that you'd be hiding among your own kind, Melon Head!" said Mark to his twin. They laughed and wrestled in the grass.

Although it was early, their mother had already hung linens on the clothesline, clipped into place with the wooden pins. Fresh sheets rippled in the slight wind. The amber sun glowed, low on the horizon, getting brighter and higher every minute.

Mike loved playing Hide 'n' Seek with his brothers. But since Tommy was only five years old, it was really a match between him

The Smart Kid

and his twin. There were plenty of places to hide around this country house; the old, red shed, that stored the push mower, with the blades that went clickity-clack; the tree fort, where the boys pretended to shoot German soldiers, just like Daddy; or the garage with the new, green Buick with the big fins on the back fenders. And surrounding the house, were open fields of tall grass. It was a young boy's perfect play land.

As they lay on the ground, the milk truck came up the driveway. Mr. Habiger smiled as he eased his stout body out of the truck. He wore a white coat and cloth cap and carried a wire basket with four bottles of bright milk. He opened the small, silver crate on the doorstep and exchanged the empties for the full bottles, topped with tinfoil caps.

The boys sat up in the dewy grass.

"Hello, Mark. How's Mr. Shale doing?" asked Mr. Habiger.

"I'm Mike!"

"Oh, it's hard to tell, you know," said Mr. Habiger with a smile.

"Dad's still sick," said Mike.

"Sorry to hear that," said Mr. Habiger, his smile disappearing. "We'll be praying for him at church. Good-bye boys." He hopped into his truck with the sliding doors, and drove away.

Mom yelled through the back screen door, "Boys come in and get ready."

The three brothers jumped to their feet and two of them ran past her into the house.

The last brother paused and smiled at his mother.

"Your bus will be here any minute. Are you ready for your big day, Michael? It's your first day of sixth grade. Aren't you excited?"

"Yes, Mom," Mike said. "What kinds of neat things will I learn?"

"You'll learn many subjects: math, history, and science and more," replied his mother. "And you'll make lots of new friends."

He was already planning what he wanted to be when he grew up: a person who helped people ... a scientist or someone like Doctor Kildare, from the radio show ...

Finally, Mike would be among the oldest students in the school. The younger students would admire him and ask him for help with their school work. And he would happily help them.

* * *

"OK, open your eyes, boys," said Mrs. Shale.

The twins stood in the doorway to the dining room. Their blonde-haired mother had just led them in, past the 1956 calendar with the big red star marked on today's date, June 2nd.

Mike and his taller twin brother, Mark, opened their surprised eyes. They saw their mom and dad, and little Tommy, along with their friends, Jay, Spike, Bill, and Sam. The twins could not have been happier. There was a birthday cake with 16 flickering candles. Inscribed in red icing were the words, "Happy Birthday Mike and Mark." Their family and friends sang the birthday song.

As Mike listened, he realized how much his friend's voices had deepened in the last year. But his had not changed.

Their mom sliced the white frosted, chocolate cake into wedge-shaped pieces and put them in bowls. She opened the new Frigidaire refrigerator with the 'separate across-the-top food freezer', as the salesman from the department store had described it, and removed a tin of ice cream. The eyes of the boys widened as she scooped big globs of ice cream onto the cake portions.

"Wow. This is great!" said Jay. The other boys silently agreed by nodding their heads because their mouths were already stuffed.

After the cake had disappeared, Mr. & Mrs. Shale gave a present to each of the twins. The wrapped gifts were obviously books. Mark opened his first, ripping off the paper. It was a dark hardcover titled *Photographer's Handbook*.

"Wow! I've been wanting to get this," he exclaimed.

Then it was Mike's turn. "I'm guessing it's a book." He unwrapped the gift, not as violently as his brother, to reveal a hardcover version of *Handcuff Secrets by Harry Houdini*.

"Wow! Thanks Mom and Dad. I'll have fun learning tricks from this." He grinned at them.

The parents left the boys to discuss boyish things.

"Hey guys, wanna see my room?" Mike asked.

Mike led them up to his bedroom, to show his collection of magic tricks. He brought his new hand-cuff book, and set it on the shelf, next

The Smart Kid

to *Close-Up Coin Magic*. They sat on the floor and talked.

Bill asked, "Hey, who do you think is going to win the World Series this year?"

"The Brooklyn Dodgers!" yelled Spike.

"They are NOT going to win. That's for sure," said Jay.

"How would you know?" Sam asked.

"Because Spike thinks that they will!" said Jay. Everyone laughed at that. Spike stuck out his tongue at Jay.

After the conversation dwindled, they went outside and played basketball in the driveway.

"Mike and I will be the team captions," said Mark. "And since Jay is the second shortest boy, he should be on my team to make it more fair."

"Yes, then Bill is on my team," said Mike.

The boys enjoyed playing basketball, but it became clear that Mike's team had a distinct disadvantage. When he passed the ball, it was easily blocked. And Mike couldn't do layups like the other boys. They didn't keep score since it wasn't a fair match.

"That's enough humiliation," said Mike. "Let's do something else."

The boys stopped the game and plopped down in the middle of the driveway/basketball court. The small pebbles in the driveway felt hot as they pressed into the bare legs of Mike, who wore shorts, as did the other boys.

"Is anyone going to that end-of-the-school-year dance?" asked Jay. Most of the boys indicated that they might, maybe, go if nothing else was happening that night.

"Hey Mikey, who are you going with?" asked Spike, as he rubbed his hand along the gravel.

Bill nudged him with his elbow. He tried to do it secretly, but everyone saw it.

Spike looked down. "Oh, yeah."

Mark said, "Hey, Shorty, Shelly Mattson will go with you again."

"How do you know that?"

"She told me."

"Yeah, but I don't need Tom Barisch yelling across the gym again to ask Shelly how much she's getting paid to baby-sit me," said Mike glumly.

"Don't let that jerk bother you," said Mark. The other boys nodded agreement.

"No thanks. I won't ever go to a school dance again."

Senator John Perkins sat in the office of the Senate Armed Services Committee chairman. The chairman had instructed his secretary to "shut the doors and don't disturb us." Perkins, a senator for nearly twenty years, waited for the older Senate chairman to sit behind his desk.

"John, your daddy was a great man, and a good Senator. I'm sorry for his passing."

Senator Perkins just nodded.

"Well, anyway, as favor to your father, I'm appointing you to the chairmanship of a Select Committee to oversee the scientists at this new experiment that Eisenhower has created called ARPA."

"Thank-you, sir. So it's a new committee."

"Yes. John, you and I know that those eggheads are not politicians or military men. Personally, I don't think that they should be given so much of the government budget. Hell, it's nearly $200 million! I don't trust 'em. I'd like to have some eyes on the inside watching this new organization. So this is my concession to your father. You keep an eye on their spending, don't let them waste their appropriations, and you get to oversee the black budget of ARPA.

"How much is the black budget portion?"

"Thirty million."

"Thanks for your trust," said Perkins with the slightest hint of a smile.

The old chairman leaned back in his chair and removed something from a drawer behind his desk. "It's yours to manage as you see fit. But from the public's view, you're just on a committee to advise and suggest directions for research projects. They don't need to know anymore. But I'll see that your directives are followed, no questions. But, just keep everything in-committee as much as possible."

The Smart Kid

"Who are the other members of the select committee?"

"Whoever. Pick who you want. Oh, the Director of DR&E wants to put someone on the committee too. I owe him a favor, so I'm passing it off on you," the chairman said as he passed a cigar to Perkins.

"No problem. We're just there to supervise anyway. Right?" Perkins smiled.

The old chairman lit his cigar and passed the lighter to Perkins. He took a deep draw on his cigar and exhaled a smoky smile.

"Right. Just supervise."

> Washington Post
> Washington, DC — Sept 13, 1958
>
> *Senator Perkins (D) of California, has been appointed to the Select Committee on Defense & Development Projects which is a temporary subcommittee of the Senate Committee on Armed Services.*
>
> *This temporary subcommittee has a supervisory role over military research and development projects through the Advanced Research Projects Agency."*
>
> *The Advanced Research Projects Agency (ARPA), created this year by President Eisenhower is an autonomous agency under the Department of Defense tasked with developing advanced military technology.*
>
> *"I'm happy to be on this powerful subcommittee to help defend our wonderful 48 states," said Senator Perkins.*

Michael, Mark, their parents, and their little brother Tommy walked through the verdant campus of the University of Iowa. Among the tall, leafy trees and the short grass, students sat reading, or walking along the sidewalks, or riding bicycles.

It was September 1958.

His mom said, "Michael, if you need anything, you make a collect-call."

"Jan," said his father, "don't treat him like a kid. He can handle it." Dad peered over his wife's head and winked. Michael winked back.

Mark carried the brown suitcase, and Mike lugged his Dad's small duffel bag from his army days. His taller twin noticed the effort to transport the heavy bag.

"I hope you get to work out at the gym while you're here. You could use a few muscles," said Mark.

Their mother said, "Mark, you could use a little tact."

His parents were dressed as if they were going to church; Dad, with his suit and tie and Mom, in her blue dress.

"Well Shorty, this is it. You're finally going to be on your own," said Mark. "How does it feel?"

"I haven't been this excited for school since sixth grade. I just hope that the other students are…nice."

"Don't you worry," said Mom. "No one needs to know your real age. You just say that you're in the Gifted Students Program."

"Yeah, that's a good way to make friends— tell them you're a teenager who's smarter than they are," said Mark with a laugh.

"Mark!" said his father sternly, and then coughed for a few seconds.

Mark shut his mouth.

His family, their worry obvious, waited for his hacking episode to diminish. After he breathed easily again, the family continued walking to the administration building.

They walked to the orientation desk, where a young brunette woman greeted them and said, "Welcome to the U of I. You and I will get along great." She giggled saying, "We have to say that to the new freshman," as she presented a packet of information to Mark.

Mark shook his head. "I ain't signing up." The college woman frowned and looked at the parents.

Michael stepped forward, hand extended. She didn't move. Michael waved his hand as he said, "Yes. I'm the freshman student!"

The young woman snapped out of her daze, smiled and handed

The Smart Kid

Michael the folder. "Welcome."

Later, the family stood outside Michael's residence hall as they said their good-byes. Michael had begged his parents not to escort him to his dorm room. Already intimidated by the size of the students on the campus, he didn't want to appear more childish by arriving with his mommy and daddy. Thankfully, they had complied.

His mom leaned down to give him a hug and whispered in his ear, "I'll miss you, Mikey."

His father smiled broadly, and shook his hand, man to man. "I'm proud of you, son."

Tommy stepped toward Michael, unsmiling.

Michael gave him an especially big hug and said, "Hey little bro, I'll write to you when I'm not busy studying."

"Or partying," said Mark, with a grin. Mark removed a small package from his coat and handed it to his twin.

"Well, *Michael*," he said, emphasizing his real name, "I got you a going-away present. I know that you enjoy reading science fiction. So here's a brand new book, just published. I think it will mean something special to you."

Michael smiled at the unexpected gift and peeled back the plain brown wrapping paper. It was *Methuselah's Children* by Robert A. Heinlein.

"Cool! What's it about?" asked Michael.

"A guy who lives an extremely long time." Mark gave a knowing nod to his twin.

Michael hugged his twin brother, said good-bye to his family and turned around to start his college adventure.

19. Philosophies

MICHAEL STUMBLED INTO his dorm room carrying his suitcase and duffle bag.

Archibald Schneider was laying on his bed, reading, with a blanket draped over his legs. He looked up from the book and pushed himself up on his elbows.

"Who are you?" he asked.

Michael dropped his bags on the floor and, with feigned confidence, said, "I'm Michael Shale, your new roommate."

"How old are you?"

"I'm eighteen," said Michael, as he forced an uncomfortable smile.

"No shit? Wow! You look like you're twelve," said Archibald.

"I know how I look. At least I'm not named after a comic book character, *Archie*," defended Michael.

Archibald jumped out of bed, walked toward Michael with a forthright directness, and faced him, only inches away. Michael was taller than him.

"You're a—"

"Whoa, Short Stop! I hope you were gonna say *dwarf* or *little person*. Right?"

"Um, yah, right."

"Good, Michael. I think we're going to get along swell. Our only problem will be reaching the top shelf in the closet!"

Archibald smiled at his new roomie.

A gloomy day, during their first week together, Michael and Archie strolled across campus. Two tall college men passed and one derided, "Hey look! The midget convention is in town!" Their scornful laughter pierced Michael's heart.

"Damn! I wish people wouldn't do that to me all the time."

"Don't worry about it, Michael. It's just a result of us being unique and them being ordinary."

Michael frowned a question at Archie.

The Smart Kid

"*For out of the abundance of the heart, the mouth speaks,*" said Archie, glancing at Michael, as they walked.

"What does that mean?"

"It means that you can discern anyone's true nature by the things they say. What's really inside of them will eventually come out. So you can see everyone's deficiency, even if it isn't physical."

"I've never considered that *everyone* has a deficiency. I thought I was the one who was different." Michael kicked at a stone on the sidewalk and watched it roll off the edge.

"Different is OK. But being bad, is bad. Having a unique appearance shows you how self-centered people are," said Archibald, the philosopher.

Michael stopped, turned to face Archie and, for the first time in years, looked down to talk with a friend.

"You mean, because we're different on the *outside*, we're able to see *inside* people?"

"Yes, now you're getting it," said Archie. "Our uniqueness reveals their badness."

"OK, I get that. What I've learned so far is that some students are just plain rude." He surveyed the campus grounds, as if he were accusing everyone in sight. They began walking again.

"I'm used to it. I've lived with it my whole life," Archie said, waddling beside Michael.

"How do you handle it?"

"Don't accept other people's judgements of you. Deflect and misdirect. And if some guy continues to be an ass, just kick him in the nuts! We're so short, there's no way to defend themselves. And in the court of public opinion, people always side with the underdog." Archie watched Michael as he summarized, "So that's my philosophy of life."

"I've only experienced this for a few years, since around age 14," Michael said, not looking at Archie.

"So what's your deficiency?" asked Archie.

"Huh?"

They both paused as Michael turned to his roomie.

"Tell me why you look so young."

"I stopped growing when I was 12. Puberty started and I stopped."

"And that's all she wrote?"

"Yes. That's all we know. Doctors are stumped." Michael stared at his feet for a moment, then turned toward Archie as he mimicked, "So what's your deficiency?"

"What the hell do you mean? I don't have a deficiency!" laughed Archibald.

Michael laughed too.

They continued walking.

Archie's attitude was a salve on Michael's pain.

Maybe the worst is behind me...

"Son of a bitch! You clumsy fool!" The Senator yelled at the secretary who had just splattered coffee over his desk.

"Oh, I'm so sorry, sir!" she said, grabbing a wad of napkins and dabbing at the mess. She cleaned it as best she could but many papers were soaked.

The thin, young woman was mortified, but her apologies had no impact on the Senator.

"I'm done with you. Go! Send in Harper."

"Yes. Sorry, sir." She scampered out like a pet dog that had been kicked.

Two minutes later, Harper arrived at his door.

Byron Harper had been the Senator's personal aide for longer than any others who had attempted the task. He had successfully survived the stinging barbs of the Senator's criticisms and complaints. That's not to say that he never got stung, but he didn't let it show. To everyone else, he appeared to be an insipid Yes-man, who mindlessly followed the Senator's gruff orders. But he hadn't become a long-time assistant of one of the most powerful men in the Senate by being stupid.

"Harper! Get me fresh copies of these ARPA proposals!" yelled the Senator, as if Harper was responsible for the spillage.

"Yes, sir. Right away." Harper gathered up the wet papers and stuffed them quickly into a folder which he took with him.

Senator John Perkins sat in his spacious third floor office of the Senate building. He stood with a slight effort and leaned his bulky body over the antique desk to snatch a napkin

The Smart Kid

abandoned by the wispy, young secretary. He removed the photo of his wife from the corner of the desk and wiped off a few drops of coffee, as he muttered under his breath, and then carefully replaced the photo at the proper angle.

He opened a drawer of his $900 Mahogany desk and removed an antique silver case from which he selected one of his favorite cigars. The Senator lit it with the gold lighter his father had given him on his first election win, in 1939, so many years ago. As he smoked his pre-embargo Montecristo Cuban cigar, he read the inscription: "Guard the Family Name". He shook his head and sneered to himself. He leaned back in his leather chair and waited, impatiently.

Harper walked in carrying a manila file folder, thick with a collection of reports, reviews and proposals.

"It's about time!"

"Yes, Sir," said Harper, setting the folder of fresh papers on the Senator's desk.

"Did these proposals come directly from ARPA Director, Ruina?"

"Yes. He's sharing them as a courtesy to the committee."

"As if he had a choice," said Senator Perkins. "Is there anything worth reading? Or is it nothing but endless solicitations from vulturous weapons manufacturers begging for government handouts?"

"Senator, as you know, private industry and university research are the heart of ARPAs technological advances. Some of these are pie-in-the-sky proposals, but there are a few theoretical opportunities that may be developed in time," Harper said.

"Time! I've been on this select committee for nearly two years now. And what has ARPA accomplished? Better missile alignment? Shit! I need something sexy to grab the attention of the news; something to brag about to the stupid sheep; something that will memorialize the Perkins name into history. Public Opinion is the life-blood of politics."

"Now that space research has been moved to the new NASA organization, we do have more opportunities for selecting projects," said Harper. "Project Defender, the missile defense program, is really important, but as you said, probably not too interesting to your stupid— um, constituents. Although Project Vela is beginning to show promise for detecting nuclear explosions in space—"

"I know all that shit! I need a project that I initiated! Something with my name on it!"

"Well, sir, since the true purpose of the committee and your budget is secret, how do you propose getting recognition for your proposals?"

"Harper, you're such a bureaucrat. It's public knowledge that I'm on this committee to advise on development projects. And with this position, I can highlight unique ARPA projects for the Armed Services committee's approval. They will just rubber-stamp anything our little committee suggests. That is what I can get recognition for: my suggestions for special Science & Tech projects. What isn't public knowledge is that my influence goes the other way too. I've got a $30 million black budget that my committee controls. And Ruina and his eggheads at ARPA know that I hold the purse strings on a significant portion of their budget. So you can be damn sure that they are going to take my proposals seriously and not nose into the special projects that our team develops. Now, don't question me again like that!"

His assistant dutifully nodded.

"Yes sir. Well, we are making progress in the mobile LASER weapon," he offered helpfully.

"Hmmm, progress? Not much!" The Senator snarled, taking another puff and blowing the smoke directly toward Harper.

"I did find an interesting article that has a hint of an idea for the development of a Super-Soldier," Harper cautiously mentioned. He watched for any glint of interest at this suggestion.

"What the hell is that?"

"Sir, you should read the article. It's in here," said Mr. Harper, tapping the folder before leaving.

Senator Perkins opened the bulky folder, stuffed with the usual military project requests. At the bottom of the stack was an article torn from a medical journal titled, *Age-Defying Kid*

The Smart Kid

Stumps Doctors.
> *Iowa City, IA — Doctors at University of Iowa Hospital are puzzled over a man who doesn't appear to be growing. Michael Shale's parents insist that this boy is nearly 20 years old. And they have his birth certificate to prove it. But you'd never know by looking at him.*
> *"All our tests have shown absolutely nothing wrong with Michael. Pituitary development appears normal for a man of his age..."*

An accompanying photo showed a boy who could not have been older than 13. The red circle, drawn around the last sentence, focused the Senator's attention:
> *One wonders about the scientific and military uses if this secret could be unlocked.*

The Senator leaned back in his leather chair, puffed his cigar, and stared at the arched doorways and ceilings in his office, as he unconsciously stroked the engraved words on the lighter, completely captivated by new ideas of military potential.

Although Michael had no interest in Psychology, he had to take it as a general education credit. He delayed registering for it until his sophomore year. Because Psych 101 was a required course, nearly fifty students attended, both freshman and sophomores, with ages from 18 to 20.

Dr. Jurgen, the professor, was distributing test results. She called the names of the each student, who then walked to the front to collect their paper from her.

"Hallson," she said.

A young man walked forward and crossed paths with another male student. They bumped. At once, a punch was thrown.

Michael didn't see the first blow, although he heard it. He was instantly aware that a fight had started in the front of the classroom, right next to the diminutive teacher. Michael jumped out of his wooden desk chair, spreading his arms, as he put his small body between the two students, who were yelling and threatening more punches. He was book-ended by the tall men, who pressed against his arms.

Every student focused on the scene.

"OK, stop, stop!" yelled the professor. "That's enough with the demonstration. Thank you."

The formerly-fighting students smiled, shook hands, and returned to their desks.

"Sorry for the little act. That was my way of introducing the next section in our Psychology class on altruism," announced the sly teacher. "And no one jumped in to break up the fight except for this boy, the smallest student in the class, Michael Shale."

The whole class was stunned at the theatrics.

The professor smiled at Michael, and asked him what led him think about trying to stop the fight.

Michael shook his head. "I didn't think. I just acted, because it was the right thing to do."

"And that, students," said the professor, "is what altruism is: not thinking of yourself, but of others."

Senator Perkins was at Old Presidents Grill drinking at a back table with four Democrat senators one night in 1960. The Grill was still promoted as 'Washington's Presidential Saloon', but it had seen better times. It didn't attract the high caliber clientele that it used to. But it was just the type of place where politicians could meet and privately discuss issues that they preferred not to have on any public record.

One of the senators was just finishing a bawdy joke about couple of blonde hookers. He slurred out the punch line and the other senators laughed theatrically.

When the men had settled down from the joking, Perkins looked at his group of four aging confidants and asked, "Do you think that there would be any military benefit to soldiers that didn't age?"

The group didn't say anything for a second, then old Senator Lattimore said, "Well, it sure as hell would make peeing easier!" The two oldest men laughed loudly at that.

Senator Emerson said, "Well, physical youth is good, but it means inexperience. If you could keep the youth but add experience, then you'd have a real soldier. What are you thinking John?"

The Smart Kid

"I've got a special project I'm working on," said Perkins.

"Is it a private black bag job?" asked Lawler, leaning in to Perkins.

Perkins nodded to Lawler, then pushed further with his questions. "What would tech like that be worth?"

One of the men whistled.

"A hell of a lot of fundraising money!" joked another of them.

Emerson said, "You couldn't put a price on it."

Senator Lattimore quipped, "Well, I'd try. I'd pay anything to be young again— or to stop my wife from aging." He laughed until Emerson shot him a glance and shook his head slightly. The other two just sipped at their drinks. Everyone got quiet for a moment.

Eventually, Lawler leaned toward Perkins, placed his hand on his shoulder, and quietly said, "Make sure you get your committee members on paper backing you every step of the way. When they know that their asses are on the line, they won't make waves. Always watch your own back first."

"Of course. CYA." Perkins smiled at his old friend.

20. Motivations

SENATOR JOHN PERKINS was scowling.

He was reading a status report on weaponizing the LASER, which had been invented three years prior.

His five hand-picked Defense & Development Projects committee members sat around the table in an ante-room in the lower level of the old Senate building, late at night, reviewing the document.

Although the director of the Armed Services Committee had said that he could pick whomever he wanted to be on the Defense & Development Projects Select Committee, Senator Perkins had to make some concessions in order to give the appearance of balance. As a result the committee consisted of only two Democrats, Perkins being one of them, two Republicans, one scientist from ARPA, and one military man.

Each man had an administrative aide taking notes. Senator Perkins's aide, Mr. Harper, was also present. Everyone watched the Senator for his reaction to the latest Progress Review from the scientists at ARPA.

The Senator had strongly suggested that ARPA move forward on developing the LASER as a weapon. It had a unique appeal that could build up the Senator's clout among other members of the Senate and his reputation with his constituents. So research and experimentation had been pushed forward through the brute force of his ego, ambition, and calling in favors from military friends.

He read,

ARPA Assessment of a LASER weapon. January, 1961.

LASER weapons deliver a large quantity of stored energy, thus obliterating their targets. A directed energy weapon (ray gun) delivers its effect at the speed of light, rather than supersonic or subsonic speeds typical of projectile weapons.

However, development of an effective power source, to generate enough energy to destroy incoming projectiles, has been a major stumbling block, along with the problem of dissipating the massive amounts of heat generated by the LASER.

The Smart Kid

In summary, significant progress has been made in LASER beam alignment and density, but current technology is inadequate to create a hand-held ray gun. Development is progressing on the truck mounted LASER, but it could be 30 years before full implementation.

"Thirty years! I thought we were making progress. What's the meaning of this?" demanded Senator Perkins.

"It means it's time to give up on the portable LASER. It's science fiction," said General Thompson. He was an experienced commander who had fought in World War 2, and was on the committee at the request of the Armed Services committee chairman to give "balance," since its purview was military budgets for secret ARPA projects. He continued, "Listen, John, I've wanted a similar weapon. When I fought in the war, we begged for advanced weaponry. We always hoped for a Lightening Shooter, just like this LASER weapon we've been funding. Hell, even the Krauts worked on a ridiculous gun that blasted lethal sound. But the technology just wasn't there, for them nor for us. Our boys had to kill the old fashioned way, with bullets and bombs. And it will stay that way for now."

"Shit!"

"Well, we're all disappointed," said the General, who wore his usual military attire. For most people, the intimidating image he presented, muscular bulk, crew cut, and stars resting on his shoulders, would have been enough to suppress any arguments. But Senator Perkins was not 'most people'.

"Sure, you don't have to be re-elected. I've got to show positive results to my constituents," barked the Senator.

"Sounds as if you don't give a damn about helping our boys, you just want to protect your own ass. Right?" responded the General.

"I wouldn't have been appointed as the chairman of this committee if I didn't care about protecting our soldiers and our country, from the damned Commies, the Chinese, and every crazy warlord in the world." He leaned forward on the oak table as he said this. He paused, but no one took the opportunity to said a word. Perkins settled back in his chair.

"Anything else on the agenda, Harper?" Senator Perkins demanded. Mr. Harper was sitting on a small chair, like a trained poodle, ready to perform a trick.

"Yes, sir. We have that last, um, biological issue," he hinted.

"OK. I need to ask the secretaries to exit the room. This topic is for committee members only," said the Senator. They waited for the administrative staff, except for Harper, to leave.

Mr. Harper handed a fat file folder to Senator Perkins.

"Gentlemen, I've been researching this subject for years." The Senator stood, his bulk casting a shadow over the table.

"The current state of our fighting force, to put it from a non-soldier perspective," Perkins said, glancing at the General, "is that we train our young men for a few months and send them out to war. Their real training occurs in the fox holes and on the battle fields. And if they survive, they become trained, true soldiers. But it takes years of experience to develop into professional killers. And for many of them, by the time they are proficient killers, they're too old; they've lost their physical edge."

The Senator paused and turned to the General. "As the military representative here, General, do you think that's an accurate summary?"

The General was not a young soldier anymore, but still spoke with vigor and confidence. "First, regarding your label of these men as 'killers': I take issue with that word. 'Killers' is synonymous with 'murderers.' But by the authority of the United States, these men are sanctioned to defend our country through the unpleasant task of killing other humans. So let's give them the respect they deserve by calling them soldiers."

Every man in the room turned to Perkins to watch his reaction to this small reprimand. Perkins stared at the General for one second too long but finally demonstrated his acquiescence by nodding.

The General continued. "Yes, recruitment and training of new soldiers is a huge budget drain. We spend hundreds of millions just to bring them up to a level of mediocrity so they've got a fighting chance." The General nodded toward Perkins, who had remained standing.

Senator Perkins scanned the faces of the men. He

paused, as if he were preparing to deliver a dramatic soliloquy in a Shakespearean play.

"What if we could change that? What if we could recruit soldiers in their youth, and train them until they have the skills of a Navy Seal team, or a top Commando unit; until they are in their best physical and mental condition and then ... stop their aging?"

Perkins paused and waited for reactions.

"What do you mean?" asked Senator Winston Timms, the white-haired Republican who was on the committee at the request of the Director of Defense Research and Engineering, to repay a favor.

"I mean, 'What if we had soldiers that didn't grow old?'"

The group looked puzzled.

"Is this a theoretical discussion— a 'What if' scenario?" asked Senator Timms.

"No. It's not theoretical. We believe that it's possible to stop human growth and aging," replied Senator Perkins.

"How? How do you know this?" asked Senator Mercer, the other Republican, as he rubbed his hand over his bald pate.

"We know of a man who has stopped aging at 12. He's now 21," said Perkins, scanning the group for reactions.

"That's hard to believe," Senator Mercer replied, looking at the only scientist for agreement.

"It's improbable, but not impossible," said Dr. Bruce Barbour, while tapping a pencil on the table. As one of the original program managers on the Defense Sciences Office at ARPA, his participation added significant authority to the committee.

Mercer snorted at that comment and said, "Are you sure you're not a politician?"

"But if true, he would be unique," Dr. Barbour quickly added.

The General listened and watched the others go after this idea like dogs after red meat.

"How can you measure aging? Is that even possible?" asked Senator Timms.

Senator Kristopher Cutler had been listening quietly during

this discussion. Sharply dressed, Cutler was also a member of the Subversive Activities Control Board, which had been created by President Truman to search out communist activities. As another influential Democrat, he and Perkins often worked together on projects. Senator Cutler asked, "So you want to engineer a bio-agent that inhibits the aging process?"

Perkins just nodded.

Finally, the General spoke. "Is this person in a test program for the military, because I've never heard of it?"

"No," said Senator Perkins. "He's a civilian with a growth disorder. We've been following his progress, or lack-there-of, for a couple of years. And we believe that, not only has he stopped growing, but he's also stopped aging."

More questions exploded from the committee:

"Can you be certain that he's not aging?"

"Could he start aging again?"

"Does this mean that he'll never die?"

"When can we meet him?"

After the questions subsided, Senator Perkins said, "I'll let Mr. Harper finish with the details. My role is merely as an idea man." He sat into his chair without acknowledging Harper.

"Oh, yes," said the aide, getting to his feet, as he pushed up his glasses. "This boy, er, man, is not in military service, yet. Although, he might be convinced to help us. His father served in the Army in the Second World War, so he may have a positive attitude toward the armed forces."

Senator Cutler asked, "Would he need to be in the military to … help?"

"He is a special case," said Harper. "And we'd want to have … control over him. So with your permission, we will send a letter to his parents requesting his co-operation. Please sign this letter and— "

"Why not send the letter directly to this young man?" asked Mercer.

"To be polite," said Perkins from his chair. "It's like asking a father for his daughter's hand in marriage."

Without any other delays, Harper distributed the solicitation letter. It was only an invitation, so there was no political reason

The Smart Kid

to avoid signing it. And every member of the committee was intrigued by the inspiring possibilities.

Senator Perkins relaxed in his chair, smiled, and unwrapped a cigar.

"Yes," said Michael. "I've got another letter!" he exclaimed, in a high-pitched voice, as he walked into his dorm room.

Carl, his sophomore roommate, sitting at his desk, looked up and nodded acknowledgment.

Archibald Schneider had been a great help and a good friend. But Michael wanted to make new friends with his next randomly-assigned roommate. Carl and he were well-matched. They both had an interest in business management. Carl was studious, creative, and continually looking for ways to make money.

Michael didn't worry about finances since his parents paid his tuition from his father's military pension. Although, to earn spending cash, he had taken a part-time job downtown as a busboy.

"It's from Mom and there's a letter from Tommy too!" Michael read Tommy's letter first. He didn't even bother sitting.

"Jan. 22, 1961.

Dear Mikey,

School is going good. Everyone is saying that I'm getting tall now. Pretty soon I'll be taller than you. I'm in the Cadets club at school. I think I'll join the army when I graduate. Dad said it made him into a man real good. And I want to be like Dad. Dad still coughs a lot. Mark is working at the downtown garage fixing cars and trucks. He said he'd rather take apart an entire 1953 Buick than spend a day taking classes in college. He said that he'll send you his Superman comics next week. I miss you. Hope to visit you,

Love, Tommy"

Michael sat on the edge of his narrow bed and turned his sad face away from Carl. He absently slid his hands over Grandma's soft quilt as he brooded over his stunted relationship with his young brother.

Carl looked up from his economics book and studied Michael. "Bad news?"

Michael forced a smile as he said, "I miss my brother Tommy."

"He's your younger brother, right?" asked Carl, turning to look directly at Michael. "Are you two close?"

"He's seven years younger than me, so growing up, we weren't close. But now, he's looking *more* like me and my twin, Mark, is looking *less* like me every year."

"Oh, I never realized that," said Carl. "So you feel closer to Tommy now?"

Michael nodded. "Yes, I started to feel a connection to him. And I became more comfortable being with boys his age than adults my age. I even considered delaying college so that I could spend time with him. But I guess I missed my chance. ..."

"Why didn't you delay college for a year?" asked Carl.

"I just had to get out of that little town. Everyone knew that me and Mark were twins. But when I stopped growing, my parents just called us brothers, not twins. It was like I got a demotion. Some people knew the truth, but others thought that Mark was my older brother. So if I had stayed in town, I would have been either the little brother of Mark, or the Freak who doesn't grow."

"That must have been tough."

"Anyway, maybe I'll be able to develop my relationship with Tommy later, after college. ..." His voice faded as he absently stroked the envelope in his hands.

Carl just nodded, put on his glasses, and turned his attention back to his book.

Michael opened his mother's letter. It was filled with boring news of the neighborhood. But near the bottom, she had written,

Senator Perkins has sent another letter requesting your participation in their medical evaluation. We've told him that you're not going for testing in Washington, DC. But he was so insistent that we decided to send him your medical records. It's for a good cause, and that should be the end of his requests. We thought you should know.

He stuck the letters under his pillow and laid on his bed. A scowl crossed his face as he stared at the ceiling.

Michael agreed with his parents' decision to deny the request. He

The Smart Kid

was tired of medical testing. Throughout his teenage years, his worried parents had him examined, probed and prodded repeatedly by their local doctor.

At first, Doctor Will had just called it 'latent development.'

"I used to be short when I was young but then I popped up rapidly as a teenager. You will too," he had said.

But after Michael turned 16, the doctor had to admit that he was stumped.

The deficient growth in his body caused a deficiency in his self-esteem. As the twins' looks diverged, his feelings about himself started changing too. Instead of being famous in his town and school, he became a notorious curiosity. He began to view himself as an aberration; a mistake. People treated Michael as they saw him. And he saw himself as people treated him: either as a little kid, or a freak of nature.

When he enrolled at the U of I, he was ready to end the emotional trauma. Michael wanted to be normal and look like others his age.

His parents had decided to make use of the large University Hospital, so they submitted him to another round of testing.

Michael was an oddity to the doctors. Word about him got out when a doctor published an article in a medical journal.

The University doctors said they were trying to create a 'genetic roadmap' that would lead to his growth. But Michael had given up hope that any 'map' would be found.

Michael was on his own personal journey of self-acceptance.

And he was a long way from his final destination.

21. Personal Issues

SENATOR PERKINS SAT at his wife's bedside in the Georgetown University Hospital. They were waiting for the doctors to return with a report.

Bernice was sitting in the bed, resting against a stack of dull-gray pillows which blended with the curls of her head. She wasn't wearing make-up but was wearing the standard dark blue gown of patients.

Bernice said, "It's strange. I don't feel sick, hardly at all. It's hard to imagine that I've got a life-threatening disease."

Her husband studied her wrinkled face a moment. "I've overcome many obstacles in my life. So let's just hang in together, OK?" He gave a serious smile, as his large hands hid hers.

Three doctors entered, their faces somber masks.

Doctor Maddock, the Head Oncologist said, "Hello again, Senator And Mrs. Perkins. This is Doctor Ellison, our radiologist. And Doctor Kitching is the head surgeon." He paused for one second.

"After the initial biopsy, and the secondary one, we have determined conclusively that you have Renal Cell Carcinoma." He waited for an indication that they were comprehending the news.

The Senator, his face a mask of non-emotion, nodded for him to continue.

"RCC is the most common kidney cancer in adults, responsible for approximately 80% of cases. The tumor is about 5 cm., which is approaching the large size. And I'm very sorry to say… that it has metastasized to the lymph nodes." The doctor paused, studying them.

Bernice, expelled a big breath of air, as she searched her husband's eyes for support.

His sad, old eyes stared back at her. He squeezed her hand.

"What can be done, Doctor Maddock?" the Senator asked.

"Well," said Doctor Maddock as he glanced at his

The Smart Kid

colleagues. "Of all kidney cancers, this particular carcinoma has the lowest response rate to treatment...Initial treatment is most commonly a radical nephrectomy, or removal of the cancerous kidney...However, because the metastases has spread...I'm afraid that isn't an optimal solution. It is relatively resistant to radiation and chemotherapy. But of course, we will still try those strategies..."

"I want you to do whatever you can, whatever it takes. I want her cured!" ordered the Senator, his hand forming a fist.

For a moment the doctors stood frozen, not knowing how to respond to the Senator's demand.

"Of course we all do, sir. But you have to face the very real eventuality of...I'm sorry," Doctor Maddock said, looking at Mrs. Perkins.

Lethargically lifting her head to catch the doctor's eyes, she asked, "What causes this, doctor?"

Doctor Maddock shrugged his shoulders. "No one knows for sure. It just happens sometimes. It comes with aging..."

Michael sat in a lounge in the student union, studying. His open book rested on the table as he scanned the sparsely populated lounge. A dozen students sat around several tables, talking. He was the only person sitting alone.

He saw a man hand a pink envelope to the petite woman next to him. She opened it to reveal a Valentines Day card; the emotion of the card clear on her face. She gave him a soft hug.

Michael remembered when classmates used to distribute valentines to everyone in their classroom at school; a different school, many years ago, when he *really* was young. A somber memory of dancing with the taller Shelly Mattson flickered through his mind.

A young man with short-cropped, dark hair, walked into the student union. His small nose, flat facial features and diminutive, abnormally-shaped ears made it obvious that he had Down's Syndrome.

He looked out-of-place as he wandered to a table encircled by four students and said, "Hi, do you want a Valentine from me?" None of the students said a word. A few shook their head.

He approached another table of students with the same offer received a similar reaction.

When he finally greeted Michael and asked him if he wanted a Valentines Day card, Michael smiled and said, "Of course I do. And I'm sorry that I don't have one for you."

"Oh, that's OK," said the man, showing, a toothy smile. Michael opened the standard store-bought card. Inside, printed in neat block letters was his name: "CASEY."

Casey said that he had a job washing dishes in the kitchen of the student union.

"Good-bye, friend," said Casey.

Michael smiled.

It's the little things...

"OK, now act like you don't know me when you walk into the bar. Do you have that letter from the doctor?" Carl asked.

"Of course," said Michael.

"If this works, I'll split it with you," said Carl, his roommate for the last two years.

They got along well. Carl didn't care that Michael could pass for a pre-teen, and Michael didn't mind that Carl smoked marijuana.

Carl slapped Michael on the back and walked into the popular bar.

Michael, outside in the cold of late February, watched him through a window, occasionally wiping away his foggy breath.

Carl joined a group of students and started drinking with them.

After several minutes, Michael walked in and leaned against the bar. The bartender hadn't noticed him yet.

"Whoa, look at that little kid!" said Carl, pointing.

The students near Carl peered across the room to where he indicated.

"Hey kid, they don't serve chocolate milk here!" taunted one student.

"He's so young that he'll have to drink his beer from a straw!"

"No. A baby bottle!" said another.

The whole group roared.

"I'll bet you ten dollars that the stupid bartender gives him a beer,"

The Smart Kid

said Carl.

"What? No way. They card everyone here. I'll take that bet!"

"Me too!" Others joined in.

"Carl, you are going to owe us so much money," said one of the soon-to-be-sore-losers.

The group watched from a distance.

The bartender talked with Michael for a minute and then shook his head.

"OK, pay up!" said a bettor.

"Just wait…" said Carl.

Michael removed a driver's license from his wallet and handed it to the bartender.

The bartender stared at it, and studied Michael. He shook his head and tossed it onto the bar. He picked up a wet towel and began to wipe the bar surface.

"Alright! Pay!" said a student.

"Just wait…" said Carl. Each of the students held their money in their hands and waited for the scene to play out.

Michael removed a paper from his wallet, unfolded it, and handed it to the bartender.

The bartender read it for a few seconds, then he threw down the towel and got a beer for Michael.

Michael smiled as he hoisted the beer and glanced in Carl's direction.

Carl was too busy to notice. He was collecting handfuls of cash from the losers.

"Look, we're not selling beer, so we're not carding anyone. All the students here can have a beer— except you! I've seen you high school students sneak in to parties and try to act like college students, but I ain't buying it, and you don't get any of my beer," said Johnny-the-Jock.

Michael didn't know the name of the muscular man who loomed over him. He was, apparently, the party host and the keg-meister.

It was the fall of 1962, the beginning of Michael's senior year. The huge party was in an off-campus house rented to football team members. Many students were drinking, smoking, dancing and laughing. And many of these students were girls.

Carl had disappeared into the crowd as soon as they had entered the house, leaving Michael feeling as out-of-place as he looked.

A record player with huge speakers wired to it blasted out Bobby Darin's Dream Lover through the smoky rooms.

Shouting above the music, the un-hospitable host yelled, "I don't know where you got it made, but you should get your money back for this fake ID!"

The man tossed Michael's driver's license. It hit Michael in the chest before landing on the floor.

As Michael stooped to pick it up, he was peering at the nearly bare legs of a gorgeous woman, wearing a mini-skirt, who was smiling down at him. He stood and smiled up at her.

"Do you want my beer?" she asked, wobbling on her heels. She indicated the glass she held by shoving it forward and sloshing beer onto the floor.

Michael resisted the urge to glance behind him to be sure that this hot chick was talking to him. But her current mental state probably prevented her from noticing how young he looked.

"OK, thanks."

As she handed him the beer, she said, "You're cute," her eyes glassy.

Michael blushed. He hadn't planned on meeting any women at this party. Why should it be any different than every other party that he'd attended?

"Well, you are very beautiful." He tossed out this statement, not knowing how it would land.

"Thank you," she slurred, lowering her eyes, and then scanning him from foot to head, as she lazily dragged her fingers through her long blonde hair.

Michael was momentarily distracted. Realizing it was his move, he asked, "Do you want to sit down and talk?" He was always more comfortable sitting; it put him at an equal height.

The girl grabbed Michael's hand and followed him to a nearby beat-up couch with cigarette holes burned in the arm rest. He sat at on

The Smart Kid

one end. She sat halfway on top of him.

"Do you mind?"

Michael looked at the 75% of the couch that was empty. "No."

"Now I'm going to do your hor-orschope," she said, poking him in the chest with her left forefinger. Her right arm around his neck held her steady.

"OK. Fine…"

His left shoulder and arm were pinned against the couch behind her back, but his right arm was free to hold the beer.

"Alright, first I need your birthdate…come on!" demanded the amateur astrologist, almost focusing on his eyes.

"June 2nd."

"Oh, so you're a Gemini, the Twins." She poked him in the chest, emphasizing the word 'twins'.

"Amazing! I am a twin." Michael tried to sound amazed and sincere.

"I knew it! Now what year were you born?" She poked him in the chest again.

Michael just smiled and considered plausible responses.

A woman wearing a string beaded leather vest interrupted saying, "Here, Lacey," and handed her a cup of beer. She had long, dark hair and gigantic hoop earrings. "Who's your little friend?" she asked with a big smile.

She was pretty, so Michael didn't mind the diminutive reference. Plus he was glad that Lacey's hand was occupied with a beer, so he wouldn't get poked in the chest again.

"Well, I don't know…" Lacey slurred out.

The un-named friend winked and grinned. "Good luck, Lacey!" she said and walked away.

"I'm Michael Shale, from Manly," he said above the laughter and music.

"I've heard of you, Michael Shale!" She smiled at him as if they were old friends.

Michael was caught off guard, his surprise evident.

"Oh yes … you're the Whiz Kid."

"I'm not really a kid," said Michael, not certain if it was in his favor to contradict her.

"You look like a kid to me … at least from what I can see." She scanned his body and then giggled. Lacey whispered in his ear and directed her half-opened eyes to the staircase. Michael followed her gaze. He took one last gulp of beer and nodded.

They left their beers, and walked up the steps into a dark hallway. When they found an empty bedroom, she immediately pushed him onto the bed. They lay sprawled across it sideways.

As she kissed him on the lips, she worked out the words, "How old are you?"

Michael didn't say anything.

"I've always wanted to make it with a freshman," she purred.

Michael didn't tell her that he was in his senior year and the same age as her.

She sat up on the bed, straddled him, and unbuttoned her blouse to reveal bare, beautiful breasts.

Michael thought he knew how he should feel. He realized this was probably every young man's dream. But it stirred nothing in him, no inclination to pursue this activity any further. And his body didn't respond like a twenty-one-year-old's.

He rolled her to her back and gave her a desultory kiss. He slid off, laid beside her, and kept his arm around her for a few minutes.

Soon she drifted into an inebriated sleep.

He left her in the room, after throwing a blanket over her.

Michael walked out of the busy party, in the warm house, into the lonely, cool night— a place where he was much more comfortable.

For the last time, Senator John Perkins came home from the hospital.

It was late. It had been a long, sad day.

His empty apartment echoed with the sound of his slow, plodding steps.

John got himself ready for bed. He opened his closet to hang up his pants. His wife's clothes were still in there, on her side, as they'd always been, but seemed out-of-place.

Staring at the full-length mirror, he saw a graying,

The Smart Kid

overweight, senior citizen wearing his pajamas.

On the edge of the bed, all his now, he sat and gazed at a photo of his wife.

John remained there on the edge, for a long time, deep in thought.

"For you, Bernice," he muttered, as he switched off the light.

22. The Plan

"WHAT THE HELL are you saying, Perkins?" yelled Senator Jerod Mercer, as he stood to face the Senator, his scowl as practiced as Perkins's.

The Armed Forces Defense & Development Projects Select Committee meeting had started civil enough that night, evaluating budgets of secret military projects in ARPA. But after several long hours, the polite atmosphere became heated.

They were in their usual ante-room in a dark corner of the old Senate building, behind locked doors. The regular attending members were present: The Republicans: Mercer and Timms; Perkin's Democratic friend, Cutler; General Thompson, and Dr. Bruce Barbour.

Prior to the discussion of the final agenda item— the one that had upset Mercer— the administrative staff had been dismissed, except for Harper.

Harper had been describing the response of Michael Shale's parents to their previous requests. "His family does not want him to come to our military medical facilities here in DC. We've already sent them two requests for his, um, Michael's, participation. They have rejected us. In fact, other than this one medical journal article, they have denied any publicity about him. They want to save him from embarrassment or unwanted attention. But they're not completely against helping us, because they did authorize the university doctors, where he's been tested, to send us his medical information."

Senator Cutler had asked, "Aren't the medical records sufficient?"

"No," replied Harper, who sat down as he nodded toward Dr. Barbour.

Dr. Barbour stood in response and said, "I have been supervising a team of scientists and doctors who are studying the data, trying to recreate the biology on animals, but so far, we've come up with nothing. We've determined that we need an actual, real human who has this condition. And as far as we

The Smart Kid

know, he's the only one, with an adult mind, and no evidence of growing old or aging."

Senator Timms, looking from Barbour to Harper, asked, "Then how do you even know that you *can* stop aging?"

Once again, Harper nodded toward Dr. Barbour, who was still standing.

"We have concluded that the cause is either a rare gene sequence or a malfunction of the pituitary gland, probably," said Dr. Barbour. "And if we were able to take tissue samples, then we may develop aging inhibitors."

"So you need ... him," stated Senator Cutler.

"I guess it's our only option now," said Dr. Barbour, who took his seat.

Harper stood. "So with your agreement, we will solicit his help with a firmer invitation."

"Define 'firmer invitation'," said Timms.

Perkins stood and Harper slunk into his usual corner chair.

"We are going to demand that he submit to our testing at a special medical lab, just as we'd conscript a soldier into military service. This issue is urgent enough to constitute a national security threat. And it's on that basis that we should authorize his conscription," said Perkins.

And that was when Senator Mercer interrupted.

"What the hell are you saying, Perkins?" demanded Jerod Mercer. "You want to target one particular person whom *you* consider a national security threat? What gives you that power?"

Perkins, impressively dressed in a tailored suit, was standing at one end of the oval table. The dark mahogany walls of the room soaked up the light from the row of overhead lights. The few wall-mounted lights did little to illuminate the room. One of them was directly behind Senator Perkins giving him a shadowy appearance to the rest of the committee members.

Perkins stopped chewing his unlit cigar and set it in the unused ashtray. "You know what gives *us* the power: The constitution of the United States. And that power invests the office of the President with the ability to take action, as necessary, to oppose all potential enemies, both foreign and domestic. President Eisenhower established ARPA as a military crystal ball for forward-looking scientists and politicians for the purpose of national defense. And we have been granted the opportunity to use our special funding for sensitive projects like this."

Every man gave Perkins his full attention.

"Gentlemen, these are extraordinary times. And we face an extraordinary challenge. The United States never wants to be caught off guard again, like we were in 1958, when the Russians launched their satellite, Sputnik. The purpose of ARPA is to *Create and Prevent Strategic Surprise.* And the protection and medical evaluation of our target, Michael, will achieve both of those goals."

For security purposes, Perkins never used Michael's last name. The Senator looked around the room before delivering the end of his response to Mercer's attack.

"And remember, ARPA is an instrument of the D.o.D. And what we're talking about is defense against a domestic source and potential abuse of that source by foreign powers."

The Senator, a skilled debater, turned the attack back to Mercer and to any others who supported his questioning.

"What gives you the power to *not* protect the security of the US? We'd expect that type of treasonous squirming from a Commie sympathizer. Wouldn't you agree, Senator Cutler?"

Cutler nodded. "The Subversive Activities board is always looking for any evidence of Communist leanings." His cool smile did little to hide the implied threat.

An accusation of treason had great power, in the same way that a mere accusation of being a Communist sympathizer could destroy a career. The legacy of Alger Hiss, the American lawyer accused of spying for the Soviets, was hyper-vigilance and fear of homegrown spies. His alleged participation with the Soviets focused the attention of the government to an inward introspection and search for Communist sympathizers.

Senator Joseph McCarthy, a Republican from Wisconsin, rose to prominence as the visible head of the political witch hunt for Communist Subversives. If McCarthy was the face of the hunt, then J. Edgar Hoover and his FBI were the boot, stomping out all political opposition, evidence be damned.

The Smart Kid

Senator Perkins's use of the terms 'Communist sympathizer' and 'treason' within the same sentence was a not-so-veiled threat. Almost any politician's career could be harmed by leaking their name to the press as having associations with suspected Communist sympathizers. The ensuing news articles and investigations to discover the veracity of the claims was enough to destroy a reputation.

His counter-attack had its desired effect; the change in Mercer's tone was evident. "Of course, we all are committed to serving our country, as demonstrated by our participation on this committee," Mercer said, his eyes darting back and forth like a nervous bird. "But I, and everyone else here, just want to be sure that the actions that we're considering today are justified. Please clarify why this man is a threat."

"OK, thank you for giving me the opportunity to clearly explain this to the committee."

The Senator began what sounded like a political speech; a speech that he had rehearsed, if not verbally, then in his thoughts many times.

"Let me be perfectly clear," Perkins continued, "the *man* is not a threat. His *biology* is the threat. He holds the secret to immortality, or at least extreme longevity. Make no mistake about it, the security of the US will be threatened if he is captured by a foreign power and they are able to decode his DNA for their own use."

"How would a foreign power even learn of him?" asked Timms.

"Senator Cutler is on the Subversive Activities Control Board. Do you want to answer that?" Perkins sat, and Cutler rose with a grunt.

"A foreign power could learn of this young man in the same way that we discovered him. The Communist spies and sleeper agents working in this country are always watching and searching for new recruits. How do you think Hiss was recruited? Someone sniffed him out, found his weakness, and turned him into an asset for the Commies." Cutler sat down as he nodded to Perkins, who rested his hands on the table and pushed his bulk upward.

Senator Perkins paused a moment as he smoothed his tie with his left hand, a favorite delaying tactic, to wait until he had everyone's attention.

"Let me continue," said Perkins. "What would happen if he was captured or recruited by a foreign enemy? First, this foreign enemy could create an army of potentially immortal soldiers. Unless they got killed in battle, they would continue, for decades, to get stronger, smarter and more experienced. Can you imagine trying to send out an army of our pimply-faced recruits against a professional Communist squad that has been fighting together for 50 years? They would have skills and confidence unlike any army in the world."

Perkins scanned the room to see if he had nailed home his first point. Their eyes were fixed on him, their curiosity obvious.

"Second, there have been world leaders— nut jobs— that have unified their people through the sheer power of their charisma and the eloquence of their dogmatic speeches, motivating their followers to blindly follow their every dictate. Hitler unified an army of stormtroopers to commit unheard of atrocities, simply through the power of his personality. What if he had not died? What if he had immortality and was still preaching his brand of hate to multiple generations of followers?"

"Imagine if a political leader such as Mao Tse-tung, Fidel Castro, or Nikita Khrushchev were able to live for hundreds of years. They could unify and lead their people for generations. Do you want to possibly give that control to an enemy? That would be a treasonous capitulation of power."

He spit the last sentence out like the words gave him a bad taste in his mouth.

"OK John, that's enough with the treason talk," ordered General Thompson. "We're all on the same side and we have the same goals. You've made a couple of good points. I think that we all see the possible threat if an enemy state were to gain this technology. Can the committee vote on this now?"

"No!" said Perkins. "I have more to say."

General Thompson sat back and folded his arms.

"Third, imagine if an enemy state infiltrated our country with sleeper agents. And imagine if these infiltrators just lived longer

The Smart Kid

than the rest of us. They could have *decades* to slip into every level of society from the local police, to the military and even to congress or our court systems. Age would be a weapon and it would be used against us to destroy our country from the inside out, like a worm in an apple."

"Damn! I never considered that!" exclaimed Senator Timms. "It's really like time would become a military weapon; a literal Time Bomb." The other men nodded agreement.

Seeing that he was influencing the committee, the Senator continued his monologue with even more passion. "Now let's turn the tables and consider how this technology will help our own country." He paused for a beat.

"Fourth, our military fighting forces, our boys in blue, will become the strongest, best trained, most experienced force in the world. We will be the threat that we feared our enemies might become with this power."

Looking toward the General, Perkins said, "I'm sure that the General agrees that this is an appealing future to consider."

General Thompson nodded agreement. "Yes. Experience is the real trainer. But that requires time; too much time."

This discussion was having a mesmerizing effect on the committee which had never had such a unique project under its control.

Perkins continued. "Fifth, consider how much stronger our nation will be with scientific geniuses like Einstein living for a couple of hundred years, or more. Dream about the technology and progress that our nation will make. I was born at a time when air flight was impossible; just a fantasy. But in my lifetime, aeronautics has advanced from no flight to orbiting the earth in a spacecraft. And I expect that the world will see the realization of President Kennedy's goal to have a man walk on the moon within this decade. In 60 years, dramatic technological progress has been made in this one industry. That is a small amount of time for History but an entire lifetime for us. Now just imagine if that 60 years was just one fourth of Einstein's life. We will be flying among the stars. And does anyone want to deter us from that grand future?"

No one said a word of contradiction, nor did they seem to

notice that the Senator had made a subtle but influential change in his phraseology from a possible future to a definite one.

So far, the Senator's eloquent and well-considered speech was a logical argument. But logic alone would not be enough to motivate the committee to agree whole-heartedly to the course he was suggesting. An emotional element would also be required. And so the experienced debater, completed his proposal with two emotionally-appealing points.

"Sixth, assess the political opportunities. Most of us are career politicians here. We want to serve our country as long as we can. We thrive on the power and the perquisites. For many of us, the only thing that is stopping us from serving for more than 40 or 50 years is old age. Why let age prevent us from continuing to do the great work of serving our nation? Do you want to become a feeble senior citizen, drooling in your oatmeal at a retirement center, remembering the 'Good Old Days' when you were in public service?"

"So you think that this formula, or whatever it is, might be developed soon enough to enable me— um, all of us, to continue in our public service for another thirty years?" Cutler seemed incredulous, his eyes widened. "Think of the legacy…"

Perkins saw that he was getting the men to look into their own hearts. So he attempted to stir up their desire like extra sugar in coffee. "Yes!" encouraged Perkins. "What do you want in life? You will have many more decades to pursue and enjoy it."

He paused to take a drink of water and secretly survey the reactions of the men. He glanced at Harper and flashed an extra-smug simper.

"Finally, have any of you had a loved one die because of, so called, old age? I have. And it's a painful, debilitating experience. It ages you years. Who would choose that guaranteed pain if they had a choice? Which of you, when you have the power, will not choose to give your loved ones the ability to live for more than a century?"

Senator Cutler looked down for a moment and mumbled, "I couldn't stand it if my wife died before me…" He glanced at Perkins before saying, "John, those are well reasoned points

The Smart Kid

and I think that everyone here can agree that protecting and using this technology is in the best interest of our nation."

Again, the other men nodded agreement.

Senator Mercer, whose nickname among Democrats was *The Mechanic* because he was always throwing a wrench into the works, said, "Although those are very strong arguments illuminating the power of this potential technology. The question really is this: Are the needs so urgent and the threats so imminent that it justifies the immediate forced drafting of this man for service to our nation?"

"Let me respond to that, gentlemen," said Perkins.

It was all very civil as they tossed Michael's future around the room like a live hand-grenade.

"I've given you seven justifications for drafting this man into our service. Now let me offer one more: for his own safety. He is a national security target. In the same way that one of our technologically advanced war planes could be stolen and reverse engineered by an enemy, so could our subject. So for his own protection we need to bring him in."

"How would we achieve that?" asked Timms.

The Senator answered, "Well, here is the precedent: Executive Order 9066 by President Roosevelt in 1942, when he authorized the internment of more than a hundred thousand potential Japanese sympathizers—"

"You can't be serious!" said Mercer, standing up at once. "That was a political travesty! It brought shame and embarrassment to our nation."

The other men seemed equally alarmed that Perkins was using this precedent to support his position.

"Gentlemen," said Perkins, raising his arms as if he were Pope John blessing his followers. "Please, let me continue…" His stare forced Mercer to take his seat.

"We have the benefit of hindsight to look back at that action. But then, our nation was facing the real threat of an enemy invasion on the very shores of California. They had no idea how the Japanese descendants would respond. And fortunately, they never had to find out. But the possibility of internal uprisings and sabotage existed and FDR and his administration dared not ignore it, even if they'd wanted. And I'm sure that FDR did not relish the potential censure by future generations, but he took this difficult action for those very generations."

"Some called it a decision by racists who had influence in his administration," said General Thompson.

Senator Perkins frowned for a fraction of a second at this swipe against his argument. But he pushed forward. "Most of them were Japanese-Americans, that's true. But it's a myth that this order was directed at one particular ethnic group. The Japanese, nor any ethnic group were ever mentioned in EO 9066. A few Italian-Americans and German-Americans who were considered a threat were also interred. The thousands of people that were temporarily incarcerated had done nothing wrong. They weren't criminals. I agree. But the Roosevelt Administration deemed them a threat to national security and exercised its sovereign authority to protect itself. And this was not simply a matter of choice, but it was a mandate in the constitution."

"But those were special circumstances. We were at war," countered Timms. "We didn't know who was a spy or a potential spy, or who might rise up against us and support an invading army of Japanese."

"Exactly. We didn't know," responded Perkins. "And we don't really know what Michael's political ties are either. What if he were to defect to Russia? We're still at war with the Russians. It's a cold, silent war, but they are still our enemy. We know that relations between the Soviet Union and the Castro regime are strong. What if Khrushchev and Castro ever decided to put Russian missiles in Cuba, aimed at Washington, just like the U.S. has placed missiles in Turkey aimed at Moscow? It's not an unlikely possibility. They would be only 100 miles off our shore. Those missiles could be used as a First Strike against us, followed by a wave of immortal soldiers for the ground assault. So don't you think that President Kennedy considers us to be at war with the Communists? You know that he does."

As Perkins argued his point, the old men in the room looked around, apparently evaluating each other's response.

"These decisions we're discussing right now *are* wartime

The Smart Kid

decisions. This is no different than our nation forcibly drafting young men into military service. That has been the S.O.P. for years. Does anyone disagree with that practice?" Perkins paused. No one said anything.

"I thought not. We are only talking about drafting one more man."

"You mean 'incarcerating' one man," said General Thompson.

Perkins again frowned at the General. In response to his argument, Senator Perkins attacked from a different angle. "Did you know that Einstein was against using the atom bomb, that led to our decisive victory over Japan?"

"Of course!" scoffed General Thompson.

"And yet," Perkins raised his hand, index finger pointing in the air, "and yet, he sent a letter to President Roosevelt to encourage the US to accelerate the development of the A-bomb."

"Yes. What's your point?" asked General Thompson.

"Einstein, a pacifist, suspected that Germany would develop an atom bomb and use it against us. He felt that the only option was for the US to develop one first. Fortunately, we defeated Germany without the bomb. But he felt that the decision was forced by the circumstances. Our subject, Michael, is like an atom bomb. If we don't do something about him now, then a foreign power may use his 'technology' against us. And that would be far worse than drafting him."

Perkins had spoken convincingly. He looked around the room. No one else countered his argument.

Senator Perkins continued. "So President Roosevelt has already given us a precedent for acting in response to this potential threat. And gentlemen, his incarceration would be temporary. The word 'incarceration' is too strong a term. It would just be a short period of medical evaluation. When we're done with our tests, he would be free to go."

"So he wouldn't be tested by ARPA scientists?" asked Dr. Barbour.

"No," said Senator Perkins. "I appreciate your initial studies of his biology. But we need to take him to a secure testing facility. And ARPA has no dedicated hospital for such a task. However, if you want to recommend some discreet, qualified geneticists, that would be appreciated."

"Would he be allowed to have visitors, like in a regular hospital?" asked Mercer.

"Absolutely! He'll be well-served." Senator Perkins displayed one of his well-rehearsed smiles.

The men in the room had relaxed. Instead of leaning forward on the table with their hands in their fists, or tensely pressing their palms to the table— as they had been doing throughout this debate— they were leaning back, or resting an elbow on the table or stroking their chin.

"Well, Gentlemen, we are on the edge— the very edge of greatness. I think that we've reached a consensus on the justifications and precedents, and I appreciate your thoughtfulness in this debate and the concern it demonstrates for the rights of this individual. Mr. Harper will now distribute the authorization letter, which will demonstrate your endorsement of this course of action and the special conscription order for everyone to sign."

Mr. Harper distributed the forms and the men began signing them.

"One more thing," said the General. "How will this conscription be implemented? Through what bureau?"

"Oh, don't you worry about that," smiled Perkins. "My team will take care of the details."

The General hesitated, then signed the forms.

Finally, Senator Perkins rested his body into his chair and lit up his patiently waiting cigar, savoring the rich aroma.

A few days later, Senator Perkins sat alone in his ornate office.

The decision had already been made.

The committee had authorized the initial invitation to Michael Shale, and they had authorized the special conscription order. They had committed themselves. Each man's name would be forever associated with that decision. They were, in effect, backing all subsequent actions that the Senator would

The Smart Kid

take on behalf of the committee— actions that the committee didn't need to know, nor would most of them want to.

The Senator knew something that the committee didn't. There was one obstacle preventing him from moving forward to his goal. Michael Shale was a college student, and, therefore, legally void from a draft call. But Senator Perkins was used to overcoming obstacles, and he knew who to call for help.

Senator Perkins knew that J. Edgar Hoover used his FBI like his own secret police force to accomplish a variety of political goals against subversives, sympathizers, and organizations that he deemed suspicious of supporting Communists. Hoover accomplished his goals under the banner of COINTELPRO, the Counter Intelligence Program. It was like a multi-featured Swiss Army knife. They created rumors, planted evidence, and published false newspaper reports against their targets, which included the NAACP, the Congress of Racial Equity, and even Martin Luther King, Jr. They also surveyed student groups and events supporting racial equality. Even Albert Einstein came under FBI surveillance because he was a member of several civil rights groups.

And Perkins intended to use Hoover's knife to cut away an obstacle.

Mr. Harper, at his door announced, "He's here."

"OK. Bring him in."

Harper escorted a young man who had a forthright gait, dark hair cut military-short, muscular arms and sharp eyes.

"Welcome, Special Agent Watts, I'm Senator Perkins."

"Oh, yes. I know, sir."

"Please sit down."

The men sat on opposite sides of Perkins's antique desk.

"How long have you worked for the FBI?"

"Ten years, Sir."

"You look too young to have ten years experience," the Senator suggested.

"I was recruited right from college."

"Did your supervisor inform you of the mission?"

"No sir. He just said to report to you and do what you say. Oh, and that it was an 'off-the-books' job." Watts smiled knowingly.

Agent Watts appeared ready to serve. He acted and spoke professionally with no hint of emotion.

"Harper, show him the file."

The assistant handed a file folder to Watts without a word. It was labeled *Top Secret: For Armed Services D&D Projects Select Committee Chairman only.*

Agent Watts opened the folder as he displayed a cautious frown and examined three photos of Michael Shale. One was dated 1953, when Michael was thirteen. He looked young, with blond hair, and indistinct features. The other two photos were dated 1958 and the current year, 1962. He looked exactly the same in all the photos.

Agent Watts asked, "I see the same kid in photos with different dates; Which date is accurate?"

"They all are," said Perkins.

Agent Watts looked at Perkins who held a serious expression. He looked at the photos again. "So are they different boys, or what?"

"No, it's the same person," said Perkins. "He's not a boy. He's twenty-two in that last photo."

For the first time since he entered the room, Agent Watts's professional demeanor momentarily cracked, as he raised his eyebrows and formed his lips to make a silent whistle. "Wow! That's hard to believe. What's his story?"

"That's all you need to know right now."

"Yes sir. What's the mission?"

23. The Arrest

FEBRUARY, 1962 WAS a time in Michael Shale's life when he was preparing to graduate with a degree in the new MBA program at the University of Iowa. Just four more months. But it was questionable if he could get hired since he still looked twelve. On the other hand, Michael wasn't worried about being drafted because the army most likely wouldn't hire him either.

His brother, Mark, never attended college. His interests were in mechanics and photography. He became skilled at car, motorcycle and truck maintenance and was hired by the city of Des Moines to repair their snow plows and other vehicles. Mark always said that if he got drafted, he'd work in the army motor pool.

Although his brother, Tom, was seven years younger and still in high school, he and Michael appeared to be the same age. He was too young to be drafted, yet.

On a frosty weekday morning, while Roy Orbison's *Only the Lonely* played quietly on the radio, there was a knock at the dorm room door. Michael opened it to the unsmiling faces of a security officer, a uniformed city policeman, and a non-uniformed man in a dark suit and tie.

"Is there a problem?" he asked, staring incredulously at the phalanx of security.

"Are you Michael Shales?" the city police officer asked, reading his name from a paper.

"It's Shale. Yes..." said Michael, swallowing hard.

"I'm Officer Nelson, this is Johnson from the campus security, and this is Agent Watts from the FBI."

"What's going— "

"Please step out of your dormitory. We have a warrant to search your room."

The FBI agent opened a suspiciously-thick satchel and removed the search warrant, which he handed to Michael.

Michael stared at it in disbelief.

The Smart Kid

He had grown up with a respect for authority, as had many students his age. Although that attitude was decaying around the country, Michael was not one to contradict uniformed officers, even if he thought they were wrong. He stepped out, wearing jeans, a t-shirt, and no shoes. The FBI agent and the police officer entered and shut the door behind them. The campus officer remained in the hallway with Michael.

Michael realized that these men must be here to investigate Carl and maybe find his joint stash.

The security officer frowned as Michael put his head to the door and listened to the intruders rummaging through things, their voices muffled.

"Is that the guy?"

"Yes."

"Geez, he looks so young."

"They can fool you."

In a few minutes the men exited holding Michael's gym bag.

"Is this yours?" asked Officer Nelson.

Apprehension cut his breathing short as he answered, "Yes."

Agent Watts reached into the bag and removed a cigar box. He opened it to reveal several bags of marijuana, a pipe, and a small notebook.

The police officer studied the notebook. "It looks like a sales list of his customers."

"What the hell is this?" screamed Michael. "That is not my stuff!"

A boy and girl who had just walked past, stopped and turned to frown at Michael. A door down the hall opened, and two boys peeked out. Someone yelled, "Pigs!" and slammed the door. The young couple hurried away.

"You're under arrest. Please turn around and put your hands behind your back."

"No! This is a mistake!"

The muscular police officer grabbed Michael's arm and jerked it behind him with uncaring force.

Michael was shocked by the unexpected, surreal start to what should have been another ordinary college day. He was certain that the police had found Carl's stash. But why was it in his gym bag? And when did Carl start selling the stuff? Was Carl really that desperate for money?

When the police officer spun him around to snap the cuffs on his wrists, Michael spied Carl walking toward him.

Carl stopped in mid-step and stared at the surprising scene.

Michael shook his head and gave him a hard stare.

Carl returned an apologetic look, waved good-bye, and skipped out the nearest exit.

As the police officer led him through the hallway, gripping his cuffed-hands behind his back, Michael thought of his mother.

The police officer brought Michael to the city jail and booked him on possession of narcotics and drug trafficking.

The jail was a dull, lifeless building occupied by a few bored officers and several angry criminals who hung on the bars of their jail cells and said nothing without yelling: questions, expletives and demands for justice.

Michael continued to declare his innocence to the officers, who didn't give a damn what he had to say. When offered a phone call, he wanted to call his mother, certain that everything would be better if he could just explain it to her.

She'll believe me, right?

Why was he doubting? He hadn't seen her since August. During Christmas break, he'd gone skiing instead of going home. Plus he had told her to stop treating him like a kid. Maybe she'd think he was selling marijuana to prove he was an adult.

He called Mark.

Mark was surprised by the charges, but he believed Michael.

Michael placed a hand over his ear to block the noise from the jail's occupants.

"OK, Shorty," said Mark, "This is a bad mistake or a set-up. I'll explain it to Mom and Dad. We'll do what we can from this side, but it sounds like they've got a story all made up about you… Don't party too much in there."

The Smart Kid

Mark always knew what to say.

A week later, Michael was on the phone again.

"Mom?" said Michael, surprised at how difficult it was just to utter that one syllable. He was standing next to a dingy gray wall in the sparse city jail, talking into a black phone receiver that hadn't been cleaned in years. The handset felt sticky.

"Is it really you, Michael?"

"Yes. I'm OK. Except, um, last week, Mark told you about the drug charges mix-up. But now there's more..."

"What is it?" asked his mother with alarm.

"Well, they accused me of selling drugs too— which you know is totally false."

"Oh my," she gasped.

My poor mom.

After a second she said, "Yes, dear, I know."

"But the charges aren't going away. It wasn't Carl's stuff like I thought. Mark says that it's a set-up and I agree."

"Why?"

"The FBI claimed that they called the names on a list found with the drugs and everyone said that they bought drugs from me. And I got notice from the college: they've kicked me out and all my stuff has been put in storage. I can't go back to school until the drug charges are dropped. Yesterday, I received a draft letter, at the jail, from a military branch called *Special Services*. It said that my draft status had changed to 1-A on the same day that the college had booted me. It came so soon that they must have sent it even before that."

He paused to let his mom consider this.

"Oh dear. Are you sure it's called Special Services?"

"Yes. The draft letter said that I've been drafted into this Special Services unit. They'll get me out of jail and get the charges dropped if I just help them. Mom, they want me because... I'm special."

"You do what you have to do. I'm sure you'll choose what's best."

"Sixty seconds more," yelled a police officer.

He spoke faster. "Mom, listen. I may be gone for a while. I don't think I'll have much freedom under their control but I don't have a choice."

"Yes. I understand, Michael."

Every time that she agreed with him, he felt guilty. Although he had stayed away from the family for months, when he got in trouble he had called his *mommy* for help, like a kid. And rather than being mad at him, Michael's mother was gracious and caring. It was more than he could take. He squeezed his eyes shut for a moment to hold back a tear drop. *Stop it! Act like a grown man, Michael.*

The guard by the door was watching him.

"Mom, I will visit you when I can, but I don't know when that will be. Listen, it's as if I'm going to war."

She raised her voice, "Well, your father still has military connections. He could try— "

"Whoever they are— I don't know yet— They said that you shouldn't try to find me or it could be bad for me."

"Oh my…" said Jan Shale, her voice fading.

"Mom, I might be gone for a long time. It may be difficult to..."

"I understand," she breathed out.

"Mom, I love you. Tell Dad too."

"I love you too, my son." Her voice was a whisper.

"Mom--"

"Time's up!" The phone went silent.

The noise of the jail faded from his attention as he continued to hold the receiver and finished the words in his head: *I want to come home. Sorry that it's been so long. I was trying to prove that I'm an adult.*

Michael hung up the phone, and hung his head, leaning against the wall. He formed his boyish hands into small fists and ineffectually pounded the wall, the sound melting into the background rabble of cops and criminals. He felt like a twelve-year-old again.

After a moment, he controlled his emotions, turned around and prepared himself for a new life.

24. Tests

"SENATOR PERKINS, SIR," said the familiar voice of Harper on the phone.

"We have him in ... custody, er, our control now."

"Finally! Is he co-operating?"

"He's very angry and demanding apologies for the drug bust. Plus he wants a written apology and explanation sent to his parents."

"What do we care? We've got him. Send the parents a letter saying that he's helping the government and he's undercover. Make it sound urgent and secret. Make 'em proud of their son's service. That will get them off our case. Also pull all the military conscription records and toss 'em. We're done with that farce. And then cover your tracks. Don't let them backtrack and find the kid— ever. Or your ass is grass! Clear?"

"Yes, sir."

"And Harper."

"Yes, sir?"

"Don't ever call me about this again. You come to me personally from now on."

"Yes, sir."

The Senator hung up the phone and removed a cigar and his special lighter. He ran his thumb across the inscription and almost smiled as he stared at the photo of his wife, who smiled back.

Michael was co-operating with the federal authorities, the government men, in order to get the drug charges dropped.

Two armed guards transported him by police car to a building in downtown Iowa City that had no sign of its purpose. They brought him to an empty room furnished with a table, two chairs and a mirror embedded in the wall. The guards left him without saying a word.

He heard the lock click when they closed the door.

He waited.

After many minutes, a middle-aged woman wearing a nurse's

The Smart Kid

uniform backed through the door, carrying a tray of food.

"Here you go ..." She had started speaking before she turned and saw Michael. Her mouth dropped open a second before she continued, "young man. I hope you like hamburgers and french fries. There's also a soda and a cup of pudding here." She gave a small smile to Michael, glanced at the mirror, and left the room.

Michael was so hungry that he ate everything, starting with the pudding. He pulled the tab off the soda can and flicked it at the mirror. He sipped as he waited. When he finished the can of soda pop, he crushed it in his hands and tossed it at the mirror— the mirror that he knew had other people's faces behind it.

After a boringly long time, a balding white man wearing white shirt and pants and a white lab coat entered the room.

"Hello Mr. Shale, I'm Doctor Bruce."

Michael said nothing.

"Thank you for your participation in this medical study. You have a key role to play in our research. Over the years there have been many studies on how to delay the aging process. Others have suffered from Syndrome-X, giving the appearance of eternal youth, but they were actually aging internally. You're the first to not age, yet still have a maturing, growing mind. A very rare find ..."

As the doctor droned on about Michael's uniqueness and the importance of the study for health and military benefits, Michael eyelids became as heavy as bricks.

"... we will be taking tissue samples, ... doing DNA analysis ..."

Michael leaned forward over the table, rested his head on his crossed arms, and fell asleep.

When Michael awoke, he was laying on a bed, looking up at a gray tiled ceiling. His head throbbed with pain. He sprung up, instantly regretting the sudden movement, and dropped back into the narrow bed and didn't try to sit up again until the room stopped spinning around him.

After several minutes, he tried again, easing himself up to a sitting position on the bed. Michael was disoriented, uncertain of the time or day. He had no idea how he got here, or where *here* was. At first, he assumed he'd been transferred to a room in the unlabeled building in Iowa City. But he was in an old classroom, with chalkboards on one wall and a pile of desks and chairs jumbled in a corner. The mesh-covered window on the west side of the room revealed a line of trees silhouetted against a grey sky.

He was not downtown.

Michael wobbled to a standing position for dizzy moment. He plopped back onto the old musty blanket. That's when he discovered that his naked body was only covered by a hospital gown.

Another wave of disorienting discomfort flooded over him. Someone had undressed him, transferred him to this room, and laid him out on a bed. He had no memory of it.

Michael eased himself to an upright position.

The room's rotation had slowed to a swirly crawl.

He scanned the room for his clothes.

A dresser rested against the wall next to a door.

A door.

His shuffling feet scraped the old wooden floor as he aimed for the door. Success.

He tried the knob. It didn't move. He yanked on the door. It didn't budge.

He was locked in a forgotten classroom. This upset him more than losing his clothes.

Clothes.

A few slow shuffles and he reached the dresser. Shirts, pants, underwear, socks— apparently his size, filled several drawers. A denim jacket hung on a wall hook above a brand new pair of sneakers.

Michael plodded back to the bed and landed in it before the dizziness overtook him again.

As the fog in his mind began to clear, he realized that his wallet was missing— gone with his clothes. So he had no identification; no student I.D., and no drivers license. He shook his head at the violation.

He scratched at the crook of his left arm and discovered needle marks, a cluster of tiny red irritations. The other arm was also red with punctures.

How long was I unconscious?

The Smart Kid

He'd been drugged, moved, stripped, robbed, and medically examined, probed and sampled. Michael felt violated and vulnerable and very angry. He wanted to kick someone.

A sickly flush of questions and confused thoughts swirled in his head. Soon the room began to spin in the opposite direction. Although he gripped the edge of the bed, he still had an uncontrollable sensation of tipping forward. Michael had to lay down again or he was going to lose his lunch.

Oh yes. He was hungry too.

Michael awoke, his mind clearer. This time he stood without feeling dizzy. He was still in the same old classroom converted to a bedroom. Another attempt at the door proved it was still locked. He pounded on it. Nothing.

Somebody had to be here, somewhere. But Michael had a growing fear that he was abandoned forever.

When he surveyed the room again, he noticed a bottle of aspirin and a glass on a worn wooden table. Why hadn't he seen that before? There was no bathroom but, hanging on the wall was a small sink, which he used to fill the glass with water and then swallowed two aspirin. As he took the pills he spied a camera mounted in the ceiling.

Facing the camera, he yelled, "Hey! I have to go to the bathroom!"

The camera stared back at him.

Michael changed into new clothes, self-consciously, aware that someone was probably watching him. The clothes were a good fit. He sat on the chair and waited.

Michael was greatly relieved when he heard someone approaching outside the door.

Keys jangled.

An unsmiling, muscular guard opened the door and said, "Bathroom break."

The guard wore a brown military uniform and a side-arm. He escorted Michael through a dismal hallway, their footsteps echoing on the yellowed tiles, as if they were the only ones in the building.

"Where am I? And why do you have a gun? Am I a prisoner?"

"Shut up!"

The gruff order shocked him into silence.

Michael was escorted along a hallway lined with glass cases filled with old framed photos of uniformed boys with unsmiling faces. The newest-looking photos were under a placard that read *Pershing Academy Graduating Class of 1952*. At one point, windows along the hall opened to a huge library with racks of books. They took a turn and came to a bathroom. The guard waited outside while Michael entered. It was a locker room with several toilets and shower stalls. Like his bedroom jail cell, the windows were wired shut with a protective mesh.

When they passed the library on their return, Michael asked, "Can I look at the books?"

The guard unclipped a radio from his belt and spoke in low tones. The scratchy words, "just watch him," came back. So the guard unlocked the library door and turned on the lights. It was a cavernous room with dozens of shelves.

Michael walked between the shelves surveying books on every subject. He found the section with historical fiction and grabbed one that he recognized.

The guard escorted him back to his prison bedroom and locked him in again.

A tray of food, utensils, and a can of soda waited on the table. This reminded Michael of the last time someone brought him food— and he woke up here. A sliver of fear entered his mind for a moment. But Michael decided that if he ate this food or not, he'd wake up here anyway.

So he sat down to eat as he opened his new library book by Paul Brickhill: *The Great Escape*.

That seems appropriate.

Early the next day, clanking keys in the lock woke Michael. He'd slept on the single cot in his new clothes.

The guard pushed open the door. "Come with me."

Michael complied.

As they walked through the hall, Michael considered what might happen if he just bolted from the guard. No doubt every door was

The Smart Kid

locked. He wouldn't get far before they caught and hand-cuffed him.

The guard escorted Michael into a darkening hallway that ended in shadows.

When they reached a pair of dingy doors at the end of the hall, the guard pulled them open to reveal one of the whitest rooms Michael had ever seen. It was a medical lab filled with shining equipment, monitors and shelves lined with medicine bottles and strange looking devices. Several men wearing blue surgical scrubs turned in his direction.

Fear started to press in upon Michael as the guard clamped on his shoulder to direct him. A cart covered with a blue cloth had gleaming surgical instruments on it; scalpels and other scary, pointy things.

The guard must have felt Michael tense up because his hand clinched harder on his shoulder directing him to a surgical table.

Michael tried to spin away as he screamed, "No!"

But he was cut off by a gas masked forced over his mouth and nose.

Everything went fuzzy.

25. More Tests

THE SENATOR WAS not happy.

Harper was with him in his office, along with Agent Watts. They said nothing, waiting for the Senator to finish his rant.

This discussion was off the books, and the other members of the Defense & Development Projects Select Committee were not invited. They didn't have to know everything that the Senator did in the name of the committee.

Harper had just reported on the progress of the medical tests.

"It's been nine damn months! And you're telling me that they haven't got squat? What the hell have they been doing—playing with themselves?" growled the Senator.

"Well, sir, that's not exactly what I said. I only said that they don't have a complete scientific report available yet. They're investigating something substantial but don't want to be too quick to make judgements yet because they're not certain if this anomaly is the cause of his non-aging. So when I said, 'Nothing to report', I didn't mean 'Nothing discovered.'"

"So you don't want to tell me what they found?"

"I don't know what their discovery is." Harper pushed his black-rimmed glasses up his nose again. The perspiration that accumulated on his brow whenever he was reporting to his boss always had this effect on his glasses. "They want to present everything at once after they have a complete report. But they need something else to help them verify their findings."

"What else do they need before they can make an accurate report?"

"Well," said Harper, glancing at Agent Watts who sat as a silent spectator away from the heat. "They've got plenty of tissue samples and have started a DNA analysis, but they don't have a good baseline to compare it to."

"Meaning what?"

"Just doing human tissue analysis has turned out to be inadequate. They need to compare his DNA to a member of ...

The Smart Kid

his family."

"What? Do you want me to get his mommy for him?"

"No, of course not," the aide stammered.

"Well, spit it out!"

"On behalf of the medical team, Dr. Barbour did some research into his family history. He was able to obtain this birth certificate." Harper reached into a file folder and handed a paper to the Senator.

The Senator leaned back in his chair and chewed his unlit cigar as he read it. "Mother of God! Why didn't we know about this sooner?"

"His family kept it secret. They never used the word; nor was it in the university report."

Senator Perkins smiled. "Watts!"

"Yes, sir." Watts stood like a soldier, chin up, hands at his sides.

"I've got another job for you."

Michael awoke, his vision blurry and his mind groggy from the anesthetics, and peered out the mesh covered window. It was a sunny day in … what month was it? He'd been brought here in February. Since then the view outside had transformed to a leafy and grassy green for a few months. But the leaves had started to fall from the trees again. Michael estimated that it was September.

He turned back to the grey ceiling and reviewed his detention time.

He had three types of days. On Medical Test Days, he'd be forcibly transferred to the white lab, sedated, and he'd wake up in his room with a painful new scar. On Recovery Days, after the medical biopsies, he was too tired or sore to do anything but lay in his cot and read a book, or sleep. At first, the Medical Test Days alternated with the Recovery Days, but as the months progressed, the number of medical tests became less frequent. So Michael was able to experience a third type of day: Recreation Day.

During Recreation Days he was allowed to exercise in the gym. On one end of the gym, weight-lifting equipment and exercise mats lay abandoned and a basketball hoop hung on the other end. Some days he'd shoot baskets and try to do lay-ups like his high school friends: Bill, Spike, and Sam. But the hoop was too high for him. Thick climbing-ropes hung from the ceiling along the side of the gym. During the first few months of confinement, Michael tried to climb the ropes, unsuccessfully. But he made it a personal goal.

His food was always brought to him in his room, served on a metal tray that reminded Michael of school lunches. The metal utensils were a fork and a spoon, never a knife. After each meal, an armed guard retrieved the tray and threw it onto a wheeled cart.

Michael was never allowed to see a TV, radio or newspaper— only the old books in the library. He read books all the time during this part of his life.

He was isolated. No one talked to him except to order him to go someplace, or stand-up, or open his mouth, or bend-over, or flex his muscles, or shut-up and be quiet. It reminded him of when he was young, adults controlling every minute of his life: wake up, eat breakfast, brush your teeth, get on the bus, go to school, blah, blah, blah. It was as if he hadn't grown up at all.

Michael felt the pain of the most recent incision from a biopsy. This time it was on his left side under the arm. He was shirtless, again — a common occurrence on Medical Test Days. He reached for the bandage with his right hand and peeled it back to check the damage they'd done to him. Just a small cut. He replaced the bandage, laid back on the cot, and tried to count how many new scars he had. By the time he got to 25 he fell asleep.

The next day Michael awoke early to the sound of jangling keys. It was too soon for another test, so he just pushed himself up on his elbows and waited as the door was unlocked and opened.

The guard stood silently in the shadow of the hallway eyeing Michael. He turned to his left and nodded as he stepped aside. Another guard appeared, directing a prisoner. This guard had, apparently, just removed hand-cuffs from the prisoner who was alternately rubbing each wrist.

The prisoner said, "Thanks a lot— Asshole!" He was shoved hard into the light of Michael's room. It was Mark.

"Mark!" Michael tried to yell, but his throat was still dry from

The Smart Kid

the medication. It came out as a whisper.

"Hello, Shorty!"

Michael sat up in bed and his twin brother, who was a grown man, bent down to hug him.

They spent the next thirty minutes catching up with each other.

Michael said, "I'm so sorry that they got you too. It's all because of me."

"Don't worry about it," said Mark. "It's not your fault that these arrogant asses think that they can incarcerate us without just cause."

"What did they say was the reason for arresting you?" Michael asked, truly wondering why the government would want his brother, a normally-aging man.

"They didn't say. They just grabbed me from work and that was it. Someone must be getting desperate."

Each of the brothers had separate cells, although they were allowed to visit each other frequently. But they each faced their invasive doctors alone. Visits with each other were the only bright spots on their gloomy days.

During one of Mark's visits to Michael's room, they were talking as they played their usual game of Dots. Mark had drawn a grid pattern of dots on a paper. They each took turns drawing a line between a pair of dots trying to create a square. Whenever one of them completed a square, he'd write his initials in it. Since they had the same initials, they used their middle names. Mark initialed a 'W' for William and Michael wrote an 'R' for Robert.

Of course, they played as adversaries who knew what each other was thinking, so it wasn't easy getting those squares initialed. Invariably, they created a pattern of corridors, and parallel lines. When Mark drew a vertical line, so did Michael. And if one of them drew a horizontal line, so did the other. It was as if they were chasing each other across the paper with parallel lines, each one rarely risking a change in direction unless forced to do so.

"Hey Mikey," said Mark. He drew a line.

"What's up?" They always spoke in low tones because they knew that every word was being monitored and recorded. Michael drew a line.

"Today I heard one of the medical techs say, 'We've almost got enough for a baseline comparison.'"

Michael thought about the meaning. He'd been wondering for weeks what the government scientists hoped to accomplish with Mark. He had a suspicion but it became a certainty.

"That's it!" said Michael as he drew a line. "They want to compare your DNA to mine, so they can see how we differ."

"Well, they're sure taking a lot of samples," Mark said, glancing at the needle marks on his arm.

"They probably figure since we come from the same family, you'd be an experimental guinea pig too."

"Who you calling a pig, Shorty?" Mark drew a line forcing Michael to draw the dreaded third side. Mark completed a box, initialed it, and took a free turn. Since they had created corridors of lines, each box that Mark finished enabled him to finish another. Like a row of dominoes, he completed a whole row of boxes, one after another.

"Well, Bro, it looks like I got you on this one."

Michael smiled. "That's OK, you earned it. You outflanked me well. But it won't happen again."

26. Test Results

THE SENATOR AND Harper waited in the usual meeting room in the old Senate building. They were expecting several doctors from the testing facility. The doctors had found something significant.

The door opened, four doctors entered and gathered around the end of the table. Senator Perkins had never seen them. He'd relied on Harper to take care of staffing issues and other details. For his own protection, he preferred not knowing every detail.

The doctor nearest the Senator wore dark pants and white shirt with a generic tie. His chosen clothing seemed more like a costume than something he was accustomed to wearing. He remained standing after the others sat in their chairs.

He cleared his throat, glanced at his colleagues, and began with, "Um ... As per your aide's request, I will just be introducing our distinguished associates, as needed. But please realize that we could not have made this monumental discovery without the help of each doctor here today. I am Dr. Xerxes Nickolas, the head of the team."

The Senator crossed his arms and nodded, closing his eyes for a second.

"Anyway," said Dr. Nickolas. "What we've found is so unexpected that we never searched for it since no one has ever seen this in a human before. It was discovered by accident. But now that we've uncovered it, we also understand how we missed it. Are you ready? This young man has 48 chromosomes!"

Dr. Nickolas paused, apparently for his audience to react with surprise, but Harper and Perkins just stared at him.

Harper broke the awkward silence. "We aren't scientists. We don't know what that means."

"What it means," said Dr. Nickolas, unable to contain his own enthusiasm, "is that this man has an *extra* chromosome pair. Humans have 46 chromosomes, organized into 23 pairs. This

The Smart Kid

subject has the usual 23 pairs, plus one extra pair of chromosomes."

He stared in wide-eyed amazement, but saw no astonishment in his non-scientific audience. "It is revolutionary to the point of almost being a new species. If I'd not seen him with my own eyes, I never would've believed that he was a healthy human. This is so significant that we won't be able to discuss all the implications today. But we will just mention the highlights. ... Dr. Mascowski?"

The only woman in the room stood while Dr. NIckolas took a seat. The middle-aged doctor brushed her brown hair away from her face as she began. "I'm going to tell you one reason why the presence of an extra pair of chromosomes in this young man is so miraculous."

"There are many ways that humans can be disabled or killed by genetic disruptions. A person could be born with less than 46 chromosomes, or genetic material between chromosomes could get switched. Sometimes chromosomes could be connected in the wrong form: backwards, or in a circle. In all such cases, the deformities or disabilities created are life threatening, if life is even created."

"In the past, when a human has been born with an extra chromosome— a duplicate of one of the regular 23 chromosomes— it has resulted in a severe disability, and often, death. For example, the disability known as Down's Syndrome is the result of an extra 21st chromosome. Hence the medical name, Trisomy 21, because there are three where there should only be two chromosomes."

Dr. Mascowski paused. "So the fact that this man has two extra chromosomes paired together and is completely healthy, is simply unique and unprecedented. But we believe the reason he's healthy is because he has all his required chromosomes, and this 24th pair is just extra genetic material that doesn't disrupt normal growth patterns." She sat and glanced at Dr. Nicholas.

"Thank-you. Now Doctor Mendenhall will describe our baseline comparisons." Nickolas nodded toward a distinguished looking man with tan skin, graying sideburns and perfect hair.

He stood, smiled, and looked directly at Perkins as he spoke.

Dr. Mendenhall said, "You know that the two subjects are identical twins. At first we didn't believe it, but a simple test proved that they are what we call Monozygotic Twins. If they had been Dizygotic, or formed from different fertilized eggs, then we would not have been surprised by their physical differences.

"We searched for every possible cause, taking many tissue samples. The only difference in their biology is the presence of the extra chromosomes in the younger-looking twin."

Perkins cleared his throat and asked, "Isn't it proof that these extra ones are the cause of the boy's anti-aging?"

"Most likely," said Dr. Mendenhall, nodding his head. "But what has us puzzled is why the older-looking one *doesn't* have the extra chromosomes. The very nature of Monozygotic Twins is that they are formed from a single fertilized egg which prematurely divides, meaning that each zygote is the same. These men should be identical, but only one of them received the extra chromosomes. This seems like an impossibility."

"So what's the answer, do you think?" asked Perkins.

"I think that we don't know enough about these special chromosomes to be sure. But I'd say that they carried instructions that prevented them from splitting apart during the special division of the cells that formed the twin zygotes."

"So you're saying that the special chromosomes were designed just to stay put and not be cloned into another twin," said Perkins.

"Basically, yes. It was encoded in the DNA," said Mendenhall.

Perkins asked, "Do you know how the young looking man got the extra pair of chromosomes?"

"We have a theory. But the explanation is as unlikely as the result. His mother may have received advanced embryonic-stimulation during pre-natal care. Or she may have been artificially inseminated with a genetically engineered specimen. This is the most likely theory because it has the lowest probability of mortality, at only 98%."

"What do you mean *98% mortality rate*?" asked Perkins.

"Only one out of every 50 embryonic-manipulations would

The Smart Kid

not result in miscarriage, proof of how difficult and novel this procedure is. So the implication is that it wasn't just a medical accident, but it was planned. It had to be. And maybe 48 to 50 other mothers also had this treatment but they resulted in miscarriages."

"So you're saying that this Shale kid was *created*, like a Frankenstein monster?" asked Senator Perkins.

Doctor Mendenhall glanced at his colleagues, as if he were looking for support, but they said nothing. "Well, I don't think that I'd use that analogy but it is true that he was purposefully created to be this way."

"Why?"

"Obviously it was to carry the genetic information in the extra chromosomes," said Dr. Mendenhall. "Someone wanted to create a person who did not age. And so the anti-aging gene is hidden in this extra chromosome pair."

"If someone had the ability to develop a longevity gene, then why make an extra pair of chromosomes?" asked the Senator. "Why not just add it to one of the existing chromosomes?"

The three doctors sitting at the table smiled at this question, which caused a scowl to cross the Senator's face.

Harper interjected, "I believe what the Senator means is: 'Why go to the trouble of creating a 47th and 48th chromosome?'" Harper looked at the Senator who didn't acknowledge his help.

"Yes. It's an excellent question!" said Doctor Mendenhall. "This was very clever. If we tried to manipulate any of the regular 46 chromosomes, it would result in a disability or death as Dr. Maskowski has indicated, because gene therapy isn't advanced yet. The smallest change in a single base pair— one out of billions— can cause disabilities or deformities. So instead, this extra genetic material has been encased in its own chromosomes so that there is no need to alter the other 46. The extra genetic code gets duplicated into every cell and performs its function, but it doesn't hinder the body's natural cell development. It really is amazing!"

Perkins showed the barest hint of a smile. "Great! So we know what causes this kid's longevity. We can use that information now, right?"

Dr. Mendenhall swallowed hard, looked back at his colleagues, and said, "Um, I think that Dr. Walz should speak to that subject. Ah, Doctor?"

An older man stood. His balding head was encircled with gray hair and he was the only doctor who had not changed out of medical clothes into more formal attire. He removed dark-framed reading glasses from the pocket of his white lab coat, before opening a folder and removing a paper from it. He referred to the page as he made his presentation to the Senator.

"The answer to your question is 'No.'" He spoke bluntly. The Senator's small smile changed to a large frown.

Doctor Walz continued. "I don't think that we can just take this extra chromosome pair out of our test subject and stick it into someone else. A chromosome is a repository for personally identifying genetic markers. Even though this chromosome was originally foreign, when it began its existence in the fertilized egg of his mother, it was passed on to him naturally, and became a part of him. And that word *naturally* is the key. Shale is alive because he was born with the extra chromosomes."

"Genetic manipulation is in its infancy— its pre-infancy. You could say that this technology hasn't even been developed yet. Or, at least the regular medical establishment is not aware of such progressive genetic manipulation. Someone has been keeping secrets. There must be some secret medical institution with advanced knowledge—"

"I understand that you're saying that a genetically engineered chromosome has to be passed on naturally to the offspring or it won't work," said Senator Perkins. "Do you mean Shale could have children that have his same condition?"

"Once again, the answer to your question is 'No,'" said Dr. Walz.

Perkins sighed and bit his lower lip.

The doctor continued. "First, he cannot pass this extra chromosome pair to children because he's sterile."

Perkins smiled. "Good."

"And, interestingly, it seems that it was no accident. It appears that, besides giving this man an extremely long life, it

The Smart Kid

was designed to cause infertility," said Dr. Walz.

Perkins continued, "What purpose does that serve?"

"Its a way of controlling distribution of the genetic material. If this extra pair of chromosomes didn't cause infertility, then there would be an exponential growth in the number of people who have this longevity chromosome. Each succeeding generation would have more than the previous. We'd see a renewal of the human race, with some lucky souls living for a hundred years or more."

The Senator furrowed his brow as he considered this news.

The doctor continued, "Someone wanted to *restrict* distribution and knowledge of this genetic technology. So we were very fortunate to even discover it."

"Why is that?"

"Because it was hidden."

"What do you mean *hidden*?" asked the Senator, not hiding the surprise in his voice.

"One of our doctors discovered it by accident. These extra two chromosomes are so small that they were designed to blend in with other chromosomes, secretly riding along, getting duplicated into every cell, and causing this growth anomaly."

The Senator stood abruptly. Dr. Walz sat in deference to him. "Let me see if I understand what you're saying, Doctor. Someone created this genetic technology to inhibit aging, but they wanted to keep it hidden so the chromosome camouflages itself with other chromosomes, and it can't get passed onto children. Right?"

The doctors nodded.

"That is exactly what I'd do with military technology," said Perkins. "I'd withhold knowledge about it from our enemies and I'd classify it as top secret. And I'd control the distribution of the technology, so it doesn't fall into the wrong hands. The creators of this chromosome are protecting it like a military weapon. It's as if we're at war against an enemy with advanced technology. But we have no idea who these creators are ... maybe."

The doctors shook their heads. "I don't know of any medical facility that has developed this technology," said Dr. Nickolas.

Dr. Mendenhall leaned forward to see Dr. Nickolas. "Perhaps

it's being funded privately—"

"—Doctors," interrupted Perkins, "is there a chance that you may be able to discover how to transfer this special genetic code to another person?"

"No! I already told you that," said Dr. Walz.

"Well now, Dr. Walz," said Dr. Nickolas, "Let's not be so hasty here. What do the other doctors think?"

The doctors looked at each other and, apparently, Dr. Mendenhall was silently nominated to answer that question.

"That is an interesting question, isn't it?" said Dr. Mendenhall, smiling again. "If this extra pair of chromosomes could get transferred to another person, we would, in effect, have a longevity factory; with the power to give long-life to anyone."

"If they have enough money!" said Perkins.

"Yes … of course," Dr. Mendenhall replied. "It could be an expensive process. But who wouldn't be willing to buy another hundred years or two?"

"So you think it's a possibility?" asked Perkins.

"Mmmm. Perhaps." said Mendenhall. "If we could figure that out, our team would be guaranteed a Nobel prize."

The other doctors raised their eyebrows in unison. They turned toward each other and started whispering among themselves.

"Doctors," said the Senator.

The doctors stopped their quiet conversation and directed their attention to Perkins.

"I have a new agenda for you. I want you to figure out how to transfer this chromosome to another person. This is your top priority now. If you succeed, your reward will be more than a Nobel prize, it will be long, long life … for us all."

Michael heard the keys jangling outside his door. He'd heard this sound so many times, for months, that he had a reaction like Pavlov's Dog. Fear gripped his heart and increased his pulse. He sat in a chair with his back rigid, watching the door.

The guards escorting Mark held him by each arm. Mark shook off their grip and yelled, "Stop holding my hand all the time! I like girls."

The Smart Kid

"Shut up!" yelled the guard, slamming the door.

Mark smirked at this brother. "I try to annoy them every day. It's my only hobby."

Michael slumped down in his chair and smiled. "Hello, Mark." Michael sat at the table, which held a colorful jumble of old books.

"How's the studying going?" Mark pulled up a chair, sat down, and extended his legs to rest on the table.

"Fine. This week I'm reading about psychology."

"Why?"

"Well, I've got to read something. And I had a class in it once. It was interesting. I even stopped a fight in my psych class."

"You stopped a fight— that's a new one."

"I'm learning … I think."

"You going to read every book in their library?"

"That would be difficult; it's huge. I'm surprised that they've abandoned this military school. What a waste."

"That's your tax dollars at work," said Mark.

"I don't pay any taxes."

"Because you haven't earned much money, except for a few part-time jobs in high school and college. But when you and Dad start withdrawing money from your huge investment windfall, then you'll pay taxes on it."

"I never see that side of it. Dad said to just rely on Mr. Monaghan to take care of the legal and financial details. I can just contact him when I need some money and he'll wire it to me."

"Nice. Oh, by the way, Bro— this may sound weird: Happy Birthday."

"Really? I've kind of lost track of time," said Michael, glancing at a makeshift calendar he'd drawn on an old chalkboard. Many of the days had 'x's on them. He walked to the board and crossed off six more days.

"Yup. We are 23. What a way to celebrate."

"Damn! That means that I've spent two birthdays in … this jail for me." Michael continued staring at the chalkboard calendar pensively as he asked, "When do you think they'll let us out?"

Mark took his feet of the table and leaned forward. "Michael, They won't. The only way out of your jail is gonna be by your own effort."

Michael turned in surprise to face Mark. "What? Not even when they're done with all their tests?"

"They don't need the political headaches that we could cause for them. Even though we don't know who *them* is yet."

"Isn't it the Special Services Division?"

"I looked it up, Shorty. That's the entertainment unit for the Army."

"Entertainment?"

"Yes. Actors and singers, to perform for the troops, like Burt Lancaster. He was in the Army's Twenty-First Special Services Division."

"But that means—"

"It was a scam, Michael. You're not really in the military because you weren't officially drafted. The same as me, you were abducted."

"Damn! Who's got power to plant false evidence and fake a draft call?"

"It's got something to do with those letters you got from Senator Perkins," suggested Mark.

"Yes, I figured he had a role."

"And he will not simply let us go when he's done."

"But we don't have any proof, so he shouldn't fear us. It doesn't make sense."

"You always appeal to logic, don't you?" said Mark. "We're in here for good, or bad. We're going to have to find our own way out."

Michael turned toward the dirty mirror on the wall and stared at his face. "I've tried. I'm trapped."

Mark stepped forward, put his arm on this brother's shoulder, and looked down at him. "But now you've got me here. *Two are better than one.* Isn't that what we said as we were growing up?"

They heard a guard outside the cell. An envelope was pushed under the door.

Michael grabbed it. "It's a letter from Mom!"

"What? Addressed to where?"

"Its got a military box office number on it."

Michael sat at the table and ripped the envelope open, and read the letter aloud.

The Smart Kid

> *"Dear Michael,*
> *Thank-you for the letter."*

"—I never sent her a letter."

"Of course not," said Mark.

> *"...For the letter. It sounds like the work that you're doing for the government is very important and secret. I was trying to find out where you are, and someone from your department contacted me and delivered your letter.*
> *I have some bad news. Your father's illnesses finally won. He died May 15th."*

"What? No! No!" yelled Michael, pounding his fist on the table.

Mark started weeping.

"Oh! And we weren't there to support her!" cried Michael.

"Shit! Damn you, Perkins!" bellowed Mark. He picked up one of the old school desks piled against the wall and threw it against a mesh-covered window, doing little damage.

Michael slumped forward and rested his head on his arms. Mark stood beside him. After several minutes of silence, Michael shuffled to the wall-sink and splashed water on his face. He sat again and finished reading the letter.

> *"I know that your service with the government prevented you from attending. And Mark wasn't there either. I've lost touch with him. But fortunately my brother and sister were able to attend and give some support, along with little Tommy. Plus there were several military friends who came to pay their last respects. It was a beautiful service. I hope to see you soon.*
> *Love, Mom"*

"I have *got* to get out of here,"

"Don't worry Michael, I'm working on it."

27. Escape

Mark Shale picked up the metal chair and, for the second time, hurled it against the window of his locked door. A crack appeared on the glass.

"I want to see my brother right now, you assholes!"

A voice from the speaker in the upper corner of his room said, "Settle down, we're bringing him now. Please be patient."

"Up yours!"

Mark turned away from the surveillance camera to block what he was about to do. He peeled at the white medical tape that held the bandage on his left hand, which he'd hurt punching the wall during an angry rant at his captors. And it was a good thing because he had a plan. He pulled a clean piece of tape off the bandage and palmed it in his right hand, sticky side out, and waited for his brother.

Ten minutes later, Mark heard the key in the door just before it opened. Michael was flanked by an armed guard on each side. Mark took a step forward and placed his hand on the door frame.

"Back up, right now!" ordered a guard.

"OK, fine," said Mark, displaying his empty palms to the guards. He smiled.

"You've got thirty minutes," said the guard, closing the door. Mark listened but didn't hear the usual click of the latch falling into place. Mark smiled at Michael.

"How you doing, Shorty?" Mark said, hiding his nervous anticipation. He knew that they were being monitored.

"OK," said Michael, as he stood with a quizzical look.

"I thought that you might want to continue our dots game— the one that we never finished."

Mark sat at the table.

"Um, I guess. Show me." Michael, still frowning, sat to face his brother.

From a notebook, Mark removed a paper that had the usual dot grid. But the page already had lines and corridors drawn on it. He

The Smart Kid

looked hard into Michael's eyes as he said, "Here's our last game. Let's see if we can finish it. Then you can get out of here."

"All right," said Michael. "I hope I win ... this time."

"I think that you might. This is where we begin." Mark pointed to a rectangle labeled, *We Are Here*. The pattern of lines and corridors formed a map of the building.

Mark drew an arrow on the map from his cell out the door and to the right, along the corridor. The arrow continued to a square labeled *Shower*, where a large *X* was scratched next to the words *humidity vent*.

"OK, if you make this move," said Mark, glancing over Michael's shoulder at the security camera, "you'll be home-free."

"But," said Michael cryptically, "I don't think I'll get to this square here because it's blocked."

"No, it's not. I'll bet if you try, you'll win this one. Do you want some nuts?" Mark removed a small bag of government-issued peanuts from his pocket.

Michael frowned and held out his hand.

Mark dumped the contents into Michael's hand. Among the nuts, were eight screws.

Michael raised his eyebrows at Mark and smiled. "Thanks. I think I will win, now."

Mark looked into his eyes. "Well, Shorty, I'm going to miss playing this game with you."

Michael stared back for a moment. "Oh, Mark. No!" Michael blinked away a tear.

"Hold it together, Shorty. Yes, it's time to finish this game. Today, you're just the right size. If you win this game against Big Brother, then you'll be winning it for both of us. Go now; I'll hold 'em off."

They both stood. Michael gave Mark a bear hug. Mark's chin rested on his twin brother's head.

"It was a good game," said Mark, his voice cracking. "I don't know when we're going to play again."

As they hugged each other, Michael whispered to Mark, "They might be able to hear me, so just listen: I've been thinking about where

I might go if I ever got out— someplace safe for a while. You will find me among my own kind. I have to rush. More will hide me later."

Michael squeezed his brother's arm and said, "Remember what I said."

Mark grabbed the metal chair, hauled it above his head, and smashed it against the camera. The lens cracked and the camera hung limply by one wire. He hopped onto the chair, grabbed the camera, and ripped it from the wall.

"Go! Just pull on the door!"

Michael complied and yanked hard on the door; it flung open. Michael glanced at his twin one last time and escaped into the hallway.

Mark knew that their captors would be sending a repair crew at any time. But they'd have no way of knowing that Michael had left, so maybe the staff wouldn't hurry. But Mark planned to be ready for them. He grabbed his helpful chair and used it one more time by jamming it under the door knob. It rested at an angle on two legs. Mark kicked the chair legs in tighter. Next he pushed the bed against the chair, and then the heavy metal table against the bed, creating a line of furniture against the door.

A four foot gap remained between the table and the wall. Mark jammed himself into the small space and sat with his back to the wall, his legs pressed against the solid metal legs of the table. He was prepared to push with his full strength when the staff came to open the door.

That should slow them down a bit.

He knew he couldn't hold out for long, but by the time they busted into the room, Michael may have had a 15-20 minute start.

Apparently, they didn't suspect an escape, because it was 15 minutes before Mark heard a guard and a repairman outside the door. The guard tried to push open the door, and then slammed his shoulder against it. Both men pushed against it. After several minutes, other guards arrived and added their shoulders.

As he sat there, listening to the guards yelling outside the door, Mark thought about how many weeks he had worked on that vent. The shower was in the old locker room down the hall and the vent was just above head level. He had used the end of a stolen spoon to work on the

The Smart Kid

screws each time he took a shower. The decades-old screws were solidly fastened, and the spoon wasn't the right instrument for the job, but he worked at it for as long as he could during his showers and then re-hid the spoon under the shower bench.

Every time Mark worked at it, straining his hands on the metal spoon, he remembered his father's words, *"Inch by inch, it's a cinch."* Once he'd removed the first of the eight screws, he had hope that the rest would come out with weeks of patient work.

He wasn't certain that the vent led to the outside, or even if there were no obstructions that might stop Michael. It was a risk, but it was their only choice. Mark knew that he wasn't going to fit in the vent, but suspected that Michael would be able to squeeze through.

First, his brother would need to jump up and knock off the vent cover, as it sat loosely in position. Then he'd have to haul himself up by his fingers with no support for his feet on the tiled wall of the shower. Maybe the notch for the soggy soap bar would help him. Mark realized that Michael was probably doing just that while he thought about it.

Two red-faced guards were jamming their bodies hard against the door. They yelled obscenities and threats. "What do you hope to accomplish? We won't let you visit together again. Damn you two! When we get in, you're going to be so sorry!"

Us two? No, *they* are going to be sorry.

Mark considered what his brother had said: *"You will find me among my own kind. I have to rush. More will hide me later."*

More what?

As Michael crawled through the cramped metal tunnel in complete darkness, his elbows, hands and knees banged against the walls and floor kicking up the thick layer of dust, making him choke and cough. He knew that he was making too much noise but had no time to move cautiously.

With no warning, his outstretched hand pressed down on nothing.

He got a head-rush roller-coaster feeling as he started to tumble forward into a sightless void.

He extended his left hand to grasp at anything in the darkness. It hit an edge of the shaft and he clung for his life, as his right hand pressed against the smooth wall on the opposite side of the shaft. His head tilted down, his feet had somehow managed to stay back on the top edge. He was entirely supported by the pressure of his hands on the opposite sides of the vertical shaft.

How to get himself righted before his arms gave out? If he let go with his left or right hand, he'd fall head-forward into the void. Michael had no idea how far he'd tumble, but he didn't want to find out.

He had to step into the shaft with his right foot and press it against the top edge. Supported by his left hand and his right foot, he was able to shift his right hand upward a few inches. After a few quick, upward jerks with his right hand, it caught the top edge of the shaft.

After he crossed the two-foot chasm, he stopped for a minute and caught his breath, and listened to his heart thump wildly. Then Michael proceeded with more caution and used his right hand like a blind man's cane testing the safety of each step.

As Michael crawled foward, he smelled fresh air. *Mark was right!*

Finally, he reached the outside vent cover. The clean air had a hint of pine. Squinting through the grille, he saw a large, metal fence with barbed-wire strands across the top.

Almost free!

Michael tried to push open the outside cover; and then slammed his shoulder against it. It didn't move. He pounded it until his hands were sore. He had no leverage to force off the cover.

He tried to flip his body around so that he could kick at the grille, but the metal tunnel was too narrow for him to maneuver.

Did I come all this way to get stuck in a ventilation tunnel? A rat in a trap.

Michael backed up until he reached the vertical shaft that had nearly finished him. He eased himself into the shaft, allowing his legs to dangle unsupported and held himself in place with his hands flat onto the metal floor of the vent. With nothing to grip, his weight began to drag him down as his hands slid along the vent.

Michael switched one hand from its precarious perch to the opposite side of the shaft, slipping down slightly, but turning 90

The Smart Kid

degrees. His arms were extended and supporting him on either side of the shaft where his body hung. He strained to push his feet against the sides of the shaft and force himself up onto the other side as he completed his rotation.

Now Michael was on the wrong side of the shaft, facing away from the outside vent cover. He backed over the hole with the utmost caution, bracing his hands against the sides of the duct and tried not to imagine falling into it. He continued backward all the way to the outside vent cover and rolled himself onto his back. Shaking from the exertion and stress, he rested.

Michael pulled his leg back intending to kick with full force, but his knee banged the inside of the air duct, his attempted kick, nothing more than a tap. After two more tries, he twisted his body to the right, placing his back against the side of the shaft. He was able to pull his knee up further, but not as far as he wanted.

He kicked at the cover as hard as he could.

On the first kick, the repercussion felt as if he'd kicked a wall of solid rock. But on the second thrust, he heard a crack. A few more enthusiastic kicks and the cover thumped to the ground. Michael slid out feet first, his body hanging against the wall and clung with his fingers inside the vent. He twisted his head to judge the distance. A drop of five more feet.

He let go. His feet jarred against the ground and he recoiled forward nearly smashing his head into the side of the building.

Outside!

Michael involuntarily smiled as he surveyed the grounds.

He ran to the section of metal fence furthest from the building and obscured by shadows of trees. The fence wouldn't be a problem, but the three strands of needle-sharp barbed wire would be. This fence wasn't designed to keep people *out* because the top bent inward. This made it impossible to scale from the inside of the compound without getting slashed on the barbed wire. He looked at the barbs and wondered if they'd bite through his thin jacket.

Michael removed his jacket and climbed the chain-linked fence until he was just below the three strands of barbed wire. With a single hand-grip on the fence, he held the jacket by a sleeve and swung it up and over the fence. It hit the top strand and flipped around the wires. The sleeve slipped down between the fence and the lowest strand of barbs. Still working with one hand, he tied the sleeves in a knot while his left hand cramped hard around the fence.

Michael nervously glanced at the building every few minutes.

When the knot was completed, he jumped down from the fence back into captivity. He searched the ground and found a stout branch. Re-climbing the fence, he inserted the heavy stick into the knotted sleeves of his jacket. As Michael twisted it, his jacket tightened around the three barbed strands. When it became too difficult to continue with just one hand, he hooked the toes of his sneakers into the fence and grabbed the stick with both hands.

He hung at a precarious 45 degree angle, like a rock climber trying to surmount an outcropping. His toes stuck into the fence and his hands held the stick twisted into the coat as his thin body stretched between. If he slipped loose, he'd drop flat on his back to the ground six feet below. This risky maneuver allowed him to rapidly twist the branch. It tightened the jacket around the three strands and forced them together until they almost touched, creating a small opening between the lowest strand of barbed wire and the top of the fence. Michael hooked an end of the stick under a strand to stop it from spinning loose.

He dragged himself upward through the narrow space. The gap between the top of the fence and the barbs was barely large enough for his thin body. As he squirmed through, a sharp barb hooked into his thin shirt. He tried to wriggle through but was held back.

Michael was stuck like a fly in a barbed web.

He reached over his shoulder and grabbed his shirt behind his neck. He repeatedly jerked it until the barb ripped free and instantly recoiled into his back. Michael cried out in pain. The barb scratched him the full length of his back as he finally pulled himself through the opening.

One more scar...

He paused, hanging on the other side of the fence, and looked at the old, brick dormitory that had been his prison for 18 months and still held his twin brother. He focused on Mark and thought,

The Smart Kid

"Thanks!" Message sent.

Michael dropped to freedom.

Mr. Harper reluctantly walked into Senator Perkins's office. "Sir, you told me to always talk to you personally about this; that's why I didn't call."

Perkins rested his burning cigar on the ashtray. "What in *The Hell* is it, Harper?"

"He got away ... sir."

"What? Which one? You mean ... him?"

"Yes, sir. He's so small that he squeezed through the humidity vent in the shower room. No one thought it could be opened. It wasn't considered an escape route."

"Well, it sure the hell turned out to be didn't it?" spit out Perkins. "Now you have really screwed the pooch, haven't you? If he goes to the police, or the press— God forbid— then we are through! Done!"

"Well, sir," said Harper, measuring his words, "Our Tactical Operations team has decided that he won't take that course of action."

"Why the hell not?"

"To the world he appears to be a little kid. No one is going to take him seriously. Should he go to the press, we can deflect any inquiries to that facility since it is mostly just government storage space. It doesn't look like a prison. And we can quickly scrub any evidence."

The Senator seemed to be considering this, so Harper pressed his point further. "He has nothing to tell the police or the media. He'll sound like a kid playing a prank. Also, and this may be his main motivation for not stirring up trouble, we still have his brother." Harper watched the Senator's reaction.

Perkins leaned back in his chair, and stroked his chin as he stared out the window.

"We've determined that Shale's only option is to go home to his mother. Since his father died two months ago, he'll want to console her. And we'll have our team waiting for him. He's got to go there. Where else can he go?"

"Yes, where?" asked the Senator, still staring out the

window. He turned to Harper. "What about the other one; is he any good to us?"

"Well, sir," said Harper, pausing to push the black-rimmed glasses up the bridge of his nose. "Um, we'll continue our tests on him. But so far, he seems to be a normally-aging man. Other than the baseline comparison, he hasn't given us any clues to his brother's anti-aging. So he may only be valuable as a hostage to keep Michael silent."

"And now that the punk is gone, do we have any valuable data that we've learned from him?"

"Well, of course we still have all the physical samples that we've taken: blood, hair, skin, and biopsies of every organ in his body."

"Every one, huh?"

"Yes. It wasn't very pleasant for him, but he was under sedation ... usually."

"So?"

"The docs haven't made any progress since the initial discovery of the chromosome differential. They've been conducting live tests on Shale to see if they can extract the genetic information in some way. But so far ..."

"In other words, we have to catch the little freak again."

"Yes sir. And now that he knows we're coming for him, it's going to be much more difficult."

"I'm sure it will be," said the Senator, as he raised his cigar and crushed it down violently into the ashtray.

28. Freedom

MICHAEL SPRINTED THROUGH a light forest that opened into a field of tall grass. He might have enjoyed a stroll through the field on that cloudless August day if he wasn't running for his life. But it was no stroll; it was a long, long jog for an unknown number of hours. There was almost nothing to hear as he ran through vacant lands, only the crunching of the grass under his feet and his heavy breathing as he pushed his muscles to their limit. He stayed off roads, cutting through fields, forests and shallow valleys that occasionally hid lazy, trickling streams. At one of these streams he paused to rest. Michael peered into the water. Below his rippling reflection he could clearly see the pebbly bottom of the stream. He scooped handfuls of cool, fresh water to his mouth. It renewed his strength and his resolve to continue.

After an hour, he came to a gravel road. He ran along it past acres of pines, oaks, and unknown trees until he was so tired that his sneakers scraped on the gravel with each lethargic step. The rumbling of an approaching vehicle made him dive into the ditch. He peaked out from the tall grass.

It was an old, red pickup truck with wooden side boards driven by a man wearing an orange cap.

Michael jumped out of the ditch at the last second and waved his hands above his head. The pickup truck skidded to a stop on the gravel. Michael approached the truck on the driver's side. The window was open.

"Young man, why are you out here by yourself?"

Michael had already resolved to say nothing that might put his brother at risk. So, in an earnest, child-like tone, he said, "Oh, uh, I was taking a walk and got lost. Could I have a ride into … town." Michael had no idea what the town was called.

"Cove Gap or Charlestown?"

Michael hesitated.

"You don't wanna go all the way up to Bear Lick, do you?"

"No," Michael shook his head, "of course not all the way to Bear

The Smart Kid

Lick. Cove Gap please."

The man smiled. "OK. Hop in."

After Michael had settled into the passenger seat, the old man looked him over from head to toe. "You walked all this way from Cove Gap?"

"Well ... I ran a bit."

"Jogger, huh?"

"Can I ask what is down that road further?"

"Nothin' anymore, as far as I know. I just came here to do some hunting." The man motioned to the rifle that hung against the back window of the cab.

The sight of it filled Michael with dread. It reminded him of the sidearms used by the police, who arrested him, and the guards that had controlled his life since February, 1962. He tried to ignore it. "Hunting?"

"Yup. Unsanctioned hunting, if you know what I mean."

Michael didn't know what he meant. Nor did he know what state Cove Gap was in. But after the man dropped him off, he walked along the road and looked at the license plates of the cars. Most of the cars were from Pennsylvania but a few had Maryland plates. An anxious search revealed a service station where Michael asked to look at a map. He discovered that he was in southern Pennsylvania. *Pennsylvania!* He had a disorienting feeling, reminding him of his first day waking up in his new prison cell.

What now?

Michael thought it unlikely that he was going to be caught, but he wasn't ready to relax yet. He needed to go ... where? *Iowa! Yes, Mom!*

The last time that he'd spoken to her was from the city jail. He'd promised to visit his mother as soon as he was able. He regretted that he hadn't spoken to his father at that time. *Dad!* Michael burned with anger at Perkins. He forced himself to stop thinking about it. There were more immediate concerns: He was a thousand miles from home, had no money, and no transportation. And he was getting hungry.

Michael expected to hitchhike all the way back to Iowa, but the thin, deserted road gave little hope for a would-be hitchhiker. He needed to reach a busy, major highway. But the one he wanted was at least 30 miles away, according to the map. With no other option, he walked west through the small town.

A school bus was parked on the street and dozens of students were scurrying out to the nearby cafe. A woman said, "This is our bathroom break before we return to Everett, so take advantage of it."

Everett! Michael had seen that city on the map; it was on the highway he needed.

He stared at the bus, wondering if he should ask for a ride and risk rejection. A car slowly eased up the road and slipped into his awareness. The tan highway patrol car was a block away, its two occupants turned their heads left and right, scanning the street.

The decision had been made for him. Michael walked toward the throng of students and mixed himself among them. Several students sat on sidewalk benches. Michael sat on a bench beside three boys who looked twelve years old. The blond boy sitting next to him wore bib overalls and a gray long sleeve shirt. Michael's heart was beating so hard he could feel it.

The patrol car passed right in front of Michael and the students. He bent down and slowly retied the laces on his sneakers, eyeing the vehicle.

The boy wearing the bib overalls frowned down at Michael. "Who are you?"

Michael's heart thumped harder.

Wow, I feel like I'm about to commit a felony or something.

Michael sat up and faced the boy. "I'm … new."

The highway patrol car pulled off the road and parked nearby. Two officers got out and started walking toward the swarming students, turning their heads left and right scanning the surroundings.

Michael's eyes flicked from the boy's face to gaze over his shoulder at the approaching authorities. He noticed the heat of the day and wiped the perspiration from his forehead.

The boy scrunched up his face as if he smelled something bad. He turned his gaze left and right searching for something or someone.

Michael's attention became divided between the uniformed authorities and the blond boy who had stood and was waving his

The Smart Kid

hands.

The teacher said, "Students, get on the bus!"

The scrunched-face kid yelled, "Hey, Mrs. Harrison!" She didn't hear him. He yelled again, attracting the attention of the patrolmen.

Michael slouched down into the bench like a scared animal.

The patrol men were on Michael's left, and the boy calling for the teacher was on his right. Michael scanned the area for a good escape route. His legs tensed, rebelling against another run.

The boy ran toward the teacher as he yelled, "Mrs. Harrison, don't go yet. I gotto pee!"

"Well, hurry up, Lester!"

Lester ran into the cafe.

Thump-thump. Big sigh.

Michael jumped to his feet and infiltrated among the surge of students shuffling toward the bus. When he got on the bus, he headed for the only empty seat near the back. He squeezed against a window, trying to be as inconspicuous as possible.

Too late, Michael realized that his window faced the sidewalk where the patrolmen were standing, looking at the students exiting the cafe.

One of them held a piece of paper. He turned it toward the other officer. Michael recognized his high school yearbook photo. They looked toward the bus. Michael turned his face away from them and slumped down in his seat. He held his breath, too afraid to lift his head to peek out the window.

As students crowded into the bus, none sat with Michael. Lester popped through the door of the bus. He walked toward the back and looked in Michael's direction. He scanned the bus one more time and finally sat in Michael's seat, as far on the edge as possible. Lester just stared at Michael with his scrunched up face.

Michael smiled at him, relieved. Alone in the seat he had been too conspicuous. He peered out the window at the patrolmen. They were showing the photo to the teacher, Mrs. Harrison. She shook her head. The officer put the photo in his pocket and turned away.

Michael shuddered, feeling like a hunted animal.

The teacher entered the bus and began counting the students. She pointed at each student as she mouthed the numbers. "... forty-one, forty-two and forty-three." Mrs. Harrison frowned and scanned the faces of the students as she stood at the front of the bus.

Michael put his head down and pressed it against the seat in front of him. He forced himself to take a few relaxing, deep breaths. He didn't look up until he heard her voice again.

Mrs. Harrison turned to another teacher, and said, "Hey! Did I miscount before? We seem to have an extra one."

The other teacher laughed. "Yeah, like that ever happens. Surely, you must have counted wrong in the first place."

"Maybe," said Mrs. Harrison. Projecting her voice over the heads of the students, she said, "Students, look around the bus ..."

Michael's felt like he couldn't breathe. He eyed the emergency exit just a few seats away.

Mrs. Harrison continued, "Make sure that your buddy is on the bus with you. ... Everyone have their buddy here?"

All the students nodded their heads, including Michael, who breathed easily again.

Still standing, Mrs. Harrison said, "OK listen! Both my class and Mrs. Jorgenson's will be expected to write a report about your trip to Buchanan's Birthplace State Park. It can be about the park or the president."

Several students moaned their complaints.

Mrs. Harrison told the bus driver they were ready and took a seat.

The grinding of the bus's gears covered Michael's loud exhalation. He closed his eyes for a few seconds. When Michael opened them, he saw Lester studying him as if he were trying to figure out a difficult math problem.

Michael looked out the window and watched the town fade into the distance. He was a twenty-three-year-old man hiding among a busload of sixth-graders in southern Pennsylvania. *Perkins will never find me now.*

"I hate writing reports."

It took a second for Michael to realize that this comment was directed at him. Lester was still looking at him, but appeared upset. Michael used to hate doing reports too, when he was in school.

The Smart Kid

"It's not so bad," ventured Michael. He didn't know why he was helping; but he was there and he had an opportunity. "Just write anything you want about the park and then write these three things about James Buchanan. Say that he was the only president from Pennsylvania."

"He was?"

"Yes. And say that he was the fifteenth president."

"He was?"

"Yes. And say that he was the only one who never got married—yes, he was." Michael pointed at Lester and grinned.

Lester's face un-scrunched. "Thanks. You're smart!"

Michael turned to face the window again, hiding his smile.

Thirty minutes later the bus stopped at the school in Everett. Mrs. Harrison announced that there were a few left-over bag lunches for anyone to take.

Michael took two and bolted out to freedom. He breathed another sigh of relief. *Michael the criminal.* He walked west along the highway, as he devoured baloney sandwiches and potato chips as if it was a gourmet meal.

The sun was shining and it was a beautiful day. *It's the little things...*

29. On The Road

AFTER A 20-minute walk, Michael reached the west edge of the town. Whenever a car approached, he faced it and stuck out his thumb. After four cars passed, a large truck pulling a semi-trailer grumbled to a stop; the air brakes hissed their greeting. Michael ran to it and opened the passenger door as he hopped unto the step and peered into the truck.

The driver frowned as Michael stared at him with raised eyebrows and a friendly smile. "Hey, little feller. Why are you out here hitching? Where are your parents?"

"Hello, sir. I'm not that little. I'm 23."

"Don't be lying to someone that you're asking for a ride!"

Michael had no way to prove what he was saying. "OK, sir, I'm sorry. Um, I'm trying to get back to my mother. My dad is dead and I was with my uncle for a long time."

"I don't think that I should be givin' no ride to a little kid who's run away from his kin-folk. Does your uncle know that you're gone?"

"He probably does now, but I had to leave him because he was mean. He hit my back with a switch." Michael turned his back to the trucker, and pulled up his shirt to reveal the long red scratch. The shirt had been stuck to dried blood and when he jerked it, fresh wounds opened. Michael winced.

"Well, that SOB! I'm sorry that you got treated poorly. I'll help you, little guy. Hop in."

Michael had never hitch-hiked, although it was a popular form of travel for students his age. But he was amazed at how easy it was. Apparently, people were eager to help a kid in trouble.

The trucker didn't ask many questions, which pleased Michael. He talked about fishing the whole trip. Lonely Roy was obviously glad for the companionship.

As Roy told non-stop fish stories, Michael had time to consider his manipulative dishonesty. He was bothered by his own deceitfulness. For the third time, he'd acted like a young boy to get help from adults.

The Smart Kid

He'd always been honest in his earlier life, but it seemed that his new life-style was forcing him to make moral compromises.

Roy drove him nearly 100 miles and nearly crazy with all the fish talk. It was further south than Michael wanted, but he was just relieved to be closer to home, and to be finally saying good-bye to the trucker.

"Thank-you, Roy!" yelled Michael up to the trucker, as he drove away. Roy had dropped him off near Morgantown, West Virginia.

The sun was a glowing orange resting on the tops of the western trees. Soon Michael would be hitching in the dark— diminishing his chances for a ride. He continued walking west.

As the darkening sky began to steal colors from the landscape, Michael lost hope of getting a lift. Behind him, the sky was dark. In front of him, a crimson glow still illuminated the western sky.

An old blue van rumbled to a stop. The side door opened and three young people about his age, his real age, looked out at him.

"Come on, brother. Take a trip with us," said the white guy with the long hair.

The others began laughing.

The driver turned and said, "Yeah man, a trip."

Michael crawled into the van. The interior of the van, from floor to ceiling, was carpeted in a vibrant orange. Blue tassels outlined the windows. Instead of car seats, the back was filled with cushions and bean bag chairs.

The three passengers in the back were JoJo, Melanie, and Franky. There were two men up front: Mack, and the driver, Otter, or Otto— Michael wasn't sure which. JoJo had a large afro hairstyle. He wore a green embroidered vest without a shirt, which showed off his muscular brown chest. Franky wore tinted glasses that may have been prescription because he kept them on every minute. And he had hair everywhere: long hair hanging from his head, a mustache, a beard, and hair sticking out of his unbuttoned shirt. Melanie was a thin blonde with straggly hair wrapped with a headband and adorned with a yellow flower.

"Where you going to?" Melanie asked.

"Iowa— But I'll take a ride as near as you can get me, please," said Michael.

"Hey, Ott! Are we going near Iowa?" she yelled to the driver. Ott said something to Mack, who pulled out a map from the glove box and unfolded it. He shook his head and mumbled something.

"Nope. Kansas City is as close as we get," said Ott.

"Yes! That would be fine. Wonderful!" said Michael. He couldn't believe his luck.

"Were you at the festival?" asked Melanie.

Michael furrowed his brow. "The festival?"

"That means *no*," she said. "We're returning from the Newport Folk Festival."

"Oh. How was it?"

"It was so awesome! We saw Dylan and Pete Seeger. And we watched the Freedom Singers and the Rooftop Singers. And I was able to walk right up to Joan Baez and talk with her when she walked along the beach!"

JoJo spoke up. "Yeah, man. The music was incessant. Everywhere you looked there was people, and instruments, and lots of love and peace between all colors. It was totally groovy. You could sleep anywhere."

"Sounds pretty good. I wish I could have been there. I really do," Michael said.

"A large group of singers," said Melanie, "both blacks and whites, got up on stage and, holding hands, sang *We Shall Overcome* in support of the civil rights movement and the victims of the Birmingham attack."

"What Birmingham attack?"

The group stared at him for a moment. Even Ott turned away from the road to glance at him. Michael thought that he had asked a bad question.

"Where have you been?" Melanie asked. "The whole country knows about the Birmingham police blasting the peaceful protesters with fire hoses!"

"Oh my. That's terrible! I'm so sorry, I didn't know. I've been … incarcerated for a long time." Michael watched for their reactions. There was an immediate softening of their faces from their previous surprised looks.

The Smart Kid

JoJo said, "That's OK, man. That means that you understand the value of freedom. Dr. King said, *'Some day we will win our freedom.'* Feels good, don't it?"

"Yes, great! Hey I heard Martin Luther King speak at the University of Iowa, my sophomore year," said Michael.

"Even better! Give me some skin, college boy." He held out his hand.

Michael gave him a two-handed solidarity hand-shake and a nod, while looking him in the eye.

"So you went to college?" asked Melanie.

Michael just nodded.

Everyone was silent for a few minutes.

From the front seat, Mack said, "Dylan is the best. He's a Freewheelin' Free Spirit."

Franky smiled and nodded his head in agreement, as he pulled a comb through his long black hair.

Twisting to face the four riders in the back, Mack continued, "Did you know that he walked off the Ed Sullivan Show? They wouldn't let him play *Talkin' John Birch Paranoid Blues.*"

"That was a righteous decision," said JoJo, scratching his bare chest.

"Hey, Mack," said Franky. "Do your Bob Dylan impersonation for our new friend."

"OK." Mack sang a phrase in a very raspy low voice, "The aaanswer my frie-end, is blowin' in the wi-ind!"

Everyone laughed.

Melanie nudged Michael with her knee. "Hey, you try it."

Michael shook his head. "No, my voice is too high."

"Don't be shy. We're all friends here," Melanie said, delicately touching his shoulder.

Michael caught his breath for a second. She'd touched his arm where he'd received numerous shots and those memories flooded his mind. She was the first friendly stranger to touch him in 18 months. The contrast shocked him.

"Thank-you," Michael smiled and stared into her blue eyes.

"Just make your voice low and gravelly," she said.

Michael cleared his throat and imitated what Mack had just done, but with surprising results. His voice sounded deep and mature. He sounded like a middle-aged man. He surprised himself.

"Whoah man! That was amazing!" said Franky.

"You sound like a different person. How'd you do that?" Melanie exclaimed.

"I don't know," said Michael. Then, in his low voice, he repeated, "I really don't know." Everyone stared in amazement.

Michael liked the group. No one asked him about his parents; they treated him like an adult. The ride was a pleasant respite from the worried run-for-his-life of the morning.

The AM radio picked up various stations along the way.

Mack lit up a joint, took a hit, and passed it to Michael. The memory of the marijuana-filled cigar box in the hands of Special Agent Watts flashed through his mind. He shook his head at the bad memory as he passed the joint to Melanie.

She raised it to her lips but stopped when she met Michael's gaze and just passed it to JoJo.

For miles, they listened to the radio. They heard the Beach Boys singing *Surfin' USA*, and The Chiffons singing *He's So Fine*; and Bobby Vinton, and Roy Orbison. And then Michael Shale and his new friends listened to Peter, Paul and Mary do Bob Dylan, as they sang *Blowin' in the Wind*.

> *How many roads must a man walk down*
> *Before you call him a man?...*

They drove deep into the night until Ott pulled over near a patch of trees grouped along a vacant side road. The guys removed blankets and sleeping bags and spread them under the stars. Inside the van, Melanie curled up next to Michael. Their faces were inches apart.

She gave him an intense stare. "You're out of prison, but you're still not free, are you?"

His eyes penetrated hers.

She removed the flower from her hair, and clipped it on Michael's head.

"Now you're a flower child. May that free your heart."

"Thanks," Michael replied with a quiet smile.

The Smart Kid

Just before he fell asleep, she touched the needle marks on the inside of his arm. "Are you off the heroin now?"

"That part of my life is over," he whispered.

She kissed him on the cheek. "I'm glad for you," she breathed out.

And Michael listened to the wind blow.

The next day, they drove for twelve hours until they reached Kansas City, around 7:00. Melanie gave Michael a hug before he climbed out of the van and waved good-bye. His hippie friends had shared their time, friendship, and food, and he was truly thankful.

Michael walked to a service station to check a map and started hitching again. It didn't take long before a tan car with a long front end stopped near Michael. He opened the passenger door and said to the driver, "I'm going north to Iowa."

"Hop in, I'll take you pretty close to Des Moines," said the middle-aged man.

Michael got in and thanked him for stopping.

The man gave him an odd look. "Are you one of them hippie teens?"

Michael realized the man was looking at the flower in his hair. He removed the flower and hair pin and stuck them in his pocket.

They had only driven north for 20 minutes, when the man, who was named Charles, said, "I'm hungry. Let's get something to eat—my treat!" He drove to an A&W Root Beer stand. He parked under the white tin car port and, in a few minutes, a girl arrived to take their order. Charles ordered a burger, fries and a root beer. Michael ordered a cheeseburger, fries and a large root beer.

While they waited, Michael asked, "What type of car is this?"

Charles grinned. "This is the last of its kind: A Studebaker Avanti. It's from the final Studebaker run. I got it from a dealer in Indiana on one of my sales trips. I paid over forty-four hundred. But it's worth it. This car has got a fiberglass body. It'll never rust. Less than 6000 were produced. It's the end of an era." He slid his hand along the dash. "Someday, when you're older, you'll have the pleasure of driving a car you love."

"I'm older than I look."

"Oh yes, I'm sure you are," Charles said, with a wink.

The girl returned, carrying a tray of food. Charles had rolled down the window, so she hung the tray on the side of the car. "That'll be 95 cents."

"Here you go, little lady. And you keep the change," Charles said, grinning at her.

"Thanks! You and your son have a great day!" She left smiling.

Michael smiled at the assumption too.

As they ate, Charles continued their previous conversation. "Well, *son*," he said emphasizing the word as a joke, "I hope that you're looking for your momma."

Michael was surprised and showed it.

"A young boy like you shouldn't be out on your own. How'd you get separated from her?"

Michael considered his response for a moment. "My uncle needed my help and wouldn't take *no* for an answer. But now I'm headed home." Just saying those words made him happy.

Then Charles said something heart-stopping. "Does he know that you're going home?"

Oh no, Of course he does!

Since his escape, Michael had been thinking that he was getting further and further from his pursuers. But instead, he was getting closer and closer to the destination that they would expect; the place where they would definitely be looking for him, lying in wait. *A trap.*

"Yes. He does," admitted Michael, resting his head in his hands.

Where do I go?

The question bothered him for the rest of the ride. He couldn't go home. He couldn't go back to college. That was the end of an era too.

He had one choice.

As soon as I'm able, I'll have to hide among my own kind. If Mark ever escapes, he'll start looking for me there.

But Michael had preparations to do first.

30. Iowa

Harper fidgeted beside Senator Perkin's desk, waiting for his boss to finish reading a police bulletin he'd just delivered. The bulletin had been sent to law enforcement agencies in Maryland, Pennsylvania and Iowa. It included a photograph of Michael Shale and described him as a juvenile criminal who had committed a drug trafficking felony.

"The fugitive is a very young looking man with an apparent age of twelve (12), with blond hair, blue eyes, 5' 4" tall, 115 pounds."

The memo ordered law enforcement officials not to intervene, but simply to track him and call the phone number.

A hand-written note read, *"No information yet."*

"Damn! It's been two days since he escaped. He could be anywhere by now!" yelled Perkins, scowling at Harper as if he were responsible for the escape.

The Studebaker Avanti cruised through the night, northward to Des Moines. Although it was late, Michael's anxious desire to start his plan kept him wide-awake.

When they neared the small city of Osceola, Charles suddenly turned the car west.

Michael gave him a surprised look.

"In a few miles we'll reach the new highway, Interstate 35. It's only completed up to Des Moines, but it will be non-stop, smooth sailing until then," said Charles. "When we get to Des Moines, where do you want to be dropped off?"

"Any exit. Charles you've been so helpful, I hate to ask you for one more thing ... but could I have a dime to call my mom?"

Charles smiled at Michael. "Is that all? I'm glad to help you reunite with her."

"Thank-you very much," said Michael.

It was nearly 11:00 pm when Charles turned off the interstate and

The Smart Kid

stopped at the top of the exit ramp, somewhere south of Des Moines.

Michael hopped out and stood alone, listening to the drone of the Avanti fade into silence. The sky was cloudless. In the starlight, Michael looked left and right. *What now?*

He was so close; he couldn't stand it anymore. Michael had to find a phone and call his mother. Throughout his two-day journey, he'd imagined just dropping in on her. *"Surprise!"* But then he'd realized that he couldn't go home; a phone call was his only option.

There was a phone booth by a darkened service station. He entered the small glass booth and pushed the door shut. A light turned on above him. It was late, but he couldn't wait until the morning. He momentarily panicked as he felt for the dime in his pocket ... there it was; one small coin to initiate his big plans.

His fingers fumbled on the dial. He could hardly wait for the return rotation of each number. Finally, it was ringing ...

"Hello?" said the sleepy voice of Jan Shale.

Michael was speechless. The last time they'd talked, he'd been away from home for a year, and had called her from jail. Since that time, he'd been out of touch for another year and a half. Would she be mad at him? He considered hanging up. He heard his own breathing.

"Mom?"

"Oh, my! Is it my Michael?"

He calmed himself. "Yes, Mom. It's Michael. I'm OK."

"Oh, thank God. My prayers have been answered! I was so worried, only receiving that one letter from you."

Oh yes. The letter.

"Did you get *my* letter?" she asked.

"Yes. I'm so sorry that I wasn't there."

"Neither was Mark. I couldn't locate him. He quit his job and vanished."

Michael took a deep breath. *Will it hurt her more to hear the truth? Does she really need this?*

"Mom, Mark was with me."

"Oh, good. I'm so glad! How is he?" She sounded tearfully happy.

Another breath. *Here goes.*

"Mom, you remember those letters that we got from Senator

Perkins?"

"Yes." It was a cautiously spoken syllable.

"I think that he had something to do with our ... time. We weren't actually *working* for the government. Someone, or some organization, had us incarcerated in an old military dormitory in Pennsylvania."

"Oh no!" she gasped.

Oh, my poor mom.

"They were doing tests on us—both of us—to see what makes me ... special. They want my anti-aging secret, Momma."

There. He had told her. *She'll probably crumble apart ...*

"I always feared something like this, since the day you were born, knowing how unique you were. I just never thought that it could happen in America." Her voice cracked.

Or was it the connection crackling?

"Mom, I'm out now. And I'm very happy to tell you that they don't know where I am."

"Oh, that's a relief. I'm so glad! And Mark?"

Michael remained silent and heard the line crackle again.

"Oh dear."

"Momma, listen, Mark has no medical value to them now. So I don't think that they'll keep him much longer." He tried to give her hope, using his voice to support her. *How did she manage without me?*

"Where are you? Do you need some money?" She sounded strong.

"Yes! Mom. Please contact Mr. Monaghan and tell him to start the funds disbursement on our investments. As soon as possible, I'll need funds deposited in my savings account at our bank. I'll notify him later about other locations to wire the money. But Mom, don't call him. Please go to his office tomorrow. He's going to have some information for you; very important information from me. And tell him to keep it private."

"He's very discreet, Michael."

"I'm counting on that. Now, Mom ..."

"Yes?"

"This is the hardest part that I have to tell you."

He heard her exhale. "OK."

The Smart Kid

"They are still looking for me. I can't come home." He waited for her to start crying.

"Oh. I understand."

She didn't seem to be falling apart.

"I have to run and hide … for a long time."

"Michael, I'd rather have you run and be free, than to risk contacting me. Your father was a military man. But he wasn't the only one in our family who served his country. My service was taking care of you boys without him, and waiting. I've done it before, and I can do it again. You go. Live your life, and grow into the man your father and I always knew you'd become."

Her words lifted him and motivated him to push forward. He was like a new hatchling in a nest, pushed out by the support of his mother and forced to fly.

"I love you, Mom."

"I love you too."

He hung up the phone, and leaned his head against the glass. The light illuminated him as he stood motionless in a glass box in the southern end of Des Moines, Iowa, under the stars.

Where to fly now?

It was nearly midnight. Michael had been walking for 20 minutes looking for somewhere to sleep. He had no money, no blanket, and no extra clothes. He was like an inexperienced homeless person, not knowing what he was searching for: a park shelter, or an abandoned house, or … something.

Michael passed through the shadow of a dark building and then it came into view: a church. He saw the white illuminated cross first. It filled him with hope. It was a solid-looking structure of old, brown brick.

Filled with expectation, he reached for the black, iron handle on the weathered, wooden door and pulled— It didn't move. Locked. Still holding the handle, he leaned his head against the door and tapped the base with his shoe and tried to think what he should do next. After a minute, he turned around, walked down the two stone steps, and away from the church as his eyes surveyed dark buildings for any possible shelter.

"Young man, do you need help?"

Michael spun around to see a man dressed in a black smock holding the door open. Light from the church poured out, illuminating Michael. He walked toward the minister, and said in his high-pitched boyish voice, "Yes. I need somewhere to sleep tonight."

The minister stepped back, motioning for Michael to enter.

"Where are your parents? Why are you out alone?" the man asked gently.

"I've been gone for a long time but I'm almost back home." That seemed to be enough for the minister.

As the man escorted Michael, he said, "For special circumstances, we allow people to sleep here." He led Michael to a small, simple room with blue walls, a table and a single bed, neatly covered with a white bedspread and a white, puffy pillow.

It looked like heaven to Michael.

"I'll come and check on you in the morning. I'm Pastor Johanson. Good-night." He walked out of the room, and left the door open.

Michael stared at the open door. *"You understand the value of freedom"*

He surveyed the room, relieved that he didn't have to sleep outside. It was a small kindness for the minister, not costing him much effort or trouble. But to Michael it was a great act of generosity and compassion.

He walked to the table. There was a Bible opened to Ecclesiastes. Michael scanned the page and stopped at an insightful phrase:

> "And a man may attack and prevail against him that is alone, but two shall withstand him; and a threefold cord is not quickly broken."

Michael wondered if a secret government committee was trying to cage Solomon when he wrote that line. He jumped to the bed, removed his shoes, and curled his legs under him.

One man can be attacked and conquered, but not three. If only ...

The minister had fed him, let him use a telephone for an important

The Smart Kid

call to Mr. Monaghan, and then sent him on his way. Michael had thanked him profusely.

Michael had one day to get to the bank by Thursday morning. An easy 100 miles separated him from his destination.

He walked down the entrance ramp, past a sign that proclaimed this new four-lane highway to be part of the Eisenhower Interstate System. Walking north on the interstate, he thumbed for a ride again. Immediately, a car approached and slowed. But it wasn't what Michael had expected.

The yellow badge-shaped logo printed on the two doors of the black Chevrolet read 'Iowa Highway Patrol.' A red dome-shaped light on top of the vehicle lit up and began to spin around. The patrol car stopped, and an intimidating officer stepped out.

"Hello, young man," his deep voice boomed, as he put on his sun glasses.

"Hello," said Michael, squinting up at him.

"Do you know that hitchhiking on the interstate is illegal?" he asked, as he put his hands on his hips, in an obviously exaggerated pose of superiority.

"Golly, no mister! I did not know that. But thank-you for telling me. I will go call my mom for a ride." Michael backed away.

"Now hold it, little boy!"

Michael froze.

"Where is your mom at?"

"Um, Story City." *Better to give him a story, than the truth.*

"That's pretty far away. This interstate isn't even completed much more to the north. You wouldn't have made it on this road. I'll call her for you. What's your name, Son?"

"Look. I just talked with her, and told her that I was on my way. So there's no need to call her again," Michael implored. He did not want his name radioed over government channels detailing his location.

"I am not going to leave you out here to try to hitch a ride home. Get in. I'll bring you to Story City."

Michael didn't move. He didn't know what to do, since the officer wouldn't be able to drop him at his mom's house, which was actually in Manly.

"Get in right now!" The officer opened the passenger door. Michael shuffled toward the car.

Each step took Michael closer to confinement in a government vehicle. He imagined the officer closing a door behind him— just like every day for the last eighteen months. The officer's brown uniform reminded Michael of the uniformed guards that had escorted him to the medical lab hundreds of times. The holstered pistol on his belt, the flashing light, the expectation of obedience to authority— It was happening again …

He panicked. He turned and ran as fast as he could away from the patrol car, heading south. Michael figured that the officer wouldn't drive against traffic to catch him.

The officer was so surprised that Michael got a good head start before the officer decided what he should do. He had paused for several seconds watching Michael run south under the overpass. Michael could have run for a mile and the officer still would have been able to see him on the flat, straight highway.

Michael glanced back as the officer said, "Oh, hell!" and climbed into his patrol car and turned it around right in the middle of the northbound lane. The wheels screeched on the gray pavement as the car made the sharp u-turn and headed south, against what little traffic there was. The patrol car crept along the edge of the road, its red bubble-light spinning. It didn't have to go very fast to catch up to Michael. An approaching car swerved, narrowly missing the patrol car which stopped momentarily.

Michael had feared he'd be overtaken any second, so he took advantage of the delay to run across the northbound lane and through the narrow median. Before crossing the southbound lane, he paused for an oncoming car. He got a momentary flash of a driver's surprised face, as the car wooshed by. Then he raced up the west side of the grassy embankment.

Michael had assumed that the patrol car would have to stay on the highway and drive to an exit ramp to follow him south, giving him plenty of time to run. Michael was wrong.

The patrol car veered across both northbound lanes with a squeal. The car's front end dipped sharply as it dived into the median, cutting

The Smart Kid

deep, dirty gouges in the grass, and then popped up on the southbound lane, with a heavy thud.

It reached Michael in less than a minute. The door flew open and the patrolman followed up the hill yelling, "Stop, you little punk! Now you're just making trouble for yourself!"

Michael ran very fast for a man with the body of a twelve-year-old. But the long-legged officer easily caught up to Michael at the top of the hill. He grabbed Michael by the collar and yanked him back. Michael got slammed backward against the ground, knocking the wind out of him.

"Ow!" Michael laid flat on his back looking up at the angry face of the patrolman. The sun was directly behind the officer's head, giving him a shadowy appearance. Michael squinted at him, and tried to catch his breath.

Through heavy breaths the officer said, "I'm sorry to … have done that to you, little guy, but you've got to learn to respect Officers of the Law!" He breathed deeply. "I was only going to give you a ride home. Why'd you run? Are you in trouble?"

He pulled Michael to his feet. They walked down the hill; the officer holding him tightly.

"Oh, um, no, I'm not in trouble … I thought … I thought that you were going to arrest me and throw me in jail for hitchhiking. Then my mom would be real mad at me," Michael said earnestly.

Acting like a kid again.

"I was just going to bring you to Story City, but now your mother needs to know that you tried to run from a patrolman." The officer was using his lecture-to-a-child voice.

Michael rolled his eyes.

The officer frowned at him, pushed him into the back seat, and shut the door.

Trapped again.

As they travelled north, the officer again asked, "What's your name, son?"

"Tommy." Michael thought of his little brother who was 16. He could pass for him.

"What's your last name?"

"Smith."

The officer called on the radio and mumbled an incoherent conversation. The officer concluded with, "OK, notify me when you contact them."

They drove for many long minutes before a voice piped in over the radio. The patrolman spoke to a distant voice for several minutes. He smacked the radio mic into its clip and burned a stare at Michael in the mirror.

"What's your real name? There are no Smiths in Story City."

"Wow. Who'd have guessed that?" said Michael with a surprised frown.

"OK. The truth, funny guy. Or I'll just take you in and book you for providing false information to an Officer of The Law."

Michael could tell by the tone that he expected to scare a little kid. He sighed. "You won't believe me."

The officer waited.

"I'm older than I look. I'm really 23. My name is Michael Shale. I've been illegally incarcerated by a secret government organization for the last year and a half. I've just escaped from Pennsylvania and I'm making my way back to Iowa. So you must understand that I can't have you take me to my mother's house because agents will be waiting to recapture me there." He took a deep breath.

The officer removed his sunglasses and stared at Michael's reflection. "Oh yes, I understand. I understand that you just told a whopper!"

Michael exhaled deeply and shook his head.

"Michael Shale, huh?" Then he called on the radio again and talked in low tones. The distant voice of the patrol headquarters said, "Detain and hold at nearest police station. Suspected drug trafficker."

It was getting worse. The agent who arrested him in college had claimed that those charges would be dropped if he co-operated. That was more than a year ago. Michael started to panic. He knew that if he was locked in the jail, then his deadly pursuers would get him released into their custody and he'd never be free again.

"OK, I was kidding! Look, do I look 23? Well, do I?" Michael pleaded.

The Smart Kid

"No."

"I'm really twelve years old. I was playing a prank. I'm really Tommy Shale from Manly, Iowa. Go ahead; verify that there are Shales in Manly."

"Oh, so now you're Tommy again? And it's Shale, not Smith? And Manly, not Story City? It sounds to me like you've been sampling your own products, Pusher," the officer said. He spoke again on the radio for several minutes.

"OK, wise guy. I'm taking you to the nearest jail. We'll hold you until we can get this all sorted out. We have to confirm your identity and find out which story is true, if any. It all sounds like a bunch of BS to me."

They drove ten minutes more to the Ames police station. When they got there, the officer man-handled him into the police station.

It was a small station. There was one man behind the counter.

"What do you got there, the Lollipop thief?" joked the middle-aged police clerk.

The unsmiling patrolman said, "I'm officer Stinson with the Highway Patrol. We have a potential drug dealer here."

The clerk behind the counter looked dubious. "Put him over there, and I'll help you get him booked."

Then he said to Michael, "But first, empty your pockets."

Michael reached into his right pocket. He had forgotten about the flower. He pulled it out and set it on the counter. He thought of Melanie. The man looked at the flower and rolled his eyes. "That's it?"

Officer Stinson patted him down and led him to a chair by the wall. There was a hand-cuff bar attached to the wall. Officer Stinson put one cuff on Michael's left wrist, and attached the other cuff to the bar, and walked back to the counter.

He said to the police clerk, "He claims he's twelve, or twenty-three."

The Ames police clerk looked up from his paperwork. "Hey! Wait a minute. I think we got a notice from the Feds about a young drug trafficker ... Yes, here it is ... Yes, this kid fits the description."

He dialed a number from the memo. The police officer spoke into the phone. "I think that we have your suspect in custody here in Ames.

Yes, that's him. No, I'm looking right at him … OK. We'll hold him for you."

He hung up and said to the patrolman, "We've got ourselves a real live federal fugitive! Yeeha! Come on, I'll introduce you to the chief. He's going to want to meet you."

They left the room.

Eight minutes later, they came back into the central lobby with the Sergeant-in-charge, laughing.

"What the hell!" yelled the patrolman. The other two men followed his gaze to the hand-cuff bar where the pair of hand-cuffs hung empty.

31. The Bank

MICHAEL RAN NON-stop, heading northwest through the city. Avoiding the main roads, he ran through yards and fields until the city was far behind him. Fear of capture usurped his plan to go to the bank. The dirt roads, meadows, and corn fields became a blur of memories until they all looked the same, and he wondered if he'd run in circles for hours.

The sun burned down on him and soaked all his energy. The run had nearly defeated Michael as he strained up a short rise, and looked down into the valley. A pair of oak trees leaned protectively over a trickling stream. It was just what he needed. After drinking two refreshing handfuls of water, he decided to lay in the shade of the oak trees for a few minutes.

When he awoke, the low, amber sun told him that it was late in the day. As he walked north along an unlabeled, dirt road, a car approached behind him. A middle-aged couple offered Michael a ride.

Once he'd settled into the back seat, and they'd been driving for a few minutes, the man glanced in the rear-view mirror. "So young man …"

And Michael knew what question was going to come out of the man's mouth.

"… where are your parents?"

"They're dead."

The man's mouth opened in surprise. He flashed a look at his wife. They didn't ask Michael any more questions. They drove about 40 miles while Michael rested in the back.

After the ride, Michael walked for several miles, until he reached a farm, just as daylight was fading. The old barn looked very inviting. When he slipped into it, several horses whinnied and shuffled nervously. Michael peeked through a small window at the illuminated red brick house, but saw no movement. He climbed to an open loft above a horse stall and hid behind a musty stack of hay that looked like it'd been there for years.

The Smart Kid

With nothing to see as he sat in the dark, Michael looked inside himself. He wondered what Mark was thinking at that moment.

Michael smiled. *He's probably gloating; taunting the guards every day about how he beat them. My escape will probably give Mark plenty of ammunition to annoy the guards for many more days.*

Michael's smile faded. He had escaped, but not Mark. Mark was incarcerated because of Michael. It didn't make sense. Guilt filled his heart.

Did I make a mistake by escaping? Why run for the rest of my life? I should have just stayed a few more months until they decoded me.

But then what? Perkins and the military would be able to create an army of immortal soldiers. The U.S. First Immortal Infantry Division. Almost immortal— like me, they could still die, violently.

Why not do my part for my country, like Dad? Why not let them weaponize me, for the good of humanity?

Hell no!

Michael realized that Perkins wasn't motivated by altruism. If the incarceration was really for military purposes, then why secretly abduct Mark and him? Michael suspected that the real issue was one that every human has faced since the beginning of time: fear of dying. Perkins wanted power over death. And Michael felt no inclination to give him that power.

I'll do everything that I can to stop him from exploiting me, even if I have to die.

Michael was starting to depress himself and gave up the unfruitful meditating.

In the dim light of the loft, he tried making a bed of hay when he found an old comic book. He held it in the starlight that fell through a diamond window. It was Captain Marvel.

Captain Marvel has super-human powers, intelligence and can do magic.

Me too— if long life can be considered a power. And compared to boys who look like me, I would seem to be a genius; Lester, the sixth grader, thought so. And maybe I can use my interest in magic to my advantage.

Michael was familiar with Captain Marvel. He was a boy who

could become a grown man. Michael had never identified with the hero ... until that night.

What would I do if I ever came face to face with Perkins? Run like hell. Or give up.

What would Captain Marvel do?

Fight.

Get real, Michael. You gonna fight Perkins, and all the secretive government machinery under his control?

No.

But I can run.

Michael realized that he had to run. *No choice.* He had to be absolutely certain that Perkins never caught him. What would men like Perkins do with his power? Abuse it.

I, Michael Robert Shale, could change history. Me.

Hiding in the darkened hay loft, Michael laughed. From high school to college, Michael had felt like a freak, an outsider. He had wanted to become a grown man. From college through his incarceration, he was a lab rat, an oddity to be studied and harvested. But, from that time forward, his attitude changed.

He had changed.

He *was* Change.

Michael was a world-changer; valuable; unique. He saw himself as he never had: a super hero.

Perkins and his team were spending everything they had to find him.

His value to the world was beyond measure. Priceless.

If my plan fails, the world could be dominated by power mongers who controlled life and delayed death—for whatever purpose they wanted. They would decide who lived for hundreds of years, and who wasn't valuable enough to merit the gift of long life. I can't let that happen, at any cost.

He had to turn around and go back. He imagined himself returning to where his pursuers lay in wait for him. After he did that dangerous thing, then he would run.

Yes. He had to get to the bank. Without financial resources he'd be quickly caught. The decision was forced: he had to go to the bank by

The Smart Kid

the next day. With luck, he might still make it at the time that his mother expected.

As he drifted to sleep in his hay bed, he thought of Melanie, the Flower Child. Michael realized that he was able to start his plan because of her kind gesture. She had saved him from capture forever by pinning a flower in his hair with a useful hair pin.

Two dark colored cars pulled up to the curb two blocks from the Bank of Northern Iowa in Mason City. Special Agent Watts stepped out, a radio in his hand. He spoke into it with a crisp military cadence. "Special Agents Ross, McIntire are you in position?"

"Yes. ... Yes, sir," came the responses.

"Which of you has the rooftop position?"

"Ross, sir."

Watts spoke into the radio again. "Now we are certain that the target will be coming here today to withdraw funds. He may have accomplices working with him, so don't only be looking for a young boy alone. Call it in if you see anything suspicious."

"Yes, sir. ... Yes, sir." Their radio responses crackled back.

The two cars, filled with agents, waited for a quiet and tense twenty minutes. The radio crackled again. "Car approaching ... and parking ... No, old man." They waited several more minutes.

The radio scratched out a static-filled voice, "Another car has entered the parking lot. ... A middle-aged woman and a young boy got out of the car."

Watts hopped into his vehicle and told the driver to pull forward a block.

"It's a blond-haired, young-looking boy ... He matches the description, sir," said Ross.

"Are you sure?" Watts asked.

"As sure as I can be from this distance sir."

"Hold your positions," Watts said. "Wait for confirmation from our spotter in the bank."

A tall man wearing an ill-fitting suit stood at a bank counter reading a brochure. He watched the woman and boy approach a teller.

"Welcome, Mrs. Shale," said the bank teller.

The tall man reached into the side pocket of his jacket.

A red light on the dash of Watts's Sedan began to blink.

"OK, that's it. It's confirmed! Wait for them to exit, we don't need everyone in there seeing this."

Several minutes later the light on the dash stopped blinking.

Watts squeezed his radio mic and yelled, "Move! Move! Now!"

The two government cars sped forward and turned the corner toward the bank. Special Agent Ross, on the rooftop, dropped his binoculars and pointed a rifle down at the suspects, eyeing them through the rifle's large scope. Special Agent McIntire ran from his position with a pistol in his hand. The cars bounced over the curb and into the parking lot, bearing down on their targets, who had just exited the bank. The cars screeched to a stop a few feet from their targets. Three agents jumped out of the cars, along with Special Agent Watts.

Mrs. Shale screamed and hugged the boy against her, just as Special Agent McIntire reached them.

Two men exited the bank and stood at the door watching the action.

"Michael Shale you're under arrest for escaping federal custody, and endangering national security," said Watts.

Mrs. Shale turned to Watts with fire in her eyes. "You stupid government apes! Michael is not a criminal! He did nothing wrong. He is not a threat!"

The boy pulled himself away from his mother and looked up at Special Agent Watts. "And I'm not Michael— You stupid government apes!" Tommy Shale laughed in his face.

Although it had been 19 months since Watts had seen Michael, he recognized at once that it wasn't him. But he removed a photo of Michael from his coat pocket, showed it to the agent next to him, and shook his head.

Watts motioned for the other agents to stand down. They plodded back to their vehicles. "Mrs. Shale, where is Michael?"

"I have no idea!" she yelled. "Are you going to arrest me too, in front of all these people?"

Watts looked toward the bank. A dozen bystanders gawked

The Smart Kid

at him. The doors of the bank burst open and a dark-haired man wearing a business suit ran out toward Watts.

"Listen here! What right do you have assaulting my customer?" the man yelled.

The audience in front of the bank was mesmerized.

Watts looked past the yelling man to the bystanders and mumbled into his radio. One of the government vehicles drove away. Special Agent Watts removed his FBI badge, and held it with his finger covering his name. "This is a national security issue, sir. It was a case of mistaken identity and we do apologize to you and your customers at the bank for the intrusion."

Watts got into his car. The window slid down. Watts, who had donned sun-glasses said, "We're watching you, Mrs. Shale." He pointed his finger at her like a gun.

The man from the bank looked at Mrs. Shale and Tommy. "He thought I was the bank manager. Mrs. Shale, do you want to explain why Michael called me and told us to be here at this time?"

Watts saw a hint of a smile on Mrs. Shale's face, before his window slid shut. The last thing he heard was Mrs. Shale's voice.

"Misdirection, Mr. Monaghan."

Meanwhile, Michael waited on a bench outside the branch office of the Bank of Northern Iowa in Forest City. He faced the parking lot. The bank behind him had been open for half an hour.

He had gotten a ride from the surprised farmer who had found him leaving his barn in the early morning. Michael had received the usual questions from the farmer. He'd told the farmer that he was trying to get back home, and he was generously offered a ride. The farmer went far out of his way to help Michael.

While Michael waited, he read his newly-found Captain Marvel comic book.

A small, blue Mustang drove into the bank parking lot. A young woman stepped out, and entered the bank. Michael remained sitting. An old Buick entered the lot. Michael ran up to the parked car, as a middle-aged couple got out.

"Hi. Excuse me. I'm wondering if you could help me please?" Michael asked in his most boyish manner.

The woman, with a purse hooked over her arm, smiled. "Yes, little boy. What do you need?"

"Well, ma'am, I'm in need of a ride. Will you be driving to the edge of the city?"

"Yes. When we're done at the bank, we'll return home on the north side. Why?"

"Oh, um, someone just stole my bicycle, and I need to go about 10 blocks north of here ... if you don't mind," Michael said politely.

The woman turned to the man. "Harold, may we give this nice, young man a ride?"

Harold nodded. "Sure."

"That's swell! Thanks! Be right back," said Michael. He abruptly turned and dropped his comic book, as he ran into the bank.

Michael scurried up to a friendly-looking teller, smiled, and said, "Hello. I want to withdraw money from my savings account." He already had a withdrawal slip completed, which he slid forward on the counter

The teller picked it up and studied it. She gave a quick smile, and looked past Michael. She scanned the bank lobby. "OK, young man, this is quite a bit of money. May I ask where your parents are?"

Michael continued to smile. "Oh, they'll be coming any minute. So could you start processing that?" The teller paused.

The older couple walked in, the woman held a purse in one hand and a comic book in the other. She walked toward Michael. "Here's your comic book." She was still ten feet away.

"Thanks!" Michael said loudly, then turning back to the teller he said more quietly, "...Mom."

The teller smiled. She withdrew three hundred dollars from the cash box and counted the twenty dollar bills as she dealt them in front of Michael. The older couple approached and waited behind Michael.

Michael grabbed the cash. He spun around to face the woman and said, "Thanks," as he accepted the comic book from her. "I'll wait outside for you. OK?"

"Fine. We'll only be a minute," said the woman.

Michael walked out the door, with no intention of stopping, glanced at the picture of Captain Marvel, and said, "SHAZAM!"

32. Deputy Kan

SENATOR PERKINS SAT at the desk of his third-floor office, scowling at the paper he held in his hand. Mr. Harper sat in a corner chair, waiting for the fury to subside.

"How in the hell did Watts botch this?" He let the paper slip to the desk.

"He only had a tap on the mother's phone, not the lawyer's. And he didn't anticipate covering the bank's branch offices because Shale made it sound like he was going to the main bank. Shale tricked him." Mr. Harper was noticeably not using the word *we*.

"Damn! Now Shale has money and he's gone, again. We were so close! What the hell should we do now?" Perkins stood and paced the room.

"Do you want to send out a national bulletin?"

Perkins looked annoyed at Harper's question. He shook his head. "We can't risk doing a national bulletin. It would draw too much attention. And I can't rely solely on my tactical ops crew because they aren't cutting it. We've got to call in some outside help from the U.S. Marshals— off the books, of course."

"Sir, how do we account for that expense?"

"Harper, we don't account for it. Just put it as part of the black budget under *technical training*. Do what you can. And if the expense gets too large, I'll use some of my own funds to make up the difference."

Harper didn't ask about the source those funds.

Perkins continued, "The decision is made. We're ramping this up. I've gone too far to stop it now. Harper, tell Watts that he's fired! Then find a discreet Marshal we can bribe."

Deputy U.S. Marshal Kan had been briefed on the subject by Harper. They both waited in Perkins's office; Harper in his usual corner chair; while Kan gazed out the window.

Perkins entered his office and Kan turned to greet him. They shook hands as Harper introduced them, saying, "This is

The Smart Kid

Deputy U.S. Marshal Kan."

"You have quite an impressive view up here, don't you?" said Kan.

"Of course. One of the larger offices too," bragged Perkins, resting a hand on his fireplace mantel.

Kan nodded and raised his eyebrows approvingly.

The Senator moved to his chair and chewed an unlit cigar, as he studied Kan. Nearly as tall as Perkins, he was dark-haired and muscular. Kan looked asian.

"Chan, you're not Chinese are you?"

Kan paused and showed a practiced-smile. "It may sound like 'Chan', but it's pronounced 'Can', spelled with a K. And no, it's not a Chinese name. I'm half-American and half-Vietnamese."

"South Vietnamese, I presume."

"Of course."

The Senator smiled. "Alright, Kan, you're the hot shot fugitive catcher. What do you have planned?"

"Well, sir, your team's initial estimation that he would go directly to his mommy turned out to be wrong, as you know. He's not stupid. It's like your team can't help seeing him from his outward appearances: as an inexperienced twelve-year-old kid. In fact, that's why he escaped too: because they underestimated him and his brother."

Perkins frowned. "Enough with the compliments Kan, what's the plan?"

"First, we will treat him as he is, a twenty-three-year-old man. He's smart. He's college educated. He's been on his own since he was eighteen, for God's sake! He knows how to take care of himself. Plus he has the advantage of being disguised as a kid."

"How do you mean?"

"Who wouldn't stop to pick up a kid who's hitch-hiking along the highway? Hell, someone might feed him too 'cause he looks so scrawny. They'll ask him about his parents, and he'll give them some sob story. There's a chance that some good Samaritan has driven him all the way to Los Angeles already."

"Then how in the hell are we gonna catch the little punk?"

"See. You just did it now, you referred to him as a young person," said Kan.

"OK, It's easy to do. So any plans?"

"Hell yes, I have plans! His apparent age is also his weakness. Consider the things he can't do that any other fugitive can."

"One, he can't drive a car, or at least not for long without drawing attention to himself. He can barely see over the steering wheel; it would look like it was being driven by the damned Invisible Man." Kan smiled. Perkins didn't.

"Two, he can't rent a hotel room. He has no ID, and no hotel will rent to a kid without an adult to pay for it.

"Three, he can't fly on an airplane without identification, and that also means that he can't leave the country.

"And four, he only has limited money— it would have been 'no money' if your team had done their job. Anyway, he has limited money and no way to earn it. What type of work is available to someone who looks twelve? What's he going to do, mow lawns for Pete's sake?" Kan smiled again.

The Senator's face was expressionless. "He may have a financial source now that is beyond our control."

"Oh, that's just great," Deputy Kan said. "I see why you need me. Your people don't have enough experience with a pursuit like this. Hell, this is all that I've done for years. The U.S. Marshal Service specializes in fugitive recovery. We capture hundreds of fugitives every day. I get into a suspect's mind and anticipate their moves. I know that you'll want to keep your team of loyal FBI agents. So, put them under the control of the Marshal's Service. I'll direct your team and catch this fugitive. OK?"

Perkins gave a nod. "I'm counting on you."

"You were right to bring me in. Because now that he has resources, it makes things much more difficult. But it will still be hard for him to travel, rent, or live without some outside help."

Perkins chewed his cigar and stared out his window.

"Also, your decision to do a police bulletin for an escaped criminal was wrong," said Kan looking directly at Sen. Perkins, who turned and scowled at Kan.

The Smart Kid

"What the hell? Didn't we do anything right? We found him, set him up, and arrested him. We studied him like a guinea pig in a cage!" yelled Senator Perkins.

"Let me finish ... sir." said Kan, lowering his voice. "As I see it, we could send out three different notices to the press, and law enforcement:

"One could say that an escaped criminal is on the loose. You tried that. It nearly worked, but only because the highway patrol accidentally had him already. The problem is that he doesn't look like a criminal. He's not threatening in any way. It's going to be difficult to get the general public engaged.

"Second, we could say that a lunatic escaped from the Funny Farm. That is better because it may catch the attention of the press, and people may be more inclined to call in tips to the authorities.

"But I think the best option is the third one: We send out a bulletin about an orphaned child who has run away from violent foster parents. He's lost and on his own. Don't say that the police are after him; say that it's Child Protective Services. Most people will cooperate if they think we're from that agency. We should create the biggest sob story that we can about this boy. Every newspaper and TV news show will run it. How could he hide then?" asked Kan with a slight smile.

"Damn, I see now what you mean about the Marshals Service. You know your shit, don't you? I think your name should be spelled with a 'c', because you *can* do it." At that compliment, Harper looked up and frowned.

"Thank-you, sir," said Kan.

Senator Perkins leaned back in his chair, and chewed his cigar as he considered the plan. "I like the last two options; we'll try it both ways."

"But sir—", countered Kan.

"You're working for me on this job. Follow orders, and you get your big fat envelope of cash!"

"Yes, sir!"

Once Michael got his cash he felt very relieved. He could travel without the risk of hitch-hiking. He walked to the bus station, and bought a ticket for Sioux Falls, South Dakota. It was a large enough city that it would have the special services that he needed. He was beginning to formulate a plan for how he was going to live.

As he rode the bus, the plan for his life took shape. He knew that it would be difficult living on his own. Everyone would ask him where his parents were every time that he went shopping, or tried to rent an apartment, or go to a restaurant. He wouldn't be able to drive a car or fly anywhere.

"And Perkins may attack and prevail against Michael who is alone ..."

Solomon was right. Michael would need to solicit outside help.

He recalled his visit to the A&W root beer stand. The girl had assumed that Charles was his dad. He needed a surrogate parent to help him. A fake parent. Someone to temporarily act like his parent. As soon as he formulated the problem in that way, he had the solution: an actor. He wondered if it would work. But he was confident that he'd always be able to find an actor desperate enough to overlook a slight moral equivocation.

There are so many places to hide, just like back on the farm. How could Perkins track me to Sioux Falls? Or Chicago? Or Bear Lick, Pennsylvania? It will be nearly impossible. After a few months, he'll probably give up searching. Maybe he'll even let Mark go. Yes, I just have to hole up here until it blows over.

The longer that he considered it, the better he felt about the crazy plan. By the time that the bus stopped in Sioux Falls, Michael had talked himself into a pleasant sense of complacency.

33. Found Him

FIVE MONTHS LATER, Senator Perkins sat in his office when his aide entered with a folder and an uncharacteristic smile. Harper handed the folder to the Senator and said, "I'm happy to say that we found him!"

The Senator scanned it and smiled. "So they're on their way right now, to pick him up?"

"Yes, sir," Harper said proudly.

"That's great! Finally!"

Harper smiled at the apparent compliment.

"How did Kan's team track him to this town?"

Harper's smile faded.

"We still have a tap on the mother's phone line," said Harper. "She got a call from him. He was vague about his location, but told her that he was safe. We were able to track the call to a limited number of telephone exchanges in Sioux Falls."

"Inform me when Kan has got him." The Senator looked down to read a paper on his desk.

"Yes, sir!" Harper turned to leave when the Senator spoke.

"Harper."

"Yes, sir?" He looked down on Perkins.

"We don't need the brother anymore."

Harper questioned him with a look, which the Senator didn't see, his eyes focused on the papers in front of him. "We've got all the data. He's just a liability now."

The Senator removed a cigar from his desk.

Harper stood motionless for a moment, ignored by the Senator. He turned away, his head down, and walked out.

The Senator lit up the cigar, took a puff, and watched the tobacco shrivel and burn to used, dead ash.

Michael sat in a small cafe in downtown Sioux Falls, feeling a pleasant sense of satisfaction from his breakfast of scrambled eggs and sausage. From the booth, he gazed out the window for several minutes. Evidence of the most recent November snowfall frosted the tops of the

The Smart Kid

buildings and parked cars.

The November 20th issue of the Argus Leader lay opened on the table in front of Michael. The "Apartments for Rent" section was marked with dozens of circles and scribbled notes. Since the previous day, when he'd bought the paper, he'd already called 15 prospective apartments, using his adult voice.

It was time to move. After five months in his apartment, the questions by his neighbors had become too intrusive: "Why don't we ever see your mom or dad?" It was only a matter of time before someone called the county social workers. He didn't want to spend Christmas of 1963 in a juvenile detention center, so he sat in the cafe, reading the classifieds amongst the smell of pancakes, maple syrup, and frying bacon.

A dark, luxury Oldsmobile Sedan pulled to a stop in front of the cafe. The sun reflected off the sunglasses covering the driver's expressionless face.

The back doors of the sedan opened and two muscular men stepped out. They looked like linebackers wearing suits and ties. They stood on either side of the restaurant entrance and waited. Another bulk of a man sat in the front seat and glanced left at his driver, and right at the impassive guards standing on the sidewalk. The engine stopped. Everyone did nothing.

Michael gulped down the last of his orange juice, and dropped some coins on the table, as he turned to the woman. "Thanks." He pulled on a light overcoat, grabbed the newspaper, and shuffled toward the door, his head down, reviewing his notes.

One of the men outside the restaurant nodded to the dark sedan. The engine started.

"Oh, little boy!" yelled the waitress, who had just dropped his dishes into a shallow tub.

Michael spun around to face her. "Yes?"

She approached him with her hand extended. "You don't need to give me such a big tip. Here … you save this for your college fund." She handed him two quarters.

Michael smiled. "Thanks! You're a nice lady." He turned and headed for the door. The waitress turned her back to him, picked up the tub, and wobbled toward the back of the cafe.

The second that Michael exited from the restaurant, they grabbed him.

He tried to spin away as he yelled, "No!" but a large hand clamped over his mouth, muffling his scream. He was lifted off the ground, his arms pinned to his side. He thrashed his feet as the gorilla-sized men carried him to the government vehicle. In a few seconds, Michael was forced into the back seat of the dark car, with the muscular guards squeezing him between them. The tires squealed on the road as the car sped away.

Once Michael was trapped in the back seat, the hand was removed from his mouth. Michael struggled against the immobilizing-grip on his arms and yelled, "Stop it! Let go of me you low-life government goons!"

"Release him," said the man in the front seat. He turned around to show a worn, serious face beneath military-cropped gray hair. "Michael, please calm down! It's OK. We're friends!"

"Oh yeah? What kind of friend forcibly abducts me without warning?"

"Yes, you're right. I apologize for that, but we had no choice. We didn't have time to explain. But we have time now. Please calm down and listen; you'll be glad for my help."

Michael relaxed a bit, glancing at the two men flanking him who were not paying any attention to him.

The man in the front seat said, "My name is General Joshua Thompson. I'm part of a government committee in charge of military development research."

"Oh, I know about that committee. You incarcerated me and my brother!" Michael spat out the words.

"Please listen. It wasn't supposed to be incarceration, just a temporary testing time. I never agreed to imprisonment," said General Thompson.

"You just said that you're on the committee."

"Yes, but your secret incarceration wasn't sanctioned by me. I am

The Smart Kid

a friend!" General Thompson punctuated each of the last four words for emphasis, and then turned up his mouth in what was supposed to be a smile.

"You're not out to capture me? You don't work for Perkins?"

"No, I don't work for him." The general's face was serious again.

"Well, what do you want?" Michael scanned the interior of the vehicle for a clue.

"I want to help you."

"Help me? How? And why?" Michael was still frowning, but intrigued.

"When my car arrived at the restaurant, we were only ten minutes ahead of another car. And the men in that one *work for Perkins*. They are part of a *team* that does secret tasks for him. They were going to pick you up. You would have been caught again— and never released. Alive." The general's voice had an alarming certainty.

"Prove it! You could just be giving me this line of crap so that I don't fight you. You're on the same committee that wants information from me. Why should I believe you?"

General Thompson stared into Michael's eyes until he had his attention. "I served with your father in World War Two."

Michael looked surprised. "You knew my dad?"

"Yes. We were in the First Infantry Division together. He saved my ass on more than one occasion. I owe him my life. He was a great man. He would have made a great general too, if he'd stayed in the army. But he always said that he wanted to raise a family ... and there you are." A smile almost formed on the general's face.

"Why would you support this committee if you're my dad's friend?"

"I didn't know your full name, or your association with Major Shale. And I didn't know the extent of Perkins's obsession with you. I don't think that anyone on the committee did."

"So," mocked Michael, "you were just an innocent bystander?"

The general pursed his lips. "History will judge my innocence or guilt. But I didn't pay attention to everything that Perkins was doing. I didn't ask enough questions, and I trusted him too much. I'm sorry."

Michael's breathing slowed. "So they were really sending another car for me?"

The general turned and spoke to the driver. The driver flipped a switch on a radio attached to the dash. After a burst of static, words became clear.

"Approaching the target area now, sir." ... static ... "Do you want us to engage him now?" ...static ... "Yes, sir. Will do sir." ... static ... "Immediately ..."

Michael waited in silence, with the other men, for two minutes wondering what the G-men would do when they discovered he wasn't in the cafe.

"Sir?" ... static ... "He's not here, sir." ... static ... "I don't know. The only person inside was a waitress and she said that he just walked out." ... static ... "OK, we'll search the streets. He couldn't be too far away." ... static ... "We'll notify you. Out." The driver flipped the switch and looked at the general.

"Good. They're not suspicious yet." the general said.

"What do you mean?"

"They are going to search that area of the city in an ever-widening circumference. When they don't find you, they'll know that you're not walking. Then they're going to contact every taxi company, bus and train depot. They have enormous resources at their disposal. Eventually they'll determine that you escaped with help from someone." Once again, the certainty in the general's voice rang true.

"But how did they know that I was at that particular cafe?"

"Once they tracked you to this city, they sent a team. A spotter probably saw you go into the cafe."

"Does that mean the spotter saw you pick me up?"

"I don't know," said the general. "We saw no one else around. If he was still there, he kept out of sight."

"So they might figure out it was you that helped me?"

"Maybe. It depends on how much Perkins trusts the other members of the committee. I became suspicious because, after we signed the letter agreeing to your conscription, we heard nothing about you. So I met with the director of ARPA. Although the Senator had said that this project ... you ... would be managed through ARPA, the director knew nothing about it. I had one of my assistants trail the Senator's

The Smart Kid

aide and do a bit of digging for me— Perkins isn't the only one with covert connections. And that's how I learned about Perkins' deception. But there are several ways that information could have leaked from the committee, ..."

"What now?" asked Michael.

"Well, I can't be conspicuously involved. I can set you up with some finances to hold you over temporarily. But that's it."

"Why? Why can't you just report what the Senator has done?"

The general looked out the car window momentarily and watched the buildings pass by. He turned back to Michael. "First, I have no proof. Even if I figured out what facility you'd been held at, they would have already scrubbed all evidence. The Senator isn't stupid. He doesn't leave trails back to himself. I'd look like a fool making accusations that I can't support. Secondly, it would out me, when I may not be suspect yet. And thirdly, my participation on this committee makes me culpable in its activities, even though the Senator instigated your false arrest and abduction without our agreement. He has signed forms in place that will prove the knowledge and participation of every member of the committee. He'll have documentation and hired witnesses that protect him and implicate me. It's standard CYA procedure."

Michael frowned. "CIA?"

"No. Cover Your Ass. It's rule number one in politics."

"What would happen to you if anyone found out?"

"Certainly I'd be dishonorably discharged, and lose my pension. Senate hearings would ensue. Criminal charges and prison time are also a possibility," said the general.

"If you report the Senator, then you go down with him?" Michael sounded surprised.

"Absolutely— unless ... unless every member on the committee united with the same story— agreeing that the Senator did this behind our backs. But the only way that Cutler and Dr. Bruce Barbour would turn on Perkins is if it was politically beneficial for them."

"Did you say 'Doctor Bruce?'"

The general nodded.

"I met him! Just before I was drugged and smuggled to the prison."

The rage boiled in Michael's heart again, and his fists tightened at the memory.

The general waited for him to calm down.

Finally, Michael said, "thank you for saving me from Perkins. I truly appreciate it."

The car drove into an open garage door of an unmarked building. The door closed behind them.

"Well, Michael," said General Thompson, "I have to leave you here. I won't be able to help you much more. I think that my access to information about you will become very restricted. Perkins will shut down as much intel as possible, once he discovers this was an inside job. But my team will give whatever you need."

"I don't need money, but I do need help with some government paperwork," said Michael.

"OK. Tell me."

"I need several birth certificates with various names and dates?" Michael said it like a question. The general's eyes narrowed. Michael feared that he had asked for too much.

"My aide is waiting in this building for you," the general said. "She will help you get your special birth certificates. Just tell her all the details. And she'll set up your own P.O. box anywhere. Where will you go?"

"Aurora, Illinois."

They stepped out of the sedan, and the general introduced Michael to his aide. He told her to "assist Mr. Shale with some special needs." He shook Michael's hand, apparently getting ready to depart.

"Thanks, General. I'm overwhelmed by your support." Michael showed a small smile.

"Do you trust me now, Michael?" The general looked down at him.

"Yes, I guess so."

"What the hell for?" yelled General Thompson, with a vengeance.

"What?" Michael was shocked by the complete change in the general's tone. *Maybe it was all an act.*

"Why the hell would you trust me? Just because I gave you some damned story about serving with your father? Anyone could have said

The Smart Kid

that!" The general bellowed his reprimand.

"What the hell are you saying?" Michael yelled back.

"Don't you know that you're being chased by a man who is completely obsessed with capturing you?"

"Of course I do. That's why I'm running all the time."

"Running? You came out of that cafe with your head down, reading the damned newspaper! That's like sticking your head out of a foxhole without wearing your helmet. Do you think you're on a damned holiday?"

"What? Of course not!"

"You need to pay attention! Perkins has many people searching for you. You are nothing to Perkins but another re-election. The secrets that you possess are all that interests him, and the people that he works for— as they would interest anyone of advancing age."

"I suspected that he had personal interests in capturing me."

"Of course. He's got all the money, fame and power that he wants. But he can't hang onto it forever. Soon he'll be dead; unless he can crack the code in you."

"Well, I'm doing my best to avoid him," said Michael, defensively.

"No. You're *not* doing your best! Pay attention! Plus ..." General Thompson paused and looked at Michael.

"What?"

"One other reason that you don't want me to go public about Perkins is because then you'll never be safe; you'll be exposed."

"What do you mean? With Perkins out of the picture, why wouldn't I be safe?"

"Do you think he's the only power-monger in DC? That place thrives on power-mongering. Also, we have intelligence to suggest that the Russians are doing selective breeding of humans to develop super-soldiers. They are treating women like breeder cattle to create the most effective strain. They are looking for biological solutions to create enhanced fighting soldiers. So do you think that they'd be interested in you?"

"Oh, my! Are you trying to scare me?"

"Wake up! Always remember that you're a rare gem. You're different. You're a man in an eternally youthful body. Evil men would steal you if they learned of your existence. Never assume that you're safe. Never stay in one location for long. Don't do anything to draw attention to yourself. And don't trust anyone! Because anyone could be working for Perkins or the Russians or Chinese. Anyone can be bought!"

"Sir," said Michael, "Did you say that Perkins represents some other people?"

"Yes. He's just a puppet for a very powerful organization of greedy social engineers."

"What organization? Who are these people?" asked Michael.

"I don't know and I can't say. They protect themselves with a veil of secrecy. It's surprising that even this much information leaked out. But Perkins wasn't that careful."

"Well what about—"

"That's it. There's nothing more!" snapped General Thompson. He paused. In a quieter tone, he added, "Now, let me show you something that you should have asked for the minute that I told you I'd served with your father— real proof."

The general reached into his coat pocket and removed a photo which he handed to Michael. It was an old, worn picture of soldiers posing side by side in front of a bar. The man on the far left was a very young version of Howard Shale. Next to him was a young and thin Joshua Thompson.

Michael studied the photo for a minute. He smiled at the general. "Thanks for showing this to me. I'd never seen that photo of my dad before."

"Neither had your mother."

"What? You saw my mother?"

"Yes. I attended your father's funeral," General Thompson said in a low voice.

"I missed it. I was ..."

"Let me tell you a story, son. And I'm not calling you *son* because you look like a kid, but because, when you serve in a hell-hole together, facing death every day, you become family. My C.O. saved my ass one time by pulling me out of a foxhole in Germany. We were about to be overrun by Krauts, and I missed the signal. He hauled me

The Smart Kid

out of there before I got skewered— just like I hauled you out today. But he did more for me. He *really* saved me by not letting me get lazy. He rode my ass every single day. For a while, I hated him for that. I thought that he was singling me out for special mis-treatment. But I was wrong. He cared about me, like a son. And he burned those harsh lessons into my thick skull to protect me. That's why I'm alive today — because of my C.O., your father. I reamed you for Howitzer Shale, because he isn't here to do it himself." The general put his hand on Michael's shoulder.

"OK. I understand what you're saying. Thanks for the … reaming," said Michael. He smiled slightly.

The general had been so helpful, Michael was afraid to ask for more help. But he had to. "Sir, what about my brother? Can you help him?"

In contrast to his imposing demeanor, the general spoke softly. "I'm sorry to tell you that your brother was no longer useful to them." He still rested his hand on Michael's shoulder, but it meant something different.

For a moment, Michael wasn't sure that he understood the implication. He stared at General Thompson. But the way that the general stared back confirmed his fear. Uncontrollable tears welled up in Michael's eyes.

"No, no! It can't be. It doesn't feel real to me!" Michael struggled to maintain his composure. He wanted to weep, but he sucked it in and shut it down.

The general waited for him to calm himself again.

Michael recalled Mark's last words to him. "Hold it together Shorty. Yes, it's time to finish this game. If you win this game against Big Brother, then you'll be winning it for both of us. Go! I'll hold 'em off."

Michael sighed deeply and got control of his emotions. He tried to imagine how he might "win this game." He couldn't. Not by himself. Perkins was too powerful and out of reach. He turned away from the general.

"One last thing, Michael."

"Yes?" Michael didn't even raise his eyes.

"Don't ever call your mother again. Don't mail letters or contact her in any way." It was a quiet order.

That command forced him to look into the general's wrinkled face. "Why not?"

"How do you think they tracked you to this city?"

General Thompson got into the sedan. The garage door opened and the car disappeared into the brightness of a fresh, South Dakota day.

The garage door closed, dragging shadows over Michael.

He stood alone, letting it sink in.

Mark is dead.

I'm half a twin.

If I stop running, I'm caught forever.

I can't ever talk to Mom.

I'm all alone.

I'm not safe. I never was. And I never will be.

34. Death

THE DOOR ON Mark's cell was unlocked and swung open wide. The guard stood in the doorway, filling it with his bulky, muscular body. "It's time to go swimming!" he snarled.

Mark sat on the edge of a chair, scratching at his full beard, which he'd started the day that Mike escaped. Every time he stroked it, he smiled, at the victory. But not that day.

Mark knew that day would come. He knew it before he'd told his brother of the escape plan. And he had suspected that Michael's escape would result in his own execution. But the only thing that mattered was Michael's safety. Years before, their father had told Mark, in confidence, that he was to protect Michael, and keep his secret from evil men. It had become his life purpose.

With a new clarity, Mark realized that he had achieved his purpose in life.

And he smiled.

Mark turned his gaze to the window, while watching the guard out of the corner of his eye. When the guard turned to the window, Mark jumped up, grabbed the chair, and hurled it.

The guard dodged it and ran into the room. A second guard exploded in behind him.

Deputy Kan arrived at the Senator's office a few minutes earlier than expected. Mr. Harper, in the front office, looked up from his desk. Neither man smiled.

"You may enter and wait for him," said Harper.

Kan walked into the ornate office, and sat in a wooden chair with hand-carved arm rests, in front of Perkins's antique desk.

A moment later, the Senator appeared in the doorway, filling its width. "Well, Kan, what have your plans amounted to? You made it sound like it would be easy sailing. But it's been five months of searching, and what do you have? Nothing! You're dead in the water!"

The Smart Kid

Kan showed no emotion. That seemed to annoy the Senator.

Perkins walked in, slamming the door, and dumped his body into the leather chair behind his desk. The two men faced off against each other. "We almost had him today. You assured me that your men were on the way to pick him up. What in the hell happened?"

"Remember, Perkins, you're the one who recruited me. And I never promised when we'd catch him. Somehow he has avoided all our public bulletins about a run-away kid. But we only missed him by minutes in Sioux Falls. He got help from someone. Maybe your committee has a leak." Deputy Kan was on the attack.

"You let me worry about that. You just need to do your job!"

"It's pretty tough to fill a leaky bucket."

Perkins glared at Kan.

Kan remained calm. "I do have a back-up plan."

Senator Perkins leaned forward a few inches, his scowl remained.

"Do you still have the brother in custody?" asked Kan.

"For a few more minutes." The Senator glanced at his gold watch. "Pretty soon his body is going to be found accidentally drowned in an Appalachian river."

Mark Shale's arms were held behind him in a murderous grip by the monstrous guards flanking him. A fresh bruise marked his face. He wasn't moving his feet, forcing the guards to drag him the entire distance to the locker room. He felt like a prisoner on death row who hadn't been given a trial, or charged with a crime, forced toward his execution.

The struggling guards began to show evidence of fatigue.

"Why don't we just put a bullet in his head and claim he died of lead poisoning?" asked one guard to the other.

"It's supposed to look like an accident, dumbass!"

The guards dragged Mark passed an army recruitment poster with the slogan, "Look Sharp! Be Sharp! Go Army!" When they reached the closed doorway of the locker room, Mark sprang into action.

Mark had been resisting the guards for so long that, when he darted forward, he surprised them, and almost broke free. As the guards held his arms, Mark ran up the front of the door. When his body was horizontal, he pushed against the door, and did a complete flip.

The guards couldn't hold him, their arms twisted backward above their heads, as Mark's body flew over them. The men fell to the floor, Mark a few feet beyond the guards. He scrambled to his feet and ran.

The guards were three steps behind him.

At every intersecting corridor Mark turned, zig-zagging his way through the building.

One of the guards yelled into his radio, as the other yelled curses at Mark.

Mark turned left into a hallway and realized too late that it was a dead end. He hoped against reason that a door was unlocked as he yanked at two before the guards careened around the corner. Mark watched the guards pause to catch their breath. He knew that they waiting for reinforcements.

Two more guards appeared behind them.

All four closed in on Mark, who backed up, eyeing them, as he slid his hand along the wall. Mark passed a fire alarm and a fire extinguisher. He jerked down on the fire alarm, and to his surprise, the alarm blared through the corridors as the sprinklers showered water. The guards looked surprised and unhappy at the involuntary shower.

It was enough of a distraction.

Mark snatched the fire extinguisher, and in one motion, pulled the pin and squeezed the trigger, spewing a white cloud at the nearest guard.

The guard's vision was so limited, that he didn't see the butt of the fire extinguisher rushing at his face until it was too late.

Mark felt a sickening thud as the canister crunched the guard's nose into his skull.

The guard screamed like death as he crumpled to the floor.

The Smart Kid

Dumbass held back as another guard ran past him.

Still gripping the extinguisher, Mark spun around and gave a back-handed swing. The canister clanged when it connected with the guard's head, knocking him flat and motionless.

Dumbass drew his pistol and took a bead on Mark.

Out of options, Mark hurled the fire extinguisher and ducked as the guard fired. An explosion of white filled the air.

Mark was blind and deaf for a couple of seconds, as was dumbass. But it was enough time for Mark to roll on the floor toward the inert guard, and probe for his holstered pistol. He used the guard's body for cover and pointed the pistol down the cloudy hall.

The sprinkling water dissipated the white cloud.

Mark aimed for the first thing he saw: an ankle. He fired twice but heard three shots. His "body guard" jolted as he took a hit intended for Mark.

Dumbass dropped his gun, screaming as his ankle shattered.

The other guard drew his weapon as three more came around the corner, guns drawn.

"What? You old fool! We can still use him!" Kan stood, looking down at Perkins.

Perkins stood. "Watch yourself, Kan! We've learned everything we can from his body."

"He has one more purpose for us. Use him as bait!" said Kan, still standing.

Perkins shook his head in disbelief. "If we let him go, he'll know he was bait, and will not go near his brother. Maybe you're not the right person for this job!" barked Perkins.

"Of course, sir. That's why you let him 'escape'. And make it convincing," said Kan, with a wink. He'd been leaning forward on Perkins's desk, but stood upright as he waited for the Senator's response.

Senator Perkins relaxed a bit, still standing in front of his chair, as he chewed an unlit cigar. "So you think that when he escapes, that he'll find his brother?"

"Exactly!" Kan sat down.

The Senator settled himself into his deep leather chair.

"But how the hell will he be able to find him alone, if we haven't been able to?"

"Well sir, they planned the escape, so they must have planned a reunion at some point. They had to." Kan gestured with his forefinger.

"You sure? Because he could become a nasty liability to us," said Perkins.

"If he thinks that he's escaped on his own effort, then he's not going to go public because then we'd have him again. He's going to hide in the shadows and meet up with his brother. So he's valuable to you as bait. He's nothing but a grub worm hanging on a hook. I say, 'Cast out the line' and watch what happens!"

Senator Perkins sat forward and called Harper.

Mark Shale's head was underwater, pinned down in a large metal tub by the strong arms of a nameless guard. With hands cuffed behind him, he held his breath, as he strained his body upward in vain.

The guard, trying to make him inhale water, punched Mark in the ribs several times. Mark moaned, keeping his mouth closed.

Another punch.

The pain was so sharp that he involuntarily gasped for breath. He sucked in death instead. Bubbles rose to the surface, like a spirit leaving his body.

The punching stopped.

At least Michael is safe, thought Mark, in the eternity of his last second on earth.

His head was hauled out of the water. Mark gagged and coughed. He fell to his side onto the wet tiled floor, unable to block his fall. He inhaled great breaths of life and viewed the locker room sideways from floor level.

A guard was speaking into a radio. He said, "Yes, sir. We've still got him ... If you'd called two minutes later ... Yes, I understand."

The next day at noon, a thoroughly depressed and defeated Michael dragged himself onto the bus bound for Aurora. With all his belongings in the backpack slung over his shoulder, he settled into a

The Smart Kid

seat near the back and stared out the window at nothing.

He had to leave town, and Aurora was as good as anywhere, or nowhere. The plan *had* been to hide from Perkins by impersonating a young student and attending a particular selection of schools in the mid-west, until Mark found him ... after they let him go. It would have been a glorious reunion.

It would have.

Michael was shocked by the extreme evil of selfish men with greedy goals. He'd been so naive.

Before his father had died, Michael had no experience with death. But in a matter of months, he had to face the loss of another family member. It was a sad, lonely feeling, and he wished that he had someone to counsel him.

A dark cloud of depression, anger, and self-pity enveloped him; engulfed him; cutting off everything else until he was the only person in the world. He ached and waited for the cloud to dissipate. But until it did, he sucked it in, and breathed the pain, because it was the only way that he could love his twin brother.

He was even beyond the point of crying. He just seethed anger and plotted revenge that would never come.

No relief. No catharsis. Only pain.

Michael decided that he would not become a fake student, as he had planned. He would not move to Illinois and set up residency in the Washington Middle School district. There was no point. He could hide anywhere in the world. *No, not really.* Michael had no passport, and little chance of getting one, until he got to the P.O. box in Aurora, and picked up his new birth certificates. That became his only reason for the trip.

He leaned back, eyes closed. He remembered when Mom used to dress them both alike to proudly show off her twins. *We attracted so much attention, until we aged. Then no one called us 'The Twins'. We were just brothers to the world. But we knew we were twins. But what am I now? What's the word for a single twin? Part of me is dead. I'm not a twin anymore. I'm just ... a freak.*

Archie Schneider, his diminutive philosopher-roommate, had said that 'Different isn't bad.' But Michael disagreed. It was bad.

As Michael began to doze off, he heard the hissing of a transistor radio far away. *He's dead. He's dead. Shot dead.* Michael thought he heard himself crying, but it was someone else.

"He's dead!" a man shouted. "The President is dead! I just heard it on the radio!"

The driver pulled the bus over to the side of the road. He turned on the radio and the news poured out of the ceiling speakers, showering everyone with the tragedy.

"... President John Fitzgerald Kennedy was shot at 12:30 pm while riding through downtown Dallas in a presidential motorcade ... pronounced dead at 1:00 pm. ... Vice President Lyndon Baines Johnson was sworn in as the 36th President of the United States, 99 minutes after Mr. Kennedy's death."

Many people in the bus openly wept. And so did Michael Shale.

After many long, sad minutes the bus moved forward again. Through the farmlands of Minnesota and the forests of Wisconsin, every flag was at half staff. Michael wondered again about the extremes to which selfish men would go for their own purposes.

Oh, to be an innocent, ignorant child again.

And the dark cloud got darker and heavier.

When Michael got off the bus in Aurora, the day was overcast and frigid. But there was the slightest hint that the sun might break through the gray clouds.

At the designated post office, Michael received his government package. Sitting on the floor, he leaned against the large window. He investigated the contents of the envelope that would have allowed him to hide as a student for the next two decades— if it took that long— until Mark found him. The first thing he saw was a hand-written note: *"Perkins changed his mind. Mark is alive. He plans to release your brother to trail him to you. Good luck. -JT."*

The sun broke through the clouds and shone on Michael. It became a bright, glorious day filled with happiness, thankfulness, and tears of joy.

Adults stared at Michael, sitting on the floor, crying with a smile on his face. But Michael didn't care.

The Smart Kid

Eventually, he examined the survival packet, created at his request. He had five birth certificates with the names Tom Howardson, Matthew Selah, Matthew Janson and others. The dates of birth ranged from 1951 to 1967, so that he could be 11, 12, 13, or 14 at any school that he chose to attend.

His plans suddenly changed. He *would* hide out as a student.

Michael would help his twin brother find him by leaving obscure clues that a similar thinking twin may catch but that a sinister, selfish Senator would miss.

The Senator would have no idea that Michael was impersonating a student and hiding among the 30 million students in elementary and middle schools. And even if he did finally realize it, Perkins would have over 100,000 schools to search. And even if the Senator discovered the pattern of schools that Michael had chosen, how could he search hundreds, in dozens of different states, to find the one school where Michael hid? It would be nearly impossible, because every few years, Michael would enroll in a new school, with a different name. He would play Hide 'n Seek for his freedom until his brother finally found him.

And the reunion would be glorious.

35. Found Him Again

HARPER RUSHED INTO Senator Perkins's office holding a memo. "Senator, we've found him!"

Senator Perkins dropped the papers from his hands and grabbed the memo. He scanned it as Harper explained, "Over the years, we've received hundreds of tips about run-away children, and escaped lunatics— just as Kan predicted. But unfortunately, they were all false leads, and time-wasters. That strategy yielded us nothing."

The Senator frowned.

"But we've also been tracking his brother as best we could for the last seven years. Either he knows that we're following him, or he's just being extra cautious, because he's been secretive, hiding his locations and activities. But we discovered that he's doing research in libraries. He's been reading community newspapers from around the country. And lately, he's been focusing on one particular city in Kansas. Our spotters interviewed the librarian after he left, and learned that he was researching schools in Great Bend, Kansas. We're pretty sure that our fugitive is at Lincoln Middle School."

"A middle school? Not an old shed in the woods or a mountain retreat? Not a series of flop houses and YMCAs across the country? He wasn't living like a homeless vagabond! Damn! We were way off. We've wasted years!" The Senator glanced at the photograph of his wife. "Dammit, that was clever!"

Perkins looked up at Harper. "Tell Kan to send in an undercover spotter to scope it out. We need this to be a well-planned and perfectly executed trap. He doesn't know we're coming, so that gives us time to get it right."

Harper said, "The team is already developing an escape-proof trap."

The Senator lit his cigar with his specially inscribed lighter and, as he flipped it shut, said, "I've heard that before …"

* * *

The Smart Kid

    Deputy Kan managed the trap at Lincoln Middle School by radio from the disguised white van parked outside the pool's only emergency exit. The school had been notified that Child Welfare Services had arrived to retrieve a run-away foster-child. The pool area had been cleared. FBI Agents guarded all the outside doors. It was time for Shale's phy-ed class. Kan was ready to spring the trap on the rat.

    Kan looked at the young agent sitting in the passenger seat and glanced back to the other agent squeezed against a windowless, side wall.

    "I wonder what the hell Shale is doing attending a middle school? How was he able to register at the school under the false name of Howardson? It's not even a very good false name, since he is Howard's son. How many other schools has he attended?"

    The agent beside him shook his head saying, "We can ask him when he's in the cage." He jabbed his thumb toward the man-sized cage which occupied most of the space in the back of the van.

    Kan spoke into the hand-held radio.

    "All agents, prepare to spring the trap." While he looked at his watch, he added, "Masterson and Keane, are you at the gym door?"

    The static-filled response came back, "Yes, but the assistant principle insisted on escorting us here, and now he wants to know why we're waiting."

    "Ignore him. When Shale is on the rope, enter, and wait at the door so he can see you."

    Long pause.

    "OK. We're headed in," said one of the agents.

    Long pause.

    "You were right! He ran to the locker room," Keane's voice crackled through the radio.

    "Great! Just block that door to prevent his exit. His only choice now is the pool," responded Kan. He smiled.

    "Yes, sir."

    Still speaking into the radio, Kan asked, "Palmer, ready to put him to sleep?"

"Yes, sir. But I just wish these dart pistols weren't single shooters. It takes too long to re-load," whined Palmer.

"Then you damn well better get him on the first shot!" Kan paused before yelling into the radio again, "And all agents, keep an open mic. I want the play by play."

Multiple "Yes sirs" blasted through the radio.

Kan turned to the agent sitting in the passenger seat. "I'm going to use the recording of this transmission as my resumé for a better assignment. I'm sick of chasing this guy for seven years."

The young agent asked, "You mean you've been chasing the same kid for seven years?"

Kan frowned. "Of course not," he said, forcefully enough to silence the lower-ranked agent.

During their wait, Kan stuck a cigarette between his lips — the stress showing on his aging face. He looked twenty years older than the others. Kan flicked a cheap plastic lighter and fumbled; it dropped to the floor of the van. While he bent forward, the radio transmissions exploded with multiple voices.

"We can hear him running toward the pool door."

"He's coming through— Oh my God!"

"Get him!"

Kan jerked his head up at the sudden chatter and banged it under the instrument console. "Damn!"

"Damn! I missed him!" another voice yelled over the radio.

"Someone, help Huntley out of the pool. And get him to the medic!" said the first voice. "Go, go, go!"

"Damn!" said Palmer. "I woulda had him if he hadn't slipped!"

Kan grabbed his radio. "Palmer, what the hell happened?"

"It didn't go exactly as planned, sir. But he's in the pool maintenance room— He's trapped."

Kan lowered the radio, cursed, and shook his head. He brought the radio to his mouth again. "OK, Palmer, make sure you've got all your men around that door before you open it."

While Kan waited during the unnerving silence, he searched the floor for his lighter. When he retrieved it, he flicked it five times, but it failed to light. "Shit."

The agent sitting in the passenger seat removed a small box

The Smart Kid

of wooden matches from his pocket and handed it to Deputy Kan, who accepted it with a nod, after tossing his lighter out his open window.

The agent glanced at Kan for a second. He looked away and then glanced toward Kan again.

Kan asked, "You're Guzman, right?"

"Yes, sir."

"What's on your mind?"

"Oh, well, I know that I'm new with this whole pursuit division. But we've got this big-ass cage here, and the team is using dart guns, but the target is a kid. Why?"

"What's your rank?"

"Special agent," replied the low-ranking agent.

"And how did you get assigned to me?" asked Kan.

"Deputy Assistant Director Manchester gave me the assignment. He called it an off-the books favor for ... someone."

"Then you know that you'll never repeat this, right?"

"Yes, sir."

"I agree that the darts and cage are overkill. But someone very high up is pushing this. And someone even more influential is directing him. This is a national security issue. This 'kid' is nearly 29 years old. He's escaped from prison, police handcuffs, and two recovery attempts."

"What's his secret?"

"Stupid-ass amateurs who judge a book by its cover." Kan looked at Special Agent Guzman with narrowed eyes, and turned away.

The radio crackled to life again. "OK, there's four of us around the door ... guns drawn ... I'm about to yank it open ... Shit! It's locked!"

Kan heard pounding and yelling. Exasperated, Kan yelled into the radio, "Stephens, get a pry bar from the van to bust that door off its hinges!"

In a minute, Special Agent Stephens jerked open the back door of the van, and spoke through the wires of the cage. "Sir, that little shit is smart and fast. But he's trapped now." He grabbed a heavy pry bar and sprinted into the school.

The radio chatter began again. "OK, it's busted open. We

found the light switch ... He's not here. Oh no! There's an open access panel in the floor."

"What the hell!" yelled Kan, "Stephens, I thought that you cased this school? You had a whole damned week!" Kan cursed under his breath again.

After a few seconds, Stephens' voice said, "I'm going down myself with the tranq pistol." Several minutes later, his voice cracked through the radio, "Oh damn. It's pitch black down here. Does anyone have a light?"

Kan tried to strike a wooden match. It broke. He busted two more matches before he lit the cigarette. He sucked at it hard, held his breath for a few seconds, and then forced the smoke from his lungs with an audible sigh.

Palmer's head popped into the window, inches from Kan, as he yelled, "Deputy Kan?"

Kan dropped his cigarette. He frowned down at it before turning to Palmer. "Why are you here?"

"Well sir, they have the access hole guarded. Even if he gets by Stephens, we still have him. But I think that we should reconnoiter the building's exterior. Stephens missed the maintenance room escape, maybe he missed something else ..."

"Get in!" ordered Kan.

Palmer squeezed into the back.

Kan stepped on his cigarette, and rubbed it out with disgust, before turning to the three agents. "No more of these pansy-assed darts. Men, shoot to stop him any way you can. Just don't kill him!"

Palmer tossed his dart gun to the floor and unholstered his Glock, as did the others.

Kan stomped on the accelerator. The wheels spit gravel.

As he drove around the building, he scanned all the exits. An armed agent stood beside each door. When he reached the west parking lot, he sped into it, and slammed on the brakes, at the top edge of a long hill.

Since the west side of the school faced sloping grass, there were no exit doors ... except one maintenance door near the bottom of the hill. Unguarded. Michael Shale was standing at

The Smart Kid

the open door, looking up at them.

Agent Stephens' crumpled body laid across the threshold.

Kan scowled. "Dammit! Stephens is going to wake to unemployment. Go, go, go!"

The men jumped out of the van labeled *"Child Welfare Services."* Kan and two others skidded cautiously down the hill in hard leather shoes. Agent Guzman slipped and thudded onto his back.

Palmer remained at the top and took aim. He fired as Shale rounded the corner.

"Damn!" said Palmer. He carefully eased down the hill. By the time Palmer had reached the bottom and turned the corner, Shale was already over an eight-foot safety fence and swinging hand over hand along the branches of a large tree.

Guzman was trying to climb the fence without success; he couldn't get a footing.

Kan studied the interlaced branches of the trees for a moment and he realized that Shale could do it.

"Guzman, get back to the van and bring the wire cutters. Open this fence!"

"Palmer, shoot that monkey! Knock him out of the tree. When he falls and gets a boulder shoved up his ass, that should stop him."

"Gladly, sir!" said Palmer. He leaned against the fence for balance. Michael Shale was a moving target, getting farther away. Palmer squeezed his trigger. The loud bang was the only result.

Shale wasn't looking at them. Kan followed Shale's gaze to the window, which was filled with the faces of children.

"OK. We're done!" he ordered.

Palmer continued to point his pistol toward Shale wriggling further toward the river. He was temporarily obscured by the branches, then he suddenly swung into view again. He just hung over the river. An easy target.

Palmer trained his weapon on Shale.

"No!"

"But sir, I've got a clear shot now," Palmer protested.

"Yes, in front of fifty witnesses to watch you gun down

someone their own apparent age," countered Kan.

"But they're just children!"

"Someday, they'll be adults. And they won't forget this," argued Kan. He turned to the agents who had gathered behind him and yelled, "Someone, drag Stephens out of that corridor!"

Palmer aimed his Glock at Shale.

Kan looked back, yelled, "No!" and swatted Palmer's gun as he squeezed the trigger.

But it was too late, the gun had recoiled from the shot.

Kan watched Michael Shale drop into the river. He didn't come to the surface.

Guzman returned and began working at the fence with a pair of wire cutters.

Kan continued watching the river, waiting for Shale's body to pop up either dead or alive. Finally, he saw Michael appear, swimming and bobbing in the fast-flowing river.

Palmer asked, "Why don't we get some boats to catch him?"

"Don't tell me how to do my job, you insubordinate ass!" Kan spit back. He turned to Guzman, "Guzman, get on the horn, call in search team beta to skim the river with a couple of boats; and you take team alpha and scour the banks of the river and all nearby roads."

Kan turned back to Palmer. "Of course the search continues! Damn! This search never ends. But by the time we get the boats on the river, it will be too late. At the speed that the river is flowing, he'll be miles away, or have climbed out anywhere along that wooded bank. If he gets to a road, dripping wet, he'll get a helpful ride from some Good Samaritan. Damn! Do you know how difficult it's going to be to find him now?"

Palmer holstered his sidearm and stared at the river.

Kan continued, "Plus, I now have the job of answering questions by this school administration about why the hell we're shooting at a kid."

Palmer, silent, faced him defiantly.

"Since you're so damned smart, you can lead a new search — a search for a job. You're off my team!" Kan yelled. He burned Palmer with his hot gaze. "Plus, I've got an even harder job: I have to give a report to Senator Perkins."

The Smart Kid

* * *

One day later, Harper and Kan cautiously entered Senator Perkins's office. Perkins looked up from the papers scattered over his desk. Harper could see that the papers were the plans and maps of the latest failed capture.

The Senator stared them down. "Well?"

Harper looked at Deputy Kan.

"He got away ... again, sir," said Kan quietly.

"Damn! How could this happen? You had a week to prepare the trap!" The Senator stood and began pacing the room.

"Well, sir, you can see on the map that the school was built next to the Arkansas river. Agent Stephens, a man from your team, missed the access door near the river. But the ravine was fenced off, and covered with rocks. It was so steep that I considered it a natural obstruction ..."

The Senator sat at his desk again.

"Deputy Kan, you are this close to losing your assignment!" Perkins used his cigar trimmer to clip the end of a fresh cigar. "One more time, and you're history!"

"Yes, Senator." Kan escaped from the office.

Mr. Harper remained in front of the Senator's desk.

"What's the next step, Harper?"

"Our tactical operations team has concluded that, since his cover was blown, Shale probably won't be hiding at schools anymore— at least not for a few years. So now they think that we *do* have to start searching the flop houses, YMCAs, and abandoned buildings, and probably rental apartments ... again."

"Oh, really? And what city do the eggheads in Tat-Ops suggest that we search?" mocked the Senator.

"All of them, sir."

36. XXi

Just before entering the New York headquarters of Chrysalis Chronology, Int., Senator Perkins squinted at the company's logo, mounted above the sliding glass doors. Piercing sunlight reflected from the large chrome letters, "XXi." The top of the building was nearly beyond his view, more than twenty stories above him.

The spacious lobby was filled with modern, chrome and glass furnishings, and the walls were decorated with floor to ceiling murals depicting the advancement of technology through history.

In a matter of seconds, Senator Perkins walked through the history of the world, passing images of pre-historic animals; pyramids and other ancient structures; historic western towns with horse-drawn carriages; modern, and sprawling cities with weaving, inter-connected roads, smoke-spewing factories, and electric power lines. And he passed glass cases protecting metallic models of transportation from past to present: a steam locomotive, automobile, airplane, and a rocket.

Medical photographs hung on the walls. They appeared to be close-up, multi-colored images of cells, enlarged from microscopic size, and colorized to create something resembling abstract art more than medical photographs.

Passing through a narrow corridor, Perkins heard the hum of machinery behind the walls just before the hot blue light of a camera bulb flashed, forcing him to pause, blinded for a moment. He was still scowling by the time he reached the reception desk a minute later.

The receptionist was a blonde woman, in her late twenties, who maintained a permanent smile. Besides the attractive receptionist, the green glowing letters of a CRT monitor caught his eye. To his dismay, an electronic resume of his professional and personal background information flickered on the screen for a moment before fading, just as a tele-type furiously punched out a document.

The Smart Kid

"Hello, Senator Perkins," said the receptionist. Her greeting exuded professionalism, as did her attire and overall demeanor.

The Senator nodded at the woman.

She ripped the page from the printer. Handing it to him, she said, "Since this is your first visit to our offices, you'll need to sign these papers, please. It's a standard non-disclosure form."

Perkins scanned it. A photograph of his own, stunned face from seconds before was printed at the top of the page. Below that, a legal document that began,

"Date: June 2, 1972.

I, Senator John Perkins, agree to the confidentiality requirements of Chrysalis Chronology Int., (hereby referred to as XXi) as listed forthwith:"

The list was long. The Senator scowled, signed it without reading it, and handed it back to the smiling receptionist.

"You may enter the elevator with the chrome logo to reach your meeting destination."

The symbol on the elevator door matched the one on the front of the building. The doors opened automatically as Perkins approached and entered. He turned to press a button for the top floor, but there wasn't one. There were no buttons. The doors pulled together, closing off the Senator's view of the receptionist.

An automated female voice said, "Welcome, Senator Perkins … approaching floor X-X-i." The movement was imperceptible, even when the elevator stopped. After a few moments the red neon letters above the door displayed *'X-X-i'*. Until the doors opened, it was questionable if the elevator had moved at all.

The first thing that the Senator saw was an expansive window that overlooked the New York skyline. But the skyline looked fresher or cleaner than usual. When Perkins stepped from the elevator into the dark hallway, lights turned on to his left, and the same female voice echoed 'This way please.' As he walked, the lights moved with him, illuminating above and before him and then turning off behind him.

The smooth, silver and glass doors at the end of the hall opened automatically. Another magical view of the city below stretched out beyond a floor to ceiling pane of glass, only blocked by an imposing chrome and glass desk. The directing lights stopped and formed an illuminated circle in front of the desk. When Perkins stood in the center of the circle, a light shone in his eyes so that he couldn't quite see the man who was seated at the desk in a purposeful shadow.

"First, thank you for allowing my clandestine participation on your very influential committee." The voice from the shadow spoke deliberately, giving weight to every word.

"Well, I want you to know that I appreciate your support all these years. Your company has been one of the main sponsors of my re-elections." The Senator did not smile appreciatively.

"Yes. We are aware of how you spend the *support* we give you. But we didn't do it to be nice. We consider it an investment … in our future. Thank you so much for coming to see me personally."

"Well, I don't like to be summoned to appear before you at a moment's notice, but in truth, I wasn't given much of a choice."

"Senator, you always have a choice. That is our working philosophy here: Freedom to choose your future."

"OK. I *chose* to come here because you won't communicate any other way."

"Face to shadow is my preferred method of communication. It's safer and cleaner."

"So what's so urgent?"

"We have learned that you had Shale in your control for more than a year, and you never notified us; you kept it secret."

"How did you … Well, I was intending to notify you after our scientists finished their experiments."

"Senator, you are an arrogant man. We know that the real reason that you never told us is because you want his longevity for yourself, and you didn't trust us to share the technology with you."

The Senator opened his mouth to say something.

"—Don't try to deny it."

Perkins frowned and closed his mouth, lips tight and straight.

The voice from the shadows continued, "We have a team of doctors ready to harvest his DNA for our own use. No experimenting necessary."

The Smart Kid

"Why do you think that your doctors can do it better than my team?" The Senator crossed his arms.

"At the risk of exposing our agenda, let me say that we were prepared because we *knew* that eventually someone with his gift would be discovered."

"How? How could you have anticipated someone like Shale? He's unique. You couldn't have predicted his existence."

"We did!"

"How could you have known?"

"Senator, I'm going to tell you something that no one outside this building knows. And I'm only telling you because you've become a partner, of sorts, with us. Decades ago, our founders seeded the population with genetic mutations under the guise of pre-natal clinics. Thousands of young mothers came to our free clinics for pre-natal care and embryonic vitamins."

The Senator stared into the shadow.

"We knew that there would be natural, random unions between the offspring of our genetic guinea pigs to create our biological anomalies. We just had to be patient and vigilant."

Senator Perkins uncrossed his arms, and almost pointed into the shadow, as he exclaimed, "Oh. I suspected that you were the cause. My team discovered your work. But we don't understand the science or the purpose."

"Nor do you need to. He is ours. Now we've learned that this little science experiment ... is in jeopardy. We want him back."

"How ... Yes, we're working on recovering Shale."

"Re-covery is a backward step. Here we move forward ... always."

"We'll be moving forward soon enough. I've got a competent team working on it." The Senator took a step back, crossed his arms, and looked at the scene out the window. "You have an impressive view way up here on the twenty-first floor, don't you?"

"You think you went up?"

The Senator blinked, and stopped breathing for a moment, as he frowned at the skyline.

"That's a pretty sharp photo you have there."

"Things are not always what they appear to be ... as our Mr.

Shale has demonstrated. He's actually twenty years older than he looks, today. It is his 32nd birthday."

Perkins uncrossed his arms. "What do you want to do—throw him a party?"

"I *want* to impress upon you the extreme importance of acquiring this ... technology. But it seems that your team has missed your opportunity of *recovering* him multiple times, over a period of *years*."

"Well, if you think this is so easy, why don't you do it yourself?"

"We don't expose our interests like that. We use other people's agendas to further our own. So our participation in this pursuit begins *and* ends with you and your committee, unfortunately."

"Well, the first time, he outsmarted my agent— whom I fired. This last time, he just got lucky. And the second time we think there was a leak, or someone helped him, we don't know who, yet."

"Time will tell. It always does."

"So you summoned me all the way here just to tell me to get my shit together?"

"No. To warn you. If your next *recovery* fails, you won't receive any more *support,* and you will no longer be useful to us."

The Senator straightened his body and peered into the shadow. "I'll handle it personally, the next time we find him." His voice was meek.

Every light went out except for one illuminating the exit door, which slid open without a sound.

Part Three
The Team

37. Planning the Attack

MARK AND MICHAEL Shale spent Monday catching up on the last 15 years. They sat on the couch in Michael's apartment, and for once in many years, they were oblivious to the passage of time. It was a glorious afternoon filled with tears and laughter. Michael told of the many schools where he'd hid. And Mark told how he had escaped.

"I noticed that the mesh covering of a window was loose on one side. I worked at it for a couple of days until I knew I'd be able to yank it off when the time was right. On a cloudy, moonless night, I yanked off the wire mesh and got out the window with a metal leg from one of the chairs. I also used that leg to leverage up a section of the outside chain-link fence that went straight into the ground for a foot. There was just enough space to wriggle through. And I've been running ever since, just like you."

"Wow, that was lucky," said Michael.

"Yes, too lucky. I suspected that they might have let me escape to lead them to you. At first, I wasn't sure. But I've always run with the assumption that they were right behind me," said Mark, involuntarily glancing behind himself.

"I know the feeling," said his small twin.

As Michael and Mark continued catching up, Mark explained how he'd spent his years searching for his brother. He did odd jobs along the way, often finding work as a mechanic at auto repair shops.

"Michael," said Mark, "You are very smart. It was genius to hide among the students. I'm sorry it took me so long to figure out your secret message to me."

"I had to be obscure about it, because I suspected that they heard it."

"Oh, they heard some of it. They asked me repeatedly if you had any special meaning in your message. And I honestly didn't know."

"I'm glad you were paying attention and figured it out." Michael smiled broadly. He couldn't stop smiling. They were silent for a moment. Michael took advantage of the break in the conversation to

The Smart Kid

retrieve some beverages from the kitchen.

"You still like root beer?" asked Michael handing Mark a can of pop.

Mark nodded. They both pulled off the tabs and set them on the coffee table.

Mark took a long swig and looked at his twin seriously. "It must have been hell for you, Bro."

"At first I was so scared of being discovered. For a long time, I feared that someone would see through my disguise and realize that I was actually a grown man. So I acted like a dumb student for a number of years. But you know what *I* figured out? It is *hard* to act stupid and uneducated forever. Things slip out. Students at the schools started calling me the smart kid. Slowly, I learned that it didn't matter if I was the smartest kid in my class, or school, because people just don't pay attention. I was very ignorant."

"When the article was published, *'The Genius Kid'*, that sure helped me to get on your trail. So I don't think you were that ignorant," said Mark.

"I remember that story. Usually, I avoided publicity, but I couldn't stop that one. But I realized that I had to let some information leak out for you to find me."

"Thanks, Bro. It's like you knew what I'd be looking for."

"Yes. Twin minds. Twin thoughts," said Michael with a wink. "But I meant that I was ignorant about people. Eventually, I started paying attention to how people act toward little kids. That's when I began to develop my purpose in life, and to understand the value of my secret identity."

"Secret identity, huh? I'm glad you found a purpose for your life," Mark said resting a hand on his brother's shoulder, momentarily.

"I remember the day I discovered the value of my hidden identity. I saw a teacher slap a kid around right in the classroom. There were no other adults in the room, just me and a few young students. But she saw nothing wrong with hitting a kid in my presence because I was just a dumb kid who didn't know enough to report it."

"So what'd ya do, dude?" Mark asked.

"First I yelled, 'Hey! Stop that!' She yelled at me, 'Shut-up or you're next!'"

"Then what?" asked Mark.

"I reported it ..."

"And?"

"Nothing happened. Either the other teachers didn't believe me, or they didn't think that any disciplinary action was required since no adult had seen it. But I think the teacher must have got wind that I snitched ..." Michael said.

"Why did ya think that?"

"I started getting F's on all my homework," Michael said, smiling.

"Well, the joke was on her. So what'd you do?" Mark asked.

"Oh, nothing ... just let the air out of all the tires on her car!" Michael blurted out. "You should of heard her swear! It was hilarious!" Michael laughed at the memory.

Mark roared. He thought that was the best course of action—something he'd have done.

Time flew by as the twin brothers shared histories all day long. Fifteen years were covered in six hours. Then they heard Charleen's pounding at the door, which startled them back to current reality.

After Charleen recovered from the multiple surprises of the Matt & Mark twins, the puzzle pieces in her head finally fit together.

"Charleen, I was running from my own brother!" Matthew exclaimed with a big smile. He stood next to his tall brother and put his arm around his waist. It was comical to call them twins. Mark looked down at his twin and rubbed Matthew's hair like he was a little kid.

"Hey. You know I don't like that!"

"Yup. That's why I do it! Missed you!" Mark grinned broadly. Charleen chuckled and shook her head.

Mark sat in the cushioned chair across from the couch. Matthew sat on the couch with Charleen.

"Now we know that you were the one sitting by the school in the truck ... Mark, why didn't you come to the school?" Charleen asked.

"I had to play it safe. I was pretty sure that the G-men were

The Smart Kid

close. So I had to be absolutely certain that they weren't lying in wait for me. It was safer to lurk in the background one more day than risk getting captured forever. But I couldn't stick around all day waiting at the school either because that would've drawn attention to me."

Charleen nodded knowingly. "It did. Our janitor noticed your truck."

Mark looked seriously at his small twin. "I saw you on the playground, though. You don't know how hard it was for me to not run over and give you a big hug. But I forced myself to be super cautious."

"And that's why you didn't show yourself at Deena Swenson's house?" Charleen asked.

"Oh, the young girl? I was planning to show myself after your little mission with her. So I snapped a few pictures and then waited for my long, lost twin to come out. But then you two took off and lost me!" Mark complained. "Charleen, I can never catch my brother."

Matthew smiled proudly.

"Wait. So you took those photos of Deena and the coach? Oh ... that makes sense now."

Mark looked at his twin. "Yes. I knew you were on a mission that I didn't want to interrupt. Once I figured out what was happening, I suspected that the photos would help you, Michael."

"Michael?" asked Charleen. A frown flicked across her face.

Mark frowned for a moment before the light dawned. "Oh, Charleen, I'd like to introduce you to my brother, Michael Robert Shale." He grinned broadly.

"Oh my! I feel so stupid," said Charleen. "Of course you weren't using your real first name."

"I'm sorry about deceiving you." Matthew showed an apologetic smile. "But you don't have to call me Michael. That would just sound weird coming from you after these two months."

Charleen nodded. "OK. Anyway, I was going to tell you that those pictures did their job— Coach Easton quit. But—"

"Oh, that's great!" exclaimed Matthew.

"But—" said Charleen.

"—One last mission accomplished, before you retire," said

Mark, with a grin.

"Yes, you're right, Mark. It *was* my last mission with the kids! I just realized …" Matthew looked up at the stack of notebooks on the shelf. "No reason to hide in the schools now that Mark has found me …"

"Nope," said Mark.

Charleen looked at Matthew, beside her on the couch, and then across the room at Mark. "So that means that you, both of you, will be moving on now? And leaving … forever?"

Matthew and Mark looked at each other but said nothing.

"Could I have something to drink, please?" she looked at Matthew.

"Oh, I'll get it," said Mark.

"No, you don't know where anything is. I'll get it."

Matthew went to the kitchen and returned with a glass of water. He sat on an arm rest on the couch. The twins watched Charleen.

And she watched them watch her. *More men leaving me.* After a moment, she regained her composure. "OK, you two, I was *going* to say that the photos got Easton to quit, but they also got me into trouble."

"What happened?" Both twins asked at the same time. They looked at each other in surprise, and then both smiled at an amazed Charleen.

"When Easton learned that he'd been followed, he figured out that it was me. So he followed me to your— this apartment. He tried to get me in trouble by taking pictures of us entering your apartment together. And he waited until I left too."

"So they know about you and me?" Matthew asked.

"Principal Heim and the school board chairman know how much time we've been spending together, and it doesn't look good. I've been suspended. I may not have a job."

"Oh, I'm so sorry Charleen. It's my fault," said Matthew. "I got you into this by asking for your help." He looked at her with sad eyes.

"No. It's not your fault. It's mine. I got myself involved by digging into the mystery of you. Actually, there is no fault because I don't regret getting to know you." Charleen looked at him with glad

The Smart Kid

eyes.

"I'm glad too," said Matthew, smiling.

"OK, OK. Enough with the Mutual Admiration Society," interjected Mark, standing. "The real issue is: Since this guy knows where Michael lives, does this constitute a threat?"

"It depends on how close the G-men are on our trail," said Matthew. "They know that I'm in the city. But they haven't narrowed their search to only Jefferson school."

"Oh yes they have!" said Charleen.

Both twins stared at her with open-mouthed surprise.

"You're sure?" asked Matthew, standing.

"Yes. That's why I finally believed you. They came to the school with a picture of you and said they were with Child Protection Services."

"Well, that's it," said Mark. "I led them to you. Now we're both at risk." He shook his head, regret showing on his face.

"Don't take the blame, Mark. It was going to happen eventually," said Matthew.

"So that means it's time to go, right?" asked Mark.

"Absolutely!" said Matthew. "It's only a matter of time before they interview everyone that ever talked to me. And that will lead them to Coach Easton, and then to this apartment."

Matthew had always felt that his apartment, like the others he'd stayed in for the last sixteen years, was his sanctuary; his safety zone. But the zone was about to be breached. The enemy could come at any time.

"It's time to pack up and leave," announced Matthew, with a finality in his voice.

Mark and Charleen eyes met, and then they turned to Matthew. Charleen asked, "You mean right now?"

Matthew nodded. "I think I need to be out of here by tomorrow."

Charleen stood and looked around his apartment at the furniture: the couch, chairs, TV and stereo consoles. "How in the world are you going to move all this furniture in a day?"

Matthew slowly scanned his furnishings. "I've never taken furniture with me. Everything I value can fit into four boxes: photos, mementos, notebooks, some clothes. But no kitchen utensils, appliances, or furniture. No microwave." He shook his head. "But of course, I'll take my Elvis album, and my new Eagles album." He smiled at Charleen.

Mark looked at his twin and then at Charleen.

The reference to their special time together made her smile back misty-eyed. "What about the four boxes?"

"Usually I ship them by bus, or the mail, to my new location. But I don't have a new location ..."

"Well, let's start packing now. We'll figure that out later," said Mark.

Matthew walked toward the bedroom closet to retrieve the well-travelled cardboard boxes. He dumped them in the living room and grabbed a stack of newspapers from the hall to use as packing paper. He brought a ball of string and a scissors, dropping them with the other supplies. They all sat on the floor around the boxes and started packing the things that were important to Matthew.

Charleen glanced at Mark. "So Mark, you were captured just because you two were twins?"

"Yes. They had Mike as the test subject and I was the baseline. We were a perfect experiment."

"That is so wrong!" she said. "How can they get away with that?"

"I guess in politics and government, the end always justifies the means," said Mark. He stood and started removing pictures from the walls.

"So Matthew, what do you think you'll do now?" asked Charleen, trying to sound casual.

"Matthew?" asked Mark, twisting to look at the others, crouched on the floor, around the boxes.

"Oh, Mark, I'd like to introduce you to your brother, Matthew Janson." Charleen gave a big teethy grin.

But her smile disappeared when Mark said, "Good one ... Char."

Charleen shook her head. "Charleen, please."

"You got it," he said, as he stepped near to hand her a framed photograph he'd removed from the wall. Then he surprised her by

The Smart Kid

tapping her shoulder with his fist, and winked at her. He turned to his brother. "I don't think I can get used to your new Matthew-name. Is that really what you want to be called now, Michael?"

"Well, it is my current name. But you can call me what you want, Mark."

"OK, Shorty." Mark walked back to the hallway to retrieve more photographs.

"Oh, great! Well, I've spent lots of time considering what to do with my life." Matthew stopped wrapping for a moment. "The Senator chasing me has, of course, made me hide out in schools, but it has done something good for me."

"Good?" asked Mark. He was holding the old picture of their family standing in front of the old house.

"Yes," said Matthew thoughtfully. "Last week Deena called me her friend. And this school year I was able to get Timmy Iverson's dad to stop hitting him. His mom became aware of the situation now. And their family life is improving. The same goes for a few other families. And Joey changed from a nerdy kid, with few friends, to a boy who is admired by the others because of the great collection of Superman comics that I gave him— "

Mark jerked his head to look at Matthew. "You gave him my Superman comics?"

"Sorry, Mark. I'd been dragging them around since I got them shipped from the college storage. So it helped Joey and me."

Charleen laughed.

"Wow, that kid has got a treasure of comics now," said Mark, shaking his head.

Charleen interrupted the sibling dispute. "OK, you're saying that you've done some good at this school with the kids. And since you've had to run from school to school, that you've helped kids in many different schools. Right?"

Matthew again looked up at the notebooks on the shelf, and nodded. "Mark could you lift that whole stack of notebooks down for me?"

Mark pulled them down and flipped through the stack of notebooks. "Hey Bro, looks like you've done a lot of work with the little twerps. But there's no way that I coulda sat through sixteen years of middle school again. I would've gone crazy with a capital K!" Mark plunked the stack of notebooks on the floor in front of Matthew and Charleen.

Matthew unrolled the string and began to wrap it around the stack of notebooks.

"Hey Bro, why are you going to bring that whole stack of old notebooks? You don't need them anymore." Mark stood over Matthew, watching him tie the notebooks together.

"Mark, I think that I'll decide what's important to me." Matthew glanced at Mark and then at Charleen. He continued, "Let me tell you a story about me. There was a time when I gave up. I stopped hiding in the schools. That was right after I almost got caught again. For over a year I just lived in a rented apartment in Madison, Wi. I had the money for it. I had stuff delivered; stayed on my own. But I was miserable. I had no goal or purpose. I couldn't make any friends, except for young kids who lived in the apartment building or who I'd see at the park. I had no adult friends. How could I?"

The others nodded; the compassion evident on their faces.

"That must have been when I completely lost track of your trail, around 1970. I think I previously tracked you to Lincoln Middle School in Kansas, right?"

"Yes. Good job, Mark. That break also helped to cool the trail for the G-men."

"Talk about a waste of time— I worked as a mechanic for a full year; used my nights and weekends to try to track you— when I wasn't out at the bars looking for women."

Charleen looked up at Mark, her mouth dropped open in surprise.

Mark shrugged his shoulders. "I couldn't spend every hour looking for him. I had to have a life too."

"Mark, I realized that, if you were going to find me, I had to hide in the schools again. But long before that decision I'd figured out that, if I must be in the schools, I'd try to make the best of it and help the students." Matthew tightened the string around the stack of notebooks and yanked at it as he tried to tie a knot. "And really, it was because of

The Smart Kid

this whole difficult trial that I started to ask myself, 'What is the purpose of life and why am I here? Why did God do this to me?'"

"So, God's out to get you, Bro?" Mark laughed.

Matthew smiled. "I mean, what's my purpose?"

Charleen smiled. "We discussed this at the Gymnastics meet. It's not materialism, or hedonism. Right?"

"Right," said Matthew.

"So the answer for you is ... what?" she asked.

"Altruism. Leaving your mark in the lives of other people that you've helped. And so *Mark*, I've left my mark in the lives of hundreds of students. And recorded it all here. This is what gives my suffering meaning."

"Hey, Bro, It's wonderful that you've decided what you want to be when you grow up. But I've spent the same amount of time, having one purpose: to find you. Now I did that."

Charleen looked up into his eyes. "Now what, Mark?"

Mark pulled up a chair, sitting on it backwards, resting his hands on the chair back. "Well, as I see it, we have two options: Keep running and hiding, like a ..." Mark glanced at Matthew, "... or fight back!"

Matthew gave the string one more strong tug, and it snapped. He held a short piece of string and looked at Mark in surprise.

"That stack of notebooks is too heavy," said Charleen, taking the ball of string from Matthew.

Matthew wasn't paying attention to the string. He focused on Mark. "Fight back? How's that supposed to happen?"

"Hell, I don't know. But I'm only 39, and I don't think I want to hide like a criminal until I'm dead."

"Or maybe just until *he's* dead," said Matthew.

"Well, that's the whole point, isn't it Bro? He wants to take you apart and see what makes you special so that he *doesn't* have to die. If he gets his way, he'll be in the Senate for the next fifty years."

"So that's really the issue?" asked Charleen.

"Yah, of course. It's a power grab. Don't believe any of this bullshit he says about Military Technology and National Security. Sure, he'll get that too. But that's not what's driving this old man," said Mark.

Charleen was surprised at the bitterness in his voice. *But if I were locked up as a lab rat for nearly two years ...*

"Listen," said Matthew. "If we run, we may only have to hide out for another five or six years until he's dead."

Mark stood abruptly, pushing the chair away. "Michael, You cannot be serious! Only six years! When I said that we had two choices, I didn't mean to imply that both were good. Fighting is the only right choice."

"Fight back?" Matthew asked. "How could we even do a thing to stop him? He's got power; the government; the authorities. He's got all the weapons."

"But he doesn't have the Right," said Charleen. "He's just got greed, and selfishness."

"No! We're together now. Let's just run! We can hide together. Why risk it?"

"Listen, Bro, I didn't find you so that I could tell you what to do. You have to make your own choice. But hiding isn't my idea of 'Happily Ever After.'"

"What are you saying?" asked Matthew. "You'd leave me now?"

Mark picked up a full box and carried it to the kitchen table, out of Matthew's sight. He spoke from the kitchen. "Do you have some string for this box? It's ready."

Charleen started to get up, but Matthew rested his hand on her arm until she sat back on the floor. "Mark, would you come here?"

Mark remained in the kitchen, silent.

Charleen remained very still, waiting for Mark's response.

Using his adult voice, Matthew said, "I asked you a question, Mark."

Mark came around the corner and stepped into the living room. "Wow! Was that you, Michael?"

Matthew nodded.

"Impressive." Mark bit his lip for a moment before answering. "Well, I'd help you get set up in some obscure hideout somewhere. But don't expect me to hole up there with you for the rest of my life. I don't feel like being a hermit in a cave or wherever. I won't do it." He

The Smart Kid

stared out the window.

Matthew stared at the floor. No one said anything. No one even moved for a minute.

Mark spun around to face Matthew. "I helped you escape so that you could be free. But now that I'm with you, it's time to change your tactic. I know that you're used to running. But you've got to man up, and hold your ground. You've got me, and Charleen here…" Mark glanced at Charleen, who nodded to him. "… so it's time to stop running. You sound like a man. But is there really one inside that small body?"

Matthew jumped to his feet. "You— you insensitive jerk!" He turned away and stared at his reflection in the decorative mirror hanging on the living room wall.

Mark stepped closer to his twin. He spoke quietly. "Michael, I never told you this. But Dad asked me to watch out for you, and to keep you safe. I helped you escape from the prison so that you could run. But being safe doesn't *always* mean running. Dad kept the world safe by fighting in the war. So what do you think that he'd do?"

Matthew turned around to face his twin, with a stern expression. "How are we supposed to attack someone who hides out in an office in Washington, DC?"

"Well," said Charleen, "You're the superhero. Let's put that super-brain to good use."

"Yeah! Now you've got the idea Charleen Baby!" said Mark, as he stepped close to rest an arm on Matthew's shoulder.

Charleen looked at them and smiled. But she smiled more on the inside at how these twins were different. Matthew was as meek as his body suggested, but thoughtful. But Mark was … something else."

"You know, all that superhero talk was just to help me to define my mission in the schools," said Matthew. "I know my limitations. We've been imprisoned before. If we try to attack Perkins, and it fails … we'll never get out. They'd kill us, rather than risk exposure of their crimes. You know that, right?" Matthew looked at Mark. Charleen looked scared.

"Let's at least *consider* a plan of attack," said Mark, who sat on the floor next to Charleen.

"Fine. I'll think about it," said Matthew, reluctantly. He started pacing the room, his head down, ignoring the others.

Charleen cut off three long pieces of string. "Mark, can you hold the ends of these strings for me?" Mark scooted closer and grabbed the strings as Charleen began braiding them together. They talked quietly and braided the string, while Matthew paced the room. Occasionally, Charleen giggled at something that Mark said.

After twenty minutes, Matthew stopped pacing, and faced the others. "Listen up. We have to get Perkins to come to St. Cloud."

"How?" asked Charleen.

"I don't know, but that's the first part. Second, we get him to incriminate himself."

"How?" asked Mark.

"I don't know."

"And third, we take the incriminating evidence to the news, police, and whoever else will listen. And 'No', I don't really know yet what that evidence will be."

"That's the plan?" asked Charleen. She looked doubtful. "You know that the last time that you and I tried to get incriminating evidence on someone we failed."

"Almost failed— if it wasn't for me!" said Mark, with a grin.

Matthew nodded. "Well, I guess we make a good team together."

"Yes," said Charleen. "I'll admit that the appearance of those incriminating photos of Coach Easton was good news."

"Hey team," said Matthew. "Let's deliver some news about Perkins. I mean, if we could get him to our little city, that would be big news right? I think that the TV station should know about it, don't you?"

Mark frowned up at his twin. "What are you thinking, Michael?"

Matthew took a step closer, forcing the others to look up at a sharp angle. "I'm not totally sure yet. But I'm certain that we must get Perkins to town."

"How do we get him to come all the way to Minnesota?" asked Charleen.

"You know that Minnesota is the Land of Ten Thousand Lakes," said Mark. "And to catch a big fish, you've got to use the right bait.

The Smart Kid

And I already know what it's like to be bait."

"What bait?" asked Charleen. But she already knew.

"Me and Michael. We'll make him an offer he can't refuse: both of us together for his little science experiment."

"Good thinking, Mark," said Matthew.

"In exchange for ... what?" asked Charleen.

"Well, your job is on the line," said Matthew.

"No! No!" Charleen raised her voice. "I am not going to buy my job back at the risk of your life!"

"Don't worry, Charleen. It's just a ploy. We don't plan on getting caught," said Matthew.

"We're going to have to ask for something else, too. Something that Perkins has to give in person," said Mark.

Charleen snapped her fingers and pointed up at Matthew. "An apology."

"Now that sounds believable," said Matthew. "We tell him that we want him to come in person to apologize to us for chasing us for years."

"No, not 'apologize to us,'" said Mark. "To Mom."

"What?" said Matthew. "She's still alive?"

"Oh God, Mike! I'm so sorry. I never considered that you mighta thought she was dead. No Bro! She's old, but doing fine at a retirement home. Ya know, she's living off the insurance money."

"You've seen her? Talked with her?" asked Matthew.

"Yes. Ever since I escaped. I visited her when I could. And sometimes I called her from a phone booth in a city that was far from where I was currently searching for you."

"But wasn't that risky?" asked Charleen. "Couldn't you have been caught again by the G-men?"

Mark smiled. "No. That is how I knew for sure that they were using me as bait to draw out Michael. They could have nabbed me any number of times, when I visited Mom. So I pretended that I didn't know they were after me, and they pretended that they weren't watching me."

"So Mom knows about me and why I haven't visited her?"

"Yes. She understands. She misses you, but she knows you'd

visit if you could."

Matthew became quiet, he brushed a hand against his eye. He walked into his bedroom and closed the door.

Mark turned his gaze from the empty hallway to Charleen, sitting on the floor. "He always was close to Mom."

"What about you?"

"I was closer to Dad. But you know, me and Michael have a connection too."

"A connection?"

"Yes, it's a twin thing. I could always tell when I was off track from finding him. I sensed that he would be in the mid-west."

"You mean you found him psychically?" asked Charleen, frowning across an open box.

"Heck no. I had to search; but I did have a feeling that I only had to search the mid-west, and in schools."

"How'd you know that?" Charleen tied off the end of the strings she'd braided and began to wrap them around the stack of notebooks.

"Because he said I'd find him among his 'own kind.' It took me a while to catch his meaning but when I did, I began searching schools. That's when I discovered an old record of him at a middle school. He used a name that was a clue that I recognized."

"But there's an impossible number of schools, how could you find him?"

"Well, at first, it was just random; like finding a needle in a damn big haystack. But after I tracked him to a few schools, using newspaper reports of exceptional children, and school photos, and other ways. ... It was something he said just before he escaped. I thought about it over and over: "I have to rush! More will hide me later."

Charleen frowned.

"I had tracked him to three schools that I was pretty sure he had attended. And they had the names: Washington, Roosevelt, and Lincoln. When I was thinking about this, a documentary about Borglum, the sculptor of Mt. Rushmore, shows up on TV. Mike had said, '... rush! More.' He actually said, 'Rushmore will hide me.'"

"Clever! How'd he come up with that?"

The Smart Kid

"He's very creative," said Mark. "Then I knew he'd only be at a relatively limited number of schools, named after the four presidents on Mt. Rushmore. That made the hunt much easier; instead of thousands and thousands, it was only hundreds and hundreds. But I still didn't know all the different names he was using for himself. And I had to make sure that the Government men didn't discover that I was looking at schools. So I had to create some false trails for them to follow. So it took a helluva long time ... If only I'd figured out his code sooner ... While I was searching schools, I tried to avoid being tracked myself. But I guess I failed."

"At least you got here before them to warn Matthew, um, Mike. Thank you. I appreciate it, more than you can know," said Charleen.

"So you and Mike, um, Matthew ... are close now?"

"Well, yes. Like friends." She thought she saw a flicker of relief in Mark's eyes.

She stood and tried lifting the heavy stack with the braided strings.

Mark stood to help, and lifted the stack of notebooks by the braided strings, testing the strength, as it dangled from his hand. He smiled at Charleen. "Nice."

The bedroom door opened and Matthew plodded toward them.

Mark and Charleen studied Matthew.

Matthew's eyes were red and his face, flushed. Speaking to Mark with a new resolve in his voice, "Not only has he imprisoned you and me, but he has separated Mom from her children for years. She already lost a husband and a son. Now, because of Perkins, it's as if she's lost her two remaining sons. ... Let's hurt this sonofabitch!"

The rest of the night was spent discussing a little of everything: more about the plan, and each person's history. Charleen shared about her life, and family. She told about the accident, and it wasn't as hard as when she'd shared in the grief group. She felt comfortable with these two men.

Two men.

She felt like she had known Mark for as long as she'd known Matthew. She found herself studying his face, and then looking at

Matthew for similarities. It was as if she were time-shifting from the past to the present; watching Matthew grow into a full grown man in the second it took her to turn her head from left to right.

It's incredible.

When it was very late, Charleen realized that the men assumed she'd stay at the apartment. She couldn't risk going out. No doubt the G-men were searching the city for Matthew. But they didn't know about the apartment, so they were safe, for the moment. So she took Matthew's bedroom, and the twins slept in the living room. As she closed the bedroom door, she heard the brothers arguing about who would get the couch.

Tomorrow it starts, she thought. And a dark fear crept into her heart.

38. Initiating the Attack

"Hey Mark, can you buy me a beer, please?"

Mark, Matthew and Charleen were sitting in the Press Bar, downtown St. Cloud, around 7:00 pm, reviewing the plan they had made the day before, and waiting for the news bulletin. Matthew's boxes had been packed and dropped at the bus station for shipping to a P.O. box in Chicago.

Mark was staring across the room at the TV, resting behind the bar. Half a dozen other patrons sat at the bar, or in booths along a smoky wall.

Matthew nudged his brother with his elbow. "Hey. Beer?"

Mark laughed. "Just like when you were in college!"

"Yes, it has been a long time since I've had a beer in public." Michael smiled.

Mark stepped to the bar, and returned several minutes later with three more bottles. Their wait had been filled with eating, drinking, and talking. But it wasn't a party. It was more like the luncheon that is served after a funeral. The seriousness of the occasion tempered their spirits.

A news bulletin flashed onto the TV.

"OK, there's the special bulletin about the escaped lunatic. Write down the number," said Mark.

Matthew had been nervously fiddling with a dime, spinning it on the table, during the wait. Finally, he took that dime and the phone number to the pay phone in the back of the bar. He dropped it in the slot and dialed the number.

One small coin to initiate our big plan.

A woman answered, "U.S. Marshal Service, Deputy Kan's office. Do you have information about the escapee?"

Matthew was surprised that they had a line dedicated just for him. "This is Michael Shale ... the escaped lunatic." Matthew waited. There was a pause.

Without revealing any emotion, the female's voice said, "Please

The Smart Kid

verify your identity."

"I was born June 2, 1940, to Howard and Jan Shale of Manly, Iowa. I have ... had two brothers Tom, and Mark, my twin."

"Just a minute." In less than a minute, a man's voice came on the line. The static-filled connection sounded distant.

"This is Deputy U.S. Marshal Kan. Are you really Michael Shale?" The voice cut through the phone line and stabbed into Matthew's heart.

Oh, what am I doing? He glanced at the exit.

"You know I am. And you know I'm in St. Cloud. And I wouldn't be surprised if you were tracing this call right now."

"Michael, we've never met, but it seems that already you don't trust me."

"Why would I trust someone who is trying to hunt and cage me like an animal?"

"Michael, you should know that my only job is to get you into custody for the purposes of national security and your own safety. I don't know what the plan is after that." He sounded so sincere and truly hurt that Matthew distrusted him.

Good act.

"You probably have a pretty good idea of what they want. And don't give me any of that BS about 'for my own safety.'" Matthew spit back.

Mark and Charleen were watching him from across the bar, their faces serious.

"No, it really is true, Michael," said the sincere-sounding voice. "Have you ever considered what would happen if the Russians or the Chinese were to catch you?"

Matthew *had* considered it, ever since General Thompson had mentioned that threat. He didn't fear it, but he needed Kan to believe him, so he simply said, "No."

"They would not be nice. Their goal would be to dissect you to figure out how to stop aging. Michael, they wouldn't care about you, or your family, or your life."

"So you're doing a favor for me and my family by catching me first?" asked Matthew, hoping to give Kan some leverage.

"Well, that is one way to put it, Michael. Once the military scientists discover your secret, you'd probably be allowed to travel wherever you want ... under the safety of the government, of course."

"No kidding? I hadn't considered how I'd need protection the rest of my life from enemy nations." Matthew paused for dramatic effect. "So you'd actually be willing to do that for me?"

He tried to sound as sincere as possible, at least as sincere as Kan. Every time Kan used his name, like they were old buddies, it made Matthew's gut tighten in disgust.

Deputy Kan continued, sounding even more friendly. "Yes, of course, Michael. I'm sure that Senator Perkins would try to make your life as comfortable as possible."

Matthew paused a moment. *OK, make this sound good.*

"My brother, Mark, and I are very tired of running. So—"

"Of course you are, Michael. It must have been very unpleasant for you all those years, with no one to talk to," said the overly-sincere voice of Kan.

"Yes, well—"

"I'm sure that you must have been lonely, since you probably couldn't have had any adult friends without taking them into your confidence. And that's a risk you wouldn't have been willing to take."

Matthew had planned to make a quick call and hang up. But Kan had mentioned a topic of great interest to Matthew. He seemed sympathetic to the hardship of the last decade. Matthew had been alone with his secret. It had isolated him. In a way, his pursuers knew him better than all of the students and teachers he'd befriended over the years. No one knew how hard it was for him, except for Mark and Charleen, whom he was watching, while listening to Kan's sickly-sweet sincerity.

Mark was tapping his watch, motioning for Matthew to hurry.

Kan was still talking. "... Michael, I know that you probably wanted to talk to your brothers or mother more than anyone in the world, but you weren't able to—"

"Yes, anyway, what I was going to say is that we may take you up on your offer, in exchange for a couple of conditions—"

"Oh, yes, of course, Michael. You didn't call to hear my

sympathies. But I do feel bad about—"

"We want a written apology to our mother, for chasing us for years and stopping us from visiting her. She hasn't seen her sons in years." He paused for a comment from Kan, but heard nothing but static. Kan's non-response added to the delay. The call was taking too long.

Mark and Charleen both stood, walked to the front of the bar, and peeked out the window.

"Second, we want Charleen Therry's job re-instated at her school, and all charges expunged from her record."

Mark and Charleen turned toward Matthew with worried looks on their faces.

"Of course, Michael. We can do those two things—"

"There's more," interrupted Matthew. "Third, we want Senator Perkins to apologize to us face to face, here in St. Cloud. We want him here within 48 hours. Notify us through the news when he's here, and we'll call this number again to set up the location where we'll meet. That's it. It's not negotiable! You won't hear from me again, until I know the Senator is in town!"

"Yes, of course. We will do that for you. Now, I'm wondering if there is anything else? Any other requests?"

Matthew frowned. Kan was being overly solicitous. *He just called my demands 'requests.'*

Mark and Charleen were scurrying toward Matthew.

"Just wait a minute. Let me discuss this with my brother—"

Mark jerked the phone receiver from Matthew's hand. He left it hang off the hook. Charleen grabbed Matthew's hand and pulled him away toward the back of the bar.

As the three of them headed for the back door, Matthew glanced toward the front window and saw flashing lights reflecting off the glass.

They ran west through the dark alley. When they reached the end, they peeked around the corner. The police were blocking the intersection so that a large, black truck could head down the one-way street in the wrong direction. That street led to The Press Bar.

A police cruiser pulled up to the curb and two officers jumped out and headed directly toward the trio.

Matthew, Mark, and Charleen jerked their heads back from the corner. "Oh, my, they're here already!" exclaimed Charleen.

Matthew grabbed her hand, and the three of them ran back down the alley. To their left, were the buildings that faced the street where the government vehicles were assembling. To their right, the businesses that faced the opposite side of the block. Directly ahead of them was the end of the long, dark alley.

As they ran toward the end of the alley, Matthew had the sense that their opportunity for escape was rapidly closing. When they approached the avenue, their only escape route, a police cruiser crossed their view. Instantly, Matthew, Mark, and Charleen jammed their bodies against the side of a building, crouching low. A short burst of a siren erupted for a second. Another cruiser leisurely passed the alley's exit and parked. The rear end of the cruiser was visible, protruding into the alley.

Doors slammed.

They were hemmed in.

The three fugitives turned and ran back the way they'd come.

As they ran west again, Mark yanked on every door they passed. All locked.

On both ends of the alley, flashing lights reflected against the buildings, casting flickering shadows. The alley exits were blocked. There were probably agents in the Press Bar already. At any moment, they may come bursting out the back door to the alley.

Fifty feet ahead of them, on the left, a door opened, and a man carried a trash can to a dumpster. He dumped the trash and returned, pulling the door open wide.

Mark sprinted forward at a furious pace.

The man entered the building, unaware of the trio running toward him.

The door eased shut.

Mark reached it at the last second and jammed his foot in the opening. As he waited for the others to catch up with him, he peeked into the building. The worn lettering on the door proclaimed "Hansen's Hardware."

The Smart Kid

Dark shadows of uniformed men appeared at each end of the alley, silhouetted by the flashing yellow and red lights.

Mark held the door for the others, and they slipped into the back of the hardware store, unnoticed. When the door closed behind them, they breathed a sigh of relief.

No one was visible in the store.

The trio started a brisk walk to the front of the store, glancing left and right as they passed dozens of empty aisles.

When they reached the front door, a voice from behind yelled, "Hey!" They all spun around to see a store employee. He added, "We're closed."

Mark flipped the lock on the door, and held it open for Matthew and Charleen.

They stepped into the street, a block away from the bar. It was silent and empty.

"They're going to be looking for at least two people together," said Mark. "So, one at a time, go in different directions. Make sure no one is following you. Meet back at Michael's." He grabbed Charleen's arm and directed her to right. Matthew turned left and walked along the street as fast as he could, without being overly conspicuous. He looked back to see Mark pull open the door to the hardware store and disappear inside.

Matthew got to his apartment first. He waited a nervous fifteen minutes until Charleen arrived. When she entered the apartment, she gave him a big hug. "Matthew, I'm so sorry again for doubting you. I'm so scared now!"

"It will be OK." He hugged her shaking body.

It was another twenty minutes before Matthew heard Mark at the door. Matthew swung the door opened before Mark had finished rapping on it. "What took you so long?"

"I went to the top of the office building and watched their operation from above. Bro, that was close! They had SWAT, local police, and a lot of black government cars surrounding that place. Man, they are good!"

"That's unbelievable!" said Charleen. "How could they have

done that so fast?"

"They had that line tapped and ready to go, for whoever called."

"All for us," Matthew added.

"Isn't it nice to be popular?" Mark joked.

Matthew shook his head.

"Oh, and one more thing..." Mark paused for a beat and said, "I think that Perkins is here."

"Really? So he was already here overseeing the operation," Matthew said thoughtfully.

"Maybe he's gonna make sure that they don't screw it up again," Mark offered, with a smile.

"Now what?" asked Charleen.

"Now we watch TV and wait for the special bulletin ..." said Mark.

Mark and Matthew simultaneously said, "... just for us." They grinned at each other.

Mark was already turning on the TV.

"Matthew could you please explain how Senator Perkins thinks that he can use you for military purposes?" Charleen asked.

"Soldiers who don't age would always be in their prime physical condition. And if they don't get killed in a war, who knows how long they could live and fight?" Matthew explained.

"OK, I was thinking about that ... How long will you live, Matthew?"

The twins looked at each other. Matthew nodded for Mark to go first.

"I'll bet you a thousand dollars that he lives longer than me," said Mark.

"The problem with that bet is that, if Mark is right, he won't be in any position to collect his winnings," said Matthew.

"It's true. Just like you, Charleen, I'm getting older every day: dying minute by minute. But my twin brother here, isn't going to die of old age."

"That should make you happy, Matthew."

"No one wants to die. But the alternative is watching everyone that you love pass away. And who would want that?" asked Matthew, solemnly. He paused briefly. "Actually, I've always had this unshakable sense that I would die tragically, or violently ..."

That sad note hit too close to home for Charleen, who became visibly upset. Matthew saw it, but it was too late. No one said anything for a minute.

The announcement on the TV broke into their silence. "We interrupt this program for a special bulletin. The dangerous mental institution escapee has been spotted in St. Cloud. All residents are encouraged to leave the downtown immediately and go home. Local downtown businesses are encouraged to lock their doors immediately, for their own safety. He is armed and extremely dangerous. Please lock your doors now. Police are on alert. Senator Perkins, who happened to be in town on government business, has offered his security detail to aid in the pursuit of this dangerous fugitive. Please co-operate with all government authorities. ... We now return to our regularly scheduled broadcast."

"There's the coded message, telling us that Perkins is in town now," said Mark.

"Hmm, that warning was smart," said Matthew.

"Yes," agreed his twin. "Clear the streets now to make it easier to spot us."

"We need to leave immediately, before the streets are empty," said Matthew. "It may already be too late." He looked grim.

Mark grabbed his pack of gear and headed out, with Matthew and Charleen right behind him.

Mark turned to his brother, gave him a one-armed hug and said, "See you at the show!" He winked at Charleen, opened the door, and raced down the steps. Matthew and Charleen took the elevator to the lobby, and exited the apartment building through the back utility room, abandoning his apartment forever.

39. Executing the Attack

BEFORE THEY REACHED the car, Matthew stopped at a phone booth and made one more important call.

One more dime, one last time.

Charleen led the short walk to Holly's car.

Matthew stopped, and stared at the Pinto. "This is our escape vehicle?"

"Yes. I took Holly's car so that I could leave school unnoticed. Why? Is there a problem?"

"Not yet."

She shrugged her shoulders.

They climbed into the compact car and drove a few blocks to a place that Charleen had been before— the Paramount Theater. They parked a block north. She left the keys in the car, and they walked the final dark, cold block. The streets were empty, like when everyone in the city takes shelter for a tornado. Snow flakes drifted to the streets, adding to the illusion of a peaceful night.

As they neared the theater, a police car came south down the street toward them. The lights began to flash, and the cruiser pulled across the road, against traffic. A beam of light from the car focused on them. A police officer jumped out of the car and approached, a silhouette against the spotlight.

Charleen let out a surprised gasp.

Matthew felt Charleen pulling at his hand. He calmly rubbed her hand.

"Hey, where are you going?" asked the gruff-sounding officer.

Matthew winked at Charleen. "Mommy, I'm scared!"

"Do you know about the warning tonight, ma'am?" asked the police officer, in a softer tone.

"Yes, Officer. My son and I were … "

"Eating," said Matthew, quietly.

"… eating downtown when we heard it. We're on our way home," Charleen said, sweet as pie, and topped it with one of her best

The Smart Kid

smiles.

The officer smiled. "OK, just checking. Hurry home."

Charleen and Matthew scurried down the street and turned a corner. They both sighed deeply.

"Secret identity?" Charleen asked.

"Award-winning smile?" Matthew replied.

They chuckled as they walked into the darkness of the alley.

By the time that they reached the back door of the theater, Mark was already there, holding a crow bar. He had opened the door with a little force. He dropped the crowbar next to a canvas bag. "We'll use that later. Charleen, when the G-men enter the front doors, you stop them from exiting with these ..." He removed a pair of chains and locks from the bag. "... and I'll be busy at the controls."

Charleen nodded, her eyes wide with fear.

"Ready for you, Shorty. I called Kan, did you make your call?"

"Of course!"

"Now we'll see if Perkins takes the bait. This is it!" Mark hugged his brother, put his arm over Charleen's shoulder, and led them into the theater.

Mark and Charleen headed to the front, while Matthew took the four steps up to the stage, into a dim space behind the rear curtain. He walked around the side of the curtain into the illuminated front stage. Although the front curtain was open, the bright stage lights made it impossible to see the theater seats or control box.

Matthew walked from the back to the front of the bare, wooden stage. In the stage wings, thick ropes stretched from the floor to the proscenium arch, attached to pulleys and fly systems. A ten-foot batten hung low, only five and a half feet above the stage. Matthew was able to guess the exact height because he could walk underneath the long metal pole, clearing it by a couple of inches. He knew that Mark had lowered it; his way of saying, "I'm ready for you, Shorty."

Matthew imagined how nervous actors must feel before an important show. But Matthew had good reason to worry about the upcoming show; his life depended on it.

I'm as nervous as a worm on a hook.

While he waited, he questioned his own ability to complete the plan. The doubt gnawed at his gut, impossible to ignore. Although he had conceived it, the plan was Mark's, not his. Matthew was good at *escape* plans, not *attack* plans.

It was fitting that he was going to face-off against the Senator on a stage. For the last fifteen years, Matthew had been acting, playing his expected role, effortlessly deceiving strangers and friends. His disguise was perfect. Too perfect. Where did the disguise end and the real man begin? The hard part wasn't fooling others, it was *not* believing his own act.

Can I face Perkins man to man? If only Captain Marvel would make an appearance tonight...

After several long, tense minutes, Matthew began to wonder if Mark had made his call when the front doors of the theater were pulled open with great force. Matthew saw the silhouette of a large man, who sauntered into the theater as if he owned it. When the doors swung shut, Matthew couldn't see anything but the spotlights. But he heard the slow plodding steps of his enemy getting closer. Matthew found it difficult to swallow. His breathing became shallow and rapid. He felt just as he had years ago when he was about to enter the Iowa highway patrol car. But, unlike that time, he didn't run.

"Come up on the stage where I can see you, or are you afraid of a little kid?" Matthew taunted. He waited with his hands in the pockets of his denim jacket.

A voice boomed from the darkness, "Remove your hands from your pockets."

Matthew removed his hands and smiled to himself. *He is afraid of me.*

Senator John Perkins ascended the steps to the stage and walked into the light.

Standing across from each other, they couldn't have contrasted more. The old, gray-haired man was an imposing size and towered over Matthew. He looked over-dressed in his tailored suit and tie, like he was ready to attend a political fund-raiser. He strode with an arrogant confidence that showed in every muscle of his face. With each step, Matthew was forced to raise his head higher to look him in the eye.

David and Goliath, thought Matthew.

The Senator stared down, impassively, at Matthew. "Am I afraid of a little kid? Now we know that's not true, don't we, Mr. Shale?"

Matthew, staring at Perkins, face to face for the first time, started to boil inside.

Run or Fight?

Matthew scanned the empty theater. He didn't usually wear a watch, but he did that day. He glanced at it, and looked toward the doors at the front of the theater.

"What's the matter? Were you expecting someone ... like a news crew?" The Senator showed a wicked smile. "My team got rid of them. National security, you know." His smile disappeared and was replaced by a look of contempt. "Maybe your brain stopped growing too. That was a pathetic attempt. I knew that you weren't really meeting to give up the race. But now its over. So easy."

Matthew clenched his hands tight and began breathing great, heaving puffs. Uncontrollably, the words gushed out like hot, boiling oil. "You! What you did was wrong! You are wrong! You are criminal! You had no business messing with my life or my family! You are an evil, arrogant, son of a bitch!" He yelled at the top of his lungs; he had no volume control. He couldn't hold it in; he had no anger control either.

"I expected as much from you. You're not just small in body, you're small in mind! You can't imagine the pressure I've had for the safety of this entire country."

"That gave you no right to imprison a boy for nearly two years. And for what? To treat me like a lab rat. I did nothing wrong! I wasn't a criminal. I didn't deserve it!" Matthew referred to himself as a kid to emphasize the gross evil of the Senator.

"You know kid, you're right. You didn't deserve it, and you didn't do anything wrong. But you were just an unlucky victim of life. And that wasn't my fault! But it was my responsibility to unlock your secrets for the safety of all the unworthy, thankless citizens of the country."

"You wouldn't have a job, if it weren't for those people that you call unworthy!"

"Don't lecture me kid! The people of this country are stupid as sheep, in need of a shepherd. They've given me power over you and them, so that they don't have to think about what I must concern myself with every day. So don't blame me. Blame the stupid sheep whose only concern is that they're safe to eat and shit their whole long life— thanks to me!"

"You're the one doing the lecturing. You talk as if you're some altruistic guardian of us all. I know this is really about you and your old wrinkled ass! You're in this for self-preservation!"

"Well, you're not as dumb as you look. If I benefit from this technology, then the world will be a better place. And I can continue protecting the stupid sheep, for as long as I live— which, thanks to you, I think will be a long, long time." His wicked smile re-appeared for a second.

Matthew's tight fists squeezed his fingernails painfully into his palms. He forced his breath out his nose in strong audible puffs, sounding like a bull ready to charge.

The Senator continued. "You're just as thankless as the rest of the country. You have this wonderful gift; the fountain of youth, and you hoard it all to yourself. You could have voluntarily shared it with everyone; with me ... and—"

"I hoard it because I despise it. This isn't a gift. It's a curse. If men like you controlled it, the whole country would be cursed. I'd rather die than let you have that power!"

"You die? That's funny," said the Senator, who didn't look amused. "No, you won't die. You think two years was long ? You're going to find out what its like to be imprisoned for two hundred years."

"So that's the extent of your *apology*? Just another threat? You have no regret in you at all!"

The Senator paused, unsmiling. "Regret? Yes. I regret that I didn't catch you a decade ago!"

Matthew looked in the direction of the control booth and nodded.

The Senator reached into his pocket and removed a small walkie-talkie. He pushed a button and said, "Get him."

The Smart Kid

Finally, the rage was too much. Matthew lost complete control. He ran to the Senator, and kicked him in the nuts. Hard.

The radio smashed to the stage as Perkins bent forward in agonizing pain. He dropped to his knees, landing eye level with Matthew. Through the pained grimace, his eyes were wide as he looked at Matthew, face to face, eye to eye.

With full force, Matthew swung his clenched right fist into the face of the kneeling man. It stung as his fist smashed the old man's nose. The Senator fell sideways to the floor, his shoulder taking most of the force, as his nose gushed blood. Matthew, the man, stood over the belittled, moaning Senator.

Senator Perkins pushed himself up to a sitting position. For the first time, he was forced to look up at Matthew. "You'll be sorry."

The entrance doors on both sides of the theater burst open, and six dark-clothed officers in full tactical gear, emblazoned with 'FBI', marched down the aisles.

Matthew sprinted upstage to the low-hanging batten, which began to rise. He jumped and grabbed it with both hands. Matthew was out of reach before an agent made it to the stage to help the Senator. *Thanks for the lift, Bro!* As he rapidly rose, his view of the theater improved.

"Where is that rigging controlled from?" yelled one of the agents. "Get to the control booth."

An agent ran up the aisle to the entrance doors and tried to shove them open but found them chained shut. He ran to the doors topping the other aisle and tried to force them open. He jammed his shoulder against the door, as he cursed and yelled, "Hey! Who did that?"

Matthew heard the clang of chains and smirked. As he rose above them, he couldn't help yelling out a victorious, "SHAZAM!"

Several of the FBI agents resembled riot police, wearing flack jackets and black helmets with reflective face shields. They were faceless soldiers just obeying orders; like the police that blasted peaceful protesters in Montgomery; or the soldiers that interred innocent Japanese families; or Mark's murderous guards. Evil-doers doing evil, in the name of goodness.

One of the helmeted officers ran to the stage, helped the Senator stand, and handed him a handkerchief. The Senator pressed it against his bloody nose and yelled, "Where the hell is Deputy Kan?"

The officer gave a muffled response and ran backstage. That worried Matthew. But he worried more about another agent who stood by the front entrance, pointing a rifle at him.

What? They can't shoot me. It occurred to Matthew that they could still do experiments on him, even if he had an arm blown off. But Matthew couldn't do anything about it. He just rose into the air, like a real life carnival game.

Shoot the monkey and get a prize. Again.

The sharp-shooter fired.

Matthew almost let go, startled by the gunshot.

The shooter's aim was true; one of the supporting ropes split apart. An end of the metal pole arced downward, carrying Matthew with it. He wrapped his arms and legs around the pole as it swung wildly. The lower end of the pole nearly hit the Senator, who was forced to drop to the floor as it swooped across the stage.

After a minute, the bottom of the pole was out of reach as Matthew was lifted higher. When it stopped rising, Matthew hung more than twenty feet above the stage, but still several feet below the catwalk.

It's the ropes challenge again. Matthew had no doubt that he could do it. Fifteen years of rope climbing in phy-ed class had prepared him for that moment.

He pulled himself up, hand over hand. But Matthew's grip on the pole decreased as the perspiration on his hands increased. With each hand that strained to pull him up another foot, he slipped back a few inches. He worked harder than he ever had on a rope.

He needed to climb two more feet to reach the more secure grip on the single rope that supported the swinging batten.

As he struggled to pull himself up another foot, he saw the marksman lift his rifle.

Matthew moved another foot higher.

The agent was lining his sight.

With only two more inches to reach the rope, Matthew's hands started to lose their grip. The pole squeaked through his cramping

The Smart Kid

hands.

Matthew was certain that the marksman would squeeze the trigger before he reached the catwalk. He'd crash to the stage when the rope busted, and maybe break a leg. But the doctors in the prison would fix him up and keep him healthy ... for the rest of his life.

Darkness exploded into the room with the bang of the rifle. It was complete blackness.

Matthew heard the shot, and waited a second to realize that he wasn't hit, and neither was the rope. He was hanging safely in the darkness.

Someone yelled, "Hey, turn on those lights! Who did that?"

Matthew silently thanked his team for the extra time to finish his climb. He pulled himself up the rope a few more feet, and reached the catwalk. He rolled to his back, and flexed his aching fingers for a second. The lights turned on as he began running along the catwalk.

Senator Perkins yelled his orders to the agents. "The back is guarded. Check for side exits. ... Bust open the front doors and get to the control room."

When Matthew reached the ladder, he grabbed the side rails, pressed his feet against the sides of the ladder and slid all the way down— almost. His burning hands released, and he fell back toward the floor, too far.

Open arms saved him from a concussion, as Matthew and a black-uniformed FBI agent fell to the ground, amid groans of pain. It was the officer wearing the full riot gear. Their faces were inches apart, but Matthew saw only his scared reflection in the dark shield.

"Run, Tommy!" said a woman's muffled voice from behind the mirrored shield.

Matthew saw his scared reflection change to open mouthed surprise. He scrambled to his feet, before the agent could stand, and pushed through the back doors.

Mark was waiting for him. As soon as Matthew ran out, Mark slammed the doors shut and jammed the crowbar between the handles of the double doors.

Charleen was sitting in the green Ford, with the motor running.

"Listen Bro, they didn't know we were in the video control

358

room, until it was too late. We've got the tape!"

Charleen waved a VHS cassette in the air.

"Go!" ordered Mark. "I'll hold them off!"

"What? You can't!" yelled Matthew. "Let's all go now!"

"Look, I gotta lead them the other way. Misdirection! Meet you back at Charleen's. You're the one they want. Get outta here!"

There was no time to argue. Matthew ran to the driver's door, and jerked it open.

"Move over, I'm driving!" he said to a surprised Charleen.

"I thought you couldn't drive."

"Watch me!"

She climbed over the center divider and shift knob, and fell into the bucket seat.

Matthew slammed the car into gear and stomped on the gas pedal, forcing the small car to spit gravel and swerve wildly as they skidded around a corner.

Mark watched them speed away and smiled for a second, until the double doors pushed forward two inches and stopped with a jarring thud. Someone began kicking the door.

Mark ran a half block to his truck.

When he started it, he jammed one foot on the brake and the other foot on the accelerator. The tires squealed and smoked. The air became cloudy with the burnt smell of rubber. When he released the brakes, the tires squealed and spun on the pavement, as black smoke spewed from his truck.

In that same second, the doors of the theater busted open.

As the truck careened around a corner, Mark glimpsed a pair of agents, motionless, watching the truck escape, but certainly unable to see how many occupants were in the truck. Just like Mark had planned.

Although Mark was driving as fast as he could through the side streets of St. Cloud, he didn't like his chances. He didn't know the city well, and it was likely that at any turn, he could find himself facing a dead end.

It only took a few minutes before the black Broncos appeared in

The Smart Kid

Mark's rear-view mirror. Red and yellow lights flashed in the front grille of the pursuing cars. As they caught up to him, Mark tried to estimate how many vehicles were following him. It looked like three; the last one would be the Senator's car.

Mark weaved and dodged his truck through the streets. He slammed on the brakes, turned sharp, and hit the gas hard, while his truck fish-tailed and the tires tossed up gravel at the vehicles that were too close.

They had left the buildings of the downtown miles behind, and had reached a residential section of St. Cloud. When he came to a long straight street, Mark gunned it, reaching more than 70 mph. At every intersection he laid on the horn as a warning. Cars in crossing intersections screeched to a stop, and pedestrians jumped away from the curb, giving way to the speeding, four-car caravan.

They were too close; close enough to start shooting.

But Mark didn't care because they were getting farther from Michael and Charleen. He was fairly certain that they didn't know about her car, or they wouldn't be chasing him.

A memory flashed through his mind. He was in the control booth taking the videotape out of the machine, and the Senator was being helped by an agent when he yelled something ... *"Where the hell is Deputy Kan?"*

Mark knew Deputy Kan. Weeks after Michael had escaped, Deputy Kan questioned him for an hour. While Kan had learned little from Mark, Mark had learned that Kan was the man assigned to re-capture Michael. He was the head of the team.

Where is he?

Oh no!

Mark slammed on the brakes and took a hard left, and another. He had to get back to Charleen's before it was too late.

It was a trap.

But first, he had to lose the government cars trailing him. *I need to change my tactic.* He raced to the commercial district, near the center of the city. *I just need the right building ...*

Mark aimed for an alley flanked by brick walls. He floored it for a few seconds, hit the brakes as he turned into the alley, and stomped on the gas pedal. The right side of the truck slammed against the brick of the adjacent building, scraping and screeching for a few ear-blasting seconds. After thirty feet, Mark slammed on the brakes, and shoved the transmission into reverse. He floored it, racing backward at top speed, unsure if his plan would work. Bracing himself with a murderous grip on the steering wheel, Mark pushed his head forward to protect from the recoil. He couldn't see what was behind him, but he knew what was coming.

Just as he reached the end of the alley, Mark felt a bone-shaking jolt against the back of the truck. His head lurched backward violently, but only tapped the back glass with a small, painful hit. The truck crunched to a stop as the tail gate smashed against the Bronco with an ear shattering explosion of metal and glass.

Mark slammed it into first gear and stomped on the accelerator. The truck didn't move, but the wheels spun and smoked wickedly.

He looked back and saw the corner of truck bed crunched upward. He flipped the shifter to reverse again, and pushed the Bronco back a couple of feet. He slammed the truck into first gear and rotated the steering wheel to the left, pulling at a different angle, dragging the Bronco a foot before the truck broke free. It jerked toward the left wall of the alley, disintegrating the front quarter panel against the brick building.

As the truck lurched forward, Mark glanced back at the damage. The Bronco had just started to turn into the alley when the truck had smashed it. The driver's side door was crushed like a pop can. The driver's head was bloody. And to Mark's surprise, the second SUV had smashed into the back of the lead vehicle. Neither one was in any condition to drive.

The Minnesota twin had hit a double! Of course, the Senator wouldn't be pursuing Mark without his security team. So Mark hit a Triple.

Maybe a Home Run!
But only if he made it to Charleen's in time.

40. The Chase

It was past 9:30 when Matthew & Charleen reached her neighborhood. As they neared the house, Matthew calmed himself and relaxed, feeling safer. The streets were quiet. It was a peaceful neighborhood filled with families unaware of the violent assault that had occurred downtown.

Matthew asked, "Do you think that they know about you yet?"

Charleen had become more relaxed also, and released her tight grip on the edge of the seat. She scanned the darkness. "If they did, I think this place would be crawling with G-men."

"Yes. I guess you're right." Matthew drove behind the house, out of sight from the front street.

As they ran into the house, Matthew said, "Just take the basics for now: money and a few clothes— in case we have to run. But if we deliver this tape to the news station, our worries will be over. Senator Perkins will be exposed for what he's done."

When they entered the kitchen, Charleen dropped her handbag, and turned to Matthew. She placed both hands on his shoulders and peered into his eyes.

She had his full attention.

"You asked me to pack my things, as if you're assuming that I'll just run with you and Mark; abandoning my job here."

Matthew showed his surprise. He *had* expected her to run with them. Ever since they'd met, he'd felt a growing bond of friendship to her. Her reputation in this school district had been permanently damaged. And last night the three of them bonded with a shared goal. He swallowed hard,

"Charleen, do you mean that this is the end for us? I have to run and, of course, you don't. I'm sorry, I just assumed ..." He looked away, not wanting her to see his disappointment.

"No, Silly!" Charleen touched his chin and directed his face at her. "What I meant was: How do you know me so well?"

Matthew breathed a sigh of relief. He smiled. "I'm not sure.

The Smart Kid

Something clicked when I saw you."

"Matthew, I'll go with you now, and once you get settled in a new place, I can come back and wrap up my affairs here, if that's what we finally decide is best. OK?"

"Thanks. I appreciate you being with me as I start a new role in life, Charleen."

She wrapped her arms around his small body. "Matthew, if we're successful in this attempt to expose Perkins's crimes, then you'll also be exposed. The world will know about you."

"Well, maybe that's good. Notoriety may protect me better than a secret identity did."

"Yes, you're not going to be secret anymore."

"That's fine by me."

The black Lincoln Town Car idled in a shadow, headlights off, under the low hanging branches of a large oak tree. It faced the yellow house on the crossing avenue, at the end of the city limits. One of the men in the car snapped pictures of the Pinto's two occupants, as it turned left from the driveway.

The black sedan crept toward the corner. When the Pinto had traveled a sufficient distance, the Town Car turned and followed.

Without warning, the Pinto turned right. It was heading out of town.

"Don't let them get too far ahead of us," came a voice from the back. "We'll trail them until the security team can intercept. We will not lose these two under my watch."

The driver glanced into his rear-view mirror. "Yes, sir."

"Hand me that radio mic," ordered the man in the back seat. The driver stretched the mic cord to him.

"Security Team Alpha, this is Kan. Do you read?"

After a burst of static came a distant voice. "Yes, sir."

"I need you to intercept the target. He's headed south out of town."

After a pause, the static filled voice said, "Sir, we thought that we were chasing the target. But there's been an accident. We're out of commission."

Kan stared out the window and cursed. Speaking into the mic he said, "Call the beta-team now. Notify me when they're in range."

"Yes, sir. And watch out for the brother in the pickup truck. He's deadly."

Kan dropped the mic and sat back in his seat.

As the two cars neared the outskirts of town, traveling along a narrow highway, the Pinto accelerated. The driver was a pro. He continued the pursuit but backed off further since there were so few cars for coverage.

"Deputy Kan, Sir?"

"What?"

"How did you know they'd escape and go back to her place?"

"Senator Perkins is a stupid ass. He trusted in his own pompous superiority and ability to outwit Michael Shale. He thinks like a puffed up politician, not like a desperate prey being hunted. Shale is very smart. I knew he'd be prepared for Perkins. And I'm glad. Now I get to catch Shale, get the credit finally, and then I can get out of this endless assignment."

The driver saw only a few cars on the road. Behind them, the bright headlights of a truck approached at high speed. When it caught up to the Lincoln, it slowed and trailed it, dangerously close. The three vehicles traveled through the darkness, south on Highway 16, a narrow winding two-lane that passed through farmlands. The Lincoln Town Car trailed the Pinto by a quarter mile. But the truck was directly behind the Lincoln.

"Sir, we have a tail."

Deputy Kan turned in his seat and saw the grille of a large Ford pickup truck filling his view.

"That's not a tail, that is a threat!"

The pickup bumped their car.

"Don't slow down!" ordered Kan.

The pickup truck bumped them again, harder. The pager and binoculars tumbled from the dash.

"Speed up!"

As the Lincoln accelerated, it closed in on the Pinto, which increased its speed too.

"OK, we're blown. Just don't lose them!" ordered Kan.

All three vehicles traveled along the highway at more than 90 miles per hour.

When the Pinto reached a slower moving car, it was forced to swerve around it, suddenly leaving an obstacle in the path of the pursuing vehicles. The Town Car swerved violently around it while the surprised drivers yelled obscenities.

The truck easily maneuvered around the slow car, accelerated, and closed in on the government vehicle again. It jerked into the oncoming lane and came up alongside the Lincoln.

The government driver saw the truck on his left seconds before it veered and smashed against them with a cringe-inducing grinding as metal scraped against metal at high speeds. The road
became littered with pieces of shiny trim, paint and metal shards.

"Dammit! I didn't expect this!" yelled Kan. He lowered the window, and unholstered his Glock. He aimed at the front tire which should have been an easy target since the front quarter panel was almost ripped away, but the truck swerved from side to side, and braked as Kan fired his weapon. The bullet shot past the hood of the truck.

The Pinto turned without warning, to the right, onto a gravel road.

The government driver hit the brakes, swerved hard and skidded, barely making the turn.

When the truck braked and turned sharply onto the gravel road, it immediately lost traction.

For a moment the speed of the chase slowed dramatically as the tires of the vehicles spun on the loose gravel. They were all within a few hundred yards of each other. Sand and dust was getting kicked up and spit by every tire. The dust cloud was enormous.

High-speed pebbles chipped the windshield of the Town Car.

Kan leaned forward, peering through the dust, barely able to see the dark-haired woman, who glanced back at him before yelling at her driver. "Look at that! The little man is driving the car. No wonder they're swerving all over the place. The midget can't drive!"

The driver checked his side mirror but saw only dust. The truck wasn't in sight— until it smashed into the back of the Lincoln.

The Lincoln slipped sideways, and the driver, not used to gravel roads, over-compensated-- causing the rear end to swerve violently in the other direction for a moment.

"Dammit! Just catch up to the teacher and the kid and knock 'em off the road, before we get taken out," yelled Kan's adrenaline-powered voice.

The driver stomped on the accelerator, bringing the Lincoln to top speed. He couldn't see the brake lights of the Pinto, until it was too late. The Town Car clipped the left side of the Pinto, smashing the tail light.

The Pinto swerved erratically, and braked, forcing the Lincoln and the truck to brake suddenly. It turned again, passing a sign that read, *"Granite City Quarry."* A second later, the car and truck turned and sped past the sign.

"OK, they're trapped now!" yelled Kan. "Finally! Do you know how long I've been trailing this little bastard? And it must be his brother behind us. This is even better— because now we've got them both again. Get us turned around and just block the entrance. I'll radio for back-up and we'll be done with them before this night is over!"

The driver was ready to obey, when he saw the grille of the truck threatening in the rear-view mirror. In a second, he realized that the Pinto was coming *toward* him. The government car was between the other two vehicles, about to be smashed on both ends. The driver jerked the steering wheel to the left as the counselor's car swerved to the right of the Sedan, and then was gone.

A wooden barricade seemed to appear from nowhere.

The driver slammed the brakes but was unable stop soon enough and the Lincoln smashed into the barricade, splitting the boards nearly in half, and busting the expensive grille.

Skidding to stop, the gravel crunched as the truck came

The Smart Kid

within inches of smashing into the side of the Lincoln.

A cloud of dust hid the counselor's car ... for a second.

There was a loud crash, and an explosion.

The dust couldn't hide the fiery wreckage at the floor of the quarry. The Pinto had swerved and smashed through the barrier and sailed downward, flipping over and smashing, rear end first, to the jagged quarry bottom.

Kan and his driver jumped out of the car.

"Look how close we came to busting through!" yelled Kan to his driver.

The driver exited the the truck. As Kan had suspected, it was Mark Shale, their fugitive bait.

Kan walked forward to view the wreckage.

Mark ran to the edge of the quarry and stared at the fiery debris, 100 feet below. "NO, NO. Michael! No!" He stood there for a minute and scanned the quarry for a path to the bottom.

Then he saw Kan.

Mark lunged at Kan, who was caught off guard. Kan, knocked onto his back, tried to pull his pistol from its holster. Mark batted it away as he jumped on top of Kan and started smashing him in the face. First, with one solid, rock hard fist, and then the other. Left. Right. Kan's face was instantly bloody. As Mark continued punching, his fists became covered with blood. Each new punch on Kan's face left a red fist print. "You son of a bitch! Murderer!"

A shot rang out and the ground beside Mark erupted in a small explosion. Dirt shot up and hit Mark in the face and eyes. He fell back, shaking his head, and rubbing his eyes.

Kan scrambled back, pushed himself up on his elbows and turned. His driver was pointing a gun at Shale. The three men remained motionless for a beat.

The two men struggled to stand. Mark steadied himself with a hand on the hood of the car. Kan stood and brushed off the dirt from his pants. His driver handed him a white handkerchief which he dabbed against his face and saw it instantly change blood red.

"Shit! You ass! You broke my nose!"

Mark just stared at the smoldering wreckage of the

unrecognizable Pinto. After a minute, Mark turned to Kan. "Kan, after all these years, you just wouldn't give up! And look what it got you!"

Kan didn't look again. He knew.

"I suppose you think that you just get to walk-away scot-free, and cover this up with the government's support." Mark seethed with anger. The venom in his voice could have killed a rattlesnake.

Kan was still dabbing at his face with the bloodied handkerchief. "I know it won't matter to you, but I never cared for this assignment, or Perkins. I didn't think that what they did to you and your brother was right— even for 'National Security'". He paused and dabbed at his face again.

Mark started walking away, but stopped, and turned back when he heard Kan's voice again.

"I never tell people my true nationality. There's still too much prejudice against us. I'm really Japanese-American. I was born in the U.S. but for nearly four years, as a teenager, I lived in a Japanese internment camp for the purpose of 'National Security.' So I know what it's like to be wrongfully imprisoned. But I had to do my job. I just didn't put my heart into it, or follow every clue we had. Maybe that's why it took me years to track you down."

He paused, straightened his body, and raised his chin.

"I know— *knew* who Matthew was, but I still always felt like I was playing Hide 'n' Seek with a kid. But it was my job. And now, you're right: this will get covered up from the public. But I'll give my full report to a Senate oversight committee about what Senator Perkins did to you ... and your brother. And I'm doing that ... for me."

He walked back to his car. Before he opened the door, he said, "I'm sorry."

The government men got into the car and drove away, leaving Mark alone, silhouetted by orange flickering light.

41. Reunion

MARK STOOD ON the edge of the quarry and cried.

Maybe if he'd never found his brother, then Michael would still be alive. "I'm sorry, Michael!" His legs gave out. He sat on the ground and cried bitterly for many minutes.

After he regained his composure, he got into his truck and found a sloping path to the bottom. The smoldering car was crumpled like a tin can. A burnt tin can. There was nothing recognizable inside the car, fortunately.

Mark remembered the words his brother had just said that night, "I've always felt that I would die tragically, or violently..." He shook his head in disbelief.

Junk was spread across the quarry base. Mark saw a suitcase, clothing, and a black satchel 30 feet from the wreck. He examined the satchel. It had the initials CAT embossed on it.

Inside, Mark found Charleen's driver's license and a picture of a Charleen and a man holding a young boy.

He also discovered a notebook. Mark stood in front of his truck's headlights and opened the notebook, immediately recognizing the hand-writing. It was Michael's. The emotions nearly overwhelmed Mark again. He read the first sentence: *"I met the new school counselor today ..."*

As Mark slowly drove to the top of the quarry, he saw the flashing lights of a sheriff's car. A news van sped through the gate. The side of the van read, *'KSTC News Channel 11.'*

Mark stopped and stepped out of his truck.

The sheriff was already standing at the edge staring down at the wreckage.

The white news van skidded to a stop and the side door slid open. A woman and a cameraman hurried out. The cameraman took up a position a few feet away, as the reporter approached Mark. "Excuse me, sir. Did you see this deadly crash?"

Mark just nodded.

The Smart Kid

"Who was it?"

"My brother."

"Oh, I'm so sorry." She motioned to the cameraman. He shut off the camera and removed it from his shoulder.

The sheriff walked over and asked the reporter, "How'd you get here so fast?"

"Police scanner," said the young, dark-haired woman. "And you?"

"Someone reported a stolen car, headed down that highway."

"I found this." Mark handed the sheriff Charleen's driver's license. He kept the notebook and photo. The sheriff took Mark's name, and asked him to stop by the office in the morning to give his report. The sheriff and reporter began discussing the crash.

Mark had no interest in the conversation, or anything, for that matter.

He dragged himself into his truck and drove out of the quarry. As he traveled along the gravel road, a taxi approached. Lights flashed at Mark. Both vehicles stopped.

Mark turned off the headlights.

The rear door of the taxi opened. The silhouettes of two people, a woman and a small boy, walked toward him.

What?

The taxi turned around and drove away.

Mark turned on the headlights. It was Charleen and Michael.

They ran to Mark and hugged him. The trio stood there for a long time hugging while tears flowed freely.

Finally, Mark asked, "How? Who was that? How'd you know?"

Michael and Charleen turned serious. Through tears and sniffles, she said, "Some very troubled students ... hiding in my shed ... we packed the car ... they stole it when we went back in the house."

Michael finished for her, saying, "We called the sheriff, anonymously. We didn't know who stole the car, at first. We also called the taxi to try to follow ... There was only this one highway that they could've taken and ... the flames were easy to see from the highway."

"But I thought it was you two! I saw a boy and woman driving in the car."

"Yes. A boy and his tall sister," said Charleen. "We found some stuff they left in my shed. It was revenge against me while they tried to get to their mother. So we knew which direction they were headed, to the Twin Cities."

"They just wanted to visit their mother?" Mark said, shaking his head.

"I don't blame them for that," said Michael.

"What about the tape? Is it burnt?" Mark looked from Michael to Charleen.

Charleen removed it from her handbag and gave it to Mark.

"That is it: The Senator admitting that he illegally incarcerated *a little boy!*" Michael said.

"And getting kicked in the nuts!" Mark said, with a grin. "Hey! You two are dead, as far as he knows."

Michael and Charleen stood speechless.

"Get in the truck and don't let anyone see you."

Mark walked back to the news reporter and handed her the tape. Before Mark let go, he said, "This tape has evidence implicating Senator Perkins in kidnapping, misuse of government resources, this crash, and the death of those two people." He released the tape into her hand.

The news woman's eyes got really big as she stared at it like it was an Edward R. Murrow award. "Hey, someone called to tell us that Senator Perkins was at the Paramount Theater, but we weren't allowed in. Was that you?"

"No. That was my brother."

"Why did he want us there?"

"Misdirection!"

Mark turned, hopped in his truck, and the trio vanished into the night.

42. Meeting Mom

"Mark, come on! We've got a few hours drive in front of us!" yelled Michael.

"OK, just a minute— It's on the news again ... There you are! ... Haha! I love it!" Mark said, pointing to the TV, as he looked at his brother, who just rolled his eyes and walked away.

The news station had reported that Senator Perkins was forced to resign due to a video recording of the Senator incriminating himself, and supported by the testimony of every member of a task force he chaired, with the most damning testimony from his own personal aide. He was being investigated by a Senate oversight committee for abuse of power, kidnapping, personal use of funds, using FBI resources and manpower for personal gain, and more.

But the best part of the report— and much to Mark's amusement it was shown repeatedly on every news station— was the scene of the Senator getting kicked by Michael.

Charleen followed Mark and Michael as they walked past a pair of twin oak trees towering over the entrance to Heritage Care Center in Mason City, IA. They knocked on the door labeled 'J. Shale'.

The old, gray-haired woman opened the door. "Michael! Mark! Oh my! Thank the Lord. My prayers have finally been answered," she said in a soft voice. She reached out her arms, hugged both of her boys and kissed them on the cheeks with tears in her eyes, as she smiled at Charleen.

"Mom," said Michael. "This is Charleen, my friend."

Mom reached an arm out and pulled Charleen into the group hug. After a long moment of tears and hugs, she cried, "Once you were lost, but now you're found. I've missed you so much. I'm glad the waiting is finally over."

"Yes, me too," said Michael.

After a few minutes, Mrs. Shale shuffled to a table in her modest room and retrieved an envelope emblazoned with a government logo.

The Smart Kid

"I received this letter from someone who worked with the former Senator Perkins. She said that he was too busy to write because he had many meetings to attend. But she said that he's sorry for the trouble he put you through and that he apologizes to me. It was so nice of her to send it."

"Her?"

"Yes. And she included a personal note to you, Michael."

"What? Let's see ... It's a hand-written note that reads,

> "Dear Tommy/Matt/Michael,
>
> "I thought that you were dead. Ten years ago, when I was 15, I saw you get shot and fall into the Arkansas River. I didn't know who did it or why. But that event changed my life. I joined the FBI and, two years ago, got assigned to a unit assisting Senator Perkins.
>
> "Then I saw you in St. Cloud, unchanged, exactly as I remembered you. And you were being shot at again. I'm so sorry for my participation in the assault at the theater. It was wrong. I tried to help.
>
> "The news reports said that you were killed at the quarry. But I'm sending this letter to your mother anyway because I have a feeling that you're a survivor.
>
> "Your friend, Michelle Hanson."

"Mark, when they were shooting at me in the theater, weren't you the person who turned off all the lights?"

Mark wrinkled his brow. "No, I was running out of the theater at that time. Besides, the main power switch was backstage. Why, who is she?"

"Someone from the security team. ... an old friend."

"Michael, I'll bet that you have so many friends all around the country now. Don't you?" Mom said.

"Yes, I guess I do. But you're the person that I've missed the most. I'm sorry I wasted so much time and was absent for so long. I know I don't look it, but I've grown into a man."

"I know honey. I'm so proud and happy for you. But you didn't waste your time, even while you were hiding. You redeemed the time for the children. Now you can be at peace with yourself."

Bob Miller

She knows me. She sees the real me.

Epilogue

A WOMAN AND a boy walked toward the Double Oaks Clinic, in northern Minnesota. She guided his arm as they traversed the uneven, stone blocks embedded into the path surrounded by Northern Pines. With its rough-hewn timbers and cedar shakes along the roof, the building resembled a hunting lodge more than a world-famous counseling center. They entered through double-doors which each had an oak tree carved into the handle.

The lobby's decor was plain, matching a traditional waiting room of an older hospital. A row of wooden chairs sat along the large picture window that revealed a forest of northern Minnesota trees and fauna.

"Please sit here for a moment while I get us registered. And behave!" said the mother. She wore a plain tweed jacket, woven with light grays and greens; nothing fancy. And it begged the question if the clinic was too expensive for her. She walked to the well-worn wooden counter and said to the young receptionist, "I'm Mrs. Freeman. I have an appointment for my son, Nathan."

"Oh, yes," said the receptionist, who wore a traditional white smock. "We've been expecting you." She pressed a gray button on her desk. In a few seconds an office door creaked open and a woman who looked to be in her late sixties, entered the room.

"Welcome, Mrs. Freeman, to the Double Oaks Clinic, I'm Doctor Shale. Please come in. Your son can wait in the lobby for a few minutes while we talk, if you don't mind. He can visit with my grandson, Michael. Is that acceptable?"

Mrs. Freeman turned to her son. "Nathan, please wait here while I talk with the doctor." He nodded.

The two women entered an expansive office with 10 foot ceilings. As they walked to her desk, Dr. Shale said, "Please understand that this is just an initial consultation. We haven't agreed yet to accept your son into the program. Let's have a chat to determine if we can help. OK?"

The Smart Kid

The old oak door slowly creaked shut behind them.

A muscular, blond-haired boy who appeared to be twelve years old was in the lobby, reading a comic book. He looked up at Nathan and said, "Hello, my name is Michael."

Nathan's hair was cut as short as it could be, as if he'd just come from a barber shop. He was dressed in a plain blue shirt and tan pants supported by a rope belt. Nathan said, "Hi," and looked at his worn black shoes.

Michael set his comic book on a wooden chair between them and stepped closer to Nathan. "Hey, I've got red licorice. Do you want some?" He held out a paper bag filled with long red licorice whips. Nathan took a piece but said nothing.

"Do you ever read comics?"

Nathan just nodded, not exuding any confidence.

Michael asked, "Do you have a favorite superhero?" After studying his shoes for a few seconds, he looked toward Michael and quietly said, "I like Super Man."

"Yes, so does my brother. I've got this comic about Captain Marvel. It's an old one. Wanna see it?" Michael passed the comic book to Nathan.

"What's it about?" asked Nathan, looking into Michael's eyes for the first time.

Michael smiled. "It's about a boy named Billy, who can become a full-grown man just by saying the word SHAZAM. Isn't that neat?"

"I guess so ..." said Nathan.

"Want some more licorice?"

"Sure!" Nathan said with rising enthusiasm.

"If you could become a man instantly, what would you do?" asked Michael.

"Well, I think that I would..."

Mrs. Freeman sat in the chair facing Doctor Shale's desk, looking worried. "Thank you for seeing me, Doctor. I've heard such wonderful stories about your clinic. Your success rate is phenomenal. I just didn't think that you'd be able to fit us into your schedule. I know you're busy."

"We are busy, and even more so now that we've announced that 2013 is our last year. My husband, Mark, and I will retire later this year."

"Yes, I heard that," said Mrs. Freeman. "I'm so worried about Nathan. Since the divorce, his grades are slipping. He just stays in his room for hours and plays video games. No one has been able to get through to him." She shed a tear as she talked.

"OK, let's discuss this a bit more..."

After several minutes of discussion, there was a knock at the door.

"Yes?" said the counselor.

Her grandson peeked his head in the door. "Grandma, is it OK if Nathan and I go outside so that I can show him my rope ladder and treehouse? We're getting along really well."

Matthew winked at Charleen.

"Yes, Michael, run and play. ... Is that OK with you?" Mrs. Freeman nodded.

Charleen Shale said, "My grandson used to be troubled too. But he found a purpose in life. And that made all the difference for him."

"It would be a near-miracle to pull Nathan out of his depression."

Charleen said, "If my grandson can get along with Nathan, then that's a good sign. I would be happy to accept Nathan into our counseling program."

Doctor Charleen Shale gave one of her award-winning smiles.

The Next Story

"I'll miss you, Matthew," said Charleen Shale, in a crackling, aged voice, as she hugged her young friend and brother-in-law. Only she called him Matthew. It was her private name for him. She kissed him on the cheek and added, "You have another life to live with new adventures." Tears rolled down her cheeks.

After a long embrace, Michael Shale released her and turned to his aged twin.

Mark looked down at his young twin. "Well, my little bro, do you remember when the family brought you to start college in 1958?"

"Yes. Feeling the same way?"

"Yup. You are going off on another adventure and I'm staying home." Mark put an arm around his wife and added, "And that is just fine by me. Now we can get some rest around here: no kid and retired from our jobs. It's like we'll be empty-nesters, Charlee."

"Yes, it will be like that," said Charleen, smiling. Then her face took on a serious countenance. "Matthew, please be careful. You may be revealing to these people that you didn't die in the car crash and they may start chasing you again."

"I don't plan on getting that close. It's just an information-gathering mission. Based on Senator Perkins's testimony, I know that he had a secret partner who was pulling the strings in the background to get me arrested. He also said that this same company has been a regular donor to the physics department at the university. So it's my only clue to these people who tried to dissect me."

"Michael, you used to always play it safe," said Mark. "But now you're going right into the lion's den."

Michael's lips pursed tight for a moment. "I have to know where I really come from. I've never mentioned this to you … Mom knew that I was special— that I was going to be special before we were born. She had said, 'I always feared something like this, *since the day you were born,* knowing how unique you were.' Even before I stopped growing, she knew. And I have to know why."

The Smart Kid

"I understand, Shorty."

"Besides, I've already got my bus ticket to Minneapolis, so I'm committed." Michael smiled and hugged his brother, the top of his head reaching Mark at chin level.

"I love you, Michael."

"I love you, Mark. Good-bye."

Acknowledgments

I started writing this novel in 2012. In 2013, I joined the Rochester Writing group in Rochester, MN. I submitted my chapters for peer review. The critiques and suggestions that I received were beyond helpful. The group helped me to see my writing from different perspectives. Since I was a new writer, the first dozen chapters reviewed by the group were pretty raw. I implemented many of the suggestions, and modified many of my scenes. I always looked forward to the critique of these writers. And I'm a better writer now because of their gracious investment of time reviewing my work.

About the author:

Like Michael Shale, the protagonist in The Smart Kid, Bob has an interest in magic tricks. He has been performing tricks since he was seven. Later in life it became his profession for more than twenty years.

Also, like Michael Shale, Bob has a twin brother. (But they've age pretty much evenly over the decades.)

Bob's mother is also named Jan.

He attended elementary, junior and senior high, and college in the city of St. Cloud, the location of the story. (Although there was no Jefferson Elementary school in the city when Bob attended.)

Even though there are similarities, it is a work of fiction, so don't read too much into it. Bob doesn't consider himself to be a smart kid, just blessed.

Bob Miller
31 9th St. NE
Rochester, MN 559066

507-281-2213
Bob@ChrysalisChronology.com
www.ChrysalisChronology.com

Proof

Made in the USA
Charleston, SC
20 December 2014